Angel Death

THE HENRY TIBBETT MYSTERIES
BY PATRICIA MOYES

Angel Death

Who Is Simon Warwick?

The Coconut Killings

Black Widower

The Curious Affair of the Third Dog

Season of Snows and Sins

Many Deadly Returns

Death and the Dutch Uncle

Murder Fantastical

Johnny Underground

Murder by 3's (including *Down Among the Dead Men,
Dead Men Don't Ski,* and *Falling Star*)

Falling Star

Murder à la Mode

Death on the Agenda

Down Among the Dead Men

Dead Men Don't Ski

AN INSPECTOR HENRY TIBBETT MYSTERY

Angel Death
Patricia Moyes

An Owl Book

HOLT, RINEHART AND WINSTON
New York

Copyright © 1980 by Patricia Moyes
All rights reserved, including the right to reproduce
this book or portions thereof in any form.
Published by Holt, Rinehart and Winston,
383 Madison Avenue, New York, New York 10017.
Published simultaneously in Canada by Holt, Rinehart
and Winston of Canada, Limited.

Library of Congress Cataloging in Publication Data
Moyes, Patricia.
Angel death.
I. Title.
PZ4.M938An   1980   [PR6063.09]   823'.914   80-13196
ISBN 0-03-057592-3
ISBN 0-03-060003-0 (An Owl book) (pbk.)

First published in hardcover by
Holt, Rinehart and Winston in 1981.
First Owl Book Edition—1982

Printed in the United States of America
1 3 5 7 9 10 8 6 4 2

Grateful acknowledgment is made for permission to
quote from *Yachtsman's Guide to the Greater Antilles*
by Harry Kline. Copyright © 1979 by Tropic Isle
Publishers, Inc.

ISBN 0-03-060003-0

For Jim

I would like to take this opportunity to express my most sincere thanks to Helen and Charles Marwick for the time and trouble that they took to research the medical data for this book.

AUTHOR'S NOTE

I HAVE WRITTEN BEFORE about the entirely imaginary territory in the Caribbean which I call the British Seaward Islands, and I want to stress yet again that the islands and all the characters in this book are absolutely fictitious. Nevertheless, some of the problems mentioned in the book are real. The plot may seem outrageous, and yet it is not beyond the bounds of possibility. Fortunately, the authorities are alert and vigilant, and I am convinced that in no territory would things reach the point described here without official intervention. Those of us who love the islands and their people pray that this will always be so.

WARNINGS

ANCIENT:

What the sage poets taught by th' heavenly muse
Storied of old in high immortal verse
Of dire chimeras and enchanted isles
And rifted rocks whose entrance leads to Hell—
For such there are, but unbelief is blind.

—John Milton, *Comus,* 1634

AND MODERN:

From: *Yachtsman's Guide to the Greater Antilles,*
1979

CAUTION: Just to be aware of all facets of cruising the high seas these days; a soft warning to the thoughtful skipper on the possibility of hijacking should be in order here. The U.S. Coast Guard advises owners of yachts cruising in the Bahamas and Caribbean to be very careful about taking on hitchhikers. . . . Even a rescue at sea should be approached with caution, and a "Float Plan" should be filed with someone who could report to the proper authority if an "arrival" were overdue.

Angel Death

THE NORTHEASTERLY TRADE WINDS blow steadily and beautifully across the island of St. Mark's, one of the gray-green knolls that breaks the shiny sea surface to form a fragmented barrier between the Atlantic Ocean and the Caribbean Sea, between the modernity of Florida and the antiquity of Venezuela. This chain of islands, known collectively as the West Indies, comprises such political extremes as Cuba and Haiti, such diverse cultures as the French of Guadeloupe, the Dutch of St. Eustatius, and the American of St. Thomas. British influence, too, has always been strong—and nowhere stronger than on St. Mark's, the principal island and seat of government of the British Seaward Islands.

Government House stands white and foursquare among the coconut palms and tamarinds, with the Union Jack fluttering bravely from its flagpole. Expatriate ladies, arriving home after driving a sick goat in a bucking jeep over miles of boulder-strewn track to visit the vet, still find time to take tea in the garden under the shade of a mahogany tree. There is a big difference, however, between these expatriates and those of former colonial times. Apart from the Governor, who is the representative of the Crown and a career diplomat, none of them ever refers to England as "home"— which is hardly surprising, since a great many of them are Americans. To all of them, irrespective of national origin, the islands are home.

The single greatest asset of the islands is their climate. Year-round sunshine and beaches of white coral sand bring in the Sybarites; the never-failing trade winds bring in the yachtsmen. Of the latter, the most intrepid sail across the Atlantic from chilly, winterbound Europe, or down the North American coast from the

1

fogs of Maine. The adventurous set out from Miami Beach or Tampa and follow the chain of the Bahamas to Puerto Rico, but the great majority fly down from the United States and charter a boat for a couple of weeks. The bare-boat charter business is booming, and St. Mark's is taking full advantage of the fact.

The most obvious outward sign of this lucrative trend in tourism is the newly built marina at St. Mark's Harbour, continually abustle with movement along the line of gleaming white hulls and curtseying dinghies. Visiting boats coming in for the night nose tentatively toward the moorings, directed by a gesticulating Harbour Master. New arrivals from New York, pale-faced and anticipatory, clutching duffel bags and crates of provisions, are shown aboard by charter-firm staff. Backward out of her berth comes a lemon yellow sloop with a merry crew on board, preparing to sail to St. Matthew's Island for dinner at the Anchorage Inn. From seaward, a dark green catamaran roars in, back from a day sail with a load of strictly nonmaritime hotel guests who have been only too happy to concentrate on the refreshments and leave the sailing to the skipper. On other boats, holiday-makers in wisps of bikinis relax on deck, making a striking pattern of bronze, white, and lobster red, depending on the duration and concentration of their suntanning. Bright burgees and ensigns crinkle in the breeze. There is a pervasive and not unpleasant smell of mingled gasoline and coconut oil.

Ashore, a spanking new building complex on the quayside houses a bar and restaurant, showers, a Laundromat, a beauty salon, a gift shop, and a liquor store. The yachtsman's every need, as the brochures proclaim, is catered to. If any visiting skipper has a grouse, it is because the one thing that the marina lacks is a Customs office. That is situated, as it always has been, on the town quay some two miles away, where fishermen unload their catches onto the old stone jetty, battered fruit boats tie up to sell bananas, mangoes, and sweet grapefruit from Dominica, and big black barges bring in the provisions, furniture, and vehicles that are the lifeblood of the island. The only other Customs and Immigration office is five miles out of town, at the airport.

So yacht skippers must come ashore with their ships' papers and passports and pile into taxi-jeeps to make the bumpy journey to the town quay to get their clearance. Once in a while, a Customs Officer will come to the marina and do a certain amount of spot-checking on visiting private yachts—but these are holiday-makers, not smugglers. There are smugglers, of course. This is an ancient stamping ground of buccaneers, pirates, contrabandists, and freebooters. However, the excise men have a shrewd idea of the identity of habitual offenders, and a sharp watch is kept. No need to upset the tourists.

Even the much smaller island of St. Matthew's has been infected by the current sea fever to the point of constructing a small yacht basin not far from the public wharf in the harbor of Priest Town. In many ways it is more convenient than St. Mark's marina, for the Customs office is on the quayside. On the other hand, it lacks the polish and amenities of St. Mark's. There are no boats for charter and no waterside facilities—only the old gray stone fish market and the new concrete police station. Visiting sailors wanting to buy provisions or have a meal ashore must walk up one of the narrow cobbled lanes to the main street of Priest Town, and even there the choice is limited and hardly inspired. There is no way of taking on water except by filling your jerrican from a single tap.

The casual traveler might wonder what prompted the elder statesmen of St. Matthew's to spend a part of the island's scant revenue on the construction of the marina; the answer is that nothing did. The marina was built and is maintained by the wildly expensive and exclusive St. Matthew's Golf Club, with the sole purpose of keeping mere mortals in charter boats away from the Club's private moorings and jetty, where weekend invasions from St. Mark's had begun to annoy the members. The presumptuous visitors were sent packing, of course, but the Club became acutely aware that its soft underbelly, so to speak, was to seaward. Now, affixed to the outer port and starboard buoys marking the channel to the Golf Club jetty are large notices proclaiming CLUB BOATS ONLY. PRIEST TOWN PUBLIC MARINA 1 MILE, with a red arrow pointing the way. So the members are left in peace and feel they are getting their money's worth out of the new facility. The citizens of St. Matthew's are pleased to welcome visiting yachtsmen and so partake of the charter-boat bonanza. Everybody is happy.

At half-past nine on a sparkling morning in January, a small and incongruous figure might have been seen, dodging with quick, birdlike steps, up and down the double line of moored boats in Priest Town marina—a little old lady, thin and very spry, wearing a navy blue cotton skirt reaching almost to her ankles and sensible tennis shoes. Her arms, tanned, skinny, and freckled with deeper brown age spots, emerged from her sleeveless white lace blouse,

3

and her big-brimmed straw hat was anchored by a pink chiffon scarf that passed over its crown to tie under the old lady's chin. Along the swaying wooden jetty she darted and swooped, her small bright eyes peering at the names on the yachts' transoms. At last, she found what she was looking for.

"Ahoy, there! *Isabella*, ahoy!" The voice was a cracked treble, thin but penetrating. "*Isabella*, I say! Ahoy!"

The *Isabella* was a graceful white ketch, which lay quietly nuzzling the end of the landing stage. She wore the United States ensign, with a British courtesy flag at the shrouds, and flew a yacht club burgee. Her home port was apparently Miami Beach, and a certificate of American registration was stuck to her topsides. She was therefore not an indigenous charter boat, but a visitor from Florida, and the fact that the Harbour Master had not tucked her neatly into a berth suggested that she was making only a short stay in St. Matthew's. There was no sign of life aboard.

"*Isabella*, ahoy!" This time, the little old lady emphasized her cry by banging on the side of the boat with her bony fist. Slowly, the cabin door opened from the inside, and a fair-haired, sun-tanned girl with brown eyes and a pretty, pert nose, appeared in the hatchway, wearing a pale blue bikini. In a voice slightly blurred, as if from sleep, she said, "Who is it? What do you want?"

"Janet Vanduren! Janet, my dear!" Beaming, the old lady flung wide her arms in a welcoming, all-embracing gesture. "How good to see you again!" The girl looked at her blankly. In a voice tinged with more disappointment than surprise, the old lady said, "You don't remember me, do you? Well, why should you? It was quite a while ago. I'm Betsy Sprague, dear. Your mother's old schoolteacher from England. I stayed at your home in East Beach . . . oh, six years ago, it must be. Don't you remember?"

The girl smiled, squinting into the sun. "Why, sure—yes, of course I do, Miss Sprague. I just didn't expect to see you here."

"You didn't? Didn't Celia write and tell you? The naughty girl—she always was forgetful."

"We've been cruising for several weeks," the girl said. "If mother did write, I certainly wouldn't have gotten the letter."

"Well, it doesn't matter, does it, now that I've found you? Yes, I wrote and told Celia that I was spending a holiday here, and she wrote back saying that you and your fiancé were cruising the Caribbean on your father's boat, and that you would be in St. Matthew's today. You see how closely she follows your itinerary, my dear, and

4

a very good thing, too. You never know, do you? And she said I must be sure to look you up while you were here and . . ." Miss Betsy Sprague paused for a necessary intake of breath.

The girl said, "It's great to see you, Miss Sprague, but I'm afraid we're just off. Ed has gone to check out with Customs and do an errand in town, and as soon as he comes back . . ."

"Of course, dear. I quite understand. You wouldn't like to come ashore and have a nice cup of tea while you're waiting for your young man?"

"It's kind of you, but really—no. I have to get the boat ready for sea." The girl hesitated. "I'm sorry I can't ask you aboard. We're really not—"

"That's perfectly all right, dear. I don't want to inconvenience you in any way. I just promised your mother that I'd try to see you, so that I can send her word that you're fit and well. And obviously you are. You do keep in touch with your mother, don't you, dear, when you're off on a trip like this? She's bound to be a little anxious, you know."

"Don't worry, Miss Sprague. Ed's at the post office right now, sending a cable to Mom and Dad. We do that at least once a week, so they know we're O.K. and where we are."

Miss Sprague beamed. "A very sensible arrangement. After all, the sea is the sea, whatever anybody may say. Well, dear, if you're leaving so soon, I think I'll catch the Golf Club helicopter to St. Mark's—just popping over for some shopping. The Secretary very kindly offered me a seat—his wife is a cousin of one of my girls, you see. So sorry not to meet your fiancé. Celia did tell me his name . . ."

"Ed Marsham. He's a New Yorker."

"Gracious me. So you'll be living in New York after you're married. Think of that. What is it they call it—the Big Banana?"

"The Big Apple."

"Apple. How curious. One wonders why. Ah, well, I'm sure you'll enjoy it. I'll write and tell your mother I saw you just before you sailed off to— Where is it you're going next?"

"I really don't know exactly. The American Virgin Islands, I expect, and then the Dominican Republic and around there."

"Not *Cuba*, I hope?" Miss Sprague lowered her voice, as if pronouncing an obscenity.

The girl laughed. "No, no. We have to be back in Puerto Rico in two weeks' time anyway, to pick up our crew."

"Your crew?"

"A couple from New York—friends of Ed's. Island-hopping is fine with just the two of us, but we need more hands for the long haul home."

"But you got down here with just the two of you?"

"No, we had two friends with us, but they flew back to the States for Christmas."

Miss Betsy Sprague beamed again. "I can see you are a really sensible girl," she said, "with a sensible young man into the bargain. I shall write and tell Celia that you are well and happy and in fine fettle." She looked at her watch. "My goodness, I must go if I'm not to keep the helicopter waiting. Good sailing, my dear. My regards to your Edward."

Hurrying up the floating jetty, Miss Sprague nearly cannoned into a tall, fair young man carrying a paper bag from which the necks of a couple of bottles protruded. He wore minuscule blue shorts and a T-shirt with the initials E.M. printed on it. She grabbed his free hand.

"E.M. Why, you must be Ed! So nice to meet you, dear! Good sailing! Good-bye!" Leaving the young man, whose name was Ernest Mulliner, in a state of some bewilderment, Miss Sprague tripped away toward the quayside and the taxi stand.

Half an hour later, gazing down from the tiny red helicopter that was flying her across the narrow strip of dark blue water to St. Mark's, Miss Sprague saw a white ketch hoisting sail as she moved out of Priest Town Harbour. At the wheel was a slim, bronzed figure in a pale blue bikini. Miss Sprague waved energetically and was answered by a wave from the girl at the wheel. Then the helicopter changed course and the yacht disappeared from sight, as Miss Sprague settled back into her seat and began quizzing the Secretary of the Golf Club as to the best shops on St. Mark's.

And that was the last that was ever seen of the auxiliary sailing ketch *Isabella*.

THE LOSS OF THE *Isabella* did not exactly make headlines. Toward the end of January, the East Beach *Courier* ran a small paragraph, as the story was of local interest. YACHT OVERDUE. FEAR FOR DOCTOR'S DAUGHTER was the headline. A week later, the paper reported that the Coast Guard search had now been abandoned, and expressed condolences to Dr. and Mrs. Lionel Vanduren of Harbour Drive, East Beach, whose daughter, Janet, must now be presumed drowned, along with her fiancé, Mr. Ed Marsham of

New York City. The yacht *Isabella*, the *Courier* noted, had been on a Caribbean cruise, crewed by Miss Vanduren, Mr. Marsham, and Mr. and Mrs. Peter Jessel of Norfolk, Virginia. Luckily for them, the Jessels had left the boat at San Juan, Puerto Rico, before Christmas. The *Isabella* then visited various islands, having last been reported in St. Matthew's, British Seaward Islands. The alarm was raised when she did not return to San Juan to pick up Mr. and Mrs. William Harman of New York City, who had flown down to help sail the vessel home to Florida. The presumption was that she had run into a sudden tropical storm or suffered a fire at sea. Just another small, commonplace tragedy. However, the Miami *Herald* picked it up and gave it a couple of lines.

The London *Sunday Scoop* would certainly never have mentioned the matter at all had it not been for the fact that it had recently been so desperate for feature material as to concoct a rehash of the already well-worn Bermuda Triangle story, which it was running on two consecutive Sundays. A sharp-eyed junior editor in Features spotted the paragraph in the Miami *Herald*, and it was decided to run it on page 3 under the headline ANOTHER BERMUDA TRIANGLE VICTIM? MYSTERY OF VANISHED YACHT. The missing pair were described as Miss Jane Vanbarten and Mr. Edward Marshall, and the boat was called the motor cruiser *Isobel,* but otherwise the story was reasonably accurate as far as it went. The main point of it, of course, was to direct the reader's attention to the second part of the *Scoop*'s analysis of the GREAT BERMUDA TRIANGLE COVER-UP (SEE PAGE 25).

Emmy Tibbett, sprawled luxuriously in bed at ten o'clock on Sunday morning with a cup of tea, a boiled egg, and the *Scoop*, noticed the item and remarked on it to her husband, Chief Superintendent Henry Tibbett of the C.I.D., who was shaving in the adjoining bathroom.

"Listen, Henry. Here's something about St. Matthew's."

Henry pulled his face sideways with his left hand and made a razor stroke through the foaming lather. He said, "St. Matthew's? The church?"

"No, idiot. The island. Where we shall be in June, if you remember."

"Oh, St. *Matthew's*," said Henry, enlightened. "What about it?"

"Another boat gone missing in the Bermuda Triangle," said Emmy. "A private motorboat with two people on board. Just vanished." She paused. "Did you read last week's article?"

"No, I did not."

"Well, I did, and you must admit there's something extremely odd going on."

Henry turned from the bathroom mirror and came to stand in the doorway of the bedroom, his face still half-covered in white suds. He said, "For a start, it's all nonsense, and to go on with, what has St. Matthew's got to do with it? The Seawards are nowhere near the Bermuda Triangle."

"Well, they're not all that far away." Emmy was on the defensive. "I mean, Puerto Rico is sort of on the edge of it. Look, there's a map here. You can see."

"Puerto Rico is a pretty long way from St. Matthew's."

"Of course it is. They only mention St. Matthew's because that was the last place the boat called before she disappeared. She was going back to San Juan to pick up some crew, so she might easily have been in the Triangle when she vanished."

"It's people like you," said Henry, "who keep these preposterous stories going. Don't you see the whole thing's just a gimmick to sell books and newspapers?"

Emmy grinned. "I suppose I do, really," she said, "but I never can resist a mystery—and there are millions of people like me."

"I get all the mysteries I need during working hours," said Henry. "I can do without them when I'm on leave, thank you."

He returned to his shaving, putting in some fancy work on his upper lip. He regarded himself critically in the mirror—sandy hair, blue eyes, generally undistinguished. A useful anonymity for a senior police officer. He said, "Did you talk to the travel agency about Early Bird flights?"

"I did. I'm making the actual bookings next week. I can't wait to get back to the Caribbean again. I wish we could go now and get away from all this muck." Emmy gestured at the steady stream of February rain coursing down the windowpanes of the ugly Victorian house, whose ground floor was the Tibbetts' Chelsea home.

"You couldn't expect the Colvilles to put us up for nothing in the high season," Henry said. "And John's getting us a pretty special price on the boat, too. I've always wanted to sail those waters."

"Are there sharks?" Emmy asked suddenly.

"Of course there are. You know that. But they only come inshore at night, to feed. That's why John and Margaret warned us last time against swimming after dark."

"I wonder . . . I wonder if that's what happened to those wretched people on that boat. I mean, if that's why the bodies were never recovered." Emmy shivered.

"Highly unlikely," said Henry.

"Well, what do *you* think happened to them? The Coast Guard hasn't found any wreckage, either."

"Then I expect it was a fire," Henry said.

"Someone would have seen it."

"Depends where they were. If they were well out to sea—"

"It says here they were cruising the islands. They wouldn't have been so far from land that—"

"Oh, for heaven's sake," said Henry. "All you know about it is one small and probably inaccurate newspaper paragraph. Get up and have your bath, and we'll go and get a beer somewhere."

2

HENRY AND EMMY TIBBETT had been to St. Matthew's before and looked forward with great pleasure to visiting the island again, and to a reunion with their friends John and Margaret Colville, proprietors of the Anchorage Inn. John—a retired English economist—and his wife, Margaret, had taken over the small, white-washed pub several years earlier, and they had made a success of it—so much so that they had decided to close down the accommodation side of the business during the normally quiet month of June in order to redecorate their six existing bedrooms and build a garden unit with six more. The restaurant and bar remained open, catering to local islanders, the staff of the Golf Club, and visiting yachtsmen.

So John and Margaret had suggested that the Tibbetts should come over from England and spend a week, free of charge, in one of the old rooms that was awaiting its facelift; and knowing they were keen sailors, John proposed that they spend the second week of their holiday cruising out of St. Mark's. A friend of his with a fleet of charter boats knew of a private boat they could have at a special price. Emmy had protested that they could not possibly afford it, but the chance of sailing Caribbean waters had proved too much for Henry. Afford it or not, one sunny day during the first week of June found them heading across the Atlantic on the first leg of the inconvenient journey from London to St. Matthew's.

When the interisland boat—the last leg—finally arrived at Priest Town the following morning, John Colville was there to meet them at the quayside—lean, very sunburned, grayer about the temples, and yet younger-looking than Henry remembered. They all piled into his ancient but sturdy jeep, and as they drove out of Priest

Town and along the winding, bumpy shore road to the Anchorage, John told them the island news. No more racial unrest, thank God, despite what was happening on some other islands. Golf Club just the same as ever—did you notice the new so-called yacht marina near the harbor? The Club put that up at their own expense to keep the hoi polloi off their jetty—can you imagine? Got a new Governor now—seems a good fellow, quiet intellectual type, not at all like old Sir Geoffrey.

"No problems, then?" Emmy said.

John frowned at the road ahead and did not answer for a moment. Then he said, "No. No problems. Oh, except that I have to warn you about one thing."

"What's that?"

"Well, I'm afraid we have another houseguest staying with us."

"Why apologize?" Henry asked.

"Only because she's slightly odd. Quite harmless and rather a dear, really." John sounded embarrassed. "An ancient lady by the name of Miss Betsy Sprague—an old schoolmistress of Margaret's. Apparently she's always been keen on traveling, so when some life insurance policy matured last year, she decided to splurge on a trip across the Atlantic, via the West Indies. She has ex-pupils scattered all over the United States—a lot of her girls married Americans during the war. Anyhow, she came to us for a week in January, and then departed for the States, and we thought we'd seen the last of her, except for a one-night stopover on her way home. However, the woman she was to have spent this week with in Florida has let her down, and she wrote to Margaret in some distress. She leaves for England on Thursday, she couldn't change her booking, and she had nowhere to go, so of course . . ."

"Of course Margaret invited her," Emmy said. "And quite right, too. We'll look forward to meeting her."

The bar of the Anchorage Inn was as cheerful and welcoming as ever, open to the cooling breeze under its thatch of woven palm leaves. Margaret Colville, presiding behind the bar, greeted the Tibbetts and prepared rum punches—the traditional welcoming drink of the islands. Emmy sighed with pure pleasure. It was all just the same. Two black men were engaged in an earnest game of darts, while others listened raptly to a radio commentary on a cricket match. A lobster-red quartet of young Americans from a charter boat planned their next day's cruise with the help of a chart spread out on the bar and gratefully accepted Margaret's offer of sunburn ointment—things had clearly gone too far for warning words about wearing long-sleeved shirts and floppy hats.

Henry and Emmy had moved from their barstools to a table on the terrace and were about to tackle the huge salad of local lobster provided by John from the kitchen, when Miss Betsy Sprague arrived from the beach like a small, untidy tornado.

"Greetings, greetings, dear people!" she chirruped, dancing up the shallow steps from the garden in her tennis shoes, her navy blue skirt flapping wetly. "Henry and Emily, isn't it?"

"Emmy, actually," said Emmy. "But it doesn't matter."

"All the way from dear old England! How exciting! I'm Betsy Sprague, the original bad penny, as Margaret must have told you." She flopped down into the empty chair opposite Henry. "Beautiful at the beach. Beautiful. You must come down this afternoon. Don't let me interrupt your meal."

Margaret came out from behind the bar. A little awkwardly, she said, "Hello, Betsy. I see you've met Henry and Emmy."

"Yes, yes, indeed. I have introduced myself, my dear. Remember what I always used to tell you girls? Never be shy about introducing yourself. People like to know to whom they are talking."

"I remember," said Margaret, smiling. "What can I get you from the bar, Betsy?"

"Just my usual rum punch, thank you, dear. Aha, lobster I see— in honor of our new arrivals, no doubt. Not that it's really lobster at all, you know," she added confidentially to Emmy. "Crayfish."

"Down here, it's called lobster," said Margaret firmly.

"Ah, well, when in Rome, I suppose . . . the trouble that double nomenclature causes . . . you don't mind if I join you for lunch, as we are fellow guests?"

"We'd be delighted, Miss Sprague," said Henry gallantly. Margaret gave him a grin and a tiny wink and went off to mix a rum punch.

"Betsy, if you please, sir. Let's have no false formality."

Somewhat surprisingly, Betsy Sprague turned out to be an entertaining and interesting companion. During her short stay on St. Matthew's, she had obviously accomplished more of a scientific and scholarly nature than the Tibbetts had ever contemplated while on holiday. She talked knowledgeably of the curious rock formations on the island—"Volcanic origin, of course. Some authorities maintain they may be late Precambrian—highly unlikely to my way of thinking. Paleozoic at the earliest, Middle Devonian more likely—what do you think, Henry? This lobster—for so we must call it—is delicious, is it not?"

She then went on to discuss the earliest inhabitants of the West Indies.

"You mean those bloodthirsty Arawaks who ate each other?" Emmy ventured.

Betsy laughed. "Oh, my dear, you *are* confused. No, the poor Arawaks were the gentlest of people. It was the fierce Caribs who wiped out the Arawaks—literally made a meal of them, as you might say—and of a good many Spaniards as well, for which I can't blame them. Did you know that the last Carib settlement still exists on the island of Dominica? Oh, very tame and practically vegetarian by now—we Europeans won in the end, of course. We always have done, up to now. We're just living to see the last of it, of course. The future lies with Africa—very sad for her, but there's no shirking historical responsibility, is there? Well, we'll be dead and gone by then. Now, which beach will you visit this afternoon?"

Betsy Sprague was not without tact. When Henry said that they had thought of paying a visit to their favorite spot at Mango Tree Bay, she at once remarked, "What a pity. I was hoping we might have made a joint expedition, but I particularly want to observe the pelicans at Long Look Rock. Another time, perhaps. So if you'll excuse me, I shall go and trouble Margaret for the loan of her binoculars." And she was off.

Henry and Emmy had a leisurely swim, did some snorkeling, and remembered not to stay out in the sun unprotected for more than fifteen minutes. Then, after a nap and a shower, they came down to the bar in the thoroughly euphoric mood of holiday-makers who know that fourteen of their precious fifteen days still lie ahead.

The Anchorage was very quiet. The Colvilles had no dinner guests, so the whole party—the Tibbetts, the Colvilles, and Betsy Sprague—were able to sit down and eat together.

As usual Miss Sprague's presence galvanized the conversation into more lively circles than island gossip and the weather. This evening she seemed intent on drawing Henry out on the subject of his profession as a criminal investigator—not from any of the more usual sensational aspects, but from a philosophical standpoint. She was interested in the interaction of minds, she said. The minds of the criminal and of his adversary, the policeman. Before they knew it, the theme of the discussion had become the age-old question of the definition of right and wrong.

"As far as I'm concerned," Henry said, "right is obeying the law, and wrong is breaking it. I'm not paid to make laws of my own, nor even to interpret the existing ones."

"What rubbish," said Betsy blandly. "You are not a mindless automaton. If you found your own conscience in direct conflict with the law, what would you do?"

"Resign," Henry said.

"Good. So I take it that, broadly speaking, you approve of the laws of Great Britain."

"Certainly. I couldn't do my job otherwise."

Betsy leaned forward. "What about marijuana?" she demanded.

Henry opened his mouth to reply, but before he could say a word, John Colville interrupted. He said, "Betsy, you're a wicked old woman. Please let's change the subject."

Betsy favored him with a mischievous grin. "I'm not saying it isn't a problem, John. Just that it must be faced."

John turned to Henry. "Betsy knows very well," he said, "that drug abuse is the current plague of these islands. Her solution is to legalize the less pernicious substances, like pot."

"Decriminalize is a better word," said Betsy. "And I wouldn't stop at just pot. What caused the rise of organized crime in the United States in the twenties? Prohibition of the sale of alcohol. How do you think organized crime is making its money now? Are all legislators mentally deficient? Outlaw something that a great many people want, and you create a vacuum that only crime can fill." She turned to Henry, fiercely. "Am I not right?"

Henry said, "Yes, I think you are. But the trouble is, every country in the world—or at least, the majority—would have to act simultaneously. Otherwise—"

Margaret broke in. "That's right, Henry. That's what Betsy doesn't seem to realize. Look at it from a practical point of view. Just supposing that the British Seawards legalized marijuana, unilaterally. Can you imagine what would happen? Every junkie in the United States would come flocking—"

"Look what happens when a state legalizes gambling—"

"Marijuana is just the beginning. It would end—"

Everybody was talking at once. Miss Sprague held up her right hand and made a small, authoritative gesture with her knife. "Children! Children!" There was silence. She smiled and went on. "When I say decriminalize, I also mean deglamorize." She addressed John. "What makes the young men on this island smoke marijuana?"

14

"Well—" John began.

Betsy swept on. "You know as well as I do. Because it's forbidden and because it's expensive and because it's considered the thing to do by the younger generation. The merchants of the stuff—pushers, as I believe they are called—take full advantage of the stupid youngsters. They keep the price ridiculously high—as a reward for taking the risks that they do with the law, of course—and when the kids haven't enough to pay for the next fix, they go out and steal money."

Margaret said, "Everybody knows that, Betsy, but what's the answer? Don't tell me you've got one."

"Of course I have, dear, but I'm afraid it might shock our squeamish lawmakers."

"What do you mean?" Henry asked. "The death penalty for pushers, or something?"

"Goodness gracious me, no." Betsy leaned forward. "Do you know how much marijuana actually costs to produce? Practically nothing. It's a hardy crop, giving high yields for very little outlay. The government could well afford to grow it and give it away."

"But I don't see how that—" Emmy's protest was easily steamrollered aside.

"I would put the whole thing in the hands of the Women's Voluntary Services. Have little booths set up on street corners, with nice ladies in sensible hats giving packages free to passersby, like those tiresome religious tracts which are so difficult to avoid in the streets these days. That would remove the glamour at one fell swoop, as well as putting the pushers out of business."

Henry laughed. "That's all very well, but—"

"Aha," said Betsy. "Now we come to the hard part. At the same time, all treatment facilities for drug abuse would be discontinued. Not another penny would we wretched taxpayers be asked to fork out to rehabilitate the perpetrators of self-inflicted injury. That's what I meant by squeamish legislators. Of course, there would be some distressing cases among the hard-drug addicts and some nasty sights on the streets. *Tant pis.* It's nobody's fault but his own if a person abuses drugs. Nor would any advertising which might encourage the glamour image to creep in again be allowed. The result? Those people who enjoy a smoke now and then would be able to indulge in their harmless habit in peace. Those who became hopelessly addicted would soon die off. There would be absolutely no barrier to prevent them from drugging themselves to death, and the sooner the better, say I. Well, what do you think of it?"

15

John said, "It's an ingenious idea, Betsy—but impractical, I fear. As Margaret said, unless all countries acted simultaneously, there's be chaos in the ones that did. Personally, I can do without all the addicts in the world coming to the Seawards to die in the streets from free drug handouts."

Betsy Sprague sighed. "So parochial," she said. "No breadth of vision. Ah, well. This is most delicious chicken, John. The hint of tarragon makes all the difference."

At lunch the following day, Henry and Emmy's account of their morning's snorkeling led easily to the subject of sharks.

"Much maligned creatures," announced Betsy. "Or so I understand. I was talking to that nice fellow in here the other day—the tall black man who does so much scuba diving, Margaret . . ."

"Morley Duprez," Margaret said. "Yes, he takes parties from the Golf Club out diving."

"Well, he told me that sharks are very shy of human beings as a rule. He finds it difficult to persuade them to show themselves for his clients. All these books and films are so much inaccurate sensationalism."

"Very successful, though," Henry said. "I suppose people feel the need for something exciting and dangerous in their lives."

"I suppose the H-bomb isn't enough for them," remarked Miss Sprague acidly.

"That's real," Emmy said. "So people try to ignore it. They prefer make-believe horrors. Look at the tremendous vogue for science-fiction movies."

Miss Sprague said seriously, "I think that is rather different. I think the popularity of science fiction springs from a feeling of inadequacy and a longing for reassurance. The world seems to be in such a hopeless and dangerous mess that people long for an extraterrestrial solution—a benign Big Brother keeping his eye on us from outer space and descending in his machine to put humanity in order."

Henry said, "That's all very well, but in some people's minds it's not fiction at all. These ridiculous theories of prehistoric visitors from other galaxies—"

"Now, wait a minute, Henry." Betsy laid down her knife and fork and spoke earnestly. "It does not do to dismiss these things out of hand simply because the idea is more than your mind can grasp. The statistical probability of other inhabited planets in other star systems is—"

16

"Oh, Betsy, *really*," said Margaret.

"Say what you like, Margaret dear, I for one am keeping an open mind."

"Into which a saucer will probably fly," said John. "Have some more apple flan."

"It's no use trying to divert me with your excellent pastries," said Betsy, helping herself to a large slice of flan. "There is a great deal unexplained in the evolution of *Homo sapiens* which the Darwinists are hard put to . . . Yes, Emmy?"

"I didn't say anything."

"No, but you have something to say, nevertheless. I can always tell. Out with it."

With a sheepish glance at Henry, Emmy said, "Well . . . I was just remembering that we're on the edge of the Bermuda Triangle here, and—"

Henry exploded. "Oh, my God, that rubbish!"

"Go on, Emmy dear."

"Oh, it's nothing. Just that the last boat that disappeared actually set out from here. The *Isobel*. I read about it in the English papers last winter. It was—"

"For heaven's sake, Emmy!" Henry sounded really angry. "A couple of young idiots blundering about the Caribbean, probably in a hired boat that they knew nothing about, lost their way and hit a rock and blew up, or something of that sort, and people like you begin spinning wild stories about supernatural powers! People who aren't capable of navigation or seamanship shouldn't be allowed to—"

"Please! Please be quiet!" Betsy Sprague's voice was so sharp, so distressed, that Henry stopped dead in midword. In the silence, Betsy cried, "You know nothing about it! Nothing! You have no right to speak like that!" And she jumped up from the table and ran toward her room, a small handkerchief pressed to her eyes.

There was a moment of dead silence after her departure. John had half-risen and appeared frozen, one hand raised in protest. Then he sat down again slowly.

Henry said, "I'm most frightfully sorry. I had no idea . . . Whatever did I say to upset her so much?"

"I can't imagine," Margaret said. "Should I go after her, do you think?"

"No," said John. "Leave her alone and get on with your meal. It wasn't your fault, Henry, old man. Goodness me, Miss Betsy

Sprague doesn't stop to bother about other people's susceptibilities when *she* gets going on a pet subject. But it's strange that she should fly off the handle like that." He sighed. "Ah, well. Just as well she's leaving the day after tomorrow. I expect she's just tired out, poor old thing. The best she can do is lie down and have a good rest."

However, it was less than five minutes later that Betsy Sprague reappeared at the dinner table. Her eyes looked a little red, but she was self-composed. She sat down and said quietly, "I am so very sorry, Henry. Please forgive me."

"I'm the one that's sorry," Henry said. "I had no idea—"

"You mustn't apologize," said Miss Sprague, with gentle firmness. "I behaved extremely badly. I embarrassed you very much, which is a gross breach of manners. Of course, you could have had no idea that the particular incident to which Emmy referred had any special significance for me. Now that I have disgraced myself, the least I can do is to explain."

John said, "Look, Betsy dear, why don't you just—"

"Explain," repeated Betsy, decisively. "It is very simple. The couple on that boat were friends of mine. At least, the girl was. I must have been one of the last people to see them alive."

"Good heavens," said John. "How was that?"

"It was when I was here in January, before I went on to the States. Do you remember the day that I flew to St. Mark's in the Golf Club helicopter?"

"Yes, but—"

"Before I took off," Betsy went on, "I went down to the marina. I was looking for a boat called the *Isabella*—a sailing ketch from Miami."

Emmy said, "The Sunday *Scoop* said it was a motor cruiser."

"That just shows that you can't believe what you read in the papers, doesn't it?" Betsy was recovering fast. "Well, the *Isabella* belonged to an old pupil of mine, Celia Dobson, and her husband. You remember Celia, don't you, Margaret? Rather a plain girl, with fair hair."

Margaret smiled. "Barely," she said. "She was a junior when I was in the sixth."

"Ah, yes. A few years' difference makes a big gap at that age. Well, after the war, Celia married a Dr. Lionel Vanduren—an American—and went to live in Florida. The *Isabella* was their boat and the girl who was lost was their daughter, Janet. I met her when I stayed with the Vandurens six years ago. Janet was cruising down here with her fiancé, and Celia knew that they were due in St. Matthew's and suggested that I should look them up. Didn't I mention it?"

"Not that I remember," Margaret said.

"Well, I couldn't be sure of finding the boat, and I was very much taken up with the helicopter ride and my shopping. However, I did find them and spoke to them. Janet was looking so pretty. Fair, like her mother, but much better looking. There wasn't much time to talk—they were just putting to sea. In fact, I saw the *Isabella* setting out from the harbor as we flew over. I didn't think any more about it until a few weeks ago, when I was in Virginia staying with Lucy Mannering and her husband. That was when I heard that the *Isabella* had been lost."

"It was in the paper, was it?" John asked.

"Oh, no. It had happened back in January. I heard about it from people called Jessel—a charming young couple, friends of Lucy's children. They had actually been crewing the boat and had left her to fly home for Christmas. Naturally, they were very upset. We talked a lot, and . . . I'm afraid it distressed me, Henry, to hear you talking about Janet and Ed as irresponsible young people not properly in control of their boat. Peter Jessel told me that Janet and Ed were both first-rate sailors, and the boat was in impeccable condition. There was no possible reason they could think of why she should vanish without trace.

"Naturally the first thing I did was to write to Celia. My letter was answered by Dr. Vanduren. He explained that Celia had had a complete breakdown, had spent several months in hospital—psychiatric, I imagine—and was now on a long visit with her mother in Shropshire. I didn't mention it to you, Margaret dear, because it seemed unnecessary—but, in fact, it was with Celia that I should have been staying this week. Of course, it was out of the question. The doctor didn't even seem to know I had been invited— or if he did, he had forgotten. Not surprising. Dr. Vanduren couldn't throw any light on what might have happened. He said Celia was always nervous when Janet and her friends went off on long cruises, and she always made them give her a precise itinerary and keep in touch by phone or telegram. In fact, when I met Ed he was just back from sending a wire to Celia from the Priest Town post office. And that wire was the last that the Vandurens heard."

"Where was the *Isabella* supposed to go after St. Matthew's?" Emmy asked.

"That's the trouble, you see. They were going to go island-hopping, as Janet put it, around the Seawards and Virgin Islands, and although they had promised to keep in touch, the Vandurens didn't worry too much when they didn't hear from them. These are very safe and sheltered waters. It was only when the boat didn't turn up in San Juan to pick up the homeward crew that the alarm was raised—and that was two weeks later. There's no record of the *Isabella* having put in at any of the other islands, so . . . well, there it is. I'm sorry, Henry. Silly of me to get so emotional."

"I understand completely," Henry said. "It's easy to take these things lightly when they happen to strangers. It's a different matter when you know the people."

"Two young lives," said Betsy Sprague. "Such a waste. I cannot abide waste."

TWO DAYS LATER, the Anchorage entered into a controlled turmoil, leading up to the departure of Betsy Sprague on Thursday morning. Her itinerary took her first in the Colvilles' jeep to Priest Town, where she would board the *Pride of St. Mark's* for the short trip to the larger island. A taxi from the harbor would deposit her at the airport, whence, given luck, a ten-seater interisland plane would convey her to Antigua. After that, she would be in the safe arms of British Airways as far as Heathrow Airport in London, where she would arrive early on Friday morning.

Her arrangements after that appeared complicated to the extreme, involving Jock Higgins's taxi and Mrs. Bastable's housekeeper who had the keys and was looking after the dog, and Miss Pelling from the village who had taken the cats—but in the course of time Betsy Sprague would once again be installed in her comfortable cottage at Little Fareham, Hants.

Margaret offered to accompany her old teacher as far as St. Mark's, for there was a wait of four hours between the arrival of the *Pride* and the takeoff of the Antigua plane. Miss Sprague, however, would have none of it.

"I know how busy you are, Margaret dear. I am quite capable of amusing myself in St. Mark's for a few hours. I shall have some luncheon and buy a few little gifts for people back home. You are *not* to worry about me."

The Colvilles and the Tibbetts all came to Priest Town to wave good-bye to the *Pride of St. Mark's* and the small, straight-backed figure standing on her deck with two well-worn suitcases at her feet. After the usual hooting and shouting, the last local boys leaped on board with a half-second to spare, and the sturdy little craft pulled away from the quay and chugged out of the harbor. The Anchorage contingent went home, with mixed feelings of relief and deflation.

About an hour later, the telephone in the Anchorage rang. John, who was balanced on top of a ladder fixing the palm-frond roof of the bar, called out, "Henry, would you answer that? I expect it's a dinner booking."

"Henry? Oh, I am so pleased you answered. You are just the person I want to speak to."

"Betsy! Where are you? Is everything all right?"

"Listen to me carefully, Henry. I am at St. Mark's marina, and *I have just seen her!*"

"Seen her? Seen who?"

"Oh, do be sensible, Henry. Janet Vanduren, of course. She's here!"

"But that's—"

"She has dyed her hair dark and she's with a different young man, but I'd know her anywhere."

"You're really sure?"

"Of course I'm sure."

"What are you going to do?"

"I'm going to speak to her, of course. Find out what in the world is going on, and at least make her get in touch with her poor mother."

"Is she on a boat?"

"Not at the moment. She's having a drink in the restaurant with this young man. He's dark and has a beard, and he's certainly not Ed."

"Now, listen to me, Betsy. You must go to the Harbour Master and—"

"I can't stop to talk now, Henry, or I may miss her. I'll call you back after I've spoken to her. Oh, Celia will be so happy!"

"Betsy, you must be sensible. Go to the—"

"Ah, they're getting up to go. She's coming this way! Now's the moment! Good-bye, Henry!"

The line went dead.

BETSY SPRAGUE HAD TELEPHONED soon after midday. Henry reported his conversation with her to Emmy and the Colvilles when they gathered in the bar for a prelunch drink, and the general mood was one of amused, affectionate skepticism.

"She hasn't called back, of course," Henry said. "It must have been a mistake."

"Poor Betsy," Margaret remarked. "She's really fearfully short-sighted, and she's getting very forgetful, but of course she won't admit it. I hope she didn't make a scene and upset the poor girl, whoever she was."

"Betsy always lands on her feet," said John easily. "I expect the young couple found it all hilarious. She's probably got herself invited on board their boat for lunch and even now is regaling them with the geology of the Seawards."

"Well, I hope she doesn't lose track of time and miss her plane," Emmy said.

"Anyhow," said Margaret, "I'm quite sure that she's thoroughly enjoying herself and that we won't get another phone call. She'd never ring us up to admit she'd been wrong. Another rum punch, Henry, or shall we eat?"

The first intimation that anything might be amiss did not filter through to the Anchorage until Saturday morning. It took the form of a telegram addressed to "Sprague." It was phoned through the post office in Priest Town, and Margaret wrote it down carefully on the message pad by the telephone in the office. The telegram had been handed in at Little Fareham on Friday evening, and the message read: CABLE WHEN RETURNING CATS INCONVENIENT PELLING.

"I'm afraid it's missed Miss Sprague, hasn't it, Mrs. Colville?" added Corfetta Johnson, the postmistress, who knew everything. "She left on the *Pride* Thursday, didn't she? Morley was over to St. Mark's that same day, so he was telling me." Morley Duprez, the diving expert, was Corfetta's common-law husband, or, in island parlance, boyfriend.

"Yes." Margaret was puzzled. "She should have arrived home early on Friday. I suppose the plane was delayed. Thank you, Corfetta. How are the children?"

"Fine, thanks, Mrs. Colville. Annelia will be in the school play next month."

"Oh, I'm looking forward to that," said Margaret. "Good-bye now, Corfetta." She hung up the telephone and went to find John.

It was the Tibbetts' last day at the Anchorage. At eleven they were due to take the boat to St. Mark's and pick up the yacht that they were chartering. *Windflower,* as John had explained, was not a regular charter boat, but a sailing sloop belonging to an American who lived in Connecticut. He kept her in St. Mark's marina and rented her out to carefully selected and personally recommended people when he was not able to sail her himself. Bob Harrison of St. Mark's Yacht Charter Service had the keys and would see the Tibbetts safely installed on board.

Accordingly, Henry and Emmy had packed immediately after breakfast and had gone down to the beach for a final swim. They came back to the inn at ten o'clock to find Margaret and John in a worried huddle around the telephone in the bar.

Margaret said, "Oh, thank goodness you're back, Henry. You can tell us what to do."

"What to do?" Henry's swimming trunks felt clammy and damp under the fresh draft from the overhead fan. "About what?"

"I'm afraid there's a bit of a crisis, Henry," said John.

"Yes, well, I'll just go and take a shower and—"

"Henry," said Margaret, "Betsy has disappeared."

"Has *what*—" Emmy, coming into the bar at that moment, had caught the last words.

Margaret explained about the telegram. John continued the story.

"I wasn't really worried," he said, "but I thought maybe I had just better check up with British Airways, so I called them in Antigua. They confirmed that a Miss Elizabeth Sprague had been booked on the Thursday flight, but never checked in for it. They

23

weren't surprised. They get all too many 'no-shows.' Bane of the airlines—people who book flights and simply don't appear. If the airlines could eliminate no-shows, the whole fare structure might—"

"Oh, John, do keep to the point," said Margaret. "The fact is that she didn't show up on Thursday, and she hasn't done so since. Nor did she check in for the Pan-Island flight from St. Mark's to Antigua."

"What about her luggage?" Henry asked.

"No sign of that, either, as far as we've been able to trace."

John went on. "The skipper of the *Pride* remembers her being on board on Thursday, and Morley Duprez spoke to her on the way over and helped her off the boat with her suitcases. He says she took a taxi from the harbor, but he doesn't know where to. He left her while the cab driver was still loading the baggage into the trunk."

Emmy said, "Well, she must surely have driven to the marina because she telephoned Henry from there."

"Why would she have gone to the marina and not into town?" Margaret wondered aloud. "She said she was going to have lunch and do some shopping—"

Henry said, "It was still early for lunch, and didn't somebody mention that there was a new gift shop at the marina? She was talking about buying presents."

"That's right," John said. "Those people from the Golf Club were talking about it in the bar the other night. What's it called, can you remember, Margaret?"

"Caribbean something . . . rather twee, I seem to recall . . . Treasure Trove. That's it. Caribbean Treasure Trove."

"I'll ring them now," said John. "Somebody might have seen her."

Margaret was consulting the small newspaper called the *Island Echo*. She said, "Here's their advertisement. Let's see—open eight to twelve and two till six. Closed Saturday morning. That means you can't get them until two. Anyway, you've got your call to England coming through."

"We'll be at the marina by two," Henry said. "We'll go to the shop and let you know if there's any news."

The telephone on the bar began to ring. "Ah," said John. "That'll be my call to Miss Pelling. Why don't you listen on the office extension, Henry? I had a devil of a job finding her number. Hello, Anchorage Inn . . . yes . . . yes, I do . . . yes, Colville speaking . . . hello, Miss Pelling?"

Picking up the phone in the office, Henry heard a sharp, very English voice. "Hello? Is that you, Betsy?"

John said, "No, Miss Pelling. This is John Colville from the Anchorage Inn on St. Matthew's."

"Well, where is Betsy Sprague?"

"I was hoping you could tell me, Miss Pelling. Hasn't she arrived home yet?"

"No, she has not, and it's most inconsiderate of her. I told her I could only keep the cats until Friday afternoon at the latest. My nephew and his family arrived yesterday on a visit, and little Pamela is allergic to—"

John broke in, "Miss Pelling, please listen. This is serious."

"I am well aware that it is serious, Mr. . . . er . . ."

"Colville."

"Mr. Colville. The poor child has developed acute hay fever, in spite of the fact that I've shut the cats up in the—"

"Miss Pelling, I'm talking about Betsy Sprague."

"And so am I. Where is she? What does she mean by staying away and leaving me with—"

John shouted. "Betsy has disappeared! Vanished! Nobody knows where she is!"

"—am expected to do with . . . What was that you said?"

Deliberately and loudly, John repeated his remark. There was a moment of silence, and then Miss Pelling said, "How very extraordinary. What do you mean by disappeared?"

"She left here to catch her plane to England, but she never arrived at the airport. She hasn't been seen since."

After a little pause, Miss Pelling said, "Well, I don't see what I can do about it."

"Has Miss Sprague any relatives or—?"

"Not that I know of. Her elder sister died last year—also unmarried, of course. She only has what she calls her girls—her ex-pupils, you know."

"Who are her close friends in the village, Miss Pelling?"

"Well—myself, I suppose, and Mary Bastable, but she's in Scotland at the moment."

"So if there had been a change of plan, you're the person she would have told?"

"I should hope so, Mr. Colville. After all, I have her two cats in my house, and what I'm going to do with them—"

"Miss Pelling, I think you should inform the police that Miss Sprague is missing."

"The police?"

"I shall do the same at this end. Now, please pay attention. Tell them that she was booked on British Airways from Antigua to London on Thursday, but she never boarded the plane. She was last seen at St. Mark's Harbour. The police here have been informed. O.K.?"

There was a long silence. The operator's voice said, "St. Matthew's? Have you finished your conversation with England?"

"No, I haven't. Miss Pelling, are you there?"

"Yes, I'm here. I must say I find the whole situation very peculiar, but quite typical of Betsy."

"Will you inform the police?"

"The police? Certainly not. I have no intention of getting involved with the police. Meanwhile, these cats—"

"Good-bye, Miss Pelling." John slammed down the receiver with unnecessary force. "My God, the stupid bitch. That'll have cost me about fifty dollars." He mopped his brow. Henry came back into the bar. "Well, there it is, for what it's worth. She hasn't arrived home."

"Then she must still be on St. Mark's," Emmy said.

"Or on another British Seaward Island," said Margaret. "She'd only be checked by Immigration if she left the Territory and went to another country."

"Which might be anywhere," John added. "We'd have to check with the Immigration people in every damned island and the American mainland as well. Let the police do it. I'm calling Chief Inspector Ingham."

Henry said, "Is that Sergeant Ingham—the chap who was in charge here last time?"

"That's right." John was dialing already. "Chief of Police on St. Mark's now. Done very well for . . . Hello, police? John Colville here, St. Matthew's. Is Chief Inspector Ingham in the office today? . . . Good. I'd like to speak to him. Yes, I'll hold on."

Henry said, "Tell him I'm coming over to St. Mark's today. I'll go and see him."

"Good idea. Hello, Ingham? John Colville . . . Fine, how are you? . . . Good . . . Lucky to catch you on a Saturday . . . Now, listen, Herbert, a rather rummy thing has occurred. . . ."

No, nothing to do with drugs. It's just that a guest from my pub seems to have vanished into thin air . . . on her way home to England last Thursday . . . left this island, yes, and got as far as St. Mark's and then . . . Oh, I know, that's probably it, but . . . an elderly lady, Miss Elizabeth Sprague, S-P-R- . . . that's right . . . booked through to London via Antigua, Pan-Island, and British Airways, and didn't show up for either flight. . . . No, she hasn't arrived in England, I've just checked by telephone. There weren't any delays in B.A. flights, were there? . . . That's what I thought. Well, she's over eighty, you see, and traveling alone. . . . That's very kind of you, Herbert. By the way, you'll get a visit from an old friend this afternoon. You'll never guess . . . What? How did you know?" John laughed. "Try to keep a secret on these islands! Oh, Morley told you, did he? . . . Yes, they've been here a week . . . No, no, purely a holiday this time. . . . They're picking up the *Windflower* in St. Mark's this afternoon, and Henry thought he'd pay you a visit. . . . O.K., very kind, I'll tell him . . . yes, let me know if anything turns up, won't you. . . . Thanks, Herbert. Good-bye for now."

John hung up and turned to Henry. "I suppose Ingham's right," he said. "Seems to regard it as a storm in a teacup. Incidentally, he knew that you and Emmy were in the islands and seemed a bit hurt that you hadn't called on him sooner. He'll be in his office this afternoon and would be delighted to see you both." He looked at his watch. "Golly, you'd better hurry or you'll miss the *Pride*."

"If this is Betsy's idea of a joke," said Margaret, "I'll never forgive her. I mean, if she's just swanned off to stay with some other old girl in South America or somewhere—"

Emmy said, "Suppose the girl Betsy saw *was* Janet Vanduren, after all? Maybe the Vandurens could shed some light on—"

"Highly unlikely," said Henry, who then added, "But do you happen to have their address, Margaret?"

"No, but I think I have Betsy's letter somewhere. I'll look for it while you go and change."

A few minutes later, as the Tibbetts came downstairs with their baggage, Margaret came out of the office with a blue aerogram in her hand.

"Here it is." She read aloud, skimming over the crabbed handwriting. "'Dear Margaret . . . forgive me for troubling you . . . people I was going to stay with in East Beach, Miami . . . death in the family . . . impossible for them to . . . wonder if I might come to St. Matthew's rather earlier than . . . will try to change my homeward bookings . . .' That's the best I can do for you. She mentioned the husband's name, didn't she? Leonard, or something."

"Lionel," Henry said. "Dr. Lionel Vanduren."

"Wife Celia, née Dobson. Address somewhere in East Beach, Miami. That should be enough to trace them. Everybody knows doctors. Though why on earth," Margaret added, "the Vandurens should have the faintest idea where Betsy is . . ."

"You never know," said Henry.

BY TWO O'CLOCK in the afternoon, Henry and Emmy had arrived in St. Mark's, lunched at a café on Main Street, and met Bob Harrison—a stout, cheerful character with a regional accent preserved unimpaired from his native Suffolk. Soon their luggage had been stowed on board the thirty-five-foot sloop *Windflower*—a comfortable, beamy boat with an uptilted bowsprit reminiscent of a Baltimore skipjack. She was fully equipped for four people, Bob explained, but two could handle her easily so long as it was just island-hopping. He'd gathered from Mr. Colville that there wouldn't be any question of extensive cruising. Henry reassured him that they only proposed the mildest of meanderings among the nearby islands, and Harrison looked relieved. Then, while Henry explored the ship and was shown the workings of the engine, winches, rigging, and heads, Emmy went ashore in search of Caribbean Treasure Trove.

She did not have far to look. The little shop was next door to the new restaurant and bar in the marina complex, and it was attractive and inviting, with its window full of bright shirts and swimsuits, straw hats, shell jewelry, picture postcards, island souvenirs, and yellow cartons of film. Emmy went inside from the bright sunshine and accustomed her eyes to the cool shade of the shop. A very pretty black girl with an hourglass figure was behind the counter selling picture postcards and stamps to a couple of elderly tourists. Emmy waited until the transaction was complete and then approached the salesgirl.

"Can I help you?"

"I hope you may be able to." Emmy smiled and produced from her straw handbag a small color photograph that she had taken the week before with her new instant-picture camera. It showed Betsy Sprague, complete with floppy hat and ankle-length skirt, sipping a drink in the garden of the Anchorage Inn. "Were you on duty here last Thursday morning, just before midday?"

"Sure, I was." The girl sounded puzzled.

Emmy held out the photograph. "Do you remember seeing this lady in the shop?"

"I don't—" began the girl, and then, "Why, yes. The old lady from England. Sure, I remember her. Came in just before we closed at noon."

Emmy beamed and began to lie fluently. "Oh, I'm so glad. She's my aunt, you see, and she was buying presents to take back to England."

"That's right," said the girl. "That's what she told me. She was on her way home. She had her baggage with her."

"I'm trying to find out what she bought," Emmy said. "Since we're buying gifts for the same people, I want to make sure we don't take back the same things . . ."

To Emmy's ears it did not sound very convincing, but the girl seemed to find nothing strange about it. She said, "I remember quite well. She was a nice, funny lady. Not at all like an American."

"Not at all," Emmy agreed.

"I mean to say, she thought everything was so expensive," the girl went on. "She just couldn't seem to make up her mind. In the end, she took some postcards and stamps, and four of those place mats." She indicated a rack holding plastic rectangles that were printed with an unseamanlike chart of the British Seaward Islands. "Then she said she had to have a nice gift for the lady who was looking after her cats."

"Ah," said Emmy. "That would be Miss Pelling. What did Aunt Betsy buy?"

"She nearly didn't buy nothing. Said she couldn't afford anything in the shop and axed if we didn't have nothing cheaper. Then I minded we had a conch on sale."

"A what?"

"A conch shell, like these here."

The girl pointed to a basket full of huge, beautifully polished seashells. They were a delicate pearly pink, smooth and whorled, and only marred—in Emmy's eyes—by the fact that somebody had engraved the words ST. MARK'S ISLAND on the satiny inner surface. "People put flowers in them," the girl added. Sure enough, one stood on the counter, balanced on three ballet-point spikes, holding a bouquet of double pink hibiscus blossoms.

"They're beautiful," Emmy said.

"They're eight dollars fifty," said the girl, more practically. "But happened I remembered we had one going for just two bucks on account it was scratched and had a point broken. So the lady took it. I recall she said her friend didn't have such good eyes and wouldn't notice." The girl laughed attractively.

Emmy thanked her and then said, "You didn't see my aunt again after that, did you?"

"She didn't come in the shop again, no. But I just see her when I come out at twelve to shut up for lunch. She down there in one of the phone booths, making a call. I went off home then. Never see her again."

Feeling compelled to repay the girl's information with at least a token purchase, Emmy bought a plastic paperweight with a rather unconvincing seahorse embedded in it. The girl put it into a flimsy paper bag with CARIBBEAN TREASURE TROVE printed smudgily across it and bade her a polite good afternoon.

Bob Harrison had gone back to his office, and Henry was sitting in the cockpit of the *Windflower,* looking out with great pleasure over the marina—a shiny bright scene of gleaming paintwork and dancing water and fluttering flags, which never failed to enchant him wherever in the world sailing boats were gathered together. He saw Emmy coming down the jetty and got up to help her climb over the coaming of the boat and into the cockpit.

Windflower did not have a very high freeboard, but even so it was quite a scramble from the unstable floating pontoon up to the deck, and in spite of Henry's steadying hand, Emmy misjudged her foothold and was caught off balance for a moment—long enough for the flimsy paper bag from the gift shop to hit a stanchion and split. With an almost inaudible plop, the plastic paperweight nose-dived into the water.

"Oh, damn," said Emmy. "Not that it matters—it's just a souvenir I felt I had to buy." She scrambled on board.

Henry was gazing down into the water, which was crystal-clear and about ten feet deep. "I can see it," he said. "I'll dive down and get it when I go for a swim. Well, how did you get on?"

Emmy told him. "It all checks out with what we already know," she said. "Betsy took a cab from the harbor to here and went to the shop to buy presents. Coming out, there's an excellent view of the restaurant, where she thought she saw the Vanduren girl. So she went over to the telephone booths and called you—the gift shop assistant noticed her making the call as she was leaving for lunch."

"And Betsy had her baggage with her?"

"I told you, the girl remarked on it."

Henry was thoughtful. "And then she left the telephone to go and speak to the girl she supposed to be Janet Vanduren—and the trail ends."

Emmy said, "The next thing is to locate that girl, if we can—but there's so little to go on. A dark girl having a drink with a dark, bearded young man." She gestured hopelessly. "There must be fifty couples like that around here every day—either off boats or hotel-based tourists. Anyhow, whoever those people were, they've almost certainly left by now—a couple of days can mean a big turnaround in population in a place like this, especially at a weekend. I suppose it might be worth asking the waitresses at the restaurant. One of them might remember something."

Henry looked at his watch. "What we have to do now is to go and see Sergeant—sorry—Chief Inspector Ingham. We'll take a taxi to the police station."

"And I'll buy some provisions in town," Emmy said. "I rather like housekeeping again, for a change."

"Well, just get enough for breakfast," Henry said. "I thought we'd dine ashore tonight. We obviously won't be leaving until quite late tomorrow, and I thought we might try the marina restaurant and ask a few questions about Betsy at the same time."

Emmy said, "Henry—you're not going to . . . I mean, start an inquiry, are you?"

"Good heavens, no. It's nothing to do with us. We're on holiday. It's a matter for the local police—if anybody."

"What does that mean—if anybody?"

"Well—" Henry paused. "Betsy's a curious old girl and quite unpredictable. She may well have taken it into her head to go off somewhere, telling nobody."

"Margaret and John are very worried," Emmy said.

"She's their friend—Margaret's, anyhow. We hardly know her. We'll ask at the restaurant this evening, and we'll tell the Colvilles about the gift shop. After that, we'll leave it to Ingham."

Emmy smiled. "I shall be delighted to do just that," she said. "Where shall we go tomorrow? I thought Tortola might be fun."

Henry gave her a sharp look. "We'll see," he said.

4

CHIEF INSPECTOR INGHAM WAS PLEASED to welcome his old friend Chief Superintendent Tibbett. His whitewashed office in the police station on Main Street was shady and cooled by an electric fan, and Ingham himself looked spruce and prosperous in his pale blue, short-sleeved uniform shirt. His shoulders were loaded with the silver epaulets of rank.

After a brief chat about old times, Henry raised the question of Miss Betsy Sprague. Inspector Ingham smiled broadly.

"John Colville was talking to me this morning," he said. "The lady is a friend of yours?"

"Not really," Henry said. "She's a friend of Margaret's. We just met her while we were staying at the Anchorage. I wouldn't worry, except that she's not young—"

"But a healthy old lady?" Ingham put in.

Emmy grinned. "No doubt about that."

"And I gather she had been on a long tour of the United States, visiting old pupils, traveling alone from place to place."

"You seem to know all about her," Henry said.

Ingham smiled. "There are few secrets in these islands," he said. "A lady with a certain . . . well, personality . . . like Miss Sprague is bound to be noticed. She spoke to many people on St. Matthew's. I find it hard to believe that any harm has come to her."

"So do I," said Henry. "On the other hand, it's odd that she didn't tell her friends in England that she had changed her plans."

"She lived with friends?"

"No, no. But there was the question of her cats—"

This time, Ingham laughed outright. "My dear Mr. Tibbett, you tell me that someone is going to pay to send telegrams to England about cats?"

"English people—" Henry began.

Ingham cut him short. "Miss Sprague has changed her mind and prolonged her holiday, you may be sure," he said. "Nevertheless, to please John Colville, I have already done some checking here. Her Immigration form has not been handed in either at the airport or the marine Customs and Immigration office, so it is virtually certain that she is still in the Seawards." He made a note on his jotting pad. "It is sure, at least, that she reached St. Mark's?"

"Yes. We've traced her as far as the marina."

"Well, I will contact the only four hotels at which I can imagine an English lady staying. If she is not at any of them, she must have returned to St. Matthew's on the *Pride*. She might have taken the afternoon boat to George Island—the third of our group—but there is no hotel there, just a beach bar and restaurant, used by visiting yachts. The most likely thing is that she is staying with friends on one of the islands. Now let us talk of more cheerful matters."

"Just one thing," Henry said. "What do you know of the *Isabella*?"

"The—? Oh, you mean the American yacht that went down in January. A very sad accident. It really had nothing to do with us."

"I thought the boat was last seen—"

"She had cleared British Seaward waters. St. Matthew's was her last recorded port of call, and she certainly left Priest Town Harbour. The alarm was raised a week later when she failed to show up in Puerto Rico, and it was the U.S. Coast Guard who undertook the search. They are better equipped for that sort of thing than we are," added Herbert Ingham, in the understatement of the century.

"And nothing was ever found—no wreckage, no bodies?" Emmy asked.

"Some wreckage was found. If you're interested, I can look it up. The U.S. Coast Guard sent us a report." He got up and ruffled through papers in a big filing cabinet. After a minute or so, he pulled out a document. "Here we are. Report from the Coast Guard . . . 'Wreckage picked up by fishing vessel *Anna Maria* on February 18 in Exuma Sound . . . strong likelihood that said wreckage formed part of missing yacht *Isabella* . . . positive identification impossible owing to deterioration . . . water damage . . .' "

Henry interrupted to say, "How much wreckage was found?"

Ingham ran his eye down the report. "A couple of planks . . . remnants of white paint still adhering . . . part of dinghy transom with letter *A* still decipherable . . . severe water damage . . . traces of fire damage . . ."

"And where is Exuma Sound?" Henry asked.

There was a big map of the Caribbean area, from Florida to the coast of South America, hanging on the wall. Ingham went over to it and pointed. "Here. In the Bahamas. Between Andros Island and Cat Island, roughly—that's where the *Anna Maria* picked up the wreckage."

Emmy said, "But that's miles from St. Matthew's! And much too far north!"

Inspector Ingham waved a large black hand. "The north equatorial current—" he began, without too much conviction.

Henry opened his mouth to speak, but Emmy got her word in first.

"What you're really saying is that there's no proof at all that the wreckage was the *Isabella*. It was in quite the wrong place and with no positive identification. And anyhow," she ended triumphantly, "Exuma Sound is inside the Bermuda Triangle!"

Ingham smiled, with some embarrassment. "Well, now, Mrs. Tibbett, you know it's often difficult to make an exact identification in cases of shipwreck. Photographs of the wreckage were sent to Dr. Vanduren, and he gave his opinion that the lettering could have been from the transom of *Isabella*'s dinghy. It does no good for these matters to drag on unresolved. The Coast Guard has to decide on a basis of probability, and as far as they're concerned, the wreckage was from the *Isabella* and the case is closed."

"Well, it isn't closed for the Vanduren family," Emmy said stubbornly.

"How do you mean, Mrs. Tibbett?"

"Betsy Sprague was in touch with Dr. Vanduren quite recently, and he said they had no idea of what had happened to their daughter or the boat."

Ingham was puzzled. "I'm afraid I don't quite understand. I had no idea that Miss Sprague was in any way connected—"

"Well, she was. And what's more—"

Henry, in a tone of voice which Emmy recognized as a warning, said, "She had no connection, Inspector. She's a friend of the Vanduren family, that's all, and she was talking to us about the *Isabella*—which is why I asked you about it. I'm glad to hear it has been cleared up."

"No bodies have been found," muttered Emmy mulishly.

34

"Even though no bodies have been found," Henry said, with a conspiratorial smile in Ingham's direction. "Well, it's been delightful to meet you again. Emmy and I will be setting off from the marina around lunchtime tomorrow, I expect. If there's any news of Miss Sprague before then, I'd be grateful if you'd let us know. It would set Emmy's mind at rest. Meanwhile, I hope we'll see you again while we're here. Good-bye for now, Inspector Ingham."

Outside in the sun-splashed street, Emmy was vehemently indignant.

"Treating me like an imbecile child! I know very well what's happened. Just because nobody official is prepared to acknowledge that the Bermuda Triangle may be—"

Henry took her arm. "My dear Emmy," he said, "I'm sorry. I just thought that you were going to blurt out that Betsy thought she had seen Janet Vanduren at the marina here."

"What do you mean, blurt? I think Inspector Ingham ought to know. If there's something mysterious . . ." She broke off and looked critically at her husband. "Ah, I see it now. You're afraid of looking like a fool."

"I don't want to get involved," said Henry. "It's no business of mine."

"Isn't it?"

"Of course it isn't. I'll phone John when we get back to the marina and tell him about the gift shop and what Ingham said. Then I intend to go sailing and enjoy myself."

"Hm," said Emmy. Then they caught sight of a shop selling hand-printed cotton in glorious Caribbean colors, and Betsy Sprague was temporarily forgotten.

They arrived back at *Windflower* soon after five o'clock, after making the promised phone call to the Colvilles, who reported that they had had no further news. They changed into swimsuits, and as they climbed ashore, with their snorkel masks and fins slung in a string shopping bag, Emmy said, "Oh, Henry. My little paperweight. Can you get it for me?"

"I think so." Henry looked down into the limpid water. "Yes, there it is. I'll dive for it. The water's obviously perfectly clean—thank God some places are serious about preventing pollution."

He put on his mask and fins and slipped into the water from the pontoon. Emmy watched from above as his hand closed around the little plastic globe. However, he did not surface at once, but seemed to be looking at something she could not see in the shadow of the jetty. Then he came up, breaking the water surface with the paperweight in his hand. He said, "Take this, Emmy. I'm going down again."

Down he went, into the sunlit water and then into shadow. When he reemerged, he was holding something in his right hand. Emmy drew in a quick breath of surprise. It was a pale pink conch shell of exactly the same kind that she had seen in the gift shop. He handed it up to her.

"Look at it," Henry said. He had taken off his mask and was scrambling up onto the pontoon.

Emmy turned the shell over in her hands. Like the shells in the shop, it had ST. MARK'S ISLAND engraved on its shining whorl, but the engraver's tool had apparently slipped, because there was a scratch running downward from the "s" of Island: besides this, one of the projecting points on which the shell could be balanced was broken at the tip. Not worth eight dollars fifty, but on sale at two bucks.

Emmy said, "The conch that Betsy bought."

"It certainly looks like it. I would never have spotted it if I hadn't gone down."

"But—why just the shell? Where's the rest of her luggage? What happened?"

"I'd say," said Henry, "that the same thing happened to her as happened to you. She was climbing on board a boat and dropped the shell, just as you dropped your paperweight."

Emmy frowned, thinking. "You mean, the young couple did invite her on board for lunch, as John guessed."

"It looks like it. Betsy and her luggage and her shopping."

"No," Emmy said. "No, that can't be right."

"Why?"

"Because Betsy would never have let her present for Miss Pelling drop in the water and stay there. She'd have insisted on somebody going down and getting it for her—just like you fished up my paperweight."

Henry said, "Quite right. But I said I'd get it for you later, when we came back from the police station. I daresay the young couple told Betsy that they'd dive for her shell after lunch, or when they got back—"

"Where from?"

"Who knows? The fact is that they never got back. Or at least, Betsy didn't."

For a moment, Henry and Emmy looked at each other. Then Emmy said, "Where was the shell, exactly? I mean, which berth do you think the boat was on?"

"That empty one opposite ours, on the other side, I would think," Henry said. And then, "All right. Let's go and ask the Harbour Master."

The Harbour Master's office was a businesslike room in the marina building, close to the Caribbean Treasure Trove. The walls were covered with charts and there was a big plan of the marina, with small paper flags indicating the occupancy of various berths. The Harbour Master—a tall, thin man with a small mustache and a light, almost brown, complexion—was explaining to a middle-aged American the procedure necessary for yachtsmen arriving from U.S. waters.

"You have to take a taxi to the town quay, sir, with the ship's papers and your passports. There you report to Customs and Immigration—"

"For Pete's sake, do we all have to go?" demanded the American. "There're six of us."

"No, that's not necessary, sir. As skipper, you can go alone—but take all the passports for stamping. Then you get your clearance, and that's all there is to it."

Muttering something about a crazy setup, the American left the office. The Harbour Master made an entry in a big ledger and then looked up and smiled at the Tibbetts.

"Yes, sir . . . madam. What can I do for you? You're chartering *Windflower* for a week, I believe. I'd be grateful if you'd let me know when your berth is going to be vacant overnight—we need space for visiting boats every evening. And don't forget to check out with Customs and Immigration if you plan to leave Seaward waters."

Henry said, "Actually, I'm after a piece of information, if you can help me."

"I'll certainly try. Something about the marina?"

"In a way. I'm trying to find out the name of the boat that was moored opposite *Windflower* last Thursday."

The Harbour Master looked not unnaturally surprised. For a moment he hesitated, then evidently decided that tourists—even if weak in the head—should be kept happy. He got up and went over to the chart on the wall.

"Let's see. *Windflower* is here, in number thirty-six. You mean the berth on the other side of the pontoon? Number fourteen?" He indicated a space on the plan that had a little paper flag marked BLUEBIRD in it.

Henry nodded. "The berth's empty at the moment," he said.

"Not for long," remarked the Harbour Master. "*Bluebird* went to George Island for lunch, but the skipper axed me to be sure to keep the berth free, as they'd be back this evening."

"So it's *Bluebird*—" Emmy began.

"Not if you're interested in last Thursday." The Harbour Master was back at his desk, thumbing through his ledger. "*Bluebird* only came in on Friday. Last Thursday . . . let's see . . ." There was a little pause. Then he said, "Last Thursday the *Chermar* was on that mooring."

"The *Charmer*?" Henry said.

"No, sir. *Chermar*. C-h-e-r-m-a-r."

"That's a funny name for a boat."

The Harbour Master smiled indulgently. "Young couples often do it," he said. "Name their boat after both their names. Happen I hear these two talking, and they called Cheryl and Martin. *Chermar*—get it? Big white motor cruiser. Well, when I say big—thirty-five foot. Nice craft." He paused, and then, with inevitable West Indian curiosity, added, "Friends of yours?"

"Not exactly," Henry said. "So they left on Thursday, did they?"

"Seems so."

"How do you mean?"

Quite suddenly, the Harbour Master became suspicious. He shut his ledger with a bang, stood up, and said, "If the people on *Chermar* aren't friends of yours, sir, I'm afraid I can't discuss them anymore. Wouldn't be proper."

"Of course, you're perfectly right," Henry said. "The reason I asked is that they left something behind at the mooring."

"Well, I wouldn't know where to find them to give it back, sir," said the Harbour Master firmly. "I could try to raise them on VHF radio, but I'd be surprised if they're still in range. They only stayed overnight—put in for a small repair, the gentleman told me." He stopped abruptly, then said, "Here, if you found something on the jetty today, it'ud be from *Bluebird*. What made you ask about Thursday? And what's the thing you found, anyway?"

"Just a souvenir," said Henry. He grabbed Emmy's hand, and the two of them were out of the office in an instant, leaving behind a highly suspicious Harbour Master. From the doorway of his office, he watched them making for the row of telephone booths. He saw Henry ruffling the pages of the local directory while Emmy fished her small-change purse out of the snorkel bag. After a moment of indecision, the Harbour Master walked back into his office and picked up his own telephone to make a call.

Inspector Herbert Ingham was on the point of leaving the police station for the day when Henry's call came through. He listened with amused indulgence and then said, "Well, that clears that up, then, doesn't it? Silly of me not to think of it before."

"Think of what?"

"That the lady might have gone off on a private yacht with friends. Funny how the most obvious explanation often . . . What's that? . . . Well, really, Chief Superintendent, I don't think I can . . . Now, see here, the lady is a free agent and able to look after herself, isn't she? If she chooses to cruise the islands with friends instead of going home to England, that's nobody's business but her own. . . . No, I can't put out an alarm call for the boat . . . Well, yes, I could inquire if she's at St. Matthew's or George Island, but . . . oh, very well . . . What's the name of the boat? . . . How do you spell it? . . . Oh, I see, one of those composite names. . . . Well, I can tell you one thing, a boat with a name like that isn't going to be doing anything except holiday cruising. This Cheryl and Martin will be a rich young couple, probably from Florida. . . . Customs and Immigration? . . . Yes, they'll still be there if you hurry. . . ." He sighed. "All right, I'll call them . . . Officer Cranstone is the man you want, he's Immigration. . . . O.K., see you tomorrow. . . ."

Chief Inspector Ingham put down the telephone, irritated. He had enough serious things on his mind without having to bother with a Chief Superintendent from Scotland Yard fussing over an old lady, who was quite obviously enjoying an extended vacation on board a friend's boat. It was with no enthusiasm that he picked up the telephone and called the Customs and Immigration office.

"Cranstone? Herbert Ingham here. There's a fellow on the way to see you, name of Tibbett . . . Chief Superintendent from Scotland Yard . . . No, quite unofficial, he's on holiday with his wife, but he's after some information, and we can't very well refuse to cooperate. . . . Yes, anything he wants to know. . . . Sure I'll be at the fish fry tonight . . . see you there, man. . . ."

The Customs and Immigration office was situated on the town quay next to the fish market. Officer Cranstone, cool and trim in white shirt and black trousers, was happy to explain Immigration procedure to Henry and Emmy.

"Skippers of visiting boats report in here to me," he said, "with passports and the ship's papers. We stamp the passports, issue Immigration cards which have to be surrendered when the person leaves the Seawards, and give the ship clearance. The Customs Officer makes a spot check at the marina every so often, but you understand we can't possibly search every boat, any more than they can go through every suitcase at the airport. These people are on vacation, and we do our best to make things easy and pleasant for them. Coming by boat is a sort of guarantee, anyway."

"Guarantee? How do you mean?"

"Well, sir, the sort of people we want to discourage are the vagrants . . . hippies and the like, and people with no proper means of support, who try to slip in as visitors and then take odd jobs and stay in the islands. That's why the airport has to be more strict. There, we demand that visitors show a return ticket and prove they have somewhere to stay and means of support. But a boat *is* a return ticket and somewhere to stay, and it's easy to check. So we try not to bother them too much."

"But you do keep records?" Henry asked.

"Of course. Here's our register of incoming boats, with the names and passport numbers of skippers and crews . . ."

"What about outgoing boats?"

Cranstone, who was chubby and good-natured, rubbed his plump chin and smiled. "Yes, indeed, sir. The skipper checks the boat out and hands in the Immigration forms."

Henry said, "Supposing the skipper of a yacht just ups anchor and leaves, without checking out?"

"He'll be in trouble at his next port of call, that's what," said Cranstone. "If he can't produce a valid clearance for his boat, he'll be liable to a stiff fine—and you may be sure the Customs will give his ship a proper going-over."

"I see," Henry said. "Well, I'm interested in a motor cruiser called the *Chermar,* which was berthed at the marina on Wednesday last week and left on Thursday. I don't know where she arrived from. Can you help me?"

"Surely, sir." Cranstone thumbed through his records and a few minutes later came up with results. "Here she is. June 18, last Wednesday. *Chermar,* thirty-five-foot motor cruiser, port of registry Annapolis, Maryland, U.S.A., last port of call British Virgin Islands, owner-skipper Mr. Martin Ross of Washington, D.C., crew Mrs. Cheryl Ross, same address, British passports."

"British?"

"Yes, sir. I remember Mr. Ross now—it's not often we get Britishers coming in on boats. He told me he was working in Washington, living temporarily in the States. But his wife was American, he told me, from Florida, if I remember right. She had two passports, American and British, and he made quite a joke of it, asking which one I wanted to see. A very nice gentleman."

"Did he speak like an Englishman?" Henry asked.

Cranstone looked puzzled. At length he said, "He spoke like a white man."

Henry did not press the point. He should have realized, he thought, that to a West Indian English and American accents are no more distinguishable than the regional variations of Creole from different islands would be to him. He said, "Did the *Chermar* check out with you?"

"No, sir. I've no record of her leaving. Mr. Ross did mention that they'd put in for a small repair and would be away again in a couple of days—but maybe the repair is taking longer. Or maybe they're still in the Seawards. You could check with St. Matthew's."

"Mr. Ross came alone to your office, with the two passports?"

"Yes, sir." Cranstone paused. "Nothing wrong about the *Chermar* was there, sir?"

"I don't know," Henry said. "I hope not."

That evening, the Tibbetts dined ashore at the marina restaurant. It was clear that people from cruising boats welcomed a chance to escape from the galley and eat ashore, for the place was crowded; and since most visiting yachtsmen stayed only a few days, Henry had little hope that any of the restaurant staff would remember an individual tourist. Luckily, however, Betsy Sprague must have stood out among the crowd of bronzed young Americans like a crow in a cage of canaries. The waitress who served the Tibbetts remembered her.

"The funny-looking old lady in the long skirt and big hat? Sure, I do recall her. I only saw her the one time. She was with two people off a boat. They'd paid their check and were leaving when she came up to talk to them. They all sat down again and I brought them drinks. Next thing I saw, they were all going off down the jetty to the boat, I reckon. The young man was carrying the lady's suitcases." The waitress, a small and very black girl with a round face and a cornrow hairdo, smiled attractively. "I remember thinking she must be a relation, like an aunt. Otherwise it seemed kind of funny that an old lady should go cruising with a young couple. But that's what must have happened because I never saw any of them again."

Henry said, "Do you think you could recognize the couple she was with?"

The waitress laughed merrily. "I could try," she said, "but, matter of fact, most white folks look pretty much alike to me. Beside, we get so many in here, different every day. The gentleman was dark and had a beard, but then most of them do. No, it's the old lady I recall."

Henry and Emmy had finished dinner and were drinking coffee when they noticed the Harbour Master—who had long since closed his office and left for the day—coming back into the marina, accompanied by a grim-looking Inspector Ingham, now in civilian clothes. The Harbour Master unlocked his office and switched on the light, and the two men went inside. Through the open door, Henry could see them in earnest conversation, poring over papers and charts on the desk. Then they both came out and made their way purposefully down the jetty.

Emmy said, "I do believe they're going to *Windflower*, Henry. They must be looking for us."

Henry stood up. "You settle the bill," he said. "I'll go and see what's up."

He overtook the two men as they were leaving the deserted *Windflower*.

Inspector Ingham said, "Ah, there you are, Chief Superintendent. Come into the office for a moment, will you?"

"What's all this about?" Henry asked.

Ingham did not reply, but led the way back down the jetty and into the Harbour Master's office. He closed the door carefully, and then said, "You'd better take us into your confidence, sir. We can't work in the dark."

"I don't understand," Henry said.

"What do you know about the *Chermar*?" demanded the Harbour Master. Not being a policeman, he was quite unimpressed by Henry's rank.

Ingham said, "You've been making inquiries about the *Chermar*—"

"Yes, but—"

"I must ask you why, sir. You told Anderson here that the *Chermar* had left something behind on the jetty, and then you simply disappeared without answering when he asked you what it was. You then telephoned me—"

"All right, all right," Henry said. "I was interested in the *Chermar*—in fact, I still am—because, as I told you, I thought Miss Sprague might be on board. That's now virtually certain. A waitress at the restaurant saw the Rosses with Miss Sprague last Thursday, carrying her baggage down the pontoon in the direction of the boat, which must have left shortly afterwards. She had certainly gone by Friday. That's my information. What's yours?"

The two black men exchanged a look, and then Ingham said, "Anderson and I were both at the fish fry this evening when the Duty Constable got word to us. She thought it might be important."

"Word about what?"

"She was listening out on VHF and heard the U.S. Coast Guard message. There's a general alert and search out for the *Chermar*. She's overdue in St. Thomas, where the Rosses should have picked up some friends on Thursday evening. When she hadn't turned up by this morning, these friends told the Coast Guard and asked them to try to make radio contact—the *Chermar* carries ship-to-shore radio. The Coast Guard has been trying for more than twelve hours now and can get no response from any area that the *Chermar* might conceivably have reached after leaving here."

"In any case," Anderson put in, "she never cleared the Seawards, either here or in St. Matthew's, so it looks like she never even set out to go to St. Thomas."

Ingham went on. "So now there's a general alert. It could just be a broken radio—but that's unlikely in view of the fact that Mr. Ross knew where his friends were staying in St. Thomas. He could easily have gone ashore somewhere and telephoned them if he was delayed for some reason. But he didn't. So it looks as though we've got another one."

Henry nodded. "Another yacht disappeared without trace. Like the *Isabella*."

"And some others," said Ingham.

The telephone bell shrilled in the small office. The Harbour Master picked it up. "Harbour Master's office . . . Yes, he's here. . . ." He held out the receiver to Ingham. "For you, Herbert."

"Ingham . . . yes . . . yes . . . well, it's only what we expected, isn't it? . . . How much? . . . How many? . . . Anybody we—? . . . Oh, no. Oh, shit. Young Duprez as well? . . . and Laurette MacKay? . . . O.K., go ahead and book them. I'll get up as soon as I can . . . right . . . be seeing you." He put the telephone down and turned to Henry. "It's time we had a talk, Chief

Superintendent. If you can help us, we'd appreciate it."

"About missing boats?" Henry said.

"That was my Detective Inspector. We had a tipoff there was going to be a lot of pot-smoking at the fish fry tonight. So he waited until I'd left—they wouldn't light up while I was actually there—and then made a bust. He's collared a whole group of youngsters with large quantities of marijuana and some heroin as well. It makes me sick."

"Kids of important people, by the sound of it," Anderson said.

Ingham put his hand on the Harbour Master's shoulder. "Kids of good friends, too," he said.

"Not—?"

"I'm afraid so, Elwin. Your boy Sebastian. You'd best get up to the station right away and see about bailing him out. Now, Chief Superintendent, as soon as I've dealt with this lot, I'll come back here. What d'you say we meet on board the *Windflower* in about an hour's time?"

"O.K.," said Henry. "We'll be waiting for you."

5

THE CABIN of the *Windflower* was roomy and comfortable, with a folding dinette table and bunks upholstered in blue canvas. Through the open hatch the tropical moonlight flooded in, making a mockery of the small kerosene lamp. Emmy had made coffee, and now she and Henry sat facing a tired, worried Chief Inspector Ingham across the plastic-topped table.

Ingham said, "Fifteen of them. Boys and girls. All under twenty. All from families I know personally." He swirled the dark coffee in his mug. "If I could lay hands on the people behind this—"

"Did any of them tell you where they got the stuff?" Emmy asked.

Ingham shook his head. "It was being sold at the fish fry, no doubt about that," he said. "Ideal, you see. It's in the open air, it's dark and crowded, and the smell of the frying fish masks the smell of the cannabis. The kids all say they bought their joints off a stranger—a white man. A tourist. I don't believe them. I think that's what they had agreed to say if they got busted. There must be local people involved, although certainly the big guys are in the States." He sighed. "This is big business, man. Last boat the U.S. Coast Guard picked up—a private yacht out of Florida, sailing out of Colombia towards these islands—she had a cargo of hash worth five million dollars on the street."

Henry said, "The young people on this island don't have five million dollars."

"I know it. This is only a small market retail, as it were. What I'm afraid of is that we're being used wholesale."

"How do you mean?" Emmy asked.

"Well, let's put it like this. A boat that's known to be sailing out of Colombia, say, back to the States is going to be searched by

45

Customs. So she wants to stash her cargo at a staging-post, somewhere nice and safe, and then bring it back bit by bit, in innocent-seeming boats. We're a small group of islands, with a small police force and a big tourist industry, mostly in charter boats. We haven't the men or the facilities to check on every damn boat that comes in or out—and even if we did have, we wouldn't want to spoil our main source of income. How many innocent cruising yachtsmen are going to come back to a place where they're treated as criminals? We're walking a tightrope, and the smugglers know it. So we're an ideal halfway stop, with a small but growing retail trade on the side. The main purpose of that is to get the kids hooked, to make sure of local cooperation in the future. The bastards."

Henry said, "Did these kids you arrested describe the man who is supposed to have been selling joints?"

Ingham grinned suddenly. "Sure. Middle-aged, not too tall, sandy-colored hair, blue eyes."

"Henry!" Emmy exclaimed.

"Could be," said Ingham dryly, "except that I happen to know Mr. Tibbett wasn't at the fish fry."

"Does the description fit anybody else you know?" Henry asked.

"No, sir. Nobody on this island. But, of course, tourists come in all shapes and sizes."

Henry said, "Supposing you describe a typical drug-smuggling operation, as you see it."

Ingham sat back and frowned into his coffee mug. "We may have this wrong, man," he said, "but this is what we think. The big guys back in the States recruit young people—probably already hard-drug addicts and willing to do almost anything for a regular fix. Attractive youngsters, from good family backgrounds, and experienced sailors. They either charter a boat, or they're provided with one, Stateside. It's just about impossible for us to pick them out from the genuine tourists. That's how it starts."

"Where do they get the drugs?" Emmy asked.

It was Henry who said, "Colombia is a good source of supply, I believe."

"Far too good," Ingham agreed. "There's really no problem about getting it loaded onto the boat and out of there. Then they turn up in our waters as vacationing yachtsmen on a first-time visit."

"First time?" said Emmy. "Always first time?"

"First and last. They don't use the same boat twice. They don't have to, there's so much money in the organization behind them. One load delivered, here or on another island. Then—poof! No more boat."

"That seems rather extravagant," Emmy said.

"A few times, the boat has been reported lost and then repainted and refitted under another name—but that's when we catch them," said Ingham. "The only sure way is to destroy the boat. You doubt that the wreckage in Exuma Sound came from the *Isabella*. Me, I don't doubt. The *Isabella* is at the bottom of the sea, and Miss Vanduren and her friend are off on another boat, with another load of horse and another identity. What's more, they now have the great advantage of being dead."

Henry said, "All right. You've got the drugs as far as the Seawards. What then?"

"Then," said Inspector Ingham, "they are picked up by another innocent-seeming private yacht returning to the States from a Caribbean cruise. It would take the most monumental Customs operation to stop this."

Henry said, "A private yacht like the *Chermar*?"

"She would have done very well. Except, of course, that she would no longer be in the hands of her real owners."

"You think that Martin and Cheryl Ross were really Janet Vanduren and Ed Marsham?" Emmy asked.

"Why not? That's the way it works."

Emmy said, "That's all very well, but Janet Vanduren was a perfectly respectable girl, a doctor's daughter . . ."

Herbert Ingham looked at her sadly. "You have children, Mrs. Tibbett?"

"No, but—"

"You think parents today know what their children do? You think a respectable father means a respectable son? Ask my friend Mr. Anderson. Ask Mr. MacKay—he's a big lawyer on this island. We busted his daughter this evening. For heroin."

Henry said, "In view of all this, I think I must tell you that Betsy Sprague recognized Janet Vanduren."

Ingham's head came up with a jerk. "Recognized? Where?"

"First of all, in St. Matthew's on the *Isabella*. And then, after the *Isabella* had been lost—here, just last week. But by then, Miss Vanduren had become Mrs. Ross and had acquired a new boyfriend."

"You never told me this," said Ingham angrily.

"I didn't want to start anything until I was sure," Henry said. "Anyhow, what difference would it have made? The *Chermar* had already sailed, and Betsy Sprague was already . . ." Henry paused. "You haven't yet told us the worst, have you, Inspector Ingham?"

Ingham said nothing, but clasped his coffee mug and studied his naked feet.

Henry went on. "Where do these new identities come from?"

"Passports can be forged, and there's a market for them among illegal immigrants." Ingham did his best to sound convincing.

Henry said, "Martin Ross told the Immigration Officer that he was British, working in Washington, married to an American wife. All that can easily be checked out. And what about the friends who raised the alarm when the *Chermar* didn't show up in St. Thomas? Do you really believe that the Rosses never existed?"

An endless pause. Then Ingham said, "You are right, of course. Mr. and Mrs. Ross existed, and the *Chermar* was their boat. They are almost certainly dead, like many others."

"Lost at sea," said Emmy bitterly.

"Exactly. Lost at sea. It happens. Try to prove it was murder, and you get nowhere. Publicize it, and you lose your tourist trade. Oh, shit," said Inspector Ingham, becoming very human and very West Indian, "those bastards. Those bloody bastards."

Henry said, "There remains Miss Janet Vanduren. If it was Miss Vanduren and not somebody impersonating her."

At once, Emmy said, "Betsy recognized her."

"Betsy's an old lady, and she hadn't seen Janet for some years—"

"If Betsy said it was Janet Vanduren, then it was." Emmy was quite definite.

Inspector Ingham seemed to come to a decision. He said, "How long are you planning on staying in the islands, sir?"

"Just another week."

"Well, sir, with your permission I'm going to ask the Governor to contact Scotland Yard and request that this case be put officially in your hands, and that you stay as long as necessary to clear it up."

Henry half-smiled. "What case?" he said.

Ingham smiled back. "Not the Rosses," he said. "That's outside our jurisdiction. It would have to be the case of the vanishing lady, Miss Sprague."

There was a pause. Ingham went on. "You see, sir, you have the enormous advantage that you're not known. Nobody on St. Mark's except Anderson, Cranstone, and myself knows who you are. You're a perfectly genuine tourist from England, and you can go on being just that. My trouble is my face is too darn well known. I can't operate freely. But you—"

"All right," said Henry. "I don't like it, but for Betsy's sake I can't refuse."

"Good," said Ingham briefly. He stood up, stooping slightly under *Windflower*'s cabin roof, and looked at his watch. "Half-past ten. I'll call the Governor right away, and he can contact England at around five A.M.—it'll be ten in the morning in London then. I daresay he'll want to have a talk with you tomorrow. I'll get Anderson to let you know where and when. From now on, you and I shouldn't be seen together. Thank you, sir."

Inspector Ingham climbed out of *Windflower*'s cockpit, and the Tibbetts watched his tall figure striding down the jetty in the moonlight.

Emmy said, "If it wasn't for Betsy, I'd be furious. We're supposed to be on holiday."

"If it wasn't for Betsy," said Henry, "I'd have refused."

JOHN COLVILLE HAD DESCRIBED the new Governor as a quiet, intellectual type, and Henry—sipping sherry with His Excellency Sir Alfred Pendleton in the airy, old-fashioned drawing room at Government House—found himself in complete agreement. Sir Alfred might be unconventionally dressed in white drill shorts and a green open-necked shirt with blue dolphins cavorting over it, but still his neat features and rimless spectacles suggested a university don.

"The Assistant Commissioner was most helpful," he said, in his slightly clipped voice, "and not at all put out at being telephoned on a Sunday morning. You are to be given every facility, and funds as well as men will be made available to you—within reason. These are not wealthy islands, as you know. I sincerely hope, Chief Superintendent, that you can help us—not only to locate Miss Sprague, but to solve our drug problem. Do you have a plan of action?"

"Yes, I do," said Henry, "and my very first move will mean funds, I'm afraid, sir. I want to go with my wife to Miami by the next available plane and talk to Dr. Vanduren. I'm hoping to get photographs of Janet Vanduren and her fiancé, among other things."

"Very sensible," said Sir Alfred, as if bestowing an Alpha. "There will be no problem about that. And then?"

Henry considered. At length, he said, "I have a theory, sir, that I

49

haven't yet mentioned to Chief Inspector Ingham. I believe that the Rosses were selected as victims for a specific reason."

"Because they resembled Vanduren and Marsham physically?"

"No, sir. They didn't. Miss Vanduren had to dye her hair and change her companion to keep up the physical resemblance. I believe the reason was that the Rosses had British passports."

Pendleton looked puzzled. "Why would that be an advantage?"

Henry said, "Inspector Ingham explained to us that he feels these islands are being used as a staging-post. The real destination of the drugs is the United States."

"Correct."

"Well, then. To bring their cargo and dump it here, the smugglers prefer United States passports because that makes them seem like genuine tourists, and the authorities don't want to harass foreign visitors. Also, British tourists are rarities and likely to be remembered." The Governor nodded. Henry went on. "However, when it comes to the second part of the trip—from here to the States—it's obviously an advantage to be British. American Customs authorities are very strict with their own nationals, but—once again—they go lightly on foreign tourists. Mr. Ross had an especially desirable status."

"In what way?"

"I checked by telephone earlier this morning with friends in Washington, sir. Not only was Mr. Ross a very real person, but he worked for an international organization, and therefore had a G-four or semidiplomatic visa. This carries Customs privileges. As Martin and Cheryl Ross, the smugglers could have waltzed into the United States with no trouble at all."

"So you think the *Chermar* came here to pick up a load, rather than drop one?" said Sir Alfred.

"She may well have dropped a load as well," Henry said, "but with British identities I'm convinced she was headed for America. As we know, she never got there. My theory is that when Betsy spotted Janet Vanduren, the couple had actually come ashore to pick up their cargo. Betsy's interference made that impossible. She had to be bustled on board, taken to sea, and murdered. Then the *Chermar* had to be disposed of posthaste—and the Ross identity with it. What I'm banking on is the fact that they're bound to try again."

"You mean, they'll come back to St. Mark's?"

"They'll have to. The cargo is still on the island, waiting to be picked up. The girl can dye her hair again overnight, the man can shave off his beard—they were only here for one night. Nobody is going to recognize them."

"They'll need new identities and another boat," Sir Alfred remarked. "It's not so easy to pick up a couple of British passports around here."

"I intend," Henry said, "to make it very easy indeed."

"You . . . what are you suggesting, Tibbett?"

"Emmy and I," Henry said, "may not be exactly young, bronzed, and fit, but we are British and we are chartering a privately owned American boat. If we trail our coats invitingly enough, I think we stand a good chance of being picked as the next victims."

The Governor did not exactly smile—Henry had the impression that he was an infrequent smiler—but he compressed his thin lips, and the corners of them tilted upward. He said, "I like that. I like that very much, Tibbett. I suppose you realize that there will be considerable danger if your plan should work."

"Of course. That's why I think I should be armed and equipped with a ship-to-shore radio, which *Windflower* doesn't possess at the moment. If my plan succeeds, police and Coast Guard should keep a constant listen-out and be prepared to act quickly. You can arrange that with the United States authorities?"

"Of course. They are as anxious as we are to catch these people." Sir Alfred stood up. "There's a plane at three for San Juan. You'll have to stay there overnight and catch the early-morning flight to Miami. You can get back to San Juan tomorrow evening, and here early on Tuesday. Your line of communication with Inspector Ingham will be through Anderson, the Harbour Master. Ingham will report to me. Good luck, Tibbett." He held out his hand. Then, almost shamefacedly, he said, "Wish I was coming with you. Not to Miami. I mean, on the boat trip."

A chord of memory stirred at the back of Henry's mind. He said, "In World War Two, sir, weren't you—?"

Sir Alfred looked at his feet and actually blushed. "Buckmaster's outfit, special operations in Occupied Europe," he said. "Spoke French, you see . . . well, good-bye, Tibbett."

DR. LIONEL VANDUREN'S HOUSE was a white-painted rambler, which sprawled attractively over an undulating green lawn in a well-to-do suburb of Miami. The doctor himself—a huge, grizzled man who seemed to be made out of rawhide—opened the front

51

door to greet the Tibbetts. He held a table napkin in his hand, explaining that he was having an early lunch—it was a little before noon—as he had afternoon surgery at one.

"Got your phone call from the airport," he announced unnecessarily. "Better come into the dining room."

Dr. Vanduren led the way into the dining room, motioned the Tibbetts to sit down, and took the chair at the head of the table, where he proceeded to attack a plate of cold ham and salad. Between mouthfuls, he said, "Now then, what's all this? Some sort of cruel hoax, by the sound of it. All I know about you is that your name is Tibbett, you're British, and you think my daughter may have been seen alive in the Seaward Islands. Well, get this. I don't care who y'are or where you're from, and you can tell that to the Queen of England with my compliments. My daughter, Janet, and her fiancé were drowned in Exuma Sound when the *Isabella* went down. Probably a fire on board. It gave my wife a complete breakdown—she's still in England with her mother—and I'm damned if I'm going to have her upset by any goddamn stupid stories that Jan may still be alive. Got it?"

Henry said, "You know Miss Betsy Sprague, don't you, Doctor?"

"That crazy old biddy who came to stay here five-six years ago? Celia's old schoolmarm from England? Sure, I remember her. What about her?"

"How well did she know Janet, Dr. Vanduren?"

"How well? How should I know. I tell you, she stayed here about six years ago. I guess you could say that she knew Jan."

Henry said, "Miss Sprague recognized your daughter on the *Isabella* in St. Matthew's marina and spoke to her, back in January. That was the very day that the *Isabella* sailed for the last time, as far as anybody knows."

"I know that." The doctor wiped his mouth on his napkin and cut himself a hunk of cheese. "The old girl wrote to Celia. Heartbreaking. With the mails taking such a time, the letter telling Celia that Jan was safe and well came just the day after we'd put out the full Coast Guard alert. It was the last positive news we had of Jan."

Henry said, "I told you on the telephone that somebody thought they had recognized Janet, alive and well and on St. Mark's Island, just last week. That somebody was Betsy Sprague."

There was a silence. The doctor sank his large teeth into the cheese and reached for a slice of bread.

It was Emmy who said, "Don't you understand what we're telling you, Dr. Vanduren?"

"I do." Indistinctly, through a mouthful of food.

"Aren't you even interested?"

Vanduren turned to Emmy, swallowed, and said, "No, lady, I'm not. And I'll tell you why. That old Sprague woman was crazy even six years ago. All that stuff about continental drift and oolithic limestone under the Everglades and giving away free drugs. Nutty as a fruitcake. I don't believe for one goddamn moment that she saw Jan again. How could she have?"

Henry said, "When Betsy spoke to her in St. Matthew's in January, Janet was blonde. But when she saw her last week, she appeared to have dyed her hair dark."

Dr. Vanduren snorted. "See what I mean? Of course it was some quite different girl. You show this old Sprague creature a selection of pretty girls and just ask her to pick out Jan. She won't be able to tell one from the other."

Henry shook his head. "I wish I could," he said, "but it can't be done."

"What d'you mean, can't be done?"

"Miss Sprague," Henry said, "went off on a boat with the girl she recognized as your daughter and a young man."

"Don't tell me she claims she saw Ed alive too, for crying out loud."

"Apparently she met Ed in St. Matthews, but he wasn't the same young man who was with Janet last week. Anyhow, Betsy went off on a motor cruiser with this young couple, and none of them has been seen since. In fact, the boat has been reported overdue, and there's a search on."

Dr. Vanduren was by now looking somewhat shaken and very suspicious. He said, "What's your interest in all this, Mr. Tibbett?"

Henry said, "Miss Sprague is a friend of ours, so naturally we're concerned about her. We happened to be vacationing in the Caribbean, so when Betsy recognized—or thought she recognized—your daughter, she phoned me and told me. Then, instead of flying back to England as planned, she boarded this boat and disappeared."

After an uneasy pause, Vanduren said, "What boat was this? Who owns it?"

"The boat was called the *Chermar,* owned by Martin and Cheryl Ross of Washington, D.C."

"Ross? Martin Ross? You don't mean the British boy who married Neil Stockley's daughter?"

"Do I?" Henry said. "It's possible. Mrs. Ross is American and comes from Florida, and Mr. Ross is British."

"Very fine attorney, Neil. Dead now, of course. Heart attack—only sixty-six. His girl, Cheryl, married this English guy. Celia went to the wedding."

Henry said, "I bought a Miami *Herald* at the airport, but I haven't had time to look at it. Want to see it? There might be something. The boat was posted missing on Saturday evening."

Dr. Vanduren almost snatched the newspaper from Henry's hand and turned the pages feverishly. He read for a moment and then said, "Jesus Christ. Here it is. 'U.S. Coast Guard puts out alert for missing yacht. The motor cruiser *Chermar,* with the owners Mr. and Mrs. Martin Ross aboard, is being sought in the Caribbean after being reported overdue in St. Thomas, U.S. Virgin Islands. Mrs. Ross is the daughter of the late Neil Stockley of Miami Beach, who . . .'" He looked up and glared at Henry. "What does this mean?"

"Another tragic yachting accident, I'm afraid, Dr. Vanduren." Henry paused. "Did your daughter know the Rosses?"

"She and Cheryl were friends at school, but after Neil died and Cheryl went to work in D.C., we kind of lost touch. They invited us all to the wedding, but only Celia was able to go." He frowned and said again, "What does it mean?"

Henry said, "I wish I knew. It appears to mean that, since Betsy was very positive about her identification, either your daughter was impersonating Cheryl Ross six months after her presumed death by drowning—or else Cheryl Ross was for some reason impersonating Janet in January."

"That's nonsense."

"It's extremely puzzling, I agree," said Henry. "It's perfectly possible that after six years Miss Sprague might not have recognized Janet, and might just have assumed that the girl on the *Isabella* must be her. But six months is a different matter, and she was quite certain that the two girls were identical." Henry paused. "Dr. Vanduren, have you a photograph of Janet that you can give me to send to the police in the Seawards?"

Vanduren pushed his chair away from the table and stood up.

"No," he said.

Emmy said, "We could get it copied and sent back to you at once—"

"I said no," said the doctor, "for the very good reason that I don't have one."

"None at all?"

"Not a one. It was Celia. She had this . . . this breakdown, and she insisted on destroying every picture of Jan that we had in the house—negatives and all. Her psychiatrist said it was best to let her have her way. I didn't feel good about it . . . but . . ." He shrugged his big shoulders.

"Are you sure you didn't keep even one?" Henry asked.

"If I did, it wasn't deliberate, Mr. Tibbett."

Henry said, "If we took a look through your desk, or wherever you keep photographs . . ."

The doctor grinned sardonically. "You're carrying on like you're suspicious about something," he said. "I don't appreciate it."

Henry said, "Dr. Vanduren, there's just a chance that your daughter might be alive and suffering from amnesia. Surely you want to help the police check it out?"

"All right, if you insist. But I tell you, every picture was destroyed."

He shambled across the dining room and out into the hall, followed by Henry and Emmy. They all went into a small and untidy study at the back of the house, where Vanduren began pulling open the drawers of an old-fashioned desk. In one of them there was a bundle of assorted snapshots—mostly of Vanduren with a middle-aged, fair-haired woman. None at all of a young, blonde girl. They were about to give up when Emmy spotted a wedding photograph. It showed a bride and groom—both dark and good-looking—laughing over the traditional cutting of a huge wedding cake. The picture was inscribed in a bold, round hand—"Sorry you couldn't make it. Next time this'll be you and Ed! Love, Cheryl and Martin."

"The Rosses!" Emmy exclaimed.

Vanduren glanced at the photograph. "That's right. Cheryl sent it to Jan."

"May I take it?" Henry asked. "It could help."

"Take it?" echoed Dr. Vanduren. "What can you do with it? You're on your way back to England, aren't you?"

Henry said, "I'd like the police in St. Mark's to see this. If you'd care to send it to—"

"I'm damned if I'm going to get mixed up in—"

"Then please let me have it," said Henry.

After a tiny pause, the doctor said, "Oh, very well. Take it if you want to."

"Thank you," said Henry. He looked at his watch. "Well, we

must be off back to the airport to get our flight. Forgive us for disturbing you, Dr. Vanduren. We felt that you ought to know—"

"Yes, yes. Very civil, I'm sure."

Dr. Vanduren saw the Tibbetts to the door with considerably more courtesy and enthusiasm than he had displayed when greeting them. On one point he remained adamant.

"You're going back to England," he said, "and Celia is there. I absolutely forbid you to try to contact her. She must be told nothing of this. Absolutely nothing. She's only just recovering, and a goddamn silly false hope like this might set her right back. Understand?"

At the door, Henry said, "Was Janet ever on drugs, Doctor? Hard drugs?"

Vanduren became very angry, forgetting courtesy. "Get out of my house, sir! Damn your impertinence! Get out!"

Henry and Emmy went back to the airport and caught the afternoon plane to Puerto Rico. They stayed overnight in the rather impersonal comfort of the airport hotel and caught the commuter flight to St. Mark's at eight o'clock in the morning.

6

By HALF-PAST NINE, Henry and Emmy were back at St. Mark's marina. As they passed the Harbour Master's office, Anderson looked up, saw them, and motioned them to come in.

He said, "John Colville has been trying to get hold of you, Mr. Tibbett. He'd like you to call back as soon as possible. Why don't you use my phone?"

"Henry?" John's voice came over the line, strong and sounding bewildered. "Where on earth were you yesterday? They told me—"

Anderson was busy rearranging the little flags on the map of the marina. Henry decided to take no chances at all. He said, "Oh, we just went to Puerto Rico for the day."

"Well," said John, "the most extraordinary thing has happened."

"What?"

"By yesterday's post from St. Mark's. Two postcards from Betsy, one for you and one for us, posted on Saturday."

Carefully keeping any surprise out of his voice, Henry said, "What do they say?"

"Just a moment while I get them."

"What does John want, Henry?" Emmy asked.

Putting his hand over the mouthpiece of the telephone, Henry said, "He has some mail for us, that's all. A couple of postcards."

"Oh." Emmy turned away, disappointed.

"Ah, hello, John. Well?"

"Our card," John said, "is a view of Mango Bay Beach—which we see every day, of course—and it simply says, 'Just to thank you both for a wonderful holiday. Love, Betsy.' Yours is of the marina at St. Mark's, and it's a bit longer and more complicated. It says, 'I was wrong about Janet—it's a couple called Ross. They've asked me on board their boat for lunch. Hope I catch my plane. If I don't, please let Celia know. Betsy.' " John paused. "What do you

57

make of it? How could she have posted them on St. Mark's on Saturday, two days after—"

Henry said, "Can you get those cards over to me here?"

"Sure. I'll give them to Morley—he's going over on the *Pride* tomorrow."

Henry said, "John—would it be possible for you to bring them over yourself, today?"

"Today?" John sounded taken aback. "Well . . . yes, I suppose so. I was going to do some painting on the new units, but if it's so important . . ."

"I'd like to have a talk with you," Henry said. "We'll be on board *Windflower* in the marina."

John said, "I was surprised when Anderson told me you hadn't sailed. What on earth made you go to Puerto Rico?"

"I'll tell you over lunch," Henry said.

While Emmy went back to *Windflower*, Henry began looking for Bob Harrison. It had occurred to him that if Betsy Sprague wanted to leave postcards with somebody to post for her, she would be likely to choose this solid, foursquare Englishman. It turned out that Bob was not at the marina tending his charter fleet, but at the small shipyard nearby where he did repairs and fitting-out. There Henry found him, tinkering with the motor of his own launch, named *Mark One*. Bob seemed glad of an excuse to straighten up and have a talk.

Henry started off by asking whether he might charter *Windflower* for at least a second week, as he found he did not have to return to England for the moment. Bob appeared delighted.

"Quiet time of year, sir," he said, "and the owner isn't coming down before Thanksgiving, that I know for a fact. I'll let him know, of course, and get his O.K.—but he'll be pleased, no doubt about it. Not good for a boat to sit in her berth months on end."

"Good," said Henry. "Now, there's another thing. A friend of ours—a little old English lady—was here in the marina last Thursday and gave some postcards to somebody to mail for her. Did you happen to—?"

"The old lady? Postcards? Ay, it was me she asked. I was coming up the jetty to go 'ome for my dinner, and she was going down it with a young couple. She was a bit behind them, and as she passed me she pushed the cards into my hand and said, 'Post these for me, please. They're stamped.' A bit . . . I dunno . . . almost furtive, I thought. Expect she didn't want to delay the young people. Next thing I saw, the boat had sailed. And now I hear tell she's gone missing." Bob shook his gray head. "Bad business. Hope the old lady wasn't aboard."

"I'm afraid she probably was," Henry said. "So you posted the cards?"

Bob looked sheepish. "Well, yes, but I must admit I forgot 'em until Saturday. I'd stuck 'em up on the kitchen shelf when I went for dinner and never noticed them again till Saturday morning. Still, postcards aren't generally that important, are they?"

Henry said, "How do you know which boat the old lady was going to?"

"Well, I'd 'ad a word with Mr. Ross earlier on. He came up to me—I was working on a boat, like—and told me they'd put in for a small repair to the engine, and could I recommend a yard to do it. I told him I'd do it myself if he brought the boat round to the yard here, and he thanked me. Funny thing," Bob added, "he never did bring the boat round. Just upped and went. Ah, well."

Henry unzipped his small overnight bag and pulled out the wedding photograph. He handed it to Bob and said, "Do you recognize that couple?" Bob studied the picture and then said, "No. Who are they, then?"

"Mr. and Mrs. Ross."

"Ah, well now." Bob grinned. "I never did see the lady, and Mr. Ross had a beard when he was here." He squinted at the photograph again. "Could be him without his beard. I can't tell, rightly. I only saw him once, and just for a moment." He smiled cheerfully. "You don't want to get too upset about the boat goin' missing, sir. It'll turn up, you'll see. Probably the radio broke, and they may be having trouble with that engine." He hesitated. "You and the wife planning on taking *Windflower* out soon, sir?"

"Yes, of course," said Henry reassuringly. "I had to go to Puerto Rico yesterday, so we've had to postpone our cruise. But tomorrow—"

"Ah, well, that's good. Good sailing, sir."

On *Windflower*, Emmy was making a cup of coffee. Henry went aboard and told her John's news about the cards from Betsy.

"From Betsy?" Emmy was overjoyed. "So she's all right! Where is she?"

"I'm afraid it doesn't mean she's all right. The cards were posted from here on Saturday."

"That's not possible."

"Yes, it is. Betsy gave the cards to Bob Harrison as she was going down the jetty to *Chermar* with the so-called Ross couple. Asked him to post them for her. He forgot to do so until Saturday."

"So the cards don't mean anything," Emmy said flatly.

"The card to the Colvilles was just a bread-and-butter thank-you," Henry said, "but the one to us was something else."

"What did it say?" Henry told her. "So Betsy did make a mistake after all." Emmy sounded downcast.

"I don't think so. Anyhow, John is coming over on the *Pride* and bringing the cards with him. Meanwhile, I must get in touch with Ingham, and I've a job for you."

"For me?"

"Yes. I want you to go back to Caribbean Treasure Trove and see if Betsy said anything to the girl there about why she was buying postcards."

"I'll try," Emmy said.

"See you back here in an hour or so," said Henry. He climbed ashore and headed for the Harbour Master's office and its telephone.

"Chief Inspector Ingham? Henry Tibbett. Look, I have to talk to you. And I want to make a phone call to—" Henry paused as a young man with red hair and a Texas accent pushed open the door, inquiring loudly about where to obtain ice. He showed no sign of leaving, following up his quest for ice with demands for information on good restaurants ashore.

Henry said, "It would be good to see you again, old man. Could I come up to your place, perhaps?"

Ingham, on the other end of the line, said, "Lack of privacy?"

"Just that. So if it's convenient—"

"The station has a back entrance on West Street. Unmarked, next to Annie's Supermarket. When will you get here?"

His eye on the young American, who seemed to be spinning out his business with the Harbour Master to unnecessary lengths, Henry said, "Oh, within the next few days. I'll look forward to it. Good-bye, old man."

He hung up and said to Anderson, "Thanks for the use of your phone. How much do I owe you?"

"Just ten cents, sir." Anderson was straight-faced. He took the small coin from Henry and returned to his other client. "Well, sir, as I was saying, the Green Turtle specializes in seafood . . ."

Henry went out of the office, hailed a taxi, and asked to be driven to Annie's Supermarket on West Street. Ten minutes later he was sitting in Inspector Ingham's office.

60

Ingham seemed amused. "Who was the sinister character listening in on our conversation, Mr. Tibbett?"

Henry grinned. "A young red-haired American who probably really did want to know where to buy ice and get a meal ashore," he said, "but that office is too damned public. Now, listen to this."

Quickly and concisely, Henry went over his interview with the Governor, his trip to Florida, and finally his telephone call from John Colville and his talk with Bob Harrison. He also advanced a theory that had been formulating in his mind.

Ingham listened in absorbed silence. Then he said, "I think you're right, sir. I think they may well come back here."

"If they do," Henry said, "how will they arrive?"

"How? By boat, by air . . . the way all tourists arrive."

"Surely not," Henry said. "An arriving tourist fills in a form, which is kept by Immigration. The stub is torn off and given to the visitor, who must hand it in when he leaves."

"That's right."

"But," Henry went on, "these people don't intend to leave—at least, not with the identities they came in with."

Ingham said, "They'll leave on a private yacht with their intended victims. The murder and identity switch will take place on the high seas."

"Exactly," Henry said. "So, as I see it, the smuggler-murderers must get into these islands illegally—that is, without going through Immigration. Is that possible?"

"Of course it is," said Ingham, with a trace of irritation. "They can get themselves put off a boat in a dinghy and rowed ashore to a deserted beach, probably early in the morning. D'you think I can patrol every beach in the Seawards with the number of men I have?"

Henry said, "O.K., we have them illegally ashore. What then?"

"How do you mean, what then?"

"Where do they stay while they're staking out their victims? They can't very well register at a hotel, even if they do have false passports."

Ingham considered. "I see what you mean," he said. "The hotel clerk would notice at once if there was no entry stamp and no Immigration stub in the passports." He considered. "Camp out on the beach? No, we don't like campers, and it would make them conspicuous."

"I should have thought—stay with friends," Henry said.

Ingham slapped the desk with his hand. "Of course! I knew they would have to have local accomplices. But who? Well, the first thing is to find out if anyone here had foreign visitors staying with them at the time that the *Chermar*—"

"No," Henry said.

"No? Why not?"

"Because by the time they got here, they'd already assumed the identity of the Rosses. The switch must have been done at the *Chermar*'s last port of call—the British Virgin Islands."

Ingham said, "So they have accomplices there, too?"

"Not necessarily. Remember that Cheryl Ross was a personal friend of Janet Vanduren's. They could have entered illegally and gone straight to the boat. But let's get back to what they'll do next time. We've got them into the Seawards. How do they leave the islands?"

"They sail off with their new friends, murder them, and—"

"Yes, but the boat and its crew have to check out through Immigration," Henry pointed out.

Ingham spoke impatiently. "Sure, that's the correct procedure, but take it from me, sir, there are boats coming and going all the time without proper papers. Why, when we did a spot check on foreign boats anchored off St. Mark's last Easter weekend—"

"I know, I know," Henry said, "but it's very important to our people that all the papers should be in order. The boat has checked in legally, with a crew of two. It must also check out legally with the same crew." He frowned. "Ah, I think I have it. A yacht could check in with the Immigration people here, sail over to St. Matthew's, check out of the Seawards from there, couldn't it?"

"Of course."

"Then that's how it must be done. The charming newfound friends—actually the hijackers—propose a short cruise around the Seawards. No need to clear Customs and Immigration. The murders are committed in British Seaward waters and the bodies disposed of at sea—and the boat returns to the other Seaward island with just one couple aboard and checks out there. The only thing that's wrong is that it's a different couple checking out; but since it's another island, it's bound to be a different Immigration Officer, and there's virtually no chance of the switch being spotted."

Ingham said, "That makes sense. Not a very happy thought, sir—people being murdered in our home waters."

Not seeming to hear Ingham, Henry went on, "But not the *Chermar*."

"I beg your pardon?"

"There's a break in the pattern. The *Chermar* left St. Mark's without checking out through Customs and Immigration and then disappeared. Betsy Sprague broke the pattern."

Ingham sighed. "That's for sure," he said. "The poor old lady stumbled quite by accident onto—"

"No," Henry said.

Ingham looked up, surprised. "How do you mean, sir?"

"Betsy," Henry said, "was a remarkable woman. Not only quick-witted, but extremely brave. Of course she recognized Janet Vanduren, and she knew the danger she'd be in if she went on board the *Chermar*. She had a fearful decision to make, there in the restaurant. If she'd flatly refused to go on board, the pseudo-Rosses could hardly have dragged her by force. She could just have walked away and telephoned you. But would you have believed her story? I'm ashamed to say, we didn't."

Ingham shook his head. "Very unlikely," he said.

"In any case," Henry went on, "by the time she'd managed to get hold of you, *Chermar* would have sailed and the Rosses would have disappeared forever. The pickup of this particular consignment would have been allocated to some other couple, and Janet Vanduren and her young man would either have been liquidated for inefficiency or transferred to another area. We'd never have found them again. Of course, Betsy would have been able to go quietly back to England and forget the whole thing—but she wasn't that sort of person. She had spotted Janet, she was being lied to, and she refused to let go—like a small terrier being tossed by a bull. What she did do, though, was leave a trail for us. She must have written those cards right there at the table, under Janet's nose. Then she gave them to Bob Harrison to post, and if he hadn't forgotten to do so until Saturday—"

"Just what was she trying to tell you?" Ingham asked.

"She'd already spoken to me on the phone," Henry said, "so she knew I'd understand. She told me, indirectly, that Janet Vanduren was going under the name of Ross. She told me the name of the boat. She told me she was going on board and might never be heard of again. She also dropped one of her souvenir gifts into the harbor, and by great good luck we found it. She also said one other thing, which I can't quite figure out at the moment."

"What's that, sir?"

"She told me to contact Janet's mother—Betsy's old pupil. Which is why I have to make a phone call to England, and not in public." He stretched out his hand for Ingham's telephone. "May I?"

"Sure, help yourself. Just ask the switchboard to give you the overseas operator."

Henry said, "It'll be about half-past four in the afternoon in London. Reynolds should still be there, unless he's out on a job."

"Give him my regards, sir," said Chief Inspector Ingham.

Inspector Derek Reynolds, Henry's assistant at Scotland Yard, had already been told about his chief's assignment in the Seawards and had agreed with characteristic good humor to postpone his summer vacation until such time as Henry returned to England. Consequently, he was neither surprised nor put out by a transatlantic telephone call.

"Mrs. Celia Vanduren?" he said. "No idea of whereabouts in Shropshire, I suppose, sir? . . . Well, I daresay we'll be able to find her. Staying with her mother, you say, elderly lady name of Dobson . . . Yes, I've got that. . . . What do I do when I've traced her, sir?"

Henry said, "First and foremost, let me know. That is, let Inspector Ingham know . . . Yes, it's the same chap . . . Yes, of course I will, and he reciprocates. . . . Police Headquarters, St. Mark's, that's right . . . Well, I want to know whatever you can find out about Mrs. Vanduren without her knowing that you're investigating . . . how long she's been there . . . her state of mind . . . in plain language, does she appear to be slightly crazy, and, if so, does anybody know why . . . if . . ." Henry hesitated. It sounded ridiculously melodramatic. "If by any chance I should . . . meet with an accident or be put out of action . . . All right, have it your own way, Reynolds, if they get me . . . go yourself to Mrs. Vanduren and tell her you have reason to believe that her daughter, Janet, is alive and active in drug-smuggling in the Caribbean. Ask her if she's prepared to cooperate in a case which certainly involves her daughter and maybe her husband as well. Tell her that Betsy Sprague . . . S-P-R-A- . . . that's right . . . that Betsy Sprague has almost certainly been murdered going after these people, and that Betsy wanted her—Celia Vanduren—to know. But do not—repeat *do not* tell her all this unless and until you hear from Inspector Ingham that I am either dead or have disappeared. Otherwise, get all the information you can and let me know through Ingham. And another thing."

"Yes, sir?"

"Try to find out if Mrs. Vanduren has a photograph of her daughter with her in England."

"I'll try, sir."

"How's the weather in London?"

"Raining, sir."

"In that case, I won't even mention what it's like here. I expect you remember."

"I do, sir. Best of luck, sir. I'll be in touch."

Henry hung up and turned to Inspector Ingham. "Derek Reynolds sends his regards," he said. "He'll contact you when he has any news. As for communicating with me, you'd better do that through John Colville at the Anchorage in St. Matthew's. I can't risk coming up here or telephoning you all the time."

Emmy was back on board when Henry returned to *Windflower*. She said, "I spoke to the girl again—she must think I'm potty by now. Anyway, all she can remember is that Betsy said something about buying postcards to take back home to show her friends some views of the islands—she picked quite a number, mostly pictures of St. Matthew's. Then, just as she was leaving, she came back and asked for local stamps for just two of the cards."

"Stamps to send them to England?"

"No. Just within the islands."

Henry said, "You can see the restaurant from the door of the gift shop, can't you?"

"Oh, yes. It's right across the courtyard from the bar."

Henry sighed. "Betsy was altogether too brave and too ingenious," he said. "I wish to God she'd left the whole thing alone and saved her own neck."

Slowly, Emmy said, "She recognized Janet Vanduren with her hair dyed dark. She went back and bought stamps for two postcards and called you on the telephone. Then she went over to talk to Janet and the young man. O.K. so far. But what made her so suspicious?"

"Wouldn't you be suspicious if somebody who was supposed to have been dead for six months turned up with dyed hair and never got in touch with her family? . . ."

The Tibbetts were still discussing Betsy Sprague and her motivations when John Colville arrived. He clambered aboard and produced two rather bent postcards from the pocket of his shorts.

"Here they are," he said, without preamble. "Yours and ours. No doubt about it being Betsy's handwriting—I've compared them with the letter she wrote Margaret."

"Yes, she wrote the cards all right," Henry said. "And gave them to Bob Harrison to post as she was going to board the *Chermar*."

John said, "And now the *Chermar* is missing. It was on the radio."

Quickly, Henry brought John up to date on all he had discovered so far. Then he said, "You know these waters, John."

"Pretty well," Colville agreed.

Emmy said, "I'll go and get lunch," and disappeared into the small galley.

Henry went on, "Well, just think. You are Janet Vanduren, masquerading as Cheryl Ross, on board the *Chermar* with your accomplice. You have been recognized by Betsy Sprague, and so you have persuaded her to come aboard, ostensibly for lunch before catching her plane to England. You know you have to get rid of her, abort your mission, sink the *Chermar,* and get yourself picked up by your mother-vessel. How do you set about it?"

John considered. "Well, I'm certainly not going to murder Betsy in the marina, so I suggest a spin to one of the uninhabited islands for a picnic. With a powerful motorboat like the *Chermar,* there'd be plenty of time to get Betsy back for her plane—in theory. Better still—there's a landing stage right beside the airport. I'd offer to put her ashore after lunch."

"Very good," said Henry. "Now what?"

"Who do you think you are anyway—Socrates?"

Henry smiled. "The Socratic method, I agree. I'm interested in leading you from one logical conclusion to another to see if we reach the same final answer. So—now what?"

"Well, we leave the marina, and as soon as we're in open waters, I suppose the male half of this charming couple finishes off Betsy. She's a frail little old lady and shouldn't take much overpowering."

"And then?"

"Scuttle the ship."

"In these waters? In broad daylight?"

"Oh," said John. "I see what you mean. No, that would be too noticeable. Sail on into more open waters, out of sight of land, and do the scuttling in the dark."

"All this with a body on board?"

"Well . . . no, I've had a better idea. Knock Betsy out with some sort of drug. Then if by any chance you're stopped by a Coast Guard cutter or a police launch, you can just say she's asleep. When you scuttle, leave her to go down with the ship. If the hulk should happen to be found, she'll be aboard still, but with no signs of violence."

Henry nodded. "Very good," he said. "Now what about you?"

"Me?"

"I mean, Janet and her friend. Who's going to rescue you?"

"The mother-ship, of course."

"How does she know where you'll be?"

"We have a—no, we bloody don't, do we? We don't have a rendezvous because *Chermar* is supposed to be on her way to the States with a cargo of drugs."

"Exactly," Henry said. "You have to break the pattern. How do you do that?"

"I . . . I communicate with the mother-ship."

Henry remembered something that Anderson had said. "By radio," he said. "Must be. *Chermar* carried ship-to-shore radio."

"That's right," John said. "A message must have gone out from the *Chermar* on Thursday afternoon or evening."

"How can we trace it?"

John said shortly, "You can't. Nobody keeps a record of every private message broadcast from ship to ship or ship to shore on these short-range sets. Most of them are simply people making dates to meet each other at a certain anchorage or to book a meal at a restaurant ashore."

Emmy, emerging from the galley, said, "I remember. There used to be a time called the Children's Hour, when people could exchange private messages. From one to two, wasn't it? You had a radio at the Anchorage and took in messages."

"That's all changed now," John said. "Boats and shore establishments use VHF, Channel Sixteen, and to have a shore-based set you need a license, and you have to keep a continuous daytime listen-out. We couldn't manage that, so we gave up our set."

"Then how do you take bookings from boats?" Emmy asked.

"By telephone. There are all sorts of people who listen out continuously on Channel Sixteen and will telephone messages through to us. The Coast Guard and Marine Police keep a twenty-four-hour watch. Then there's WAH—private licensed marine operators who monitor all the time. The various yacht charter firms listen out in daylight hours to keep in touch with their own boats. There's never any danger that nobody will pick up a Channel Sixteen message."

Henry said, "So it's also the channel used for SOS and Mayday calls?"

"Oh, yes. But they're pretty rare, fortunately. As I said, the great majority of messages are private."

"Which," Henry said thoughtfully, "are overheard by a lot of people, but never logged or recorded."

"How could they be, old man?" John appealed for reason. "Of course, if a Mayday is picked up, the police and Coast Guard will record it . . . but private messages . . ."

"What's the range of these radios?" Henry asked.

John considered. "Generally about twenty-five miles over sea—that's to say, without obstacles in the way. Round about here, there's usually an island to block transmission, so it's more like twelve or fifteen miles. People doing long trips usually have a booster to give them a better range, and round-the-worlders have a ham radio operator's license and special equipment—"

Henry said, "No. Our people wouldn't have anything like that. The most inconspicuous and ordinary possible. Does this give you any ideas, John?"

John grinned. "Socrates again? O.K.—yes, it does. For the moment, two. First, if *Chermar* got a message to her mother-ship, the mother-ship must have been close by. Within ten miles, I'd say. Second, if *Chermar* could send such a message, quite unexpectedly, and get a reply, it must mean that whenever an operation is being carried out, there must be a mother-ship cruising around nearby, keeping a listening watch."

Henry nodded approvingly. "A sensible arrangement," he said.

Emmy added, "And the message would have been sent at an inconspicuous time—somewhere around midday, so that it would be lost among all the other private communications. I mean, a private message sent in the middle of the night, when only police and Coast Guard listen out, would attract too much attention, wouldn't it?"

"Right again," Henry said. "Well, I suppose there's just a very faint chance that somebody listening might remember *Chermar*'s message."

"It's an unusual name for a boat," Emmy said. "That might help."

"I don't imagine," Henry said, "that the name of the boat would be used. There would be a code name for both ships, and the message would sound like something perfectly ordinary. The chances of tracing it are minimal, but we'll try."

John said, "Surely by now this is a matter for the police, isn't it? I mean, we're only amateurs—" He broke off, seeing Henry's widening grin. "Oh, sorry. I'd quite forgotten. Even so, it must be the local police—"

"This is just between ourselves, John," Henry said, "but my position is now official. I'm on loan from Scotland Yard, investigating Betsy's disappearance."

"Thank God for that," John said somberly. And then, "But what can you do? You have no more facilities than the local police."

"As Ingham pointed out," Henry said, "I have the great advantage of being an unknown face and a bona fide tourist. I also have a virtual hot line to C Department in London, which may be helpful."

"I wish to God there was something Margaret and I could do."

"There is. For one thing, you can provide us with a base on St. Matthew's, and you can be a channel for passing information to and from Inspector Ingham. I had to go up to the police station today to telephone the Yard, but I don't want to do it too often. And then there's another way you can help."

"What's that?"

"You can make extremely discreet inquiries as to whether any of the local residents of St. Matthew's has an English or American couple staying with them, as houseguests."

John looked surprised. "What good would that do?"

"Never mind. I just want to know. If such people arrive, let me know at once. I want to know who they are staying with, what their names are, and what they look like. It may be fairly difficult, as they'll be lying low. Above all, don't arouse any suspicions. Just keep your eyes and ears open."

"O.K., I'll do my best."

Henry went on. "Now, when you get back to the Anchorage, please call Ingham and tell him I want to know whether anybody listening out on Channel Sixteen remembers a message sent out on the Thursday afternoon when Betsy disappeared. The message would sound innocuous, but it would be canceling some sort of arrangement and making a rendezvous. All calls to and from Ingham should be made from the office, where you can't be overheard. And Margaret should watch out that nobody in the bar picks up the extension phone to listen in."

John said, "It's incredible—that somebody would actually do away with poor old Betsy. And anyway—isn't all this a bit elaborate?"

"Not for the characters we're after. This is a big operation, John, with big money and organized crime behind it."

"Here in the Seawards?"

"The Seawards are part of it, I'm afraid," Henry said. "So will you be a good fellow and act as a relay station for me?"

"Oh, well. If you say so."

Then Emmy served lunch, and afterward John Colville made his way back down the landing stage to catch the boat for St. Matthew's. He was preoccupied with his own thoughts and was certainly unaware that his movements were being carefully watched by the occupants of another boat in the marina.

7

THE NEXT MORNING, *Windflower* left her berth at nine o'clock. The Harbour Master had been asked not to put another boat in her space, as she was only going for a day sail. It was a typically lovely West Indian day, with only a slight swell and a steady breeze from the northeast. Henry and Emmy had a thoroughly enjoyable sail, picnicked on George Island, and returned late in the afternoon.

Windflower's reentry into St. Mark's marina was not very elegant. Emmy had trouble getting the sails down outside the harbor, and Henry failed several times to start the motor, so by the time the boat was approaching the mooring, considerable shambles had broken out on board. Somehow, the sloop was maneuvered into her berth, but had it not been for assistance from Bob Harrison and the Harbour Master, it seemed unlikely that she would have been successfully moored without damage to herself or another boat. Trying to ignore the smirking faces of expert sailors on other boats, Henry and Emmy went below, changed into fresh clothes, and went ashore to the marina bar for a drink.

The bar was not crowded, but it began to fill up as more boats came in for the night and their crews came ashore. Henry and Emmy sat at the bar, drinking Daiquiris and discussing how tricky it had been to handle *Windflower* with just two people aboard. Nobody approached them or tried to speak to them.

Under cover of casual conversation with his wife, Henry was taking careful note of the other drinkers in the bar. Bob Harrison was there, chatting to a good-looking, middle-aged American couple. From the snippets of talk that he could overhear, it seemed to Henry that they were discussing the possibility of chartering a yacht for a few days. They mentioned the name of their hotel and asked Bob to call them there.

71

At the far end of the bar was a large party of young people of mixed nationalities—Henry caught snatches of French and Italian as well as Puerto Rican-accented Spanish. They were obviously all off the same boat—either a large charter or a small cruise ship—and seemed innocent of anything except making a lot of noise. More interesting were the half-dozen or so other couples who sat at tables and talked about the day's sailing. They all appeared to be American, all in varying stages of suntan, ranging in age from teens to forties. None of them seemed either sinister or interested in the Tibbetts. Henry wondered, and was still wondering, when the waitress came up to tell them their table for dinner was ready.

It was when they were halfway through their meal that the waitress approached.

"You are Mr. Tibbett?"

"That's right."

"Telephone call for you. You can take it at the desk."

"Thank you," said Henry. He stood up. "You go ahead, darling. Don't wait for me."

Several heads turned, from other tables and from the bar, as Henry made his way to the reception desk.

"Henry? This is John."

"Ah, hello, John. What's new?"

"I've had a word with Herbert. He's found out more about that radio set you were interested in."

"Oh." Henry sounded doubtful. "I'm not sure that I want to buy it, you know. I told him so."

"I know, but he wants you to look at it just the same."

"Oh, all right. Where and when?"

"Buccaneer Bar, half-past nine this evening."

"O.K. Thanks a lot, John."

Back at the table, Emmy raised her eyebrows slightly. Henry, gathering up his table napkin, said, "That was Colville from the Anchorage. About that radio we were thinking of getting for the boat."

"Oh, yes? Any good?"

"I don't know, but he says he's located one. We'll go and see it this evening."

After dinner, Henry and Emmy went back to the bar. A local calypso band had assembled and its members were tuning up, laughing, and engaging in youthful banter and horseplay. Soon, they launched into some spirited reggae, and the polyglot young

72

people began to dance. Henry and Emmy joined them, and Henry was about to suggest that they should leave for the Buccaneer when a tall, graying man with a small mustache came up to the bar. Standing beside Henry, he ordered two rum punches.

As they were being prepared, he said, without looking directly at Henry, "Saw you had a spot of trouble getting in today." He spoke with an exaggeratedly English accent.

"Yes, I'm afraid we didn't do very well," Henry admitted.

"Big boat for two people to handle," remarked the newcomer. "Need a third hand at least."

"We're beginning to realize that," Henry said.

The tall man turned and looked Henry full in the face from shrewd, bright blue eyes. "British, aren't you?" he said.

"Yes, we are."

"Thought so. Can't mistake the accent. Not many of us in these parts. Taking a vacation?"

"Yes. We're just here for another week." Henry hesitated. "And you? You sound as though you might live here."

"Here?" The man laughed. "No, not here. Not on this island. Just in these parts, as you might say. Thank you, dear," he added to the barmaid, who had appeared with the rum punches. He pushed some dollar bills over the counter. "Keep the change. Yes, my wife and I are expatriates—what you might call Caribbean beachcombers—since I retired. Live on our boat."

"That must be a wonderful life," Emmy said.

"Oh." Henry was a little flustered. "Please allow me to introduce my wife, Emmy. My name's Henry. Henry Tibbett."

"Delighted to meet you, sir . . . ma'am. I'm Colonel Montgomery, known to my pals as Bill. That's my wife, Martha, over at the corner table. Won't you join us for a drink?"

"It's very kind of you," Henry said, "but I'm afraid we're just leaving."

"Making an early start tomorrow, eh?" asked Montgomery. He added, with a booming laugh, "Early to bed, early to rise . . . ," as though it were a witticism that he had just invented. "Well, another time, perhaps. You'll be coming back to St. Mark's?"

"Oh, yes. We're based here. We're really only doing day sailing."

"Then we shall certainly meet again. Our boat's the *Ocean Rover*. Look forward to seeing you."

Montgomery picked up his drinks and threaded his way back between the tables to the corner where his wife, a stately lady in white trousers and a magenta overblouse, was sitting. Henry took Emmy's arm and led her out of the bar into the scented night.

As they crossed the marina gardens to the taxi stand, Emmy whispered, "A nibble, do you think?"

Henry squeezed her arm. "Too soon to say. Maybe."

The Buccaneer Bar was a very different proposition from the marina bar—small, dark, crowded with people and noise and the strident beat of canned disco music. It was, in fact, a part of the big Harbour Prospect Hotel, but coming in from Main Street and going down pink-lit stairs toward the din, one might imagine that one was entering an independent and certainly popular discotheque.

Henry and Emmy struggled to the bar, ordered drinks, and waited. There was no sign of Herbert Ingham—nor, indeed, of anybody they knew. The crowd was mixed, black and white, mostly young, all informally dressed. Despite a halfhearted attempt at air conditioning, it was extremely hot.

Looking around it occurred to Henry that this was a curious place for Inspector Ingham to have suggested for a rendezvous. The Inspector would surely be a most conspicuous figure in this place, and many of the young people looked as though they might well have been victims of the recent big bust at the fish fry. However, Henry knew Ingham well enough to trust that he knew what he was doing.

It was at about ten minutes to ten that a tiny, very pretty black girl came up to the bar. She smiled enchantingly and said, "Mr. and Mrs. Tibbett?" Henry had to lip-read the words over the blanket of sound.

He nodded. She smiled again. "My name is Festina. Festina Ingham. My father is expecting you. Please come. Follow a little behind me."

She turned and made her way across the small dance floor to the far side, where she disappeared behind a heavy red plush curtain. Henry and Emmy paid for their drinks and followed her. They pushed their way around the curtain and found themselves at the foot of a flight of stairs. This obviously led up toward the foyer of the hotel proper, which was built on the landward side of the steep hill that sloped down to the harbor. They rounded a carpeted bend to see Festina standing awaiting them. She was on a small landing where the staircase took a turn to the right, and she had her hand on the bar of a big door marked EXIT. She smiled again.

"Come. This way."

A moment later they were out on the grounds of the Harbour Prospect Hotel. Without a word, Festina led the way up winding paths between sweet-smelling tropical shrubs until they reached a parking area. It was empty except for a small, dark sedan.

"This is the lowest of the parking lots," she said. "It is used very little. Please get in."

She opened the back door and the Tibbetts got in. Festina then installed herself in the driver's seat, started the car, and maneuvered expertly out of the parking lot. She said, "Father thought it would be best like this. He knows you do not want to go to the police station, but he thinks you should talk to Pearletta."

"Who is Pearletta?" Henry asked.

"He will explain." Festina swung the little car out of the big main gates of the hotel and began to climb the precipitous hillside away from the sea.

Emmy said, "Where are we going?"

"To Pearletta's house," said Festina. They drove on in silence.

About ten minutes later, when the harbor looked like a glittering toy far below them and the temperature had dropped several degrees because of the altitude, the little car swung off the road and headed up a dark driveway. It rounded a bend, and there was a small, brightly lit house perched on the edge of a giddy height—on an outcrop of rock jutting out from the hillside, with a fantastic view over the sea and down to the lights of the town.

Festina parked the car, and as the engine died, the door of the house opened, and Henry recognized the massive silhouette of Inspector Ingham framed against the light.

Festina said, "Hi, Papa. I have them."

"Good." Ingham came up to the car. "Come in, please. Sorry I had to do this in a roundabout way."

"Very sensible." Henry climbed out of the car, following Emmy, who was already at the balustrade, looking down at the panorama below. "You think you have something?"

"I hope so. Please come in."

The house was small and cheerfully furnished, evincing a very West Indian taste for brilliant colors and a certain amount of clutter. Henry noticed with appreciation some pen-and-ink sketches, roughly filled in with bright watercolor, of local scenes—of boats and flowers and fishes. Not the work of a great artist, perhaps, but of a very talented amateur.

A girl got up from the sofa to greet the Tibbetts. She was plump and coffee-colored—not beautiful, but made attractive by the merriment and good humor in her dark eyes and round face.

Ingham said, "This is Pearletta Terry, Mr. and Mrs. Tibbett. Pearletta is one of our two women police constables."

Pearletta beamed, and Henry and Emmy shook her hand and professed themselves delighted to meet her.

Ingham went on. "Pearletta was listening out on Channel Sixteen at the police station last Thursday afternoon, and . . . well, you tell them, Pearletta."

"First, come and sit down and I bring you a drink," said Pearletta. "Beer or rum and Coke?"

Henry and Emmy accepted a beer apiece, Festina opted for rum and Coke, and Inspector Ingham specified a Heineken from the bottle. "Keeps it cooler," he explained to Henry. "No sense pouring cold beer in a warm glass."

When the drinks had been served, Pearletta said, "Well, Chief Superintendent, the Inspector came and axed me if I remember any of the private messages that afternoon, and I told him no. There was no SOS or Mayday, so I only listen with half my ears, like. Then the Inspector says could he see my logbook for that day—so I got it out, and here it is."

With something of a sense of drama, she picked up a desk diary that had been lying facedown and open on the coffee table and handed it to Henry. It was open at Thursday, June 19. Apart from a couple of entries recording routine checks with the Coast Guard, there were no entries. What there was, however, was a drawing—half-doodle and half-comic-strip. It showed a stylized starfish with an anthropomorphic face, gazing apprehensively skyward. One tentacle was clasping the handle of an open umbrella, and fine sloping lines indicated rain falling.

Henry studied it with an appreciative grin while Emmy peered over his shoulder. Then he looked up and said, "Well?"

Pearletta twinkled at him. "You see my starfish?"

"Yours?" Henry said.

Emmy said, "So you did all these lovely drawings, Pearletta?"

Proudly, Ingham said, "Pearletta is a local artist as well as a policewoman. Several of the souvenir shops are selling her pictures."

Pearletta showed no false modesty. "I like to draw," she said. "I draw what I see on the island. And sometimes I draw for my own fancy . . . fantastic." She laughed.

Henry said, "But what—?"

Pearletta cut him short. "When I show the Inspector my book, he ax me, 'Why you draw this starfish T'ursday afternoon, Pearletta?' 'Why not?' I tell him. And then I remember."

"Remember what?"

"T'ere was one message I had forgotten, but the starfish make me remember. I t'ought it funny. This is a lady from a boat, and she talk to a next boat, and she is saying t'ey must cancel plans for picnic today because of the weather. And I t'ink—weather is fine today. Why change plans—that's silly."

Henry was leaning forward, deeply interested. "Did the other boat answer?" he asked.

"Sure. A man's voice. Something like O.K., too bad, meet in usual place this evening. That's all."

"And why draw a starfish?"

"Because," Pearletta said, "that was the name of the boat the lady call. 'Calling *Starfish,* calling *Starfish,*' she keep saying. And then the message about the picnic. And I t'ink it's funny, and I make drawing of starfish in the rain. But t'ere's no rain T'ursday."

Henry said, "What was the name of the boat that sent the message?"

Pearletta shrugged. "I never remember. Just the starfish."

Ingham said, "As soon as Pearletta brought me her notebook and told me this, I started making inquiries." He stopped, and although Henry had not spoken, he added in parenthesis, "Don't worry, I trust Pearletta completely." He smiled at her. "I have told her that we may be on the track of smugglers."

"Good," said Henry. "Go on."

"Well, I have made sure that there was no boat called *Starfish* checked in either here or in St. Matthew's—and if the message came from a normal yacht radio, it wouldn't have had a range outside the Seawards. So it looks, Mr. Tibbett, as though by great good luck—and Pearletta's weakness for doodling—we've probably traced the message. *Starfish* would seem to be the code name for the mother-ship."

"Have you taken any other action?" Henry asked.

"Not yet. I wanted to consult you first. My idea is to circulate the Coast Guard and WAH, asking them to listen out for any *Starfish* messages and report at once—"

"No," Henry said.

"No? But—"

"Too many people," Henry said succinctly. "Too many chances that the smugglers will hear we are interested in *Starfish.*" He noticed Ingham's indignant expression and added, "I don't mean to say that any of these people is indiscreet, but such a request would be written down, and pieces of paper can be left lying about. You must see, Inspector, that it's too big a risk."

"Then what do you suggest?" Ingham sounded slightly huffy.

Henry grinned. "I suggest you put out a highly unpopular order to your own station," he said.

"What's that?"

"That for a test period of say, one week, *all* Channel Sixteen messages should be logged."

"But we never—"

Henry said, "We're agreed that these messages will go out in the daytime so as to be inconspicuous, so you needn't worry about listening out at night. You can simply say it's an exercise in case it ever had to be done in an emergency. I daresay there will be grumbling, but at least there won't be any indication of which messages you're interested in. What sort of a watch system do you have?"

"We don't," Ingham said. "The radio is in the police station, and it's kept switched on. Whoever is there listens out in case of May-day calls."

"All right. Don't change that. Just make sure every message is logged, and have the log submitted to you every day at noon and seven in the evening."

"Suppose the message comes through early in the morning," Ingham objected. "By the time I saw the log, the transmitting boat would be miles away—"

"Doesn't matter," Henry said. "The important thing is the gist of the message. Of course," he added with a smile, "if Pearletta is on duty herself, she can let you know right away if she gets a *Starfish*."

"Sure." Pearletta's eyes were twinkling with excitement.

"What will the others think about this logging?" Henry asked her.

"Oh, there'll be some sour faces," said Pearletta airily. "Do them good. All most of them t'ink about is limin' all day."

"Liming?"

"Having a good time," translated Inspector Ingham. "O.K., Mr. Tibbett. I'll do as you say."

The Tibbetts said good night to Pearletta and walked with Ingham out into the starry night. Henry said, "What do you know about a Colonel and Mrs. William Montgomery, middle-aged, living on board a boat called *Ocean Rover*? Based somewhere in the Caribbean, but not here. Possibly British."

"Possibly?" It was Emmy who broke in. "He definitely said he was British, Henry."

Ingham said, "I've never met them, but the *Ocean Rover*'s often in St. Mark's. I don't know where she's based—want me to check with Cranstone?"

"Might as well," Henry said. "But you don't know anything against the Montgomerys?"

"Nothing. They're well liked, I understand."

Festina drove the Tibbetts back to town and dropped them at the front entrance of the Harbour Prospect Hotel. From there, they made their way back down through the gardens and finally into the Buccaneer Bar, where they had a drink and emerged again onto Main Street to find a taxi back to the marina. As far as Henry could judge, their visit to Pearletta's house had been unobserved. To all intents and purposes, they had dined at the marina, gone into town for some disco dancing, and come back by taxi at half-past eleven.

The marina was dark and quiet. The band had packed up and gone off to play at a livelier spot in town. The yachtsmen had either followed it for further merrymaking or had gone back on board for an early night in preparation for dawn sailing. The moon, on the wane but still brilliant, shamed the harbor lights and laid a pathway of shimmering silver over the water. The sky was dark and velvety, and the stars seemed within arm's reach.

Walking down the jetty to *Windflower*, Emmy suddenly felt a surge of emotional and personal resentment against the people who were polluting these islands. The waters might be pristine and the air pure and sweet—but greed and corruption and even murder were worse than smog, and just as insidious.

Henry, for once out of phase with her thoughts, said, "You're very quiet, darling. I'm sorry—another holiday spoiled. You know I didn't want it this way. I didn't want to get involved."

Almost fiercely, Emmy said, "I'm glad we're involved. I cared about Betsy and I care about this place. We couldn't just have gone home and done nothing."

Henry put his arm around her shoulders and gave her a little hug. He had not missed her use of the pronoun "we."

8

SEVEN O'CLOCK. It was a shining morning, for once nearly windless. Outside the marina, the rippled water turned from silver-gray to blue, reflecting the deeper color of the sky as the sun rose higher. Henry and Emmy breakfasted in the cockpit, and by eight o'clock Emmy had washed up, cleared away the dishes, and was preparing to go and buy food at the commissary. Henry lit his pipe and climbed ashore to take a leisurely walk around and look at the boats.

He spotted the *Ocean Rover* almost at once—not in a slip but tied up alongside the harbor wall, a favorite spot for boats paying a brief visit in clement weather. She was a big, old-fashioned ketch, gaff-rigged, with heavy cotton sails, and her comfortably broad beam promised spacious accommodations below. A slow, sturdy sea boat, stiff and reliable in bad weather but sluggish in light airs, Henry reckoned. A very suitable boat to serve as sport and home for a middle-aged couple.

Bill Montgomery was already on deck, making some sort of adjustment to his jib halyard. He saw Henry, waved, and called out, "You going out today?"

"Yes. As soon as my wife gets back from shopping." Henry strolled alongside the *Ocean Rover*. "Nice boat you've got there."

"She's a steady old lady," said Montgomery. "No frills, but all the solid virtues. Like her owners, what?" he added, with a bark of laughter. Then, "Care to come for a spin one of these days?"

"Love to," said Henry. "Are you staying long in St. Mark's?"

"Oh . . . depends. See how the spirit moves us. And the weather, of course. Heard this morning's forecast?"

"I'm afraid I didn't listen," Henry said. "The weather always seems to be beautiful down here."

Montgomery gave a reproving snort. "Don't you be too sure," he said. "It can change, you know, with very little warning." He looked at the sky. "Might get some rain later today. Thunder, even. There's a tropical wave out in the Atlantic to the east of us. Never can tell what path it'll take."

Henry said, "Of course, you're right. One should always listen to forecasts. You think we're in for bad weather, then?"

Montgomery scanned the sky again. "Not before this evening" was his verdict. Then, "Is this your first time in the islands?"

"We were here once before, several years ago," Henry said. "That's to say, in St. Matthew's."

"Ah. You know St. Matthew's, then?"

"Not well at all. We spent a few days there before we came here this time—"

"Ah. So you didn't fly into St. Mark's?"

"No. We took the boat from Antigua to St. Matthew's."

"Don't blame you. Nicest way to approach these islands, by water." Montgomery gave the halyard a final tweak and secured it to a cleat on the mast. "There. That should do it."

From belowdecks, a woman's voice called, "Breakfast's ready, Bill." It was a strange accent—almost like refined Cockney. Quite at odds with the aristocratic accents of Mrs. Montgomery.

Colonel Montgomery winked at Henry. "Duty calls," he said. "Best be getting below. Good sailing. See you later." He disappeared down the companionway.

When Henry got back to *Windflower,* there was no sign of Emmy, but a young couple, hand in hand, were standing on the pontoon gazing at the boat with undisguised admiration. They turned as Henry approached and smiled shyly. The girl, in her twenties, had dark red hair and the fair complexion that often goes with it. The young man's blond head was bleached almost white by the sun, and his hair hung to his shoulders. Both wore tattered blue-jean shorts and faded pink shirts, and their feet were bare. Although they looked clean, any Immigration Officer in the world would have been wary of admitting them. Henry, not being an Immigration Officer, smiled, nodded briefly, and clambered on board.

The couple hesitated a moment, and then the girl stepped up to the boat and said breathlessly, "Do please excuse us, but . . . is this your boat?"

"Only temporarily," Henry said. "We've chartered her for a week or so."

"She's beautiful," said the young man simply.

Slightly surprised, Henry said, "Yes, she's a nice boat. But there are much newer and grander ones in the marina—you only have to look around."

The couple exchanged a quick glance, and then the girl said, "She's a Lancaster thirty-five, isn't she? Built in Baltimore?"

"Yes, I believe she is. I really don't know that much about—"

Eagerly, the young man said, "My father used to have a Lancaster thirty-five. I learned to sail on her."

"She was a fabulous boat," the girl said. "Harvey took me out on her once."

Harvey said, "Dad had to sell her four years ago. We miss her so much. She was like one of the family—wasn't she, Jilly?"

The girl nodded. She said, "Would you think it awful of us . . . I mean . . . could we come aboard for just a moment?"

If Henry felt any skepticism, it was not apparent. He smiled and said, "Of course. Let me give you a hand. I think there may be some coffee left over from breakfast."

When Emmy arrived back with her bulging shopping bag, she found quite a party going on in the cabin. The young couple, who had introduced themselves as Jill and Harvey Blackstone, were ensconced on one of the bunks with mugs of coffee and were reminiscing freely. Henry had already learned that they were both Marylanders, that Harvey's father was a Baltimore lawyer and Jill's a businessman in the same city. Casually, Henry asked if they were on holiday in the islands.

"Oh, yes," said Jill. "It's our first visit to the Caribbean. We've heard so much about it."

The young man nodded in agreement.

"You're staying here on St. Mark's, are you?" Emmy asked.

"That's right."

"At a hotel, or—?"

The young people exchanged a slightly embarrassed glance. Then Harvey said, "Actually, we came down here to camp. But . . . the people are so nice . . . somebody offered us a room in his house for nothing. One of the local people."

Henry smiled. "You did land on your feet," he said. "Who is it?"

"Well, I should have said, his father's house. The old man is Anderson, the Harbour Master. We met his son, Sebastian, on the beach—he was out diving for lobsters." There was a tiny pause. Then Harvey Blackstone put his coffee mug down and said, "You don't mind if we smoke, do you?" He pulled a strangely battered cigarette out of his pocket.

Emmy, who was busy at the stove with her back to the others, began to say, "Of course not—"

But Henry cut her short. He said, "I'd rather you didn't, if you don't mind. Not on my boat."

Harvey said, "Of course. I understand." The cigarette went back into his pocket. "Well, we mustn't keep you any longer. I expect you're off for a sail."

"Yes," Henry said. "We're just leaving."

Jill said, "Will you be back?"

Emmy laughed. "God willing," she said.

Jill was embarrassed again. "I only meant . . . I mean . . . will you be coming back to St. Mark's, or are you going down island . . . ?"

"Just a day sail," Henry assured her. "We'll be back."

When the young people had gone, Emmy said, "What a nice couple."

"Yes." Henry sounded abstracted.

"Oh, Henry—you don't suspect *them,* do you?"

Henry smiled at her. "You must learn," he said, "to suspect the least suspicious. That's how these people operate."

"But Henry—"

"They're not staying in a hotel, but with locals. They say it's their first visit to the Caribbean, but did you notice how the girl came out with the expression 'down island' quite automatically?"

"She probably picked it up from her host—"

"Sebastian Anderson, who was busted at the fish fry," said Henry. "And you realize they were about to light up a joint just now?"

"No, I—"

"That may just have been to test us. I don't know. Look, Emmy, I'm not accusing those two of anything more than smoking a little pot, but from now on we can't take *anybody* at their face value. Why did they pick on our boat? Because Harvey's father had the same model. A plausible pretext, but very easy to invent. One thing I'm prepared to bet—innocent or not, they want a sail on this boat, and they're going to do their damnedest to get it."

Ocean Rover left harbor ahead of *Windflower,* with the Montgomerys waving energetically as their yacht sailed past the end of the floating dock. By the time *Windflower* was out of the harbor, *Ocean Rover* had disappeared, and it was impossible to tell whether she had rounded the northerly or southerly headland protecting St. Mark's Harbour. Presumably she must have turned north, since when *Windflower* turned southward, there was no sign of *Ocean Rover*. The Tibbetts sailed to Seal Island, another small uninhabited member of the Seawards group, where they shared an anchorage and a coral sand beach with two other charter boats.

Henry and Emmy swam, snorkeled, and sunbathed and then came back on board for a picnic lunch. By half-past four they were motoring back into St. Mark's marina, managing *Windflower* somewhat more handily than the previous day, but still with a certain amount of flurry which indicated that an extra pair of hands would have been welcome.

Bob Harrison was pottering about on *Mark One* in a neighboring berth. When he saw the Tibbetts, he turned with a wave and called, "Mr. Tibbett!"

"Yes, Bob. What is it?"

"John Colville's been trying to get you on the blower. Can you give him a call back, like?"

"Certainly I will. Thanks, Bob."

Henry did not go to the Harbour Master's office, but called the Anchorage from one of the public telephones that Betsy Sprague had used for the same purpose the previous week. When John answered, Henry said, "Ah, hello, John. Look, I think I'd better call you in future. It looks a bit odd—you phoning me every day."

"I'm sorry, old man, but you did ask me—"

"I know I did. It's just that I think it would be less conspicuous if I made the calls. I'll keep in close touch, don't worry. Now, what do you have for me?"

"Several things. Hang on, I've got it all written down." There was a pause. Henry could hear the sound of cheerful voices from the Anchorage bar in the background. Then John said, "Here we are. Well, Ingham called me at five to ten this morning. He has checked up on *Ocean Rover*. Home port, Tampica. Owner, William Montgomery, holder of British passport but thought to be of American origin, though this is only hearsay. Seems the Montgomerys have lived in Tampica since the Second World War. *Ocean Rover* checked into St. Mark's on Tuesday—two days ago. Previous port of call, St. Thomas, American Virgin Islands. Local people know the boat and the people well. She does a lot of cruising. No further information at the moment."

Henry had been making notes in a small pocket diary. He said, "Thanks, John. That's useful. Anything else?"

"I'll say there is. Herbert called back at ten past twelve—seemed quite frantic to get this message to you. Does the name *Starfish* mean anything to you?"

"Yes," said Henry. "What about it?"

John was obviously reading from his notes. He said, "Police station logged a *Starfish* call at ten A.M. this morning. Not noted by Inspector Ingham until log checked at midday." In parenthesis, John added, "He sounded really mad. Said something about that would show you. Anyhow, message read, '*Starfish* to *Cockleshell*. *Starfish* to *Cockleshell*. Are you receiving me? Over.' Voice female, probably American, but reception not very good owing to approaching bad weather area. Answer (faint), '*Cockleshell* to *Starfish*. Receiving you. Over.' Answering voice, male American. Female voice, 'Hi, there, *Cockleshell*. Feel like meeting for picnic today, usual place, around half-past one? Over.' Male voice, 'Sure, *Starfish*. Be seeing you. Out.' That's all, but Herbert Ingham seemed to think it was plenty."

"Yes," said Henry. "Very interesting." He glanced around to see that he was not being overheard. The telephones were in half-egg-shaped, soundproof booths, but it was by no means impossible for a bystander to catch the conversation. However, there was nobody about. Through the glass door of the gift shop, Henry could see the girl assistant languidly polishing the countertop. In the terrace restaurant, two waitresses lounged against an empty table, giggling and exchanging repartee with the young man from the reception desk. The marina was deep in its midafternoon doldrums.

Into the telephone Henry said, "You'd better call Ingham back, John. Thank him and tell him that his information is very useful. Better assure him that we couldn't have done anything about intercepting the rendezvous even if we'd known sooner—and that anyway there'd have been little point. The important thing was to get the message. Then ask him if he'll do some more checking for me. A young couple by the name of Blackstone—Jill and Harvey. Visitors from the States—hippie-type—arrived within the last few days, probably by air. They're not staying at a hotel and would have registered with Immigration as camping. Tell him to try the airport first, and if there's no record of them there, ask the harbor office at St. Matthew's. It's possible that they didn't check in at all, and if that's so, I want to know about it, and fast." He looked at his watch. "I'll call you back at half-past seven to see if there's any news. Sorry about all this, John."

John said grimly, "If I can do anything to help nail the people who got Betsy, it's pure pleasure, I can assure you. Give Emmy my love. Good-bye for now."

Back on board, the Tibbetts had just made themselves iced tea and were preparing to come up and enjoy it in the cockpit when they were hailed by a familiar voice from the pontoon.

"Tibbett? Mrs. Tibbett? Bill Montgomery here. Sorry to disturb you . . ."

Henry and Emmy scrambled up the companionway. Emmy said, "Hello, Colonel Montgomery. You got back early, I see. Won't you come aboard?"

"Matter of fact," said Montgomery, "I just came over with a message from my good lady to ask if you wouldn't come and have a drink on *Ocean Rover*. We plan to be off at first light tomorrow, weather permitting."

"Weather?" Emmy echoed. "The weather's always perfect, isn't it?"

Montgomery cocked an eye toward the eastern horizon. "Take a look over there. Quite a bit of dirt blowing in from the Atlantic. We'll get rain very soon."

Sure enough, although the sky overhead was clear, dark clouds were beginning to build up toward the east. Bill Montgomery went on, "We had intended to get at least as far as St. Matthew's this evening, but I don't like the look of that lot. So we plan to turn in early and hope it'll blow itself out during the night. Tomorrow we have to be off—meeting friends in Anegada on Sunday, and it's sixty miles and a beat most of the way. So this looks like our last chance to get acquainted."

Quickly, Henry said, "That would be very nice—thanks. When shall we come over?"

"Soon as you like, old man. Before the rain starts." Montgomery gave one of his sudden roars of laughter, brought his hand to his forehead in a mock-salute, and strode off toward the shore.

Ocean Rover, the Tibbetts discovered when they boarded her about an hour later, was a supremely comfortable boat. Old-fashioned and beamy, her saloon was fitted out in well-worn varnished wood, with bright brass oil lamps and fittings. The galley boasted a battered, much-used stove and a refrigerator; both worked off bottled gas. Through an open door leading forward, the Tibbetts got a glimpse of a good-sized sleeping cabin with a built-in double bed and plenty of hanging space, and a door leading even farther forward presumably opened into the fo'c'sle. In the saloon, shelves of books were kept in place by removable wooden fiddle bars, and crockery and glasses were stowed in specially made racks. It was immediately obvious that this boat was not a sporting toy, but a home.

Mrs. Montgomery, tall and statuesque in white trousers and a loose yellow overblouse, introduced herself in what might have been an Australian accent as Martha. She welcomed the Tibbetts with a pleasant but slightly managerial air, seated them on one of the bunks, and relayed their acceptance of rum punches to her husband, who went and busied himself in the galley.

Martha Montgomery sat down facing Henry and Emmy across the gleaming teak table and said, "So you are from England. How interesting. Whereabouts do you live?"

"We're Londoners," Henry said.

"Dear old London. Many years since we were there. And what's your job?"

"I'm in business," said Henry, with affable vagueness.

"Oh, yes? Import-export?"

"Sort of."

Mrs. Montgomery seemed less than satisfied with this answer, but she did not press the matter. She turned to Emmy, "And Mrs. Tibbett—or may I call you Emily?"

Emmy grinned. "If you like," she said, "but actually my name is Emmy. Short for Emmeline, believe it or not."

"How quaint," remarked Mrs. Montgomery, with a quick smile. "Emmeline. Delightfully Victorian. And are you Victorian enough to stay at home, Emmy, or do you have a job like so many women these days?"

"I don't think I'm particularly Victorian," said Emmy, "but I don't have a job. Not a paying one. I do quite a lot of volunteer work."

"And look after your husband and children," said Martha approvingly.

"I look after my husband," Emmy said. "We've no children."

"Sometimes wish we hadn't," remarked Bill Montgomery loudly from the galley. "Perishing nuisance most of the time. Either they're too young and round your feet all the time, or they're grown up and getting into all kinds of trouble—"

Martha laughed, a little too loudly. "Bill will have his little jokes," she said. "He's really crazy about our two. Stella is a nurse—she works in New York—and our son, Robert, is a civil engineer in Florida. They've both done very well."

"And both settled in the States," said Henry.

"Yes—well, they were brought up in these parts, and really, let's face it, for all the God-Save-the-Queenery the Caribbean is part of the United States. At least, it's in her sphere of influence, if you like. After all, we even use American dollars as currency, don't we?"

"Here we are. Three rum punches." Bill Montgomery emerged from the galley with three pinkish drinks in glass beer mugs. He set one down in front of his wife and gave the other two to his visitors. "I'm having a Scotch myself. Been too long in these parts to—"

He was interrupted by a sudden, deafening thudding on the cabin top. Abruptly, the sky had darkened so that it was barely possible to see across the saloon, and at the same time, rigging began to thump and twang against the mast as a fierce squall of wind whipped down on the boat.

"Forehatch, Maggie!" shouted Montgomery. Mrs. Montgomery disappeared with surprising agility into the sleeping cabin, while the Colonel closed and battened down the main hatch and companionway. By the time he had done so, he was drenched, even though he had not left the saloon. He grinned at the Tibbetts.

"When it rains, it certainly does rain," he remarked.

Martha had reappeared and was lighting the oil lamps with a long taper-match. The saloon was dry and snug and the varnished woodwork glinted in the lamplight, but the incessant drumming of the rain made conversation virtually impossible.

After a few minutes, however, the rain decreased to a steady patter, and Colonel Montgomery said, "You were right, Maggie. Pretty silly we'd have looked trying to get to St. Matthew's in this. Ah, well, one thing about the weather here—it may get ugly, but it doesn't last long." He turned to Henry. "You were saying that you know St. Matthew's."

"Was I? Well, yes, we've been there for a few days, that's all."

"Beautiful island," said Montgomery. "Like it better than here. Smaller. Less sophisticated."

"Less?" said Emmy. "What about the Golf Club?"

Montgomery waved a hand. "The Golf Club," he said, "to all intents and purposes doesn't exist. It's an enclave for its own people.

They never come out onto the island, and nobody else ever goes in except as servants. It brings money to the island without getting in anybody's way. Ideal, if you ask me. Why, these islands could go independent, turn Marxist, join the United States, anything you like . . . it wouldn't make an atom of difference to the Golf Club. The island couldn't get on without the income it brings, and the Club ignores the existence of the island."

Martha Montgomery then asked what part of London the Tibbetts lived in, and the conversation developed into the mutually exploratory exercise normal among strangers meeting for the first time. The Tibbetts learned that the Montgomerys had lived in Tampica ever since the Second World War. Prior to that, Montgomery said, he had been a regular officer in the Royal Engineers. Since it was obvious that Montgomery had not been of retiring age in the late 1940s, Henry asked whether he had left the army to take a job on the British island. Montgomery replied with a brief yes, and changed the subject.

The Montgomerys learned that the Tibbetts were chartering *Windflower* for at least another week—that they might even stay longer. Their plans were uncertain, and they had not booked definite return passage to England.

"We've no family expecting us back," Henry explained, "and I've told my assistant in the office to expect me when he sees me. That's the advantage of being one's own boss."

Emmy explained that although they were enjoying themselves immensely, they were finding *Windflower* something of a handful. They had no boat of their own, but had done a certain amount of sailing with friends in England. Henry gently sounded out Bill on the topography of the better-known cruising areas of the English south and east coasts, but got no response.

Indeed, Emmy thought to herself, they had baited their lines to the absolute limit of plausibility and had not got as much as a nibble. It seemed that the Montgomerys were just what they said they were and no more.

Then the rum punches were finished, the rain stopped, and the sun struggled through a thin layer of high cloud on its way to the western horizon. Henry and Emmy got up to go and were not pressed to stay. Nor were they offered the customary tour of the boat. They said their good-byes and jumped down from the deck onto the quayside.

They were still walking back to *Windflower* when the next squall blew up, apparently out of nowhere. One moment, the sun was still shining; the next, the sky darkened, there was a distant rumble of thunder, and the rain began to come down in great heavy drops. Henry and Emmy put their heads down and began to run.

Going down the floating pontoon toward *Windflower*'s berth, Henry almost collided with a man who was running in the opposite direction, toward the shore. The man was wearing a bright yellow oilskin jacket with a hood, and apart from the fact that there seemed to be a lot of him, Henry barely noticed him. The important thing was to get back on board, out of the thundering downpour.

Henry reached *Windflower* ahead of Emmy. He jumped aboard and pushed back the hatch cover to open the companionway door. As Emmy climbed aboard after him, she happened to glance toward the shore. The man had reached the shelter of the marina buildings and stopped to get his breath. He pushed the hood back from his face and turned for a moment to look at the line of moored boats. Then he thrust his hands into his pockets and strode off toward the parking area and the taxi stand.

Henry said, "For heaven's sake, come aboard, Emmy. Everything's getting soaked—"

Emmy said, "Henry. It was him. I can't be mistaken. It was him."

"Oh, come on, woman." Henry almost dragged his wife into the cockpit and gave her a helping shove down into the cabin. When he had closed the hatch against the rain, he shook his wet hair and began to peel off his sopping shirt. He said, "Now, what's all this? Who was what?"

"That man, Henry," Emmy said. "The man who was running up the pontoon."

"What about him?"

"He took his hood off," Emmy said, "and I recognized him."

"Well, who was he?"

"Dr. Lionel Vanduren," Emmy said.

9

IN THE CABIN there was a moment of silence. Henry was looking at Emmy with a curious stare, at once blank and intense. He said, "So you thought you saw Lionel Vanduren. So what?"

Emmy grinned teasingly. "Oh, nothing. I just thought it might be of interest."

"Minimal interest," said Henry. "Now get changed into whatever decent clothes you have because we're going out."

"Out?"

"Certainly out. Where else?"

"But Henry, it's pouring rain, and—"

"The Buccaneer Bar," Henry said. He was already rummaging in the clothes locker for the pants and shirt that he had reserved for dancing nights at the Anchorage.

Catching the spirit of the thing, Emmy opened her suitcase and found a bright blue wraparound skirt and a white blouse. She said, "This is fun, Henry. But why—?"

"Why shouldn't we have some fun?" demanded her husband. And then, "Do you know, Emmy, I feel absolutely marvelous. Better than I have for years." He paused and then said, as if making a discovery, "I've been very tired."

"I know you have," Emmy said at once. "I've tried not to nag—but you really needed this holiday. Oh, I'm so glad. You mean—we're just going to go out and dance and have fun, just for ourselves, and not because there may be a criminal lurking in the ashtray?"

"Just that," Henry said. "I thought we might dine at the Harbour Prospect first."

"You never had a better idea," Emmy assured him.

They had just ordered cocktails and were studying the menu at the Harbour Prospect, sitting beside the great plate-glass window that looks out over St. Mark's Harbour, when Emmy looked at her watch and said, "Oh, Henry. It's half-past seven."

"What of it?"

"Well, oughtn't you to call John Colville? You told me you'd arranged with him to—"

"Oh, to hell with John Colville," said Henry.

Afterward, Emmy decided that this was the first moment when she felt a tiny coldness around her heart. But memory is deceptive, especially when aided by hindsight. It is unlikely that she registered anything at that precise moment, other than pleasure at Henry's obvious enjoyment of their evening out. At any rate, she had the elementary good sense not to refer to the telephone call again, and soon she and Henry were enjoying an excellent dinner with champagne.

"Champagne?" Emmy asked.

"Why not?"

"Why not indeed?" Emmy laughed, drained her glass, and tried not to notice how many traveler's checks Henry was signing to pay the bill. Then they went down into the throbbing darkness of the Buccaneer disco.

At one o'clock, Emmy said, "Well, that was marvelous, but it's time for home." She had danced like a teen-ager, she had drunk rather more than she had intended, and the thought of her quiet, comfortable bunk on board *Windflower* was extremely inviting.

Henry, on the other hand, seemed perfectly fresh. He had had very little to drink, but he was laughing and sparkling as Emmy could never remember before.

He said, "Home? Rubbish. Come on, this is a real jamming session."

At two o'clock, Emmy said, "I'm sorry, Henry. I just have to go back to the boat. I'm tired."

"I can't think why I bother to take you out if you insist on leaving just when I'm beginning to enjoy myself."

"O.K., then," Emmy said. "Why don't you stay on, and I'll take a taxi back to the marina."

In all her years as Henry's wife, Emmy had discovered that he never did anything without a reason. Obviously, it was part of his strategy this evening that she should go back to the boat, leaving him at the nightclub. "He might have told me," she thought—and then, "No, I wouldn't have been able to react so naturally if I'd known beforehand."

"Yes," said Henry. "Why don't you do that?" The blank look had come into his eyes again, and he was gazing across the rapidly emptying room toward the bar, where a group of young people were sitting. Emmy saw that it was Jill and Harvey Blackstone, with another young white couple whom she did not recognize.

Quickly, Emmy got up and made her way to the door. As she went out, she cast a quick look back into the disco, just in time to see Henry getting up from his chair and going over to the quartet at the bar. In the taxi, Emmy's principal thought was—"I might have known that it wouldn't be anything as simple as just an evening out." At that point, she did not realize how accurate she was.

Emmy was only vaguely aware of Henry's return to *Windflower,* but she heard the clatter of his feet down the companionway and opened her eyes for just long enough to see through the porthole that the eastern sky was streaked with light. About five . . . she drifted off to sleep again.

When she woke properly, it was to a delicious smell of coffee and the sizzling of bacon. She struggled through mists of sleep and a slight hangover to see Henry standing in the galley, an apron around his waist and the frying pan in his hand. He was wearing blue denim shorts and a crisp white shirt, and was whistling to himself as he set the pan down on the flame and broke a couple of eggs into it.

Emmy propped herself up on one elbow. She said, "Henry . . . what on earth . . . ?"

He turned and grinned at her. "Ah, you're awake at last. Breakfast's nearly ready. Then we'll go for a swim."

Emmy looked at her watch. "Henry . . . it's only half-past six, and you didn't get back until . . ."

"Oh, I haven't been to bed. Just washed and changed. Terrible the time people waste sleeping. Quite unnecessary."

Getting out of her bunk, Emmy said, "Well, you obviously had a successful time last night. You might have told me."

"Told you what?"

"That you knew the Blackstones would turn up, and that I should make myself scarce." She smiled and stretched. "I was very nearly very cross with you."

Henry looked at her. "I don't know what you're talking about," he said. "I stayed on because I wanted to stay on. And the

Blackstones and the Carstairs are coming sailing with us today. Nice people."

Emmy shrugged. "Oh, all right," she said. "Don't tell me. But who are the Carstairs?"

"The couple who were with the Blackstones. They're here on a boat, but they've got engine trouble and she's had to be hauled out for repairs. Here we are—coffee, bacon and eggs, bread and butter. What a wonderful morning."

It was a wonderful morning, with the sky rinsed by the rain and the island green and moist, the breeze cool and fresh.

Sitting in the cockpit, with his breakfast plate on his knees, looking out across the channel toward St. Matthew's, Henry said, "I've been thinking."

"What about?" Emmy asked through a mouthful of egg and bacon.

"About me. Us. We don't have enough fun."

"That's what you said last night."

"Well, everything's going to change. I shall retire and we'll build a house down here on this island."

Emmy sat up straight. "Henry, that's crazy. You've another ten years or more—"

"I've put in enough service to get a good pension. I don't intend to go on working until I can't enjoy myself anymore. And living here—"

"But we don't have the money to build a house here."

"We have the leasehold on our London flat. Sell that, make a down payment here, and get a mortgage—"

Emmy felt her head swimming. She said, "Look, Henry, be reasonable. We could never afford the mortgage payments on a loan like that if you retired on a reduced pension. Oh, I know it's a wonderful idea, but—"

Henry put down his knife and fork and said, "I thought as much."

"As much as what?"

"Just like last night. You insisted on going home. You had to sleep, of all things. Now you're just the same. Making difficulties. Refusing to believe in me." He stood up. "I can do anything."

"Henry—"

"Anything. If I'm not hampered by miserable, whining people like you. I've told you what I'm going to do. I'm going to sell the London lease and come to live here. You can do what you like."

The nightmare was closing in. Emmy said, "Henry, I'm only saying that I don't see how we could afford—"

"Ah, but you haven't heard the best part. The pension will only be the beginning. What do these islands need?"

"I don't know. What do they need?"

"A free-lance inquiry agency. What the Americans call a private eye." Henry patted himself on the chest. "Me. Meet the Tibbett Private Investigation Bureau. I can make a fortune."

Emmy began to laugh. "You are a clown," she said. "For a moment, I really began to take you seriously."

Henry looked at her, unblinking. "I am absolutely serious," he said. "I am resigning from Scotland Yard, and I will sell our London leasehold—"

Chilled again, Emmy said, "But you can't."

"What do you mean, I can't?"

"It's in our joint names. You can't sell that leasehold on your own. You have to have my signature."

"Oh, so that's it, is it? Let me tell you, I can do anything. Anything. And I have no need of somebody like you hanging round my neck like a bloody albatross. I may as well tell you, I've arranged with Bob Harrison to rent *Windflower* for another three weeks, and I shall probably go down island with the Blackstones and the Carstairs. You may do what you like, so long as you keep off this boat and out of my sight. I don't want to see you anymore. Do you understand that?"

Trying to keep her voice steady, Emmy said, "I don't know what's got into you, Henry, but I'll certainly keep out of your way, if that's what you want. I'll go back to the Anchorage."

"I don't give a damn what you do," said Henry.

As she walked up the jetty, carrying her suitcase, Emmy passed the young people—the Blackstones and the Carstairs—making their way down toward *Windflower*. She smiled, a small embarrassed smile, which they returned. At the marina, Emmy rushed for a telephone and dialed the Colvilles.

"John? Oh, thank God. This is Emmy."

"What's the matter, love?"

"I . . . I don't know. John, I think Henry has gone crazy."

"Crazy? How crazy?"

"I can't tell you over the telephone. John, can I come back to the Anchorage—on my own?"

"Of course you can. Right away?"

"As soon as I can get there. The boat comes over this afternoon, doesn't it?"

John Colville said, "There's something really bad and wrong, isn't there, Emmy?"

"I think so, John."

"Where are you now?"

"At the marina."

"Where's Henry?"

"On the boat. He's going off sailing with four young people we met here."

"O.K. Give me the number of your phone booth and stay right there. I think the Club helicopter is coming over this morning, and I'll see if I can get you a ride back on it. I'll call the Secretary and get back to you."

"John," said Emmy, "you are the original archangel."

"We do our best," said John, sounding more cheerful than he felt. "Now, stay there and I'll call back."

As Emmy looked down from the little helicopter—the same one that had taken Betsy Sprague to St. Mark's six months earlier—she saw *Windflower* leaving harbor. She could make out quite clearly the five figures—Jill and Harvey Blackstone, the two young unknowns named Carstairs, and Henry, energetic and efficient in his blue denim shorts.

Emmy looked and thought, "What's happening to me? What's happening to me?" And then, "It must be my fault."

Margaret Colville met Emmy at the Golf Club, where the helicopter alighted gently on a smooth green lawn. The two women embraced briefly, and then Margaret said, "Well, Henry's loss is our gain. It's marvelous to have you back." And, after a small pause, "You don't have to explain anything unless you want to. Just come and stay with us for as long as you like."

Emmy laughed a little unsteadily. "I wish I could explain," she said, "but I can't. I don't have an explanation. Henry has lost his mind."

"I find that very hard to believe," said Margaret.

"So do I," said Emmy, "but I've seen it and you haven't."

"What's he doing?"

"He . . . he's suddenly become a totally different person. Let's go back to the Anchorage, Margaret. I'll try to tell you, when I can sort it out a bit for myself."

A little later, sitting at a table in the Anchorage bar, Emmy tried.

"It's not that he's ill," she said. "On the contrary. He seems tremendously well and fit and full of energy. Too much energy. He says he needs no sleep. He says he can do anything. He wants to sell the lease to our London flat and come and live here. He says he'll open a private detective agency."

Margaret said doubtfully, "Well, I suppose there might be some sense in—"

John Colville, who had been talking on the telephone, came over to the table. He kissed Emmy and then said, "Well, Henry seems to be starting something."

"What do you mean?" Emmy asked.

"That was Bob Harrison on the telephone. It seems that Henry went to his house at five o'clock this morning, banged on the door until Bob came down, and then demanded to be allowed to charter *Windflower* for another three weeks. Bob says his speech was very slurred. He thought he was drunk. Bob made some soothing noises and sent him off, thinking that he'd just had a night out and would go off to bed. But when Bob got to the marina, just a little while ago, he found that *Windflower* had sailed, and he's very worried. He's responsible to the boat's owner, after all, and charterers are supposed to be hand-picked. He took Henry on my recommendation. It puts us all in a difficult position."

Emmy could think of nothing to say except, "I'm sorry, John."

"You?" John smiled at her. "You've got nothing to be sorry for. Now, when did this start?"

"Just yesterday evening," Emmy said. "We'd been for drinks on board *Ocean Rover,* and when we got back Henry suggested going out to dine and dance. Well, that was fine with me, and we thoroughly enjoyed ourselves, but then he refused to come home, and . . ." Miserably, Emmy recounted what had happened.

"Has he ever behaved like this before, Em?" John asked.

"No, never. It's absolutely unlike him. And now he's turned against me—"

Firmly, John said, "That's unimportant, Emmy."

"Unimportant? How can you say that?"

"I say it," said John, "because Henry is obviously ill. Get him cured, and this hostility towards you will disappear."

"I don't think so. Maybe this is something that has been festering, deep down, all these years—"

"Nonsense, Emmy." John spoke sharply. "Henry is ill, and he

needs medical treatment. Don't ask me what's wrong with him, because I'm not a doctor. But I'm going to call one."

"Oh, no, John. Please don't."

"Emmy dear," Margaret said, "we must. We don't have anything very fancy on these islands in the way of medical care, but we've a good G.P. Let John talk to him."

Dr. Daniels was, indeed, a good G.P., but of very little use in the present situation. He pointed out that Mr. Tibbett was not his patient, that he was apparently in good physical health, and that all he had done was to have a small quarrel with his wife and go off sailing with friends. He really didn't see what he could do, and he advised Mrs. Tibbett not to worry. He would send over a sedative for Mrs. Tibbett—she appeared to be the one who needed treatment.

John Colville swore mightily as he put down the telephone, but he had to admit that the doctor had given him a reasonable reply. It was not evidence—legal or medical—simply to insist that Henry Tibbett would never behave in such a way.

"Stay here with us anyway, Emmy," John said. "Something will happen, one way or the other."

What happened was a series of telephone calls. Inspector Ingham telephoned several times, wanting to know what had become of the Chief Superintendent and why all communication seemed to have been broken off. He wanted to notify Henry that his inquiries about Jill and Harvey Blackstone had been negative; that is, that the couple had never checked in officially at any Immigration office on the Seawards. This could be important information—and where was the Chief Superintendent?

John replied diplomatically that Henry was conducting an investigation and in the course of it had gone off sailing with the Blackstones and another couple called Carstairs. He imagined that it must be important for Henry to remain incommunicado and suggested that Ingham should keep in touch with the Anchorage. Herbert Ingham, who was nobody's fool, agreed grudgingly.

The next caller, on Sunday morning, was the Governor no less. Sir Alfred Pendleton was upset and also curious. He wanted to know whether Mr. Colville had any idea what Chief Superintendent Tibbett was up to.

"No, sir. I really don't know. He's off on his boat, and—"

"He certainly is," said Sir Alfred tetchily. "He's also making a damned nuisance of himself."

"Really, sir? How?"

"I've had complaints from George Island. It seems that *Windflower* went there yesterday and broke just about every regulation concerning anchoring, riding lights, and so on. That wouldn't matter so much except that Tibbett and his young friends have been behaving in such an extraordinary manner—"

"Drunk, do you mean, Sir Alfred?"

"It seems not." The Governor sounded puzzled. "The owners of the beach restaurant say that they just seemed to be . . . well, crazy. Not drunk. In the end, the restaurant people called the police launch from St. Mark's, but by the time it arrived, *Windflower* had upped anchor and sailed off. I'm absolutely baffled. After all, Tibbett is a senior police officer from Scotland Yard, and he's supposed to be conducting an inquiry here."

John said, "There must be a reason, sir. Either Tibbett is doing this deliberately, or else he's under the influence of—something. Could it be marijuana, do you think?"

"Certainly not." Sir Alfred was positive. "I'm no expert, but I've seen enough pot-smoking among the youngsters round here to recognize the symptoms. Generally it makes them very gentle, sleepy, withdrawn, and quiet. Your Henry Tibbett and his crew were loudmouthed and destructive—and yet not drunk. I don't understand it, but I'm issuing a warrant for Tibbett's arrest if he shows up in Seaward waters again."

It took John Colville quite a while to get Sir Alfred to agree to postpone this drastic action, at least until Henry Tibbett had had an opportunity to explain his strange behavior to the authorities.

The next call came from Herbert Ingham once more. It was imperative, he said, that Henry Tibbett should contact Inspector Reynolds at Scotland Yard. Reynolds had been able to get in touch with Mrs. Celia Vanduren, and he had important information for the Chief Superintendent. Where the hell, demanded Ingham, was he?

"I only wish I knew," said John Colville.

10

THAT NIGHT Emmy borrowed Margaret's alarm clock to wake her at five A.M., so that she could put through a telephone call to Scotland Yard. It would be ten o'clock on a Monday morning in London—a time when there was a good chance of finding Inspector Reynolds at his desk.

When the bell woke her, Emmy got up, put on jeans and a shirt, and crossed the cool garden to the bar. The first glimpses of golden daylight were beginning to take over from the silver of the tropical moon. In the distance, the sea was shirred with ripples, and somewhere a rooster was crowing. It seemed incredible that in the midst of all this beauty and tranquillity, Emmy should be in the grip of a nightmare. She shivered and hurried through the bar and into the office where the telephone was kept.

Inspector Reynolds was in his office. He greeted Emmy with the emotion of a shipwrecked sailor sighting a lifeboat.

"Mrs. Tibbett! Oh, thank heaven you've called. The A.C. is in a terrible state. What on earth is happening?"

"I thought you could tell me," Emmy said.

"I've important information on the case, yes. But it's the other business that none of us can understand."

"What other business?"

"The telegram. What does it mean? Is it some sort of code? I mean, the Chief Superintendent can't be serious."

Emmy said, "Inspector Reynolds, I haven't seen my husband for two days. I'm as much in the dark as you are. Tell me about the telegram."

"You mean, you don't know?"

"Of course I don't."

"This gets more and more mysterious," said Reynolds. "Well, it arrived this morning, sent on Saturday from the British Seaward Islands, and addressed simply to the Assistant Commissioner—just his title, no name, which is strange, considering how friendly he and Mr. Tibbett are. I'll read you the text." There was a pause, with a distant rustling of paper. "Are you there? O.K., here goes. 'KINDLY ACCEPT MY RESIGNATION EFFECTIVE TODAY STOP REMIT PENSION PAYMENTS TO UNITED SEAWARDS BANK ST. MARK'S HARBOUR ACCOUNT HENRY TIBBETT INVESTIGATION BUREAU STOP ON NO ACCOUNT REMIT ANY MONIES TO MY WIFE'—and it's signed, 'TIBBETT, MANAGING DIRECTOR HENRY TIBBETT BUREAU.' "

There was a pause. Emmy was speechless. Then Reynolds said, "You can imagine the effect it's had. The whole place is buzzing. I suppose this bureau is some sort of a cover—"

Emmy found her voice. She said, "Inspector Reynolds, you may be entirely right. Henry may be conducting some sort of very clever inquiry and putting up an enormous cover. But if he is, I can only tell you that he hasn't taken me into his confidence, any more than the Assistant Commissioner." She paused and swallowed. "Or Chief Inspector Ingham on St. Mark's. Or the Governor of the Seawards. As far as I can tell you, my husband has gone out of his mind."

"But Mrs. Tibbett—!"

"I know it's hard to believe. But either Henry is putting on such an act as never was—or he's crazy." Emmy paused. "The Governor wants to issue a warrant for his arrest. My friends and I have persuaded him not to do that for the moment, but—"

"And then," said Reynolds aggressively, "what's this in the telegram about not paying anything to you? I can't—"

Trying to sound calm, Emmy said, "That's all part of it, Inspector. Henry says he wants nothing more to do with me."

"But that's—"

"Understandable," said Emmy wryly. "It has nothing to do with the present situation."

"Now, Mrs. Tibbett, you mustn't—"

"Please, Inspector, I hope you're right, but for the moment, forget it. The situation between my husband and myself is purely personal. Meanwhile, whatever is happening to him is obviously part of the case he's involved in. So if you have important information—well . . . can you give it to me? In his place, as it were?"

There was a long pause. Then Reynolds spoke, and Emmy could

sense his red face from the other side of the world. "I don't really think I can, Mrs. Tibbett. I'll give the information to Inspector Ingham, and he can pass it along to you or not as he thinks fit."

Emmy felt as though somebody had poured a bucket of cold water in her face. For the first time in more than twenty years, she was not being treated as Henry's alter ego, his unofficial personal aide. Just when Henry needed her most, she was being snubbed and shunted off onto a sideline. With a big effort, she said, "I'm sure you're acting quite correctly, Inspector Reynolds. Do please call Inspector Ingham and give him all the details—but not before about two o'clock your time, or you'll get him out of bed. Good-bye, Inspector Reynolds."

Emmy did not wait to hear Reynolds's reply. She put down the telephone—being very careful not to slam it—and then laid her head on the office desk and began to cry, quietly and without hope. It was so that Margaret Colville found her a few minutes later, when the sky had become even lighter. Margaret had made a pot of delicate China tea, and—still in her dressing gown—had walked across the courtyard with two steaming cups.

Margaret sat down opposite Emmy and said, "Tea."

Emmy sniffled and raised her head. "Thanks, Margaret."

"You'd better tell me. You can't carry this alone, you know. What did London say?"

Emmy said, "Henry is either crazy, or he hates me in a . . . a really vicious sort of way, Margaret. But what is really important is that I think he is in terrible danger. And I don't know what to do about it. Nobody can help us."

"The doctor—"

"John tried the doctor. You know what happened."

"Well, of course, without any sort of proof . . . Henry might just be off on a joyride."

"Maybe he thinks he is," said Emmy grimly.

Margaret said, "You don't believe that, do you, Emmy?"

"I'm trying not to." Emmy gave a fair imitation of a smile and stood up. "I'm awfully sorry, Margaret. You had no right to expect this sort of thing when you invited us for a week's holiday, and I don't intend to inflict it on you anymore. You go back to bed, and I'll go for a walk. I'll be back for breakfast. Please don't worry. I'll be fine."

The hour between five and six in the morning is magical almost anywhere in summertime, and in the perpetual summer of the Caribbean it can hardly fail. Emmy walked down to the beach, not consciously observing but becoming aware of the daily miracle of life waking from darkness to light. A million tiny creatures stirred among the coarse grasses, piped up in the mango and mahogany trees, and skittered across the freshly washed shore. Behind the eastward hills, the glow deepened. Then, suddenly, the sun was up—and the land and sea lost their nocturnal grayness and broke into blue and pink and gold.

"This happens every morning," Emmy said to herself. "Why do I have to be almost suicidal before I bother to get up and look at it?" The thought made her smile, which was an improvement.

Hardly realizing in which direction her steps were taking her, Emmy followed the closest path along the seashore, toward Priest Town. She could not be said to be thinking or reasoning—because in a situation of utter unreason, there was no hypothesis from which to postulate. Her thoughts took the form of a silent scream. What am I to do? What am I to do? What is happening to Henry? How can I help him? Oh, God, what am I to do?

A deeper, less emotional corner of her mind registered the fact that she was now bringing the deity into it; this steadied her and provoked another small, invisible smile. She remembered the old saying that there are no atheists on a battlefield. All right, this is my battlefield. I am at bay, and there's nothing to do but stand and fight. The thought cheered her, even though she knew it was spurious. Before she realized it, Emmy was approaching the small streets and houses of Priest Town, and she could see the gray stone Customs House—now closed and shuttered—the new police station, and the small yacht marina beyond it.

It was half-past seven, the sun was up, but the air was still pleasantly cool. Priest Town was rising, stretching, and going about its business. On the quayside, half a dozen fishermen were preparing their boats for sea. Trucks carrying construction materials were beginning to roll out to building sites up in the hills. Jeeps and small cars were taking people to work. And along the jetty, people on boats were slowly waking and climbing up into the cockpit to breathe deeply, stretch, and look at the morning. One or two were even ashore already, and . . . Emmy suddenly stiffened, took another look, and broke into a run. The tall, slightly stooped figure on the pontoon was unmistakable.

Emmy nearly called his name aloud, then realized that he was too far away to hear her. He was walking up the row of moored yachts toward the quay, peering intently at each boat as he passed it. As Emmy came hurrying toward him, he gave her a brief look and obviously dismissed her. In her cut-off jeans and white shirt, she could have been a tourist off any sailing boat—and she was quite clearly not the person that Dr. Vanduren was looking for.

Before Emmy could reach the yacht basin, the doctor had inspected the last boat, found it unprofitable, and crossed the quay to disappear up one of the narrow alleys leading to Main Street. By the time Emmy arrived, there was no sign of him. She made a quick search of the area, but her quarry seemed to have vanished. The shops and cafés were not yet open, so she concluded that he must have gone into a private house.

No matter, thought Emmy. He must have entered the Seawards through Customs and Immigration, and she remembered that the entry permit required visitors to list their address while in the islands. She had only to ask Inspector Ingham to locate Dr. Vanduren for her.

Feeling happier and wondering why she had not thought of tracing the doctor sooner, Emmy made her way back to the Anchorage and breakfast.

Emmy had intended to put through a call to Inspector Ingham after breakfast, but he forestalled her. She was still drinking her last cup of coffee when John came out of the office to tell her that the Inspector was on the line for her.

"Mrs. Tibbett, I do implore you to help us." Ingham sounded near the end of his tether.

"Help you? How can I help you?"

"Your husband and his crew sailed *Windflower* into St. Mark's yesterday. It was reported to me by the Harbour Master, but in deference to you and to Mr. Colville, I took no action. The next I heard was that some sort of fight had broken out in the marina restaurant—there was a general disturbance, and property was damaged. By the time my men got there, *Windflower* had sailed off again. As far as I can make out, she ploughed her way through a cluster of small sailing dinghies engaged in a Sunday afternoon regatta. It caused utter chaos and several of the dinghies were overturned. What are you laughing at?"

"I'm not," gulped Emmy apologetically. "I think I'm a bit hysterical. To think of *Henry*—"

"And now," added Ingham, "*Windflower* has disappeared. Naturally, she never cleared Customs and Immigration, but as far as we can make out she is no longer in Seaward waters. I shall have to put out a general alert for her apprehension."

Emmy, having mastered her ridiculous impulse to giggle, said,

"Inspector Ingham, I'd like to see you. There's something I want to ask you. Suppose I come over on the *Pride* this morning?"

"An excellent idea, Mrs. Tibbett. I was going to suggest it." A little pause. "As a matter of fact, the Governor would like a word with you. Maybe you can help us. Frankly, I'd rather cope with any number of drug-runners than a top-rank policeman gone berserk in charge of a boat."

The mail, brought up by Corfetta's daughter from the post office, contained a very formal letter and a sheaf of documents from a solicitor in St. Mark's. Mr. Henry Tibbett, he wrote, had instructed him to send the enclosed documents for Mrs. Tibbett's signature. The documents required Emmy to relinquish all claim on the leasehold of the Tibbetts' London apartment and to make over the lease to the Henry Tibbett Investigation Bureau Ltd., St. Mark's, British Seaward Islands. Emmy sighed despairingly and put the papers into her suitcase.

When Emmy came down from her room, Margaret was in the bar, setting it up for the day's business. She said, "Any more news?"

"About Henry, you mean?"

"What else?"

"More of the same, only worse," Emmy said. She told Margaret about Ingham's phone call. "So I'm going over today on the *Pride* to see the Inspector and the Governor."

"I hope you're wise," Margaret said.

"How do you mean, wise? The Governor wants to—"

"Perhaps you didn't hear the weather forecast this morning," said Margaret.

"No, I didn't. But you can see what a lovely day it is—" Emmy looked up at the serene blue of the sky. "It's always perfect here."

"No, it's not," Margaret said. "Most of the time it's good, except for a few heavy downpours in the rainy season. But there are such things as tropical storms and hurricanes, you know."

"Surely not at this time of year. I thought the hurricane season was in September."

"No, officially it starts in July. But the weather doesn't always go by the calendar."

"Are you trying to tell me that there's a hurricane threatening the Seawards?" Emmy was laughing.

Seriously, Margaret said, "Not immediately. But the forecast this morning said that Tropical Storm Alfred—the first of the season—was becoming organized and would probably be upgraded to a hurricane today. It's out in the Atlantic seven hundred miles southeast of Puerto Rico, and if it continues on its present course, it'll pass north of us—but we can't be sure."

Emmy said, "I thought these islands were never hit by hurricanes."

"They haven't been for thirty years," Margaret said, "but tropical storms are unpredictable—they can change course without warning, and this one is too close for comfort."

Before Emmy could answer, John came into the bar. He held a piece of paper in his hand, which he consulted. "Just heard the latest from the Miami weather station," he said. "Good morning, Emmy. Tropical Storm Alfred now Hurricane Alfred with highest sustained winds of ninety miles per hour and gales extending a hundred miles north and fifty miles south of the center. Present location 11.3 degrees north, 52.5 degrees west, traveling northwest at ten miles an hour. Hurricane watch is in effect for Windwards, Leewards, and Seawards."

Emmy said, "What exactly does all that mean?"

"It means," said John, "that with luck it'll stay well to the north of us, although we'll probably get the tail edge of the gales."

"And without luck?"

"If the course changes to a more westerly direction—well, we could get it."

"When?" Margaret asked.

"Not before tomorrow. We've plenty of time to take precautions. I think we should board up our eastern windows and—"

Margaret said, "John, Emmy has had more bad news about Henry. She's planning to go over to St. Mark's today to see the Governor. Is that safe, do you think?"

"Safe enough today," John said, "but get back this evening, or you may find yourself stranded."

On board the *Pride of St. Mark's*, most of the gossip was concerned with the possibility—regarded by the islanders as extremely remote—of the Seawards being struck by Hurricane Alfred. There were jokes at the expense of Sir Alfred Pendleton, the storm's namesake; people reminded each other that it was thirty years since the last such occasion, and a group of youths pretended to go into an exaggerated panic over the appearance of one small cloud on the horizon. The rippled sea was calm and deep blue, shading to aquamarine as the *Pride* churned steadily through the shallows outside St. Mark's Harbour. Soon the passengers were ashore and

Emmy was walking through shady streets up the hill to the police station.

Inspector Ingham greeted her with a worried smile. He said, "Ah, glad to see you, Mrs. Tibbett. The Governor is expecting us both right away. I've got my car outside, so let's get going."

Emmy said, "Just a moment, Inspector. There's one thing. While we're with the Governor, can your people find out from Immigration whether Dr. Lionel Vanduren is on the islands and what his address is?"

Ingham looked steadily at Emmy for a moment. Then he said, "If he checked in through the airport or either harbor, we'll certainly have a record. But what makes you think—?"

"I'm pretty sure I saw him here in the marina the day before— before my husband started behaving so oddly. With all that's happened, I quite forgot about it, until I saw him again this morning on St. Matthew's."

"What do you imagine he would be doing here?"

"Looking for his daughter," said Emmy.

Ingham gave her a curious look, then picked up a telephone. "Sergeant . . . oh, it's you, Pearletta. Check with Immigration, will you, if a Dr. Vanduren, first name . . . ?" He turned inquiringly to Emmy, who said, "Lionel." "A Dr. Lionel Vanduren from Miami has checked in by sea or air within the past week. If so, let me have details of dates and where he's staying. O.K.? Thank you, dear." He hung up the phone and stood up. "Let's get going then, Mrs. Tibbett."

Little was said on the way to Government House. Soon Emmy and the Inspector were sitting in the same drawing room where Henry had been interviewed by the Governor, and a few minutes later Sir Alfred himself came in.

"Inspector Ingham . . . Mrs. Tibbett . . . I am very glad you were able to come over. I felt I should talk to you personally. This is a very bad business."

"It certainly is," Emmy agreed.

"Have you any explanation as to your husband's behavior?"

Emmy shook her head. "I feel sure there *is* an explanation," she said. "Either Henry is doing this deliberately for some good reason, or else it's . . . oh, I don't know. I simply can't believe that he's gone off his head."

The Governor looked at her quizzically. He said, "Mental breakdowns are not infrequent, you know, even in apparently stable people. And I believe there's something called the seven-year itch—"

"Henry and I have been married for twenty years."

"Well—perhaps I used the wrong expression. I mean the phenomenon of middle-aged men quite suddenly cutting loose and behaving . . . well, in an eccentric manner. And, of course, there's another possibility."

"What do you mean?"

"Your husband," said Sir Alfred, "told me that he was making every effort to contact these supposed drug-runners. Trailing his coat was the way he put it. I am tempted to think he may have succeeded."

Emmy nodded.

"Now," Pendleton went on, "I believe there is a great deal of money involved. In fact, I know it. The criminals concerned—if they should have found out your husband's true identity—might be prepared to pay a great deal to . . . to buy his cooperation."

Miserably, Emmy said, "I can't even feel angry with you for suggesting that, Sir Alfred. You see, you don't know Henry like I do. I can't blame you for suspecting—" Suddenly she turned to Inspector Ingham. "Did Derek Reynolds call you from London?" she demanded.

"Inspector Reynolds? Yes, he did."

"What did he say? He told me he had important information."

Ingham appealed mutely to Sir Alfred, who smiled and said, "I think it would be unfair not to tell Mrs. Tibbett, Inspector."

Embarrassed, Ingham said, "I think I should tell you, sir, that Mrs. Tibbett thinks she has seen Dr. Vanduren here and on St. Matthew's within the past few days."

Sir Alfred looked at Emmy with raised brows. "Really, Mrs. Tibbett? Are you sure?"

"Not absolutely," Emmy admitted, "but if it's not him, it's somebody extraordinarily like him."

Inspector Ingham said, "I'm having Immigration check on arrivals in the last week, sir. We'll soon know."

"Then keep me posted," said the Governor, dryly. "Well, Mrs. Tibbett, Inspector Reynolds's news is that he has located Mrs. Celia Vanduren. Ingham has the details."

"She's staying with her mother, a Mrs. Dobson, in a village called East Chudbury in Shropshire," said Ingham.

"Well, we knew that," Emmy said. "I mean, that she was in Shropshire with her mother. Is that all?"

"No, it's not," said Ingham, with emphasis. "The Inspector spoke to the lady himself, and he reports that she doesn't seem to be in the least ill or hysterical. She told him that she only came to England because her husband insisted that she do so. She says she never had hospital treatment after Janet's death, and that if anyone was having a breakdown, it was Dr. Vanduren himself. She strongly denies having destroyed photographs of her daughter, and in fact she has one with her. It's now on its way to Scotland Yard, where Reynolds will get it copied and send it to us here by way of a British Airways pilot en route to Antigua. Unfortunately, there's no quicker way of getting it to us."

Sir Alfred, who was engaged in filling a curly briar pipe with tobacco, looked at Emmy and said, "You were actually there, were you, Mrs. Tibbett, when Dr. Vanduren made those remarks about his wife?"

"Yes, I was."

"Then we can only assume that Dr. Vanduren was lying," said the Governor. There was a pause. "And now you maintain that he is here in person. Very curious. Unless, of course . . ." He rammed the aromatic tobacco into the bowl of the pipe with great concentration, leaving his unfinished remark hanging in the air.

Angrily, Emmy said, "You mean, unless Henry and I are both lying? Both in the pay of the drug ring."

"My dear Mrs. Tibbett, I would not suggest such a thing. However, my main purpose for asking you to come here was so that I could explain to you personally why I am proposing to issue a general alert for the arrest of the yacht *Windflower* and her crew."

Emmy said nothing.

Ingham said, "It's necessary, Mrs. Tibbett. Apart from anything else, there's the possibility of Hurricane Alfred hitting us. For the Chief Superintendent's own sake—"

Emmy became aware that the Governor was looking at her intently from behind the protective smoke screen of his now-lighted pipe. She said, "I'm sorry. Of course you're right, Sir Alfred. Things can't go on like this."

The tension seemed to relax a little. Pendleton said, "I'm glad you see it like that, Mrs. Tibbett. Let's hope that your husband has a proper respect for my namesake, and that *Windflower* is in some safe anchorage. Let's hope, too, that you are right and there's a reasonable explanation for all these goings-on." He smiled. Emmy managed to smile back. "Well, now, you'll be going back to St. Matthew's today, I imagine."

"Yes. On the afternoon boat. You can always get me at the Anchorage."

"Unless the storm hits and we all lose our telephone lines," Sir Alfred remarked. "Barring that, we'll keep you up to date on any developments. Equally, I know you'll tell us at once if you hear from your husband."

"Of course."

The skies were still serene as the *Pride of St. Mark's* forged her way back toward Priest Town, but the wind was getting up, whipping the seas so that the tubby boat bucked and rolled with an uncomfortable motion, and the trip took longer than the scheduled half-hour. John was at the jetty to meet Emmy. He looked worried.

"Glad to see you back," he said. "Things don't look so good. Friend Alfred has intensified and speeded up. Should still pass to the north, but closer and sooner than we thought. Incidentally, Herbert Ingham has been trying to get you on the telephone. You're to call him as soon as you get in. He left a number for you to call. He's not at the police station."

"Did he say what he wanted?"

"No. Sounded a bit grim, I thought."

"Oh, dear," said Emmy, and then was silent.

Inspector Ingham did indeed sound grim when Emmy contacted him on the telephone. She had been surprised to find that the number she dialed was that of Government House. After a few clicks and buzzes, Ingham came on the line.

"Mrs. Tibbett? I am with the Governor. He would like a word with you."

"The Governor? What on earth—?"

"Please hold the line."

"Hello, Mrs. Tibbett. Pendleton here. I have some rather . . . disturbing news."

"About Henry?" Emmy's throat was dry with fear.

"In a way. This afternoon, a woman police constable on radio watch intercepted another *Starfish* message. You understand what I am talking about?"

"Yes." Emmy was almost whispering. "What did it say?"

"This time it was to *Starfish,* rather than from her. It came, ostensibly from a boat called *Anemone.* You, being English, will know that 'windflower' is another name for the wood anemone. Local people would not connect the two—for them, anemones are strictly sea creatures. *Anemone* informed *Starfish* that she had had

110

a very successful cruise, but in view of the weather was planning to return home. She hoped they might meet as arranged."

"Any time or place mentioned?"

"No. The rendezvous must have been fixed in advance, and some simple code must have indicated the date and time. The interesting thing was the voice of the speaker."

"What do you mean?"

"Policewoman Terry reports that it was masculine and British. She has met your husband, Mrs. Tibbett, and it is her impression that it was him speaking."

"But that's—"

"I have another piece of information. Inspector Ingham has made a most thorough check with Immigration. Dr. Lionel Vanduren is definitely not in the Seaward Islands."

"But—"

"I have kept perhaps the most significant part until the last, Mrs. Tibbett. At the end of the *Starfish* message, the speaker from *Anemone* mentioned that *Starfish* should not bother to make contact with a person referred to only by the initial *E*. His final words were 'She is making her own arrangements.' What do you make of that?"

"I . . . nothing. I don't know what to make of it."

"I must be frank with you, Mrs. Tibbett. At the least, you owe us an explanation. I have given instructions that you are not to be permitted to leave the British Seawards, and I shall be obliged if you will take the boat over here again tomorrow. I will see you in my office at midday, and I hope that by then you will have decided to be entirely frank with us."

Wretchedly, Emmy said, "Very well, Sir Alfred. I'll see you tomorrow."

But, as it turned out, tomorrow was too late.

11

COMING BACK FROM St. Mark's on the *Pride,* Emmy had noticed that the sunshine had taken on a curious metallic quality, which gave the usually friendly land and seascape a sinister harshness. During the afternoon, following her unhappy conversation with Sir Alfred Pendleton, this brassy unreality deepened until it almost matched the nightmare going on in Emmy's mind.

There was no consolation to be had from the Colvilles because they were far too busy, and Emmy was grateful that she was coopted without question to help in the hurricane precautions. At such a time, it was merciful to be kept occupied and not bothered with questions.

As it was, the Colvilles and Emmy and the skeleton staff of the Anchorage worked hard and fast, with a transistor radio always at hand giving out the latest weather bulletins. In the office, a big chart was spread out and pinned to the desk, and over it a bold line in marker-pen ink traced Alfred's progress as he made his inexorable way across the last miles of the Atlantic Ocean toward the slender string of islands that form the eastward boundary of the Caribbean Sea.

Sheets of plywood were brought out from the garden shed, sawed into segments to fit over north and east windows, and then battened into place with long nails driven through transverse exterior beams. Margaret and Emmy assembled quantities of candles and matches, which they stored in the kitchen. They also filled every available receptacle with drinking water—jugs and saucepans as well as jerricans.

"There won't be any lack of water," Margaret explained, "but we rely on an electric pump to get it up from the cistern, and the electricity will be the first thing to go."

"Surely," Emmy said, "we can draw water up from the cistern in buckets."

"Until the cistern cracks and the water either runs out or gets polluted," said Margaret. "You'll find a couple more casseroles in the back pantry. Best fill them."

Glass windows on the south and west sides—the lee sides of the building—were crisscrossed with adhesive tape, so if they did blow out there would be less danger of flying glass. Stacks of tinned food were brought down from the storage shed to the main hotel building, where Emmy and the Colvilles proposed to take shelter. Outside, vulnerable objects such as wheelbarrows and stepladders were upturned, laid flat, and where possible tied down. The jeep was parked so as to be out of range of any tree or building that might fall on it. All the time, as the sinister sunlight faded, the wind grew stronger, and black clouds came crowding in from the east.

The radio kept up its unending stream of information. St. Matthew's Golf Club had mobilized its entire fleet of launches as well as its helicopter to ferry members to St. Mark's for evacuation by air. Many guests from the Harbour Prospect Hotel had already left the island—all available aircraft were running a shuttle service to San Juan to airlift visitors to safety. All seagoing craft should seek and remain in safe shelter, paying special attention to anchors and mooring lines. Residents were advised to take all appropriate hurricane precautions. Stocks of candles and tinned food should be laid in, in case of power failures.

Emmy's mind, as she worked, ran around like a spinning prayer wheel. Oh, God, take care of Henry. Oh, God, let him be safe in harbor.

By five P.M. the radio reports had become distinctly sinister. The Seawards, along with other islands, were now under a hurricane warning, which meant that the arrival of hurricane-force winds was imminent. By six o'clock, John had driven all the staff members to their homes, and it had started to rain. The besieged garrison of the Anchorage sat at the bar, had a drink, and listened to the wind and rain. It all seemed very unreal. Even Emmy could recall worse weather conditions on this island, and it occurred to all of them that in the absence of the radio's alarming predictions, they would not have taken the weather situation at all seriously.

John cooked a simple meal and opened a bottle of good wine. The rain grew heavier, pounding on the tin roof so as to make conversation difficult, and the slender bushes of hibiscus and oleander

113

bent gracefully under the gusts of wind. Still nothing frightening happened. Nobody mentioned Henry.

At ten minutes past ten, when Emmy and the Colvilles were enjoying a cup of coffee and a brandy, there was a sudden screaming increase in the force of the wind. Simultaneously, a massive clap of thunder and blast of lightning, and all the lights went out.

"Here he comes!" John shouted. "Inside, everybody, and get the shutters battened down!"

They were only just in time. Even though they had been sitting in the sheltered bar, on the protected side of the building, the wind hit with such force that it was all that Margaret and Emmy could do, pulling together, to close and bolt the door to the office, where they now retreated. There was no longer any hope of getting to the bedrooms above by way of the outside staircase. The office, kitchen, and downstairs cloakroom would be the hurricane hole for the three inhabitants of the Anchorage until the storm had passed.

Thanks to the precautions taken, the windows were boarded up, there was a good supply of food and water, and by the light of several candles the quarters looked positively cozy. Margaret and Emmy had brought three mattresses down to the office, together with pillows, sheets, and light blankets. The radio continued to pour out advice, weather bulletins, and updates on the position of the hurricane. The siege was on.

The worst part, Emmy thought, was the noise. The building was actually standing up very well to the tremendous buffeting of the wind, and apart from a slight rattling of the window boards, all would have been peaceful inside the office had it not been for the banshee howling of the gale outside. Like a shrieking maniac, the wind was clawing and tearing at everything it encountered—trees, vehicles, wires, buildings. Dull thuds and metallic crashes from outside told the shelterers that property was coming under fire and suffering. The radio, having given Hurricane Alfred's latest position as one hundred miles to the southeast of the Seaward Islands, moving northwest at twelve miles an hour, was now filling in time by playing a steel-band rendering of "Island in the Sun," perhaps with unconscious irony or possibly with deliberate black humor.

The ringing of the telephone took them all by surprise. Emmy had taken it for granted that telephone communication would have been cut off.

John answered it. "Colville. Yes . . . yes, Sir Alfred . . . yes, she's here, I'll put her on. . . . What? . . . Not too bad, so far.

How is it with you? . . . Good . . . No, it doesn't sound too hopeful, does it? . . . Just a moment, here's Emmy . . ." He held out the receiver.

"Emmy Tibbett here."

"Ah, Mrs. Tibbett. I thought I should call you while I could to let you know that our appointment for tomorrow is naturally cancelled." Sir Alfred cleared his throat. "Now, I don't want you to worry any more than you have to. I'm sure there'll be an explanation. We've no news of *Windflower,* but she must have been in Seawards waters today for that radio message to have been picked up here. Well, no news is good news, even in this weather."

"But, Sir Alfred—"

"So we'll just have to presume that she's safely holed up somewhere—"

"Sir Alfred!" Emmy was shouting into the telephone. "Don't you understand, that message—" The phone went dead.

John said, "What's the matter, Emmy?"

"Damn it. The phone's gone now."

"Well, we were lucky to have it for so long. What did he say?"

"Oh, he was trying to be kind. There's no news of *Windflower,* but he thinks she has to be in the Seawards, because of the *Starfish* message."

"That sounds logical," said John.

"But it isn't!" cried Emmy, near tears. "I was so upset about everything that I wasn't thinking straight earlier on. I've only just realized that that message couldn't have come from *Windflower.*"

"Couldn't? But with the call sign *Anemone—*"

"Oh, I'm sure it was from the smugglers," Emmy said. "But it couldn't have been sent from *Windflower* for the very good reason that she doesn't carry a VHF radio. So *Windflower*—and Henry— may be absolutely anywhere by now!"

"Just about anywhere," said John, "is better than here tonight."

It was a very long night. The radio kept up its continuous coverage, with updates on Alfred's position. The black track on the map snaked closer and closer to the island of St. Benedict, to the southeast of St. Matthew's, and at midnight the Seawards radio announced that Radio St. Benedict had gone off the air after a final frantic message that their transmitting tower was toppling. The only communication with the island was now by ham radio operators, who were manning their sets around the clock. If the hurricane continued on its present course, it might be expected to hit the British Seawards around dawn, with winds up to 120 miles per hour.

All the time, the noise grew louder until it was difficult to hear the radio, even with the volume turned fully up. An extra-loud crash on the roof indicated that something had fallen on it, probably a tree.

Margaret said, "There's absolutely nothing we can do but sit here and hope, Emmy. Do try to get some sleep."

"Margaret's right," John put in. "Tomorrow's going to be one hell of a day, whatever happens. I'll make some cocoa—thank God we cook with bottled gas—and I suggest you take a couple of aspirin and at least lie down."

Emmy managed a tired smile. "All right," she said, "but I won't sleep."

She was wrong. Against all odds, she drifted off into unconsciousness, almost lulled by the incessant screaming of the gale. Her last thought was to wonder if the little white pills had really been aspirin, or something stronger. Emmy slept.

When she woke, sickly gray daylight was filtering through the taped-up windows. Margaret was sound asleep on the mattress beside her, while John sat at the desk, making notes as the radio continued to drone out its messages. He looked up, saw Emmy, and smiled.

"Good morning, Emmy."

"I did sleep," said Emmy wonderingly. And then, "Am I dreaming, or is there just a bit less wind?"

"You're not dreaming," John said. "We've had a small miracle. Alfred took a turn towards the north at three-thirty A.M. He's passing us right now, but about forty miles away. We're feeling his southern side, with winds of only about eighty miles an hour."

Emmy sat up stiffly. "Only!" she echoed ruefully.

"To the north of the eye, it's blowing over a hundred," said John. "So be thankful. Like a cup of tea?"

"I'll make it."

"O.K., you do that. I want to stay with the radio."

As Emmy filled the kettle from a jerrican, she heard the latest radio announcement. Alfred's position was forty-two miles north of St. Mark's, moving north-northwest. Grim reports were beginning to filter through from St. Benedict via the indefatigable ham operators. A score of confirmed deaths, many thousands left homeless, severe flooding. Hurricane warnings now in force for Haiti and the Dominican Republic. Damage to the British Seawards so far reported light—windows broken, roofs off, roads impassable due to flooding and fallen trees. Then the parochial messages, bringing it all so close to home.

"The school of St. Michael and All Angels will be closed today. All nonessential government employees on St. Mark's should not, repeat *not,* report to work this morning. The Carib Supermarket in Priest Town will not open today. Civil Defense authorities inform motorists that they should use their vehicles only in emergencies. The road between Fat Cow Bay and Plumtree Bay is impassable due to fallen trees. The coast road between Priest Town and Mango Tree Bay on St. Matthew's is flooded and should only be attempted by four-wheel-drive vehicles in extreme emergencies. The following banks and commercial offices have told us they will not be open today . . ." The exhausted voice of the announcer droned on. He had been on duty for fifteen hours without a break. Outside, the sky lightened slowly, as if with reluctance. The kettle boiled. Emmy made tea.

By seven o'clock the wind had diminished appreciably. Emmy reflected on the relativity of human reactions. There must be a fifty-mile-an-hour gale blowing, a greater force of wind than she had ever before experienced, and yet it seemed almost mild in contrast to the storm's earlier fury. Margaret woke up and had a cup of tea, and John even ventured out into the bar to inspect the damage. Emmy followed him cautiously.

Even in the shelter of the bar, which had two solid walls, it was difficult to walk against the force of the wind. The palm-leaf section of the roof had blown off completely, scattering the garden with untidy brown fronds and leaving a bent and gaping skeleton of girders open to the gray skies. Sure enough, a big mahogany tree had fallen across the roof of the office, but it did not appear to have done very much damage.

The garden looked like a battlefield—plants uprooted, small trees and shrubs laid flat, plump green and yellow papayas rolling forlornly in the streams of rainwater that cascaded down the hillside and toward the beach. Flower beds had become sloughs of mud, and the wooden gates at the head of what had been the driveway were wrenched from their hinges and lay half-submerged in mud and sand. But the jeep was still there, even though its canvas roof was ripped and flapping. There were no broken windows or doors blown in. The bar was still standing, although all the stools had blown over and were rolling around the concrete floor.

John turned with some difficulty to Emmy and smiled. Against the wind, he mouthed rather than shouted, "We've been lucky." Emmy nodded and smiled back.

It was then that Emmy saw a tall figure in bright yellow oilskins, bent nearly double against the wind, making his laborious way up the ruined road toward the Anchorage. She grabbed John's arm.

"Look! Somebody's coming!"

"Good God," John shouted. "It looks like Morley. What on earth—?"

Morley Duprez had reached what had been the gateway and was struggling through the remnants of the cattle guard, sinking nearly up to the top of his black rubber boots. Raising his head against the wind, he saw John and finished the last few yards to the comparative shelter of the bar in a stumbling near-run.

"Mr. Colville! Mr. Colville!" Morley's voice was tossed away contemptuously by the fury of the wind.

John grabbed the black man's arm and pulled him through the door and into the haven of the office, where he stood dripping water and oozing mud, fighting to catch his breath. Emmy, following the two men, managed with a struggle to close the door behind them.

Margaret, sitting up on her mattress with her cup of tea, said, "Morley! How on earth did you get here? What's the news? Have some tea."

She scrambled to her feet and began pouring.

Morley Duprez said, "Mr. Colville, can you help us?"

"Of course. Anything I can do. What is it?"

"Thanks, Mrs. Colville." Morley buried his nose gratefully in the steaming mug. Then, "It's a boat, Mr. Colville. A yacht. Washed ashore in Bluefish Bay and breaking up. There's just a chance we can do something to save her if we have a four-wheel-drive vehicle with a tow bar."

"My jeep?"

"Yes, Mr. Colville. Priest Town is mashed up, man. Most jeeps thrown over, broken good."

Margaret said, "What about the Golf Club? They have better vehicles—"

Between gulps of tea, Morley said, "Know the Club Service area? Down near the water?" Margaret nodded. "All their vehicles in there . . . flooded out. Not one working till afternoon at best."

John said, "You've been to the Golf Club, have you?"

"No, man, no way. I'm goin' there, but I hear what happen them vehicles."

"You heard? From whom?"

Morley shrugged. "Fellow work there," he said briefly. Clearly, hurricane or no, the mysterious island grapevine was operating.

Emmy opened her mouth to ask a question, but John forestalled her. "This boat—know anything about her?"

"Not much. Daniel Markham saw her at first light this morning—you know he house looking down to Bluefish. White sailboat, that's all he say. He come find me, and I come by you."

"Anybody aboard?" said John.

"Daniel don't see nobody, Mr. Colville, but he don't know for sure."

Seeing Emmy's face, John put an arm around her shoulders, gave her a quick squeeze, and said, "There are thousands of white yachts in the Caribbean, Emmy."

"Yes, but—"

John became practical. "The question is, Can we get the jeep out of here and down to the bay? Have you seen the road, Morley?"

"It's not good," Duprez admitted, "but with four-wheel you gotta chance, man. We pass by pick up young Melville—he a good strong boy. He be waiting us."

"O.K.," said John. "Margaret, can you find my oilskins and boots? And those two lengths of fifty-foot rope we bought. The steel towing cable is in the jeep. Better bring my toolbox and the first-aid kit as well."

Emmy said, "I'll come with you, John."

"Don't be an idiot," said John, not unkindly. "You'd only be in the way."

"John," Emmy said, "I'm not being sentimental or hysterical. I know I'm not a trained nurse, but I do have a first-aid diploma, and if there *is* anybody on board—"

Rather surprisingly, Margaret said, "Emmy's right, John. You and the other men will be too busy with the boat to care for the people. Emmy can have my oilies and boots."

"Oh, all right." John sounded unconvinced, but too preoccupied to be bothered with argument. He said, "Now, Margaret, you must get in touch somehow with the Golf Club."

"How? We've no telephone—"

"Write a note to the Secretary and get it to Irving, just down the road. The wind's moderating all the time—you'll soon be able to walk that far. Tell him to pass it on—he'll see it gets there by a system of relays."

"What am I to say in it?"

119

"Tell Peter that there's a boat washed up in Bluefish Bay and that I've gone down with Morley and Melville. There may be casualties on board, but in any case we may not be able to get the jeep up again once we're there. So ask him to send the helicopter to look for us just as soon as he can."

"O.K.," said Margaret.

John pulled his oilskin jerkin over his head and got into his rubber boots. Margaret handed a similar but smaller outfit to Emmy, with a grin and an encouraging wink. Emmy did her best to smile back. By the time she was suitably outfitted, and Margaret had given her the first-aid box with a rundown on its contents, the two men were already outside, fighting through the storm to the jeep. Emmy hurried after them.

If the wind had abated slightly, this advantage was more than made up for by the fact that it had once again started to rain—heavy, warmish, tropical rain blown almost horizontally by the gale, which smashed into eyes and faces and made it virtually impossible to see. From the shelter of the bar, Margaret watched the three figures struggling toward the jeep, finally making it. After a moment of indecision, the engine turned over, hiccuped, turned over again, and finally roared into triumphant life. The windshield wipers, ineffective as blades of grass against the deluge, began sweeping manfully over the streaming glass. The lights went on. John leaned out from the driver's seat to give his wife a thumbs-up sign, and slowly the jeep began to move through the squelching morass of the drive.

To leave the Anchorage by the official exit was out of the question. The heavy gates had blown down across the cattle grid, blocking the way and buckling the stout steel pipes. Torrents of mud and water had weakened the concrete sides of the pit under the grid, which would, in any case, have formed a trap from which even the jeep would never have escaped.

"Hold on!" John shouted to Emmy. She grabbed the snatch bar as John, in four-wheel drive and low gear, headed the jeep across what had once been a lawn. In happier times, the Anchorage gardens were protected against invasion from sheep, goats, and cows not only by the cattle grid at the gate, but by a thick hedge of oleander bushes. These plants are poisonous to livestock—a fact which the animals seem to know by instinct, for no beast will venture through an oleander thicket. Outside the bushes, a decorative but flimsy white paling fence marked the boundary of the inn's domain.

The oleanders had been beaten down by the wind and rain, but the fence still stood. The jeep went through it with a splitting and cracking of wood, and so—with a broken section of white-painted plank resting on its hood—found itself on the battered track that had once been the dirt road from the Anchorage to the beach.

Never the best of roads, this now resembled the bed of a fast-flowing river. Great rocks and boulders were strewn haphazardly over it, and deep ruts had appeared where the wind and water had carved their way through the gravel. The jeep butted and leaped, lurched and jolted, as John peered intently through the drenched windshield, trying to pick the safest path. Every so often, an extra-strong gust of wind took the vehicle sideways on, making it rock dangerously and cant still further over.

From the back, Morley Duprez screamed, "Here!"

John pulled up as a short, burly figure in black oilskins came fighting its way out from the doorway of a small wooden house, which seemed to have lost half its tin roof. Morley leaned down from the back of the jeep and with strong hands helped the other man over the tailgate. Then he yelled, "O.K., John. Take her away," and the jeep resumed its slow and agonizing progress.

The first serious obstacle was a fallen tree—a biggish white cedar with a trunk about a foot in diameter and a bushy straggle of smaller branches. It had fallen across the track between two rocks, giving no hope of circumnavigating it by taking to the undergrowth. The three men climbed out of the jeep to inspect the obstruction.

Unfortunately, most of the roots were still in the ground, and there was no way of manhandling the tree out of the way. John struggled back to the jeep and found his handsaw in the bag of tools. It took them, taking turns, half an hour to saw through the trunk. Then, with Emmy lending what help she could, the main body of the tree was dragged out of the way. By then, the jeep wheels had sunk deep into the mud. John engaged the lowest gear in four-wheel drive, while the others stayed outside, slipping and losing their foothold in the mire as they pushed. With a roar and a convulsive leap, the jeep finally freed itself and gained the comparative stability of a stony patch of track. The passengers scrambled aboard and the journey went on.

After what seemed an eternity, the indomitable little vehicle breasted a steep rise, and at the same moment the rain stopped, allowing a slight improvement in visibility. John braked the jeep to a halt, and all four passengers got out, walked the few yards of flat ground at the top of the hill, and looked down toward the sea.

Far below them, huge breakers crashed in great lazily flying clouds of white spray against a small crescent of pale sand, protected on either side by gray rocks that strode out into the angry waters. Beyond, the sea faded into invisibility, until only a vague impression of white seething on steel gray could be seen. And in the center of the crescent, lying on her side, was the hull of a boat that had once been white.

As each roller came crashing in from the sea, it lifted the hull momentarily, only to drop it again with sickening force onto the beach. The mast was no more than a broken matchstick trailing over the side. A few broken spars, lighter than the hull, had already been washed up to the high-water mark. Even from where they stood, the watchers could see that the hull was beginning to split and the decks to spring and buckle. Without immediate help, the yacht would very soon break up into mere splinters of driftwood.

Emmy grabbed John's arm. "It looks like *Windflower*," she screamed.

"Are you sure?"

"Almost."

John nodded briefly. Then he pointed downhill and said something to Morley which Emmy could not catch. She looked down after his pointing finger, and her heart turned over. The road this far had been bad enough, but the way down seemed totally impassable.

It had always been a steep and curving track that led down to Bluefish Bay. Even the moderate rains of a normal October had often put it out of action as far as cars were concerned, and jeeps could only manage it with difficulty. Now, it seemed to Emmy, it was about as navigable as Niagara Falls. Streams of rainwater ran down it, bowling stones and rocks along in their path. Larger boulders straddled the track, and deep rifts and ruts made traps for wheels. John, who had his binoculars slung around his neck, was inspecting the path through them, his face grim. He turned and said something to Morley, who nodded. Emmy pulled at John's arm.

"Can I have the glasses?"

John nodded, slipped the leather strap from around his neck, and handed the binoculars to Emmy. Then he continued his discussion with Morley and Melville. Emmy trained the glasses onto the battered hull which might be *Windflower*. So absorbed was she that John had to shake her arm twice before she lowered the glasses and turned to him.

Putting his mouth close to Emmy's ear, John shouted, "Road's too bad. Not worth the risk for an empty hull. We're going back."

"No!" Emmy yelled.

"What?"

"Look! There's someone on that boat!"

"Where?"

"Look through the glasses. In the cockpit, half out of the cabin door. Look when the seas slue her round!"

John took the glasses and looked intently. Sure enough, for a moment, as the waves lifted the hull and swung it slightly sideways, he caught a glimpse of something black. Could be a tarpaulin, a sailbag, a collapsed inflatable dinghy. A heavy, inert mass wedged half in and half out of the open cabin door. It could also be a body in black oilskins.

John lowered the glasses and turned to Morley Duprez.

"Get in," he said. "We're going down."

As Emmy climbed back into the jeep, she noticed a piece of white paper on the floor—presumably it had been dislodged from under her seat by the violent movement of the vehicle. She picked it up and saw that it was a page from the monthly magazine issued by the Tourist Office of the British Seaward Islands in order to promote business. She read, "The climate of the British Seawards is ideal. Year-round, warm temperatures and sunny skies bless our fortunate islands, while the gentle rainfall is just enough to—"

"Hang on to your hats!" John shouted. "Here we go!" As he let in the clutch, the heavens opened, and the downpour began again—this time for real.

12

HENRY TIBBETT AWOKE TO a cacophony of sound. It was every bit as loud as, but different in quality from, the screaming inferno that had been his last conscious memory. It had been a hell of violent movement, of being tossed and buffeted at the mercy of some gigantic, screeching, uncoordinated force. Now, there was movement—less violent, more jolting—and the noise, although intense, had a sort of orderliness about it. A rhythm. A throb. He opened his eyes and saw nothing but blackness.

He was apparently lying on his back in some sort of small room or cabin, which shook and pulsated and threw him this way and that. He became conscious of sodden clothes around his body, but also of some warm, dry wrapping that enclosed him completely. A blanket. That was what it was. A blanket entirely wrapped around him, covering his head so that he could not see. Feebly, he raised a hand and tried to brush it away.

At once, the dark covering was pulled back. The cabin—or whatever it was—lurched sideways, rolling him over onto his face. He became aware of gentle hands righting him, easing him onto his back once more. He opened his eyes and found himself looking straight into Emmy's face, not a foot from his.

"Emmy . . ."

"Henry . . . don't try to talk . . . just lie still . . . we'll soon be there . . ."

Henry shut his eyes again and tried to think. Emmy. Something about Emmy. Emmy brought back strong feelings of antagonism. Emmy was against him. Emmy was his enemy. No, that was stupid.

Emmy was his wife. Emmy . . . suddenly a great feeling of relief surged through him. Emmy . . . everything would be all right. He couldn't remember what had been wrong, but something had been very wrong indeed and was now going to be all right again. . . . The moment of consciousness passed. In the small cabin of the Golf Club helicopter, Emmy wept tears of relief.

The pilot, battling gamely against the still-gale-force winds, turned and grinned at Emmy, pointing downward. Emmy looked out of the window, through the streaming rain, and was able to make out the lawns of the Golf Club rushing up to meet them as the helicopter touched down. With a bump and a skid in the mud, the little red insect came to rest and was at once surrounded by eager hands and voices. Henry was borne away. Emmy smiled at the pilot.

"I don't know how to thank you."

"All part of the service, ma'am. You'd best go with your husband. I'll be off to get Mr. Colville and the others from the beach."

The wind had moderated considerably, but the rain pelted down more heavily than ever. In Margaret's yellow oilskins, Emmy squelched her way across sodden bogs which had once been lawns to the Secretary's office, where a harassed girl clerk informed her that the Golf Club was no better off than anywhere else on the island when it came to communications. All telephone lines were down. There were no boats running. The helicopter was available only for emergency rescue services, like the one in progress from Bluefish Bay. Not before tomorrow at the soonest could a flight to St. Mark's be contemplated. Emmy, without regret, decided that she had done her best to communicate with Sir Alfred Pendleton and Inspector Ingham. For the time being, St. Matthew's was incommunicado. She made her way back to cottage No. 23, where she knew that Dr. Daniels was examining Henry.

The Golf Club cottages were built in the form of two-room suites—living room, bedroom, and shower. The living-room section of No. 23 was empty when Emmy entered it, and the door to the bedroom was closed. Behind it, Emmy could hear the muted voices of Dr. Daniels and his nurse and the splashing of water as taps were turned on in the bathroom. After a few minutes the doctor came out, drying his hands on a linen towel embroidered with the Golf Club's logo.

He said, "You are Mrs. Tibbett?"

"Yes. How is he?"

The doctor, kind-faced and white-haired, smiled encouragingly. "He'll be all right. He has a severe concussion and there are cuts and bruises, but nothing broken. For the moment, I've given him a sedative."

"But I have to speak to him!"

The doctor shook his head. "I'm afraid not, my dear. Out of the question. What he needs now is complete rest. He should be in hospital, and I'm arranging for him to be taken to St. Mark's as soon as any form of transport can make the journey. Meanwhile, he must stay here and sleep. You can sit with him if you wish, but even if he regains consciousness, I absolutely forbid you to try to talk to him. Nurse Quarles will come back with more sedation every four hours. I can't leave her here, much as I would like to, because we have a lot of other calls. Praise God, this island has been lucky—but there are a lot of minor casualties, and we're needed at the office." He shot Emmy a piercing look from bright blue eyes. "You look exhausted," he said.

"I am, rather," said Emmy. "It was quite a drive down to the beach, and after we got Henry out of the boat, it seemed like a hundred years before the helicopter arrived. There was no hope of getting the jeep up again, you see."

Dr. Daniels seemed to make a decision. He said, "Wait here with your husband, Mrs. Tibbett, until I can find somebody competent to come and sit with him. Then go and get some rest yourself. Doctor's orders. There's nothing useful you can do here. Right?"

"All right. Thank you, Doctor."

When the doctor and the nurse had gone, Emmy opened the door of the bedroom and walked in. Henry was lying on his back on the bed, looking like a small boy asleep. The Golf Club had produced from somewhere a pair of bright green silk pajamas several sizes too large, into which Henry's supine body had been rather clumsily bundled. He was breathing evenly and appeared very peaceful. His face, hands, and legs were liberally decorated with gauze and adhesive tape, and his sandy hair fell disarmingly across his forehead. Emmy took off her oilskins and rubber boots and washed her face and hands in the shower. Then she pulled a rattan chair up to the bedside and sat down to keep watch.

It was after one o'clock in the afternoon when Henry opened his eyes. For a moment, he seemed unable to focus. Then he looked straight at Emmy and said, "What are you doing here?"

"Making sure that you keep quiet," replied Emmy cheerfully.

Henry had started to struggle into an upright position. Suddenly, his eyes grew wild and frightened. He clutched Emmy's hand. "Emmy . . . it is you, isn't it?"

"Of course it's me."

"Must tell . . . must tell Ingham . . . Governor . . . eighty-two . . . where's Ingham? Where am I? What are you doing here? Get out . . . danger . . . eighty-two . . ."

"Everything's all right, Henry," said Emmy, soothingly. "It's all over. You're safe now."

"Don't understand . . . must tell . . . Governor . . . eighty-two . . . *Who's that?*" The last words were a scream of terror. Emmy looked up, surprised, to see that the door behind her had opened, and Nurse Quarles was coming in, followed by a young black woman whom Emmy did not know.

"Here we are then, Mrs. Tibbett," the nurse said, with professional calm and good cheer. "Come to relieve you and give Mr. Tibbett his medicine."

On the bed, Henry was writhing and moaning. "No . . . take her away . . . don't let her in . . . must tell Governor . . ."

Nurse Quarles was preparing a hypodermic syringe. Ignoring Henry, she said in a low voice to Emmy, "Has this been going on for long?"

"No . . . he's only just woken. He seems very distressed."

"Perfectly natural." The nurse was unemotional and businesslike. She turned to the bed. "Now, then, Mr. Tibbett. Just a small injection . . ."

Against Henry's screamed protests, which pierced Emmy's heart like a knife, Nurse Quarles took his arm, rolled back the pajama sleeve, made a quick swab with alcohol, and injected the syringe. Within seconds, there was silence again. Henry slept.

"There." The nurse straightened and regarded her patient with satisfaction. "He'll get quite a few more hours of peaceful sleep with that. Mrs. Tibbett, this is Ilma Rogers." She gestured to the young black woman, who smiled shyly. "Ilma will sit with Mr. Tibbett until five o'clock to give you a break. The doctor says you should have a good meal and a rest. I have my jeep here—I'll drive you back to the Anchorage, if that's what you would like." Seeing Emmy about to protest, she added, "He won't be conscious again for several hours. Ilma will call the Secretary if anything unusual happens."

"How will I get back here at five?" It was a foolish question, but the only one that occurred to Emmy.

"No problem, dear." Nurse Quarles spoke briskly, as if to a nervous child. "The Golf Club jeeps—some of them—are back in operation, and the Secretary has lent one to Mr. Colville, so the Anchorage has transport. Come along now."

Too tired to protest, Emmy allowed herself to be ushered outside and into the waiting jeep.

The route from the Golf Club to the Anchorage Inn lay through the center of Priest Town, and Emmy was appalled to see the desolation. Plate-glass windows had been shattered, leaving gaping black holes, although the actual glass had been swept from the roadway; battered cars and twisted bicycles had been dragged off the main thoroughfares into unsightly roadside heaps; many of the flimsier buildings were roofless; and everywhere twisted girders, broken tiles, and splintered wood littered the little town. Driving along the quayside, Emmy could see that many of the moored boats had suffered damage, which was now in the process of being repaired as well as possible by the owners.

It was by chance that, driving along the quay, Emmy happened to glance up toward Main Street. It was up this alley, she remembered, that Dr. Vanduren had hurried—was it only yesterday morning? It seemed an age away, in that unreal epoch Before the Hurricane. And . . . there he was. Coming out of the front door of one of the small houses flanking the narrow street.

"Stop!" Emmy shouted.

Well trained, Nurse Quarles stopped the jeep before asking why.

"Thanks so much . . . just drop me here. . . ." Emmy was out of the jeep and up the side street before the nurse could open her mouth. When she did, it was to say, *"Well!"*, and then, philosophically, "Ah, well, she's had a hard time, poor dear."

And the nurse, who had a West Indian's placid acceptance of life as it comes, let in the clutch and drove home to her lunch. She had fulfilled the doctor's orders to the letter. Meanwhile, what Mrs. Tibbett did was her own affair.

The doctor had turned onto Main Street and appeared to be heading for a small café—the only one bold enough to reopen so soon after the hurricane. Stone-built, in the center of a row of houses, and with wooden shutters instead of glass windows, it had suffered little or no damage. Presumably the proprietor thought it worthwhile to open up, even in such a ghost town. The door was ajar, and a blackboard beside it announced, "Stewed chicken and rice, fungi, maubee. Business as usual." A small boy in ragged trousers was sweeping the step with a broom larger than himself.

Emmy caught up with the hurrying figure, then slowed her pace until she was walking alongside him. She said quietly, "Dr. Vanduren, I presume?"

The doctor did a violent double take, a mixture of surprise and momentary fear. Then he looked at Emmy and said, "Who are you? I know you."

"I'm Mrs. Tibbett," Emmy said. "My husband and I visited you in Florida a few days ago."

"You were on your way back to England." Dr. Vanduren sounded accusing. Emmy noticed, with a little surprise, that both of them were talking in urgent undertones, even though Priest Town was virtually deserted.

"No, we weren't," Emmy said. "And what are you doing down here in the British Seawards?"

"It's no business of—"

"Oh, yes, it is," said Emmy grimly. "You're looking for your daughter, aren't you?"

"My daughter is dead."

"Don't waste time, Dr. Vanduren. You're looking for your daughter. I was looking for my husband, and now I've found him. I think that they have probably been together."

"Together?"

"Have you any money?"

The doctor was by now looking at Emmy with distinct apprehension.

"Money? I don't quite—"

Suddenly, Emmy grinned. "I've had quite an adventure in the hurricane," she said, "with the result that I find myself here with no cash on me. However, if you can pay, we might go into that café and have some food and do some talking."

Dr. Lionel Vanduren gave a sigh of relief. He could hardly be said to grin, but he managed a smile. He said, "I've a few dollars in my pocket. I think it would cover a modest meal."

"Good," said Emmy. And that was all she said. Soon they were both sitting at a table in a corner of the small café, having a jugful of maubee—the delicious local drink brewed from tree bark, yeast, and spices—waiting for their order of chicken, rice, and fungi.

The food arrived. The small boy put it on the table and withdrew. Emmy and Dr. Vanduren looked at each other across the table, and Emmy said, "Well?"

"Well, what? I really think, Mrs. Tibbett, that it's up to you to explain." Lionel Vanduren took a drink of maubee. "I confess to being entirely mystified."

Emmy said, "You know—or at least you suspect—that Janet is alive. Otherwise you wouldn't have come down here looking for her."

The doctor speared a chicken leg and gesticulated feebly with it. "One grasps at straws . . ."

"Oh, no, one doesn't." Suddenly Emmy was very firm. "You knew very well that Janet was alive when we came to see you. You told us all sorts of lies—and then you heard about Cheryl and Martin Ross. That made a difference, didn't it?"

Emmy was guessing wildly, but for the first time she knew what Henry meant—what Henry used to mean—when he talked about his "nose." The instinct that, without pulling together all the loose ends, told you that you had to be right, that this was the only way things could have happened. Afterward, Emmy wondered what would have happened if Dr. Vanduren had simply said, "My dear lady, I am here on a vacation and got caught by the weather. I have no idea what you are talking about," and had got up and left. But she knew he wouldn't, and he didn't.

Instead, he looked at Emmy with eyes so tragic that they seemed to come from the bottom of a well of tears and said, "I never thought it would come to this. I never thought of murder."

"Murder, Dr. Vanduren?"

Not taking his eyes from hers, the doctor said, "Can I trust you? I have a strange feeling that perhaps I can."

Emmy said, "Trust me with what?"

"The truth. That is, the truth as far as I know it."

Very carefully, Emmy said, "You've mentioned murder. If you mean, can you trust me to cover up for a murderer, then the answer is no. I've been a policeman's wife for too long—"

Vanduren stiffened in terror. "Policeman? Your husband is a policeman?"

"He was. Apparently he has just resigned."

"Resigned? Why?"

"I wish I knew," said Emmy, very sincerely. "Probably for the same reason that your daughter—"

"You know nothing about my daughter!"

"That's true. But I have a feeling that she and my husband are both . . . victims. I want to help him, and you want to help her. Please tell me the truth, Dr. Vanduren."

There was a long silence. At last, Vanduren said, "How much do you know about phenylcyclohexylpiperidine?"

It was Emmy's turn to do a double take. "About *what*?"

"Phenylcyclohexylpiperidine. Usually shortened to phencyclidine, or PCP. Known on the streets as the peace pill or angel dust." Dr. Vanduren laughed raspingly. "Angel dust! Where do they find these euphemisms? I can see that you are an innocent abroad, Mrs. Tibbett. PCP is a drug derived from a veterinary anesthetic. It can cause hallucinations and, if not properly treated, coma, respiratory arrest, and death."

"And you mean that people take this for pleasure?" Emmy asked incredulously.

"Some people find hallucinations pleasant," said the doctor dryly. "And in small doses certain individuals report feelings of well-being and agreeable sensations. However, PCP is most often used by pushers as a cheap substitute for other hallucinogens such as LSD and STP. It is also used as a weapon."

"A weapon?"

"In large quantities," said the doctor, "this drug is a killer. In smaller doses, it is a personality changer."

"Go on," said Emmy quietly.

"Not everybody," said Vanduren, "welcomes having his personality changed. But it can be very useful for an enemy to use such a drug on an unsuspecting adversary. Tetrahydrocannabinol—THC, the main active ingredient of marijuana—will not affect the personality. That is to say, moral values remain intact, even under the influence of the drug. The same is not true of PCP. It is available—to those who know where to buy it or how to make it—in the form of a tasteless white powder or liquid, which can either be mixed with marijuana or introduced into almost any food or drink. Under its influence, people will behave in a completely uncharacteristic manner. To give you an example, it has been said that the Manson family used it to obtain the lease of a property from the owner, who imagined he was getting a simple dose of LSD." The doctor paused. "Did I say 'simple'?"

He passed a hand over his brow, and Emmy thought he was going to burst into tears. She dared not speak for fear of interrupting the flow.

After a moment, Vanduren said, "Why am I telling you all this?"

Emmy said, "You've told me nothing yet, except the properties of certain drugs. How does Janet come into it?"

An endless pause, Then Vanduren said, "Janet is a beautiful girl, Mrs. Tibbett. A beautiful, kind, lovely girl. It's not her fault—what she has become."

"A murderess?" said Emmy.

Vanduren recoiled physically. "Don't say that! You don't know. I don't know. All I do know is that I have been living in hell for six months, and now . . ."

"Now?"

Vanduren sighed and shrugged his big shoulders. "I shall kill myself, of course," he said quietly. "But I must find Janet first."

As a tentative nudge, Emmy said, "The *Isabella* was your boat, wasn't she?"

"Yes, she certainly was. A thoroughbred, a sturdy sea boat yet sweet to handle. A little bit of me died with the *Isabella,* Mrs. Tibbett."

Without saying anything, Emmy refilled the doctor's glass from the jug of maubee. She felt she was getting somewhere at last. Vanduren drank and then said, "I can see them now, setting off from the East Harbour. Jan was at the helm—she's always been a fine helmswoman, even when she was a teen-ager. I waved to them and they waved back—Jan so fair and Ed so dark, what a couple they made! The all-American dream." Nostalgia was giving way to cynicism again. "Well, so much for dreams. You know what happened next. Lost at sea. Missing, presumed drowned. Wreckage picked up in Exuma Sound. Oh, that was part of the *Isabella*'s dinghy, I don't doubt it. That was that."

Softly, Emmy said, "But that wasn't that, was it, Dr. Vanduren? What happened next?"

Again the shifty, pleading look. Then Vanduren said, making a decision, "What does it matter? Someone will have to know someday. We—Celia and I—we'd gotten over the worst. We'd accepted what had happened. And then these men turned up."

"What men?"

"How should I know? D'you think they told me their names? Organized crime, no doubt about that. Mafia. First, they made me send Celia away to England."

Surprised, Emmy said, "Made you? How could they make you?"

The doctor looked down into his glass, which he was holding in both hands, swirling the light brown liquid. He said, "Most people have a skeleton in the cupboard somewhere, Mrs. Tibbett. Something that they would prefer not to be known. In the case of a doctor, it can mean total ruin—one's livelihood lost forever. It wasn't a big thing—a youthful indiscretion. Illegal overprescription of drugs. I had even forgotten about it myself. But these men had documentary proof. They could have crucified me . . . me, with my middle-class practice and my beautiful family . . . pillar of society, valued member of the community . . . Jesus! Besides, they told me that Janet was still alive."

Emmy nodded sympathetically. "I understand," she said. "So you persuaded your wife to go to England. Then—?"

Vanduren swallowed painfully. "They told me that Ed was dead, but that they had Jan, alive. That she had, in fact, joined them. They brought a letter from Jan that was—well, it was obscene. But in her writing and composed by her, no doubt about that. She referred to family matters that nobody else could possibly have known." Vanduren paused. "I am a doctor. I also, alas, know all too much about drug abuse. My patients are wealthy, professional people, and their children . . ."

Emmy said, "Janet had been on drugs before, had she?"

"Nothing serious. Only pot, like all the rest of them—an occasional joint at a party. It distressed Celia very much, but my feeling was that it was less harmful than alcohol. I'm on several committees advocating the legalization of marijuana."

"Like Betsy Sprague," Emmy said.

"That old imbecile? No, I'm not that nutty, thank you. Legalizing is one thing, but giving it away on street corners . . ."

"I'm sorry," Emmy said. "I interrupted. Do go on about Janet and the letter from her that these men brought you."

"Yes. Well, as soon as I read the letter, I suspected that they had my daughter on some kind of mind-bending drug. PCP was the obvious one. They wouldn't admit or deny it. They simply said that if I didn't do as they said, they would expose my youthful peccadillo, and they would 'deal with' Janet."

"Kill her?" Emmy asked.

The doctor shook his head. "Nothing so simple," he said. "With Janet dead, I'd have nothing to lose. I could go after them. I knew all along that 'dealing with' Janet meant something worse than murdering her. To gain time, I said I'd go along with them and do as they asked."

"Which was?"

"Can't you guess? I was to be a distribution point for drugs in Florida. As a doctor, I was of great value to them. I could actually get the stuff legally—some of it. Drugs found in my office could be legal. And I could distribute the rest from the same foolproof location. No street corners for these boys. You can see why I've been living in hell."

Emmy said, "When did you decide not to go on with it?"

The doctor shook his head slowly. "I didn't really decide," he said. "I just realized that I was getting in deeper and deeper and not helping Jan at all. Celia wanted to come home, and I didn't know how the hell I was going to handle that. Then you and your husband came to see me and told me about Cheryl and Martin Ross, and that Jan had been recognized. That did it."

"How do you mean?"

"Up till then," said Dr. Vanduren, "I thought they'd just gotten Jan into drugs and drug-pushing. But after I spoke to you people, I realized that it was far worse than that. They'd carried out their threat to deal with her. They'd turned my daughter into a murderer. I knew then the only thing for me to do was to come down here and find Jan and get her away from them somehow, and into treatment. And when I've done that, I'm going to blow the whole racket sky-high. I'll go with it, of course, but it'll be worth it." The doctor looked at Emmy and almost smiled. He said, "Well, I've come clean with you, Mrs. Tibbett. Now, how about your angle? Just where do you come in? And what's a British policeman doing investigating U.S. citizens in the Caribbean?"

"It didn't start as an investigation," Emmy said. "We were just here on holiday." As she spoke, it seemed a whole time-dimension ago that she and Henry had arrived so happily at the Anchorage.

"So—what happened?"

Emmy explained. She told the doctor about Betsy Sprague, about her supposed sighting of Janet, and her subsequent disappearance. About Henry's suspicions and his appointment from London to take over the case. She mentioned the theories of the local police on the role that the Seaward Islands were probably playing in drug-running. For some reason that she herself could not define, she did not mention *Starfish* or *Ocean Rover* or the Montgomerys, Blackstones, or Carstairs. She did, however, tell Dr. Vanduren about *Windflower,* about the theory that the Rosses had been chosen as victims because of their British passports, and how she and Henry had been putting out feelers in the hopes of being selected by the smugglers.

Vanduren said, "Well, what happened? Were you approached?"

Tentatively, Emmy said, "It's hard to say. We met a few

people—apparently innocent people. And then, quite suddenly, my husband went off his head."

"Off his head?"

"Yes."

"What were the symptoms?" Vanduren was intensely interested.

"Euphoria. Frenetic energy. No desire to sleep or rest. Crazy plans and schemes—absolutely unlike his usual character."

The doctor was nodding vigorously. "Typical," he said. "PCP, being administered in small, regular doses. Your husband doesn't smoke marijuana habitually?"

"Of course not!"

"Then it would have been administered in food or drinks. What did you do?"

"I tried to reason with him," Emmy said.

Vanduren frowned. "Worst thing you could have done."

"Well, how was I to know—?"

"Oh, I'm not blaming you, but still you couldn't have done worse. I suppose he turned against you."

"Yes."

"And you say he resigned his job."

"He sent an extraordinary telegram to Scotland Yard." Emmy grinned ruefully. "They're inclined to think he's creating an elaborate cover for some great investigative coup, and they're trying to break the code of the telegram."

"That's the trouble," said Vanduren. "When something like this happens, people simply can't grasp the fact that a personality can be changed. They flail around trying to find a logical explanation—and when all else fails, they fall back on lunacy. But they'll learn. Personalities can be changed chemically."

In a small voice, Emmy said, "Is the change . . . permanent?"

"Not permanent, no. Unless the drug is used persistently—in which case it will probably cause death in quite a short period, as I told you. Once a person stops taking the drug, his personality will return to normal. There's a snag, though."

"What's that?"

"PCP is a drug that remains in the body. Anytime up to several months after the last dose, the patient may revert to atypical behavior for a while. The important thing for him and his family is to know that, so they can deal with it if it happens."

"My God," said Emmy. "To think that there are people who'd deliberately do that to somebody—"

"That and worse, my dear. Far worse. Well, I must say it sounds as though Janet and your husband have been given the same treatment. In her case, to turn her into a tool through which they could use me. But in your husband's case—?"

Enlightenment dawned on Emmy. "Of course," she said. "They found out who he was. Who we were. We must have been pretty close behind them because they didn't just kill Henry. That would have caused quite a stir, since he's a senior police officer. Much better from their point of view was to destroy him—destroy his personality and his credibility. After the way he's been behaving, nobody is going to believe a word he says. Very clever," she added bitterly.

"Oh, yes," said Dr. Vanduren sadly. "Don't underestimate them. They are very clever, and they have a lot of money." After a pause, he added, "You say that you have found your husband."

"Yes, I have."

"Where is he now?"

"He's at the Golf Club, under sedation and waiting to be flown to the hospital on St. Mark's. He was alone on *Windflower* when she was caught in the hurricane, and it's a miracle she was washed up on a beach before she broke up or went on the rocks."

"Is he rational?"

"He was only conscious for a few minutes while I was there," Emmy said. "He didn't sound exactly normal, but who would? He seems to be trying desperately to tell something to the Governor."

Vanduren said, "Either he's still under the influence of the drug, in which case he's probably talking nonsense. Or he's not, in which case nobody will believe him." He suddenly became brisk. "Well, Mrs. Tibbett, what are you going to do now?"

"I . . . I don't know," said Emmy. "There's a warrant out for Henry's arrest. Scotland Yard doesn't trust me any longer, nor do the Governor and the local police. I feel—"

Quite sharply, Vanduren said, "You'd better stop feeling sorry for yourself, Mrs. Tibbett. And so had I. You know, I feel remarkably better for having met you."

"Thank you," said Emmy. "Well, what do you suggest?"

"For myself," the doctor said, "I shall find myself a room on St. Mark's, as soon as I can get over there. That big hotel would be best—most anonymous. The Harbour Prospect, isn't it?"

Emmy said. "You seem good at anonymity, Doctor. Immigration swears you're not in the Seawards."

Vanduren smiled grimly. "My masters had the foresight to provide me with a new set of U.S. documents, in case I had to disappear. I had the elementary good sense to use them when I came down here. As far as the Seawards are concerned, I am Leonard Venables, import-export agent of Seattle, Washington." Then, suddenly, "What do you mean—Immigration denies I am here? What on earth gave them the idea that I might be?"

Embarrassed, Emmy said, "I'm afraid that was my fault. I told the Inspector I thought I had seen you, and I asked him to trace you."

"Damned idiot," said Vanduren harshly. Then, "Well, at least you've been honest enough to tell me. So the Inspector has checked and reported that I am not here. Is that it?"

"Yes."

"Right. You will tell him, when you get the chance, that you saw the suspected Vanduren again today. You spoke to him and at once realized that you had been mistaken, and that he is simply a total stranger bearing a superficial resemblance to Dr. Vanduren. Understood?"

"Yes. But—"

"If you give any hint to the authorities that you know I am here, I will make sure that your husband disappears—permanently, this time. Don't think that being in hospital will protect him, Mrs. Tibbett. My masters have long arms, and I have only to hint that he is a potential threat—"

Emmy said steadily, "I won't give you away, Dr. Vanduren. By the way, what do your masters, as you call them, think about your sudden absence from Florida?"

"That's no problem. No new consignment is expected for a couple of weeks. I have left word, by my usual system of communication, that I have gone briefly to England to look after my sick wife. They have instructed me to behave normally, and that would be normal behavior. They know that Celia is being troublesome, and they undoubtedly think that I have gone to keep her quiet, by one means or another. They know very well I will be back. They know the stranglehold they have on me."

"Incidentally," Emmy said, "the British police have traced your wife. They report her as being perfectly well and calm, and she has given them a photograph of Janet, which is being sent here. So they know that you lied to us in Miami."

"Ha!" said Vanduren. "Intelligent thing to do, going after Celia. Your husband's idea, no doubt."

"Betsy Sprague's, in fact," Emmy said.

"The first crack in the case." Vanduren sounded thoughtful. "Somebody knew that your husband was a policeman, and that Celia had been traced. I daresay that was what decided them to take action against Mr. Tibbett. Who knew?"

"Nobody," said Emmy.

"Don't be silly, Mrs. Tibbett. Somebody knew."

"I mean—nobody who could possibly come under suspicion. Myself, Inspector Ingham, my friends the Colvilles, the Governor . . ."

Vanduren gave a sardonic grin. "Every man has his price if it's large enough."

"So you say," remarked Emmy coldly. Then, "So you're going to stay at Harbour Prospect. When I can get to St. Mark's, the first thing I have to do is report to the Governor."

"Why?"

Thinking quickly, Emmy said, "He doesn't even know yet that Henry has been found. Naturally, he'll want to know all about it, and what Henry has been saying to me."

Vanduren nodded. "Good. You should also tell the Governor what you think has been the matter with your husband. Tell him that a doctor has explained the symptoms to you."

"What doctor? Doctor Vanduren?"

"Mrs. Tibbett, I have already warned you—"

"All right, all right. I was only joking. But seriously, surely there couldn't be any harm in the Governor knowing you are here?"

"Certainly there could. Who knows whom we can trust?"

"Sir Alfred Pendleton is a career diplomat—"

"Civil servants are badly paid and corruptible."

"And I've known Inspector Ingham ever since—"

"That is immaterial. I am Leonard Venables of Seattle, and you can invent a fictitious doctor for your purposes. It is bad enough," Vanduren added, with a dark sort of humor, "that you and I have to trust each other."

Emmy sighed. "Very well," she said. "And meantime . . ."

"Meantime . . . you are staying at the Golf Club?"

"Heavens, no. The Anchorage Inn."

"Well, spend as much time as you can with Mr. Tibbett. Make a careful note of his symptoms. Did you notice if the pupils of his eyes were dilated?"

"No, they weren't," said Emmy promptly. "He had a funny sort

138

of blank stare, but his pupils were O.K. Does that mean that he wasn't drugged?"

"Not at all. One of the many peculiarities of PCP is that the pupils remain normal or even smaller than usual. The blank stare is also typical. How was his voice?"

"Slurred," said Emmy. "He sounded a bit drunk."

Vanduren nodded. He said, "Get the doctor to check his respiratory rate and depth, pain and temperature sensitivity, and let me know the results."

"Where will you be?" Emmy asked. "Before you get to St. Mark's, that is."

"Never mind where I am. I'll keep in touch with you."

Dr. Vanduren did not say good-bye. He pushed back his chair, stood up, walked over to the counter, and paid the bill. Then he strode out the open door and into the empty street.

13

FOR A FEW SECONDS AFTER the doctor had gone, Emmy sat quite still, marveling at the unnatural silence after the clamor of the hurricane. A dog barked somewhere, and there was the sound of spasmodic hammering; a man's voice called out to a companion; but there was no background electrical hum, no mechanical music, no aircraft buzz, above all no traffic. Almost like Pompeii, the island had been severed in an instant from outside contacts. Consequently, the sound of a jeep engine on Main Street appeared loud and remarkable, and Emmy went to the door to see who it was.

It was Margaret, at the wheel of a gold-painted Golf Club jeep. She saw Emmy, pulled to an abrupt stop, and jumped out.

"There you are! Where on earth have you been? Nurse Quarles told us she'd dropped you off on the quayside—"

Emmy said, "I . . . I was hungry. I saw the café open and decided to have a meal."

"Why on earth didn't you come back to the Anchorage for lunch?" Margaret was incapable of hiding the fact that she was puzzled, worried, and rather cross.

"Oh . . . I don't know . . . I'm sorry . . . I'll just get my jacket . . ."

Emmy went back to the table and picked up her oilskin jacket, which she had slung over the back of her chair. Margaret, following her, suddenly blurted out, "So you didn't lunch alone?"

There was no denying the two dirty plates, the two used glasses. Emmy, aware of being a hopeless liar, said, "No . . . actually, I . . . I met a friend, strangely enough."

"A friend?"

"Oh, just a man we ran into in Washington. An American called Venables. He's down here on holiday."

"In Washington?" Margaret echoed. "While you were staying with us? I don't remember anybody in Washington called Venables."

"No," said Emmy hastily. "You didn't know him. We met him at the Kennedy Center one evening. Quite a coincidence that he should be on the island."

Margaret looked at Emmy curiously, but all she said was yes. And then, "Well, now I've found you I'll drive you back to the Anchorage."

The entrance to the Anchorage was still unusable. John, with a couple of helpers, was busy turning his crash-exit through the fence into a beaten track for vehicles and putting up a rough-and-ready barbed-wire gate to keep out marauding livestock.

As Margaret and Emmy drove through, he barely looked up from his work. "Ah, you found her. Well done. How's Henry?"

Emmy opened her mouth to reply in some detail, but quickly realized that John was too busy to listen. So long as Henry was alive and under medical care, there were too many other things to worry about. She said, "He's going to be fine."

"Good. No, don't park the jeep, Margaret. I'm going to need more barbed wire. Can you get down Mango Bay Road?"

"I think so."

"Then go and see if Harry has any. He's the only person on the island who might be able to help. Tell him I'll buy any he's got, up to a whole roll. And on the way back . . ."

The Colvilles were deep in discussion. Margaret got into the jeep and drove off again, and John went back to work. Feeling deflated and desolate, Emmy went up to her bedroom. The winds were now no more than Force 5 or 6—less than 30 miles an hour—and the rain had thinned to driving drizzle. Emmy lay down on her bed and closed her eyes. The hair-raising drive down the ravine to the beach, the shock of finding Henry's limp body in *Windflower*'s cockpit, the enormous relief of realizing that he was still alive, the hopeless attempts to get the jeep back up the hill, the seemingly endless wait for the helicopter—all this had been at least stimulating, at least shared. Now she felt let down and very much alone.

Grasping at rationality, she tried to sum up the situation. She had a husband, alive but suffering from a concussion, and still—or so it seemed—under the influence of a pernicious drug. Also under arrest, as soon as his medical condition improved, unless she could convince the Governor to change his mind. She had Dr. Vanduren, half-crazy with worry and guilt, at one and the same time promising help and threatening retribution. Hardly a reassuring ally. Thanks to him, she had already had to lie to Margaret, and she was unhappily aware that the latter's suspicions had been quite properly aroused. Soon she would be telling more lies to Alfred Pendleton and Herbert Ingham. Unless, of course, she ignored Vanduren's orders and simply told the Governor the truth. But then Henry . . . she had already seen what could be done to destroy Henry. She could not possibly take the risk.

At a quarter to five, Margaret drove Emmy back to the Golf Club. The ride was silent and unhappy. Emmy longed to tell her friend the truth, but two reasons kept her dumb. Not only Henry's safety, but also the fact that she did not want to burden the Colvilles with the responsibility of knowing too many facts. If she told anybody, she decided, it should be Sir Alfred himself.

To Emmy's surprise, the Secretary of the Golf Club was there in person to meet the jeep as it turned into the gateway by the security guard's hut. He came up with a slightly sheepish smile.

"Mrs. Tibbett? You've come to see your husband, I expect."

"Of course."

"Well, I've some good news for you."

"Good news?" Emmy glanced briefly at Margaret, but got no response. "What do you mean?"

"Just that he's no longer here."

"What?"

"He's in the hospital at St. Mark's, where he can get all the best treatment."

Emmy felt stunned. "But how—?"

"Our helicopter pilot decided he could make the journey, now that the weather has moderated," the Secretary explained. "We couldn't contact you, since all the phones are down, and it was a question of taking off right away to get back before dark."

Emmy was shaking. She climbed out of the jeep. "I think it's monstrous," she said. "You had no right to move him without consulting me. Why didn't you send to the Anchorage for me? I could have gone with him."

The Secretary said unhappily, "I do appreciate your point of view, Mrs. Tibbett, but there wouldn't have been room in the helicopter. The police officer—" He broke off, going very pink. "We don't know how long this break in the weather will last, and the Governor was very insistent over the radio—"

Emmy turned to Margaret. "Don't you wait," she said. "I know you're terribly busy. I'll stay here and talk to the Secretary and find my own way back."

Margaret hesitated. "If you're sure . . ."

"I'm sure."

"Well—all right then. Good luck." With a sudden, warm smile that did Emmy's heart good, Margaret put the jeep into gear, turned, and made off down the rutted road.

Emmy faced the Secretary. He was new since her last visit to St. Matthew's—a large, fair-haired Englishman with a small mustache and a diffident manner. She said, "Perhaps we could go to your office and talk?"

"Oh, yes. Certainly. By all means. Just over here—we can walk."

"I'm afraid I don't know your name," Emmy said, as they made their way across the damp lawn.

"Whitely. Peter Whitely. I've been here just two months. In here, if you please. Now, do sit down. Can I get you a drink?"

"Frankly, I'd love one," Emmy said. "I need it."

"Of course. Very understandable." Peter Whitely opened a cupboard to reveal a well-stocked bar. "Scotch? Rum? Martini?"

"A Scotch and soda would be marvelous," Emmy said.

Whitely poured two drinks and brought them to the desk. "Your good health, Mrs. Tibbett. Now, what is it that I can explain to you?"

"Everything," Emmy said. "I don't know where to begin. First of all, you said something about the Governor. You've been in touch with him?"

"Yes, by VHF radio. Our Harbour Master has a set."

"Of course," Emmy said. "Well, what did he say?"

Whitely twirled his mustache awkwardly. "The fact is, Mrs. Tibbett, the Governor was anxious to get Mr. Tibbett over to St. Mark's as soon as possible."

"I see. And with a police escort. So he wasn't taken just for medical treatment."

"Well . . . er . . . no. Not entirely. The Governor wants to talk to Mr. Tibbett."

"That's mutual," said Emmy. "My husband wants to talk to the Governor."

"Well, that's good," said Peter Whitely, brightening.

"So," Emmy went on, "how can I get to St. Mark's?"

"Well, now, that will depend on the weather. If things still look good tomorrow—"

"What do you mean—if?" Emmy asked. "The hurricane has

passed us, for goodness sake. You don't expect it to turn back, do you?"

"Oh, haven't you heard?"

"Heard what?"

"Why, I thought everybody knew. Haven't you been listening to your radio?"

"Please," said Emmy, "just tell me what you're talking about."

"Tropical Storm Beatrice," said Whitely. "A new disturbance getting organized out in the Atlantic. Following the same path as Alfred. She may hit us any time from tomorrow onwards, depending on her speed and direction. That's why we felt we must take advantage of—"

"But that's ridiculous," Emmy protested. "We couldn't have two hurricanes within—"

"I'm afraid we could, you know. When the weather conditions are just right, they come marching over one after the other, I fear. But I do promise you, Mrs. Tibbett, that if it's humanly possible, we'll get you to St. Mark's by helicopter first thing in the morning. We're planning to take all our members who are still here—if we can get them out of St. Mark's by air before Beatrice arrives, so much the better."

Emmy said, "Can you get a message to the Governor for me?"

"Yes, I think we can manage that. It has to go through the police station on St. Mark's, of course."

"Then tell him," Emmy said, "that I'll be over in the morning if the helicopter flies, that I've important information, and that I must see him. Can you do that?"

"Can do, Mrs. Tibbett. Can do."

"You've been very kind." Emmy felt sorry for poor Mr. Whitely, the innocent messenger with bad news to deliver. He hadn't done badly. "Now, can you get me back to the Anchorage?"

"Well, Mrs. Tibbett—if I might make a suggestion—it might be better if you stayed here overnight. If the helicopter does fly in the morning, it'll be pretty early—"

"What about my things? And letting the Anchorage know?"

"I could send someone down to the Anchorage to pack you a suitcase and bring it back here. No sense in going yourself. As a matter of fact, I've reserved Number forty-five for you—we've no lack of empty cottages, I fear. I'll show you down there and send your suitcase along when it arrives. Then we hope you'll enjoy dinner . . ."

So it had all been arranged, Emmy thought cynically. How the Governor imagined that she might disappear from an island virtually cut off by the hurricane, she had no idea, but Sir Alfred was playing it safe. She remembered the para-military security posts at the Golf Club gates and the stout fence to keep out intruders. On their last visit to St. Matthew's, she and Henry had joked about the fact that the Golf Club, one of the most expensive resorts on earth, was very much like a superluxurious maximum-security prison. Now, it seemed to be fulfilling that function in fact. She thanked Mr. Whitely and allowed herself to be conducted to her million-dollar cell.

The next morning, the weather was ominously calm. Miami weather station reported that Beatrice had been upgraded to hurricane status, and that the Seawards, along with other islands, should maintain a hurricane watch. No immediate danger threatened, however. It would be late that night at the soonest before Beatrice struck land.

The Golf Club was eager to disembarrass itself of its few remaining guests—all of whom were far too affluent and important for the Club to risk them suing for material or bodily damage due to negligence during the storm. The airport on St. Mark's had been hastily cleared of debris and one runway declared open. The helicopter would fly a ferry service to it, so long as the weather held. The exodus was on.

As it turned out, Emmy was not allocated to the first flight, which took members who had to make a connection for Los Angeles in San Juan. The second flight, however, left soon after nine o'clock, bearing Emmy and her suitcase as well as a Senator and his wife en route to Washington, D.C. The ferry service, the pilot explained, was strictly to and from the airport. There was no possibility of taking Emmy into the town of St. Mark's Harbour, and she wondered how she was going to get there.

She need not have worried. As she climbed out of the helicopter, a trim figure in blue uniform stepped forward. Woman Police Constable Pearletta Terry.

"I have a jeep, Mrs. Tibbett. The Governor would like to see you right away."

During the drive back to Government House, conversation was kept to a minimum—and neutral topics at that. Pearletta told Emmy that St. Mark's had been even luckier than St. Matthew's. Very little damage—only a few roads blocked by flooding and fallen rocks and trees and a handful of broken windows. Electric power had already been restored.

Emmy mentioned Hurricane Beatrice, and Pearletta agreed that they would be extremely fortunate to get off so lightly next time. However, the storm was still out at sea, and nobody could predict her exact course. Emmy asked whether boat traffic between the islands had been resumed, and Pearletta replied that as far as she knew, the *Pride* would be making her normal run that day.

"Tomorrow—who knows?" she added. After that, the two women rode in silence into St. Mark's Harbour.

The Governor was waiting for Emmy. One of the drawing-room windows had been blown out and was blocked with a sheet of plywood, making the room dim and gloomy, despite the fact that the electric light was burning. Sir Alfred appeared reasonably dim and gloomy himself. He greeted Emmy briefly and then said, "You must be very relieved that your husband is alive, Mrs. Tibbett."

"Of course I am. But—"

"You have seen and spoken to him, Mrs. Tibbett. You must be aware that his mental state is—"

Emmy interrupted. "Sir Alfred, please listen to me. I think I know what has been wrong with my husband."

"A mental breakdown," said Sir Alfred dryly. "That would be the most convenient, wouldn't it?"

"No," said Emmy. She experienced a spurt of anger, which did her good. "You must listen. I've been talking to a doctor friend of mine who has wide experience with hallucinatory drugs, and he thinks that Henry has been under the influence of something called PCP. I can't remember the chemical name—it's one of those words that goes on forever. Anyhow, this is a very dangerous drug and a personality changer, and the symptoms seem to fit."

The Governor looked at her—a hard stare which she did not find reassuring. He said, "Who is this doctor friend, Mrs. Tibbett? Somebody on the island?"

Emmy had prepared herself for that one. "No," she said. "His name is Duncan. He used to be Chief Medical Officer of Tampica. Henry and I met him in Washington on the Ironmonger case." She hoped that her venerable friend Doc Duncan would forgive her for thus taking his name in vain. She also felt sure that he was not an expert on hallucinatory drugs, but it was the best she could think of on the spur of the moment.

Sir Alfred said slowly, "I've heard of Dr. Duncan. He's well known in this part of the world." Then, "How did you manage to contact him? The phones have been out of service."

Emmy said, "I spoke to him just before the hurricane, sir. I was about to mention it to you on the phone when we were cut off." She found, somewhat to her alarm, that lying became easier with practice.

"Well," said Sir Alfred, "we'll have to check this out. I'll mention it to Dr. Harlow at the hospital. He may be able to do some tests. It would certainly explain—quite a lot. On the other hand, you must admit that it is only a theory. There are other possible explanations for your husband's extraordinary behavior."

"I can't think of any."

"Can't you?"

"No, I can't."

"I am wondering," said Sir Alfred, "whether this whole business may not have been in the nature of a diversion."

"You mean, you still think Henry is in the pay of the Mafia—?"

The Governor looked at Emmy in mild surprise. "The Mafia?" he repeated. "That's the first time I've heard anybody mention the Mafia in connection with this case. Have you any reason for thinking they may be involved?"

Mentally, Emmy cursed Dr. Vanduren. She said, "No special reason, Sir Alfred. Just that when one hears of big sums of money and drugs and murders—well, one assumes that organized crime is in there somewhere."

"Yes," said Sir Alfred slowly. "Murders. That was how Chief Superintendent Tibbett came to be involved at all, wasn't it? Investigating the disappearance and presumed murder of Miss Elizabeth Sprague."

"And the Rosses and maybe the crew of the *Isabella*—"

"Those two boats were lost at sea, Mrs. Tibbett. As I recall, nobody mentioned murder until your husband turned up with this story about Miss Sprague."

Emmy said, "Henry didn't turn up with any story. Betsy Sprague disappeared. John and Margaret Colville—"

"Yes. The Colvilles." Sir Alfred sighed gently and took a piece of paper out of his pocket. "Mrs. Tibbett, I think the time has come to be quite frank with you. I hope that you'll return the compliment and be frank with me for a change."

"I don't understand you."

"I must tell you that telephone service on both islands was reconnected earlier this morning. One of the first calls I received was from your friend Mr. Colville. He had just had a telegram from England, phoned through from the cable and wireless station. Shall I read it to you?"

"Please do," said Emmy.

Sir Alfred consulted the paper in his hand. He read: "VERY WORRIED NEWS HURRICANE ALFRED HOPE YOU SAFE AND WELL PLEASE RING OR CABLE REASSURANCE LOVE BETSY."

"What?" Emmy drew her breath in a sharp gasp.

Sir Alfred continued. "This was handed in at Little Fareham, Hampshire, yesterday afternoon, English time. Your friend Miss Sprague is obviously at home, safe and sound, and has been for some time."

"I . . . I simply don't understand it."

Ignoring her, Sir Alfred went on. "Had it not been for the hurricane, nothing would have been heard from the lady for several weeks, even if she wrote as soon as she arrived home. You know how long the mails take. I mentioned the word *diversion*. Perhaps I should have said *hoax*." There was a pause. "I don't appreciate having my leg pulled, Mrs. Tibbett, even by so distinguished a practical joker as your husband."

"Does Henry know about Betsy?" Emmy demanded.

"Not yet. He is barely coherent. Apparently."

"You think he's shamming? Just pretending to be crazy?"

"That's for the doctors to decide, Mrs. Tibbett. We will check on this mysterious drug of yours. It's possible that he is or has been under its influence. It would give a certain credibility—to his incredibility."

"Are you saying he may have taken it deliberately?"

Sir Alfred sighed again. "My dear Mrs. Tibbett, I don't know. Nor do I know why Miss Sprague did not catch her original flight to Antigua—nor, indeed, by what route she left the island and returned home. We are doing our best to check on things while we still have communication with the outside world. By tomorrow, we are likely to be cut off again, possibly for a longer period." Impatiently, he added, "I have more important things to worry about. Just admit that this has been an elaborate deception."

Emmy said, "I can't admit what I don't know. I must see Henry. Then I'll talk to you again, Sir Alfred."

After a pause, the Governor said, "Very well."

Emmy said, "Is Henry under arrest?"

"My police force is very small," said Sir Alfred icily. "In the present emergency they have more pressing duties than guarding a demented prankster in hospital. Your husband is not to leave the island—not that he could do so, for by the time the doctors allow him to leave the hospital, we will certainly be without communications again." Pendleton cleared his throat. "I'm sorry, Mrs. Tibbett. I'm afraid my patience is wearing thin. Very possibly all this has nothing to do with you. Just wait here, please, and I will arrange transport to the hospital for you."

Alone in the big, dark drawing room, Emmy found her mind racing, trying to adjust to the new realities. Of course, it was wonderful news about Betsy—if Betsy had really sent that telegram. Surely John would have telephoned her by now. Must check with the Anchorage right away. If Betsy was home, how had she arrived there? Would Dr. Vanduren be able to get to St. Mark's before the second storm arrived? Where were the Carstairs and the Blackstones who had been on *Windflower* with Henry? So many questions, so few answers.

Emmy walked to an unbroken window and stood looking out over the churning water of the channel—gray and steely now, no longer a deep, translucent blue. She was lost in thought and did not hear the door opening, so Sir Alfred's voice made her jump.

"Mrs. Tibbett."

"Yes. I'm ready."

"Just one moment. I have spoken to Dr. Duncan in Tampica."

"Oh," said Emmy.

"He confirms," said the Governor, "that he met you and the Chief Superintendent in Washington during the Ironmonger case. However, he says that he has not been in touch with you since. He is not an authority on hallucinatory drugs, and he has never discussed them with you. If you did, in fact, get this information, it was not from him. Well, Mrs. Tibbett?"

Emmy said, "All right. It wasn't Dr. Duncan. That's the only thing I lied to you about, Sir Alfred. I can't tell you who it was—not for the moment."

"I have also spoken again with Mrs. Colville. She tells me that you met and lunched with some strange man in Priest Town yesterday. She says that when she asked you about him, you came up with a palpably false story. She and her husband are both extremely disturbed, Mrs. Tibbett. They regard themselves as your friends, and they trusted you implicitly. This is why they said nothing about your mysterious friend, until I told them about your deception concerning Dr. Duncan."

Feeling desperate, Emmy said, "I *will* explain, Sir Alfred. I really will, as soon as I've seen Henry. I beg you to believe that this isn't a hoax. Something very serious is going on."

The Governor gave her a long look. But all he said was "There is a jeep and driver waiting to take you to the hospital. I shall expect to hear from you."

14

FROM THE OUTSIDE, St. Mark's General Hospital was an attractive Victorian building standing in several acres of coconut-palm groves a mile outside the town of St. Mark's Harbour. It had been painted white so that its turrets and curlicues and other follies made a pleasantly frivolous pattern against the blue of the tropical sky.

Inside, however, two things were immediately obvious. The first was that Florence Nightingale's enlightened ideas on hospital building had had as little effect here as in the gloomy confines of Netley Military Hospital in England. In vain had Miss Nightingale fought to have Netley built as a series of small pavilions, with plenty of fresh air and privacy for the patients. The Establishment had won that battle, constructing huge, infection-prone wards that were mistakenly thought to be easier to administer. Here, in this far-flung outpost of Empire, similar bureaucratic characters had done their best to emulate British stupidity: fortunately, the smallness of the whole complex had perforce steered them away from hundred-bed wards, but they had done what they could to make the place uncomfortable.

The second obvious fact was the lack of funds available to the hospital. It was clean—but that was about all. The inevitable green and cream paint was peeling from the walls, a lot of the furniture was broken, wash basins were cracked, and curtains were ragged. Hurricane Alfred had not helped matters by breaking several windows and causing a small flood in the main foyer. With a sinking heart, Emmy approached the dingy cubicle marked RECEPTION, introduced herself, and asked if she might see Henry.

At once, a third and much more promising fact emerged. The premises of St. Mark's General might not be grand or even efficient, but the staff was exceptional. The lovely young black woman behind the desk gave Emmy a sweet smile and said, "Of course, Mrs. Tibbett."

"I wasn't sure about visiting hours—" Emmy began.

"Why you must be anxious to see your husband. You can come at any time—remember that. We're always pleased to see you."

At that moment, a tubby man in a white coat hurried by, and the receptionist hailed him. "Oh, Dr. Harlow—"

"Yes, Sandraleen? What is it?"

"This is Mrs. Tibbett, Doctor. I wondered if—"

"Ah, Mrs. Tibbett." The little Englishman took off his glasses and beamed at Emmy. "I'm just on my way to your husband's floor now. I'll show you up."

Climbing the worn stone staircase, Emmy said tentatively, "Did Sir Alfred Pendleton—?"

"I've just had him on the telephone. He tells me you think your husband might have ingested phencyclidine."

"It was suggested to me as an idea," Emmy said. "What do you think?"

"An interesting theory," said the doctor. "Yes, it would account for a great deal."

"You're familiar with it, are you?" Emmy said. "This frightful stuff called PCP."

The doctor shrugged. "I'm afraid so," he said shortly. "Had a couple of bad cases recently—young people, of course. And there are more who never come for treatment—frightened we'll find out about their drug habits. Most of them buy it as a cheap substitute for LSD, you see. They seldom get to a hospital unless they've actually gone into a coma, and friends or family get so scared that they bring them in."

"What I mean," Emmy said, "is that you can make tests and find out one way or the other."

The doctor shook his head. "I doubt it, Mrs. Tibbett."

"But surely—"

"Unless your husband got himself a fresh fix at the Golf Club," Dr. Harlow remarked, "he can't have had a dose of phencyclidine since—well, since a considerable time before he was rescued off that boat. That was yesterday morning, I understand."

"Yes. About half-past eight."

"Then by now blood and urine tests might well be negative."

"Oh," said Emmy. And then, "Well, anyway, that would mean that he's completely over the effects."

152

The doctor stopped walking and took Emmy's arm. "I'm afraid not, Mrs. Tibbett. There's a recorded case of a patient going into a coma and finally dying five days after the last ingestion. The postmortem showed no trace of the drug. However, in that case, the patient was already in hospital being treated for a phencyclidine overdose, which was diagnosed when he was admitted. Otherwise, the cause of death would have been a complete mystery. In fact, it's believed that far more deaths occur from PCP overdose than anybody realizes. The use—or rather abuse—of the drug has been going up significantly."

Emmy said, "We're lucky to have an expert on such an abstruse subject, Dr. Harlow."

The doctor looked at her with sharp suspicion for a moment. But all he said was yes. He put his hand to a door handle. "Here we are."

"How is he?" Emmy felt guilty that she had not asked this question much sooner.

"When I saw him last, he was asleep." Harlow's voice was quite without expression. "Before that, he appeared drowsy and incoherent, as I would expect after a concussion and sedation." A little pause. "It certainly wouldn't have occurred to me to test him for a drug overdose. Now, of course, we'll do what we can. But don't be disappointed if the results don't prove anything, one way or the other. Well . . ." The doctor turned the handle and pushed the door open. "Nice to meet you, Mrs. Tibbett." He hurried off down the drab corridor.

Henry had been put into one of the smaller wards of the General Hospital. There were no such things as private rooms, but while the principal medical and surgical wards held thirty beds apiece, this smaller unit catered to a mere eight patients.

Three of the cots contained children—small, bandaged figures, all apparently asleep, with just a dusky hand or a few black curls visible against the grayish white of the much-laundered sheets. Emmy wondered if they were casualties of Hurricane Alfred. Of the other beds, two showed humped forms of adult men, also hidden by sheets and apparently unconscious. In another bed, a young black man sat propped up by pillows, reading a comic magazine, while on his nightstand a transistor radio thrummed out a reggae beat. This did not seem to disturb the other patients in the least. The seventh bed was not strictly speaking occupied—that is to say, a very old black man with grizzled white hair and minimal teeth was sitting on the edge of it. He wore blue-and-white-striped pajamas,

153

leaned on a stick, and was conducting a rambling conversation with some invisible companion. The eighth bed was surrounded by rickety chintz screens, and Emmy made her way between them.

Henry was lying on his left side, as he always did when sleeping. Apart from the green silk pajamas (which actually belonged to Peter Whitely of the Golf Club), he looked absolutely normal—precisely, in fact, as he looked every morning in his old Chelsea bedroom when Emmy came to wake him with his early cup of tea; and, as every morning, he woke at her entry. He stirred, opened his eyes, smiled at her, and said, "Hello, darling. Morning already?"

Emmy smiled back. "Lunchtime, actually," she said. There was a wooden chair with a broken back standing by the wall. Emmy pulled it up to the bedside and sat down. "How do you feel?"

"Feel?" Henry blinked. "I feel fine. I . . ." He put up his hand to rub his eyes and caught sight of the green silk pajama sleeve. For a moment he looked at it in disbelief, then from it to the bed, the screens, and finally Emmy. He said, "Where the hell am I? What's happened?"

"You're in hospital, Henry. You had an accident."

"An accident?"

"On a boat. You remember *Windflower*?"

"Of course. We were cruising . . . down island . . ." He passed a hand over his forehead. "Something about . . . something about bad weather from the east . . . what happened, for God's sake?"

Gently, Emmy said, "There was a bad storm, darling. The boat was wrecked and washed ashore. Luckily, John and I found you."

Henry had struggled into a sitting position. He said, "What do you mean, you found me? You must have been on board."

"No, Henry, I wasn't with you."

"You weren't? Why not?"

"Well . . . you decided to go off cruising with your friends, so I went back to the Anchorage . . . don't you remember?"

"Wait a minute." Henry lay down again and closed his eyes. He seemed to be concentrating fiercely. At last he said, "Have I had a concussion or something?"

"Yes. Yes, that's what the doctor said."

"Well, you must think me an almighty idiot, but really I can't remember much. You say I went off without you? I must have been crazy."

"No," Emmy said, with a vehemence that surprised even her. "No, not crazy, Henry." She took his hand, and he grasped it as if it had been a life belt. "Now, you're just to relax and not worry, but as and when you do remember anything, you must tell me. It's . . . it's quite important."

"What am I expected to remember, for heaven's sake? At least give me a clue."

Emmy hesitated. "Well . . . your young friends. The Carstairs and the Blackstones. Do you remember anything about them?"

Henry looked surprised. "Of course," he said. "The Blackstones came on board in the marina. Jill and . . . what was his name? . . . oh, yes, Harvey. What about them?"

"I think they were sailing with you," Emmy said.

"Sounds possible," Henry said. "They were very keen on the boat, remember? What was the other name you said?"

"Carstairs. You . . . we met them in the Buccaneer disco. Friends of the Blackstones. You said they might be sailing with you, too."

Henry shook his head, as if trying to free it from a swarm of bees. He said, "Somebody else. There was somebody else. Can't remember . . ."

"Never mind," said Emmy quickly. "You've done very well with the Blackstones."

"I'm trying my best," Henry said. "Anything else?"

"Well . . . what about the Henry Tibbett Private Investigation Bureau Ltd.?"

"Oh, that. That was just a fantasy . . . I mean, I'll have to retire one day, and I thought it would be a fun way of making a living. It was never more than . . ." A cloud passed over his face. "I remember now . . . you had some bloody silly objection to it . . . you wouldn't help me . . . you're so damned unenterprising and discouraging and . . ." Henry buried his face in his hands. Then he looked up, straight at Emmy, and said, "I think I am a little crazy, Emmy."

"No, you're not." Emmy was very firm. "You've had a bad experience, and you need to rest and not worry." Tentatively, she added, "The bureau is a splendid idea for the future, but you're not retired yet . . . are you?"

"Retired? Of course not. What a fool idea. I've got another . . . oh, about ten years to go . . ."

Emmy smiled, bent forward, and kissed her husband. "That's just wonderful," she said.

"Can't see what's so wonderful about it," Henry said. "After all, it's nothing new. Nothing's changed."

"I know," said Emmy, "that's what's wonderful."

At that moment a trim black nurse in a crackling, very short-skirted white uniform put her head around the screen. "Excuse me, Mrs. Tibbett," she said with a dazzling smile. "I have to ask you to leave for a little while. The doctor wants to see Mr. Tibbett now."

"Of course. I'll go and get some lunch. I'll be back, darling," Emmy added quickly to Henry, who was holding her hand in a vise-like grip.

He relaxed and smiled. "O.K. See you soon."

Emmy said, "There's no . . . ? I mean, you don't have any message—"

"Mrs. Tibbett, please . . ." The nurse was as charming as ever, but a trace more authoritative.

"—for the Governor or anybody?" said Emmy.

Henry looked bewildered. "The Governor? Why on earth should I have a message for . . . ?"

"Mrs. Tibbett, I really must ask you—"

"All right, all right. I've gone." Emmy disappeared around the screens and bumped straight into Dr. Harlow. "Hello, Doctor. I'm just off."

The doctor beamed. "How do you find the patient, Mrs. Tibbett?"

"Fine, Doctor. Doing splendidly."

The old man was still conducting his dribbly monologue, the transistor still blared, and the children still slept as Emmy escaped from the antiseptic atmosphere of the hospital and into the sunshine of the street.

Emmy took a taxi to the marina and was delighted to find that at least one of the public telephones produced a dial tone. Within seconds she heard Margaret's voice.

"Anchorage Inn. Can I help you?"

"Margaret, it's Emmy. I'm in St. Mark's. Henry's here, in hospital."

"Oh . . . hello, Emmy." Margaret sounded embarrassed and quite unlike her usual self.

Emmy said cheerfully, "All right, Margaret, I'll explain my mysterious lunch guest in due course. For the moment, I can't, so please don't ask me. Now—did you manage to contact Betsy?"

There was a little pause, and then, in a rush and a return to her normal voice, Margaret said, "Oh, Emmy, we've been so worried. Did the Governor—?"

"Yes, he did, and of course you've been worried, and so have I.

Now, we may not have much time, so tell me, and fast. Did you speak to Betsy?"

"John did. She's safely home."

"Thank God. But what happened?"

"That's the strange part. Apparently—nothing."

"Nothing?"

"Except that Betsy simply . . . lost a couple of days."

"What do you mean?"

"Well, John says that at first she simply said she was glad to hear we were safe. Then he asked her about her late arrival home, and she said she didn't know what he was talking about. You know Betsy—she'd never admit that she's getting a bit senile and might have been confused. In the end—about a hundred and fifty dollars later, John thinks—she admitted that she'd had what she called a 'funny spell.' "

"What did she mean by that?"

"It took a frightfully long time to get it out of her, but as far as John could make out, she remembered nothing from the moment she arrived on St. Mark's on the *Pride*—that was on Thursday, of course—until she woke up in a bedroom in the Puerto Rico Airport Hotel. Her baggage was there, and her passport and airline ticket were laid neatly beside her bed. Her reservation had been changed to take her to London via New York on Sunday. By discreet inquiries at the desk, she discovered that it was Saturday morning, and that she had arrived the previous evening."

"Saturday! So she lost two whole days!"

"Apparently," said Margaret. "But she must have been functioning during those days because everything was in order. She'd changed her bookings to fly to New York on Saturday, stay overnight at one of the airport hotels, and travel on to England on Sunday."

"What about Miss Pelling and the cats?"

"Betsy admitted that Miss Pelling had been somewhat put out and had taken the cats to a boarding cattery. But—well, you know Betsy. She didn't intend to make a fool of herself. She imagined she had changed her plans and then for some reason forgotten about it—had a spell of amnesia. She pretended to Miss Pelling and everybody else that she had simply decided to come home on a later date by a different route, and the whole thing was forgotten in no time. If it hadn't been for the hurricane . . ."

"So," said Emmy, "we've all been made to look like fools, or worse. Especially Henry."

"How is Henry?"

"Better, thanks," said Emmy briefly. "What's the latest weather bulletin?"

"Beatrice is headed this way, I'm afraid. Should pass us tonight. Where are you staying, Emmy?"

"I . . . I don't know yet. Yes, I do. I'll get a room at the Harbour Prospect until my cash runs out."

"Now look, John and I can always help—"

"Yes, and you may have to," said Emmy. "I'll keep in touch if I can. If I can't, it'll be because of the hurricane, and nobody will be presenting bills or cashing checks. Now, Margaret, will you do something for me before the telephone goes off again, as it's bound to."

"Of course. What?"

"Call Scotland Yard. Talk to Inspector Reynolds—you remember Derek? Tell him to get hold of Betsy and put her through a wringer to get anything she can remember—with the aid of a good doctor. Tell him you suspect Betsy may have been drugged with PCP. That's right. P like Peter, C like Charlie, P like . . ." Emmy glanced up and over her shoulder. She had a sudden and irrational feeling that her conversation was being overheard, but there was nobody in sight except Anderson, the Harbour Master, chatting to an obviously worried young American about the coming hurricane. Emmy went on. "Tell Derek that Henry is going to be fine. Tell him that Betsy may be in danger if anybody suspects that she's . . . oh, damn. Tell him not to trust *anybody*. I mean *anybody*. This is serious, Margaret. O.K.?"

"O.K.," said Margaret, a little dubiously. "But Emmy—" There was a click and Margaret realized that she was talking to herself. Emmy had hung up.

Emmy stepped out of the phone booth and almost into the arms of Inspector Ingham. She smiled brightly. "Hello, Inspector Ingham. Lovely afternoon. Calm between two storms, I suppose."

"Mrs. Tibbett . . . I was looking for you . . ."

"I'm just going over to the restaurant for lunch," said Emmy. "Will you join me?"

"No . . . that is, no, thank you. I've already eaten. Mrs. Tibbett, the Governor would like—"

Striding briskly toward the restaurant, Emmy said, "I've already seen the Governor, Inspector Ingham."

"Yes, but . . . there's been some further development . . ."

"Just for one, please," said Emmy brightly to the waitress who stepped up to greet her. "One for lunch, that is. My friend may take a drink. Yes, this will do nicely. Bring me a glass of white wine as an aperitif, please. Do sit down, Inspector. Wine for you, or beer?"

"Beer," muttered Ingham, sinking into the chair opposite Emmy's. "Now, Mrs. Tibbett—"

"Henry is *much* better, I'm delighted to say." Emmy went on relentlessly, wondering how long she could keep it up. "And I'm sure you've heard that Miss Sprague is home safe and sound after all. Mr. Colville has spoken to her, and it was all a silly misunderstanding, so—"

Forcefully, Ingham said, "What happened right here, in this restaurant, last Sunday was not a misunderstanding, Mrs. Tibbett. I'm glad that your husband is feeling better, but it doesn't change the fact—"

"He quite often gets these little attacks," said Emmy blandly. "Nothing to worry about."

"That," said Ingham, "remains to be seen. Meanwhile, the Governor wants you to know that we've got a line on your husband's confederates."

"Oh." Emmy was jolted out of her playacting. "Really? What?"

"You seem interested."

"Of course I am."

"Well . . . the couple called Carstairs have been in touch with us. They are in St. Thomas, U.S. Virgin Islands, and they propose to lodge a complaint."

"A complaint? Against whom?"

"Against your husband and the people known as Blackstone, who were also aboard *Windflower*. According to the Carstairs, Mr. Tibbett and the Blackstones virtually kidnapped them."

"What an extraordinary story," said Emmy. And then, to the waitress who arrived with drinks, "Thank you. I'll have a rare steak, chips, and salad, please. And a glass of red wine with it. Another beer, Inspector? No?" The waitress departed, and Emmy went on. "Extraordinary. You checked up on these Carstairs people, of course?"

"Of course," replied Ingham stiffly. He took a drink of beer. "Katherine and Lewis Carstairs from Virginia. They arrived in their boat, the *Katie-Lou,* from St. Thomas a week ago. Checked in through Customs and Immigration, everything perfectly in order. Then they took the boat to a local yard for some small repairs and booked themselves a room here at the marina for a couple of days until their boat should be ready. Apparently that was when they met the Blackstones, and later your husband. It was proposed that the five of them should take a short cruise on the *Windflower*. That was when the fun began."

"The fun?"

"I was speaking figuratively. Far from fun, in fact. To condense matters, they accuse both Mr. Tibbett and the Blackstones of being under the influence of drugs or alcohol or both during the entire cruise. The incident here on Sunday was the last straw. The Carstairs demanded to leave the *Windflower,* but they say that the others manhandled them back on board. Later, after the dinghy race episode, things got so bad that nobody was speaking to anybody else. The next morning, they woke up to find themselves off the coast of St. Thomas. The Blackstones, they say, ordered them to pack their things, then simply put them into the dinghy and told them to row ashore. *Windflower* then set sail and disappeared, heading east. It was that afternoon, you may remember, that we intercepted the *Anemone* to *Starfish* message."

Emmy said, "And that evening the hurricane hit. So the Carstairs have only just been able to get through here. They telephoned the Governor, did they?"

"No, Mrs. Tibbett. They telephoned me with a formal complaint."

"Well," said Emmy, "I really can't see what they have to go to the law about—especially as I presume the Blackstones have disappeared."

"Right."

"Have you made inquiries about them?"

Inspector Ingham looked exasperated. "How can we? They landed illegally in the Seawards. We have nothing on them—no passport numbers, addresses—nothing."

"I can tell you a bit about them," Emmy said. She wrinkled her brow, remembering. "Harvey Blackstone is the son of a lawyer, practicing in Baltimore. Jill comes from the same city."

"How do you know this?" Ingham was suspicious.

"They told us, the first time they came aboard, before . . . all the trouble."

"If they told you, Mrs. Tibbett, then I imagine the information will not be of much value. As far as I am concerned, they are a couple of hippies, if not worse."

"You could check it out, all the same," said Emmy. "And you might ask Mr. Anderson."

"Anderson?"

"Yes, the Harbour Master. They told us that they had come here intending to camp, but that young Sebastian Anderson had invited them to stay at his home."

"Why didn't you tell me this before, Mrs. Tibbett?"

"I . . . you didn't ask. I didn't think the Blackstones were important."

Ingham drained his beer and stood up. "I will check," he said, "if I get the chance, with this new hurricane developing. But I think it will be useless. We may indeed trace some Blackstones in Baltimore, but you can be sure they will not be the same people as the two young criminals on board *Windflower*. As for Anderson, I will ask him, of course, but his son is not . . . well, never mind. I will ask him. Meanwhile, Mrs. Tibbett, you are staying on the island?"

"Of course. I'm taking a room at the Harbour Prospect."

"Good. It would be better if you did not leave the Seawards just now."

"I understand that I am not allowed to leave the Seawards, Inspector."

"Well . . . I suppose that's one way of putting it. . . ."

"It's the only way of putting it, Inspector Ingham," said Emmy. "Don't let me keep you. I see my lunch is arriving."

15

As SOON AS she had finished lunch, Emmy went back to the telephone and called the Harbour Prospect Hotel. Not surprisingly, they had plenty of rooms vacant and agreed to reserve one for her. Then she asked if Mr. Leonard Venables was in the hotel. His room number was called without success, whereupon the switchboard operator promised to have Mr. Venables paged. Sure enough, within a few minutes Emmy was talking to Dr. Vanduren.

"Mr. Venables? This is Emmy Tibbett."

"Ah. Glad to hear from you. Where are you?"

"St. Mark's marina, at the moment. I'm on my way to the Harbour Prospect. I shall be staying there for a few days."

"But—"

"I'll be checking in very soon," said Emmy. "Perhaps we could meet for a cup of coffee in about half an hour."

"I'd be delighted. You'll find me on the terrace."

The required deposit on Emmy's room at the Harbour Prospect left her with fifty dollars in traveler's checks and twenty-one dollars in cash. In normal circumstances—since the room, without service or meals, cost thirty-five dollars a day—Emmy would have been reduced to nervous hysteria by this state of events. As it was, however, she found herself feeling perfectly calm. She had enough to worry about, she felt, without concerning herself over mere cash. She established herself with her one suitcase in the pretty room that overlooked the harbor and then took the elevator down to the restaurant and went out onto the terrace, where the few remaining guests of the Harbour Prospect were having their coffee.

Dr. Vanduren was sitting alone at a remote table, and he welcomed Emmy warmly.

"Delighted to see you, Mrs. Tibbett. So you had your interview with the Governor. What have you to tell me?"

Emmy related her talk with Sir Alfred Pendleton, his subsequent exposure of her lie about Dr. Duncan of Tampica, and finally the news that Henry had been transferred to St. Mark's General Hospital, and Dr. Harlow's view that it was probably too late for definitive testing for PCP.

Dr. Vanduren listened in silence and then said, "Well, we can't win 'em all, can we?"

"No," Emmy agreed, but added, "Still we don't have to lose the lot."

"What do you mean?"

"First, I'm in an impossible position so long as you won't let me tell anybody you're here and that I'm in touch with you."

"I can't help that. My instructions remain the same. What else?"

"Well . . . I told you just now . . . Dr. Harlow says that any tests taken now may well reveal nothing, even though PCP intoxication had taken place."

"That's true," Vanduren agreed. "Still, with the behavior that your husband is exhibiting—"

"He's not," said Emmy.

"He's not?"

"I saw him before lunch. He was perfectly normal. His speech is just as usual. The only thing that's wrong is a memory blackout, which is apparently to be expected after a concussion."

"But earlier, at the Golf Club—?"

"When I first saw him, just after he regained consciousness," Emmy said, "he was very much under the influence of . . . something. He was desperately trying to convey some message to the Governor. Now, he doesn't remember a thing about it."

"Did he give any hint of the message?"

"Nothing sensible. He mentioned a number—eighty-something. Nothing else."

"Goddamnit," said Dr. Vanduren succinctly. "Do you think he talked about this urgent message to anybody else?"

"I'm sure he didn't," Emmy said. "For one thing, I was the first person to see him after he woke up. And second, he wouldn't have given such an important message to somebody he didn't trust completely. He was pretty dubious about giving it to me," she added ruefully. "He still had the remnants of a hostile attitude towards me. In fact, a bit of it showed up again even today."

Vanduren said, "It is a very great nuisance. It is unlikely that he will remember any more now. If only we had some way of jerking his subconscious memory into action—but we've nothing to go on."

Emmy said, "Dr. Vanduren, do the names Blackstone or Carstairs mean anything to you?"

"Blackstone? Carstairs?" The doctor thought for a moment. "No, I don't recall either of them. Should I?"

"No. It was just a vague hope." Emmy hesitated and then said, "I may as well tell you. The Blackstones and the Carstairs are two young couples who were on *Windflower* with Henry. The Carstairs have since turned up—it appears that Henry and the Blackstones quarreled with them and put them ashore on St. Thomas in the dinghy, shortly before the storm. The Blackstones then disappeared, leaving Henry and *Windflower* to battle out the hurricane. I think," Emmy added, "that your daughter, Janet, may have been the so-called Mrs. Blackstone."

"You saw them?"

"Yes. They came on board for coffee. And I caught a glimpse of them the same night at the Buccaneer disco."

"Can you describe the girl?"

"Redhead," said Emmy. "Very fair skin to match. Freckles."

Vanduren sighed. "Doesn't sound like Jan," he said, "except for the fair skin. But most things can be faked these days."

There was a pause, full of depression. Then Emmy remembered some happier news. "Oh, I forgot to tell you. Miss Betsy Sprague is alive and well and home in England."

Dr. Vanduren's face broke into a big smile. "Well, for Lord's sakes," he said. "How did that happen?"

Emmy told him. "I think she may have been fed the same drug," she added. "What do you think?"

"Very likely. Very likely. Amnesia is a typical symptom. I'm puzzled, though. Why wouldn't they have killed her? They killed the Rosses."

"When people are a little mad," said Emmy, with feeling, "who knows what they'll do?"

Then, having accepted the doctor's invitation to dine with him at the hotel that evening, Emmy finished her coffee and took a taxi back to the hospital. It left her with twenty dollars in cash.

Henry was sleeping when she arrived, so Emmy pulled up the rickety wooden chair, sat down, and tried to read a paperback thriller that she had bought in the hotel lobby. Her thoughts, however, were more occupied with the weather bulletin, also posted in the lobby, which advised guests that Hurricane Beatrice was now only one hundred miles east of the Seawards, moving at a brisk fourteen knots in a westerly direction. Hotel residents were asked to be inside the hotel by nine P.M. at the latest. They would be told by the hotel staff what precautions to take for their safety. Emmy hoped that the hospital staff would be equally efficient. She looked out of the window, and with a sickening feeling of déjà vu, she recognized the brassy sunshine and the cloud formations on the horizon. In the narrow bed, Henry stirred and opened his eyes.

"Ah, there you are. Must have dropped off."

"Yes, you did. I went to lunch. How do you feel now?"

"I feel O.K." There was a strange note in Henry's voice, a puzzled tone. "You were telling me . . . *Windflower* was wrecked . . ."

"That's right. There was a storm—a hurricane, in fact."

"Christ," said Henry. Then, "Where are the others?" Suddenly agitated, he began to struggle up in bed. Emmy put out a hand to soothe him.

"The others? What others? You were alone on board."

"No, I wasn't. The others . . . Harvey and Jill. Where are Harvey and Jill?"

"Nobody knows," said Emmy.

"But—"

"They weren't on *Windflower* when the hurricane hit, or they'd have still been there when we found you," Emmy said firmly. "Darling—do you feel strong enough to let me tell you a few things?"

"Of course I do."

Emmy smiled at him. "All right. The best news first. Betsy Sprague is alive and well. She's back in England, and John has spoken to her on the telephone."

"That's impossible."

"Wait a moment." Emmy put out a restraining hand. "Listen. Betsy had much the same experience as you did. She lost two whole days."

"She did what?"

"She remembers nothing between arriving on St. Mark's on Thursday and waking up in San Juan on Saturday. Her phone call to you . . . going on board *Chermar* . . . it's all gone. Just a blank."

Henry said, "They killed her."

"They didn't, Henry. We thought they had, but—"

"They did. He said . . ." Henry buried his face in his hands. "Damn, damn, damn. Why can't I remember. I catch a glimpse of something, and then it's gone. Like trying to remember a dream. What did I just say?"

"You said you were certain Betsy had been killed because he said . . ."

"He said what?"

"I don't know. That's as far as you got."

"Who is 'he'?"

"Henry, I don't know. I'm just repeating what you said."

Henry leaned back, exhausted. He said, "All right. Go on. Tell me some more."

"Well, you've been behaving pretty oddly over the past few days."

Henry smiled broadly. "I've had fun," he said.

"Maybe you have. You've also caused a lot of trouble and nearly got yourself killed. Never mind. Try to concentrate. What about the Carstairs?"

"Who?"

"The other couple who were on the boat with you, along with the Blackstones. You pointed them out to me at the Buccaneer Bar the night before you . . . left."

Henry shook his head. "Sorry. Doesn't mean anything."

"O.K. What about a message from *Anemone* to *Starfish*?"

"*Starfish*. I remember *Starfish*. That was the code name in the message that Pearletta heard. But that was before . . ."

Emmy said, "There was another message, while you were away. It was from *Anemone* to *Starfish,* and Pearletta thought she recognized your voice sending it. It came the day before the hurricane hit us. There was also mention of somebody with the initial *E,* and of course the Governor thinks that's me." She smiled and squeezed Henry's hand. "It would help if you could remember something. Anything."

Henry shook his head hopelessly. "Not a thing."

"Yesterday," said Emmy, "when you regained consciousness at the Golf Club, you were desperately trying to get some message to the Governor. Can you remember anything about what it was?"

"So that's why you . . ." Henry lay back on the pillows. "It's no good, Emmy. It's all gone."

"The only thing you said was a number. Eighty-something."

"Eighty-two," said Henry, promptly.

"So you do remember!"

"I . . . what did I just say?"

"You said eighty-two. What does it mean? Eighty-two what?"

Henry put a hand to his forehead. He said, "It's gone again. What could it be?"

"A radio wavelength?" Emmy was guessing. "A location . . . eighty-two degrees longitude . . . where would that be?"

"I've no idea. You could look it up. At this latitude, somewhere in the Gulf of Mexico, I should think." Henry sighed. "Sorry, darling, to be such a washout."

"You're not a washout at all," said Emmy warmly. "It's just that—well, you seemed to think that you had something tremendously important to tell Sir Alfred and Inspector Ingham, and you've obviously stumbled on something pretty big and nasty concerning drugs—"

Suddenly Henry said, "Nobody'll believe me . . . nobody, ever again . . . that's what he said. Nobody . . . ever . . . whatever I say . . . in any case, won't remember . . . you won't remember . . . will remember . . . eighty-two . . ." His voice, which had been growing more slurred and indistinct with every syllable, finally petered out. His head lolled.

Emmy ran out of the ward and almost collided with Dr. Harlow in the corridor. She said, "Doctor, please go and look at my husband. I think the drug is affecting him again, and he may be in a coma."

"Wait here," said Harlow, and he went into the ward.

A couple of minutes later, he came out again. "No cause for alarm," he said. "He's just sleeping normally. Better leave him for a bit—mustn't overtire him. Oh, by the way, those tests were negative."

"Oh," said Emmy.

"However, as I said, that doesn't prove anything, one way or the other." The doctor gave Emmy a brisk nod of farewell and went off down the corridor.

Emmy went downstairs and asked the receptionist if she might use the telephone. The receptionist was very sorry—but the hospital had only one outside line, and it was not allowed to be used for private calls. Emmy would find a public telephone at the post office in town.

At that moment, a taxi drove up bringing visitors to the hospital. Emmy hailed it and further depleted her small supply of dollars by getting the driver to take her to Government House.

The Governor was busy, but not too busy to see Mrs. Tibbett.

Within minutes, Emmy was in his office, recounting Henry's amnesia and his occasional bursts of apparent partial recall. She said, "The best explanation I can think of is that eighty-two refers to a location of some sort—maybe a degree of longitude."

There was a large map of the Caribbean area hanging on the wall of the office, and her eyes went instinctively to it. Sir Alfred was already on his feet, and they examined the map together. Eighty-two degrees west ran down the center of the so-called Florida panhandle—the peninsula jutting out into the Gulf of Mexico and terminating in Miami and the Florida Keys. Southward, the line of longitude crossed the island of Cuba.

Sir Alfred said, "It's quite interesting—as degrees of longitude go." Emmy sensed a smile in his voice, and her heart lifted a little.

She said, "Inspector Ingham tells me that these people called Carstairs have contacted him."

"Yes. Making a great fuss, I understand. They don't really interest me, Mrs. Tibbett. However, I would like to know what has become of the other young people."

"The Blackstones?"

"That's right. They arrived illegally, from nowhere, and they seem to have gone the same way. Our only line on them is through Anderson, the Harbour Master, and all he knows is that his son picked them up on the beach." The Governor paused. "Frankly, Mrs. Tibbett, now that we know that Miss Sprague was not murdered nor even harmed, but is safely home, I think the moment has come—well, to concentrate on getting through our imminent hurricane and forget the rest." Another pause. "I am sure your husband meant well, and I am perfectly aware that we have a drug problem on the islands—but apart from the fact that some young people were picked up smoking marijuana at a fish fry last week, there seems very little to go on. Two boats, the *Isabella* and the *Chermar*, have been lost at sea with their crews, which is very sad but not, I fear, unusual. We'll go on looking for the Blackstones, but I'm afraid that if they were on the *Windflower*, they were probably victims of Hurricane Alfred. When the photograph of Janet Vanduren arrives from England—and heaven knows when that will be, in present weather conditions—we will circulate it and keep a lookout for the young lady, should she be alive." Sir Alfred's tone of voice made it clear that he considered this a very remote possibility. "Meanwhile, as soon as the doctors pronounce Mr. Tibbett to be fit, and communications are restored, I think your best plan is to take him quietly home. He has undoubtedly had a

168

breakdown of some sort, from whatever cause, and he needs a period of rest and quiet. I think he can safely leave us to cope with our own problems here in the Seawards." Sir Alfred smiled. "I am trying to be as fair as I can. You can forget any question of arrest. Just . . . leave us alone, please, Mrs. Tibbett. Do you understand?"

"Yes, Sir Alfred," said Emmy.

The Harbour Prospect Hotel seemed to be keeping its cool admirably, even under the threat of Hurricane Beatrice. The dining room was not crowded, but neither was it deserted. The only obvious precautions were some taped-up plate-glass windows. As Emmy and Dr. Vanduren sat down to dinner at eight o'clock, the wind had not even started to blow hard. But the island was holding its breath.

"Well, Mrs. Tibbett?"

"Well, nothing. The Governor has decided that Henry has had a mental breakdown and should go home to England and have a nice long rest—thus leaving the British Seawards with nothing to worry about. As I told you, Betsy Sprague is alive and well, and since Henry was staying on here to investigate her disappearance—" Emmy suddenly looked up from her delicious dish of local baked fish and said, "Dr. Vanduren, am I perhaps going mad myself?"

The doctor gave her a big grin. "No, Mrs. Tibbett. But you are beginning to see what we're up against. Very clever people, with almost limitless financial resources and a great flair for . . . what can I call it? Public relations, I suppose. Making everything appear perfectly normal and—even if they are caught out—trivial at the worst. A little marijuana or cocaine carried in a small private sailing boat. Nothing to make a great fuss about."

"But—"

"But multiply that sailing boat by a few thousands, and you get a different picture. Enlist a few reputable doctors, like myself . . . get a whole generation of young islanders involved . . . you see how it goes. Each incident is small in itself—that's what makes it so smart."

"Well," Emmy said, "one thing's for sure—nothing much can happen until Hurricane Beatrice has been and gone. Alfred was bad enough, but in a curious way I'm almost ready to welcome Beatrice."

"I know what you mean," said the doctor.

"You do?"

"Better the devil you know than the one you know you're going to have to face," said Vanduren. "Will she hit us tonight, do you think?"

"More likely early tomorrow," Emmy said.

"Best get some rest while we can, then," said Vanduren. He finished his meal and stood up. "I'll be off to bed, if you'll excuse me. Plenty to do. Room twenty-two." He pulled a big key with a hotel tag on it out of his pocket. "Twenty-two, plenty to do. Do you ever use mnemonics? I find rhymes are useful."

Emmy hardly noticed him go. Something was stirring at the back of her mind. Mnemonics. Henry used them, too—made a rhyming phrase which would keep a number or a name in his mind. Or made a number . . . eighty-two . . . eighty-two . . . something was there, but Emmy couldn't find it. She reviewed mentally all the conversations she had had since Henry's breakdown. With Inspector Ingham, with Dr. Vanduren, with the Colvilles, with the Governor, with the Harbour Master, with the Golf Club Secretary . . . Eighty-two . . . And suddenly she got it. She jumped up from the table, ran to the front desk, and asked if she could order a taxi to take her to the hospital.

The front desk, in the form of a bored-looking young black man, was surprised. The hurricane was imminent, and guests had been asked to stay indoors.

"I know that, but I have to get to the hospital. My husband is ill."

Convinced by this argument, the young man agreed to call a cab, and a few minutes later Emmy was climbing the now-familiar steps up to St. Mark's General. She hoped that visitors really were welcome at any hour.

She need not have worried. The hospital was ablaze with lights and noisy with voices. It seemed to be quite a social center, and a small matter like a hurricane was not going to discourage the gregarious instincts of British Seawarders.

The screens around Henry's bed had been removed, and Emmy was relieved to see that he was awake and sitting up, looking much better and reading a three-year-old *New Yorker* magazine, which was the best in the way of reading material that the General had been able to dredge up. He looked up and beamed as Emmy came in.

"Darling! What a splendid surprise. I thought you'd be barricaded in your hurricane shelter by now. Isn't this a marvelous hospital?"

"Henry, I—"

"Where else in the world would you get live guitar music in a public ward at this time of night—let alone a pretty nurse dancing to it as she takes your temperature?"

"Henry—"

"Much as I dislike being ill, I'd sooner do it here than anywhere. Do you know what the nurse who brought my dinner said?"

"No, and I don't care!" Emmy was shouting, but failing to make any great impression against the competition of the guitar-player and his friends.

Henry, suddenly serious, said, "Sorry, love. I was a bit carried away. What's the problem?"

"Eighty-two," Emmy said.

"Eighty-two? What about it?"

"You mean—you've forgotten again? Or already?"

Henry said, "I'm sorry, you're talking in riddles. What's eighty-two?"

Patiently, Emmy explained. "When we first got you ashore from *Windflower,* you were trying to get a message to the Governor."

Henry looked puzzled. "Yes, you told me that, but I can't remember—"

"This afternoon, you remembered that part of the message had to do with the number eighty-two."

"Did I?" Henry's brow wrinkled. "Isn't it awful? I just can't remember—"

"Eighty-two," said Emmy, "was a rhyming phrase to help you remember something else."

"It was? What, for heaven's sake?"

"I think I know," Emmy said, "but if you could remember it on your own, that would really clinch it."

"Give me a clue, then."

"The name of a boat."

"Of a boat? Eighty-two?"

"Rhyming with eighty-two. What rhymes with eighty?"

"Matey . . . Haiti . . . Katie! That's it! Katie! Eighty-two, Katie-Lou!" Henry was silent for a moment, studying his wife's face. Then he said, "Katie-Lou. What the hell does it mean?"

"I'll try to tell you," Emmy said.

16

WHEN EMMY HAD FINISHED there was a longish pause. Then Henry, who had been lying back with his eyes closed, opened them and said, "Yes. I don't remember much, of course. In fact, very little. But it's coming back, in patches."

Emmy said, "You remember that it was the couple who called themselves Carstairs who were the villains."

Henry smiled feebly. "No, not really. But I do remember that it was desperately important for me to hang on to the name of their boat—*Katie-Lou*."

"As far as we know," Emmy said, "she's still here, in St. Mark's. She was brought in for repairs. Of course, the hurricanes will have upset the Carstairs' plans—but sooner or later, they'll have to come back and get her. Filled to the brim with drugs, I suppose."

"I suppose so." Henry sounded very tired.

"Then there's the question of the Blackstones. You don't feel that there was anything wrong with them."

"What do you mean, wrong with them?"

"I mean, they were victims, like you."

"Yes. Yes, I think so. They didn't constitute a menace at any rate."

Emmy frowned. "One thing puzzles me," she said.

"Only one?"

"Oh, a million things. But one, right here and now and off the top of my head. All right, so the *Katie-Lou* is here to pick up a load of marijuana and take it to the States. I know that's not a praiseworthy thing—but would it have got you so desperate to tell the Governor. You went on as though it was a matter of life and death."

"*Katie-Lou* was only part of it." Henry spoke slowly. "If I could remember *Katie-Lou,* I thought I could remember the rest. But it seems I can't."

A nurse, unflappable and smiling, had come into the ward. She switched off the transistor radio and calmly unplugged the electric guitar with which a young islander had been entertaining his sick friend. Then she said gently, "I'm afraid I have to ax all visitors to leave." She smiled enchantingly. "Hurricane Beatrice is very close now, and everybody is axed to go home and stay there until the danger is past. We'll take good care of your friends and relatives in the hospital, and we hope to see you tomorrow."

"Well," said Emmy, "that's that for tonight. I'll be back in the morning, weather permitting. Maybe the . . ." She stopped, thinking better of her intended remark. Instead, she bent and kissed Henry's forehead.

The wind was getting up as Emmy and the other visitors walked down the steps in front of the hospital. Several taxis were waiting, and people who did not have their own cars piled into them, more or less indiscriminately. Everybody was going back into town. One by one, the others called to the driver to stop, got out, paid their fares, and hurried off into the darkness. At last, Emmy was alone in the cab. They were on the waterfront, and already the seas were pounding loudly against the harbor wall.

"Where to, lady?" asked the driver—a big, untidy man with a large grin and broken teeth.

Emmy hesitated and then said, "How long do you think we have?"

"How long?"

"Before the hurricane hits."

The driver leaned out of the window and cocked an eye at the sky. He said, "Hard to say. About half an hour, I guess."

"I have to get back to the Harbour Prospect," Emmy said, "but I'd like to pay a short call somewhere else first."

"O.K. by me, lady. Where?"

"Bob Harrison's boatyard."

"You're the boss." The driver was already putting the car in reverse. "But it'll be all shut up, you know. Bob doesn't live at the yard."

"Never mind. Let's go."

The boatyard was dark but not silent. The ever-increasing wind was already rattling the wire-mesh gate and shaking the corrugated-iron roofs of the big sheds. Noisiest of all were the flapping tarpaulins shrouding the half-dozen boats that stood on wooden cradles ashore, like stranded whales. Big waves were crashing up the normally sheltered slipway, and on the dark water beyond other boats strained at their moorings, while rigging thrummed against masts and strained ropes creaked.

"Just wait, please," Emmy said. "I won't be long."

"Better not be," remarked the driver ominously. He lit a cigarette and settled himself behind the wheel. Leaning against the wind, Emmy walked up to the gate of the boatyard.

The gate was padlocked, as she had feared it would be, but there did not seem to be any barbed wire along the top of it. However, it was a good eight feet high. Emmy looked around and found an empty wooden crate lying by the side of the cul-de-sac road. She dragged it to the gate and climbed onto it. With its extra height, she could just get her arms over the round metal bar that formed the top of the gate. Clumsily, she tried to hoist herself up, but her arms were too weak.

Behind her, a male voice said, "What's all this, then?"

Emmy let out a small squeak and fell to the ground, knocking over the crate. She turned to see the cab driver standing there.

"Oh! It's you. I thought . . . I mean, you must be surprised—"

"Lady," said the driver, "you drive a cab, nothing surprises you. Want a leg up?"

"I just . . . I mean, I only want to see if a certain boat is there—a friend's boat . . ."

"You want a leg up, or you don't? Like I said, there's not much time. How you planning to get back over?"

"I thought I'd be able to find something to climb on."

"If you don't, I'll pitch that box over to you and then grab you from this side. Up we go, then."

Strong arms clasped her waist and heaved her upward. A moment later Emmy was over the gate and in the yard.

It only took her a couple of minutes to locate *Katie-Lou*. She was out of the water on a cradle near the gate—a sleek sailing ketch about fifty feet long, stoutly built, with a broad beam and a central cockpit, which promised comfortable sailing in rough weather. The name, KATIE-LOU NORFOLK VA., was painted in black on the white transom. Even in the dark and against the black sky, Emmy could see that the boat was equipped with a radio aerial. She had seen all that she wanted to see. She also noticed, happily, that there was a small stepladder alongside the boat, enabling the workmen to climb aboard. She had started to lug it over to the gate when the taxi driver's voice stopped her.

"Hey, lady, you want to give yourself away? You put that ladder back and come climb on the box." Lightly, he pitched the crate over the fence. "That's it . . . bring it up to the gate . . . climb on it and get your arms over the top . . . here we go . . . easy, see?"

It was not exactly easy, Emmy thought, but she made it. When she was safely outside the fence, the driver found a long stick and pushed it through the wire mesh, giving the crate a hefty shove that sent it tumbling away from the gate. Then he threw the stick down in the grass by the roadside.

"You think of everything," said Emmy, full of admiration.

The driver grinned and winked. "I can see you haven't had no proper experience," he said. "Find what you wanted?"

"Yes, thanks."

"Then we'd best be going."

In the taxi, speeding up the hill to the hotel, Emmy said, "I really am very grateful. You were splendid."

"Nothing, lady. Nothing at all. By the way, my name's Shark Tooth."

"Is it really?"

"No, but it's what they call me. So anytime you need a cab, you just ask for Shark Tooth. Call the main stand by the jetty and ax for me. O.K.?"

"O.K.," said Emmy. The car took the final upward bend before the hotel, and the wind caught it abeam, rocking it dangerously. Shark Tooth, with careless expertise, regained control and carried on with no loss of speed, but he said, "Here she comes, man. Here's Beatrice."

The big glass doors of the hotel were not only taped, but locked. However, there was a night bell, and the clerk had remembered that Emmy was out visiting the hospital and was waiting to let her in.

She had started to walk up the stairs to her room when she noticed sounds of merrymaking coming from the bar which led off the main foyer. It was not yet ten o'clock, and obviously the hand-ful of guests still in the hotel had decided, like any group of strangers threatened by an outside force, to band together and make the best of things. After a moment of hesitation, Emmy came back down the stairs and went into the bar.

There were about twenty people there, chattering with slightly frenetic cheerfulness. Behind the bar, somebody had pinned a large map of the Caribbean, and the bartender was marking Beatrice's latest position on it with a felt-tip pen. With a definite sinking of the heart, Emmy saw that the black dot was only about forty miles east of the Seawards, and the hurricane was headed straight for them.

The portable radio on the bar kept up a continuous stream of talk. Beside it, his ear cupped in his hand, sat a small, bald American who kept muttering, "Quiet down, won't you, fellas? I can't hear . . ." In a remote corner by himself, Dr. Vanduren sat at a small table, nursing a drink. Emmy went over to him.

"So you decided to stay up and wait for the hurricane after all, Doctor?"

"Yes. Yes, it seemed silly to go to bed, when . . . where have you been?"

Emmy had forgotten that her clothes might bear signs of her expedition into the boatyard. However, as with the matter of available cash, she found herself feeling unusually calm. She said, "I went to the hospital to see my husband."

"But with the hurricane coming—"

Emmy said, "Dr. Vanduren, I know a lot more now than I knew when we had dinner together." She paused, searching for words. When they came, they sounded banal. "Can I trust you?"

The doctor smiled and sighed. "Ah, that's the question, isn't it? Can I trust you, can you trust me? Can we trust the police, or the Governor? Can they trust each other?" He raised his glass to his lips, drank deeply, and then suddenly banged the glass onto the table, causing the would-be radio listener to break into a plaintive, "Aw, cut it out, will you?"

Vanduren smiled across the table at Emmy. He said, "Somebody has to start somewhere. Let's trust each other, Mrs. Tibbett."

"Then you must let me tell the Governor—"

"I said 'each other.' " All the hostility was back.

Emmy looked at him and thought she had seldom seen anybody so tired, so without hope. She said, "All right. Each other. I am virtually certain that your daughter, Janet, is currently going under the name of Mrs. Katherine Carstairs of Norfolk, Virginia. God knows where the real Mrs. Carstairs is. Katherine and Lewis Carstairs own—or owned—a boat called the *Katie-Lou,* which is currently hauled out of the water at Bob Harrison's yard here. I have no idea whether Bob is involved—or indeed, anybody else. All

I do know is that the boat is now—or soon will be—filled to the brim with an important consignment of drugs that have been hidden on this island, waiting to be ferried to the States. I also know that the Carstairs telephoned Inspector Ingham from St. Thomas . . . no, that's not true. I know that he told me they did—"

Dr. Vanduren smiled sardonically. "That's a bit better," he said. "You don't know, do you?"

"No, but one thing that's certain is that the boat is still here."

"You know that?"

"Yes."

"How? They may not be in St. Thomas. They may have sailed her away this afternoon."

"No. She's here."

Vanduren shrugged. "Since we have decided to trust each other, I suppose I must believe you."

Emmy smiled. "If you must know, I broke into the yard a few minutes ago, with the help of a charming and resourceful cab driver. The boat is there."

Dr. Vanduren gave her a curious look, but all he said was "Good. Go on."

"Well, since the boat is here, they will have to come and collect her when the hurricane has passed. It's perfectly obvious that no mail is going to arrive for weeks, so we can forget that photograph of your daughter that's being sent from England. Only one person can identify her, Dr. Vanduren, and that is you."

Vanduren opened his mouth to say something, but there was a sudden, earthshaking rumble from outside and all the lights went out. There were a few, quickly stifled feminine screams which turned to embarrassed laughter as the bartender produced matches and lit a row of candles that had been placed along the bar. The man who had been listening so avidly to the radio now turned up the volume. Even in the sanctuary of the Harbour Prospect Bar, it was difficult to hear against the screaming of the wind outside and the periodic crashes as trees and roofs and electricity poles came down.

"Ladies and gentlemen, I'm sure we don't have to tell you that Hurricane Beatrice is now approaching the British Seaward Islands and should pass over us within the next two hours. If anybody has not so far taken shelter, do so now. I repeat, take shelter *now*. This is Tim Shannon of Radio Seawards, telling everybody in these islands to take shelter at once. Hurricane shelters have been established at the following locations: St. Michael's Church, Priest Town, St. Matthew's; The Anchorage Inn, St. Matthew's; St. Mark's High School, Harbour Front, St. Mark's; The Astoria Cinema, Main Street, St. Mark's; The Methodist Church Hall, North End, St. Mark's. Do not attempt to drive any vehicle of any sort. Many roads are already impassable, and vehicles can be deathtraps in hurricane-force winds. If your home is not secure, make your way on foot *now* to the shelter nearest you. If possible, however, stay indoors and take all necessary precautions. All glass windows and doors should be taped diagonally with strong plastic or paper tape . . ."

The erstwhile revelers in the bar had fallen silent. There was a feeling of mass guilt, as though to sit out the hurricane in the comparative security of the Harbour Prospect Hotel was in itself a discreditable act. It was almost a relief when the radio announcer said quite calmly, "Tim Shannon here, Radio Seawards. Our engineers tell us that our transmitter tower can't last much longer. Sorry, folks, but I think that at any moment—" Then there was a crash, followed by silence.

After a shocked pause, people began to talk again. Suddenly they did not feel so guilty. If Radio Seawards—a sturdy concrete building on a hillside above the harbor—could suffer damage, then so might the Harbour Prospect Hotel. They were in some—even if minimal—danger, and it was a good feeling. Drinks were ordered, and people began to speculate on possible devastation to the hotel in a much more cheerful frame of mind. On one point there was general agreement—it would be tempting fate to go to bed on an upstairs floor. The bar—or perhaps, even better, the discotheque downstairs—were the sensible places to be.

Emmy became aware that Dr. Vanduren was looking at her intently. She said, "I'm sorry. You were going to say something, before . . ."

"I was going to say, Mrs. Tibbett, that I will help you in any way I can to find my daughter."

"Thank you, Doctor."

"And now, I'm going to bed, whatever anybody says. I'd rather risk being blown from here to St. Matthew's than sit up all night in a hurricane with this bunch."

Emmy smiled. "I agree," she said.

In the lobby, as the doctor climbed the stairs to his room, Emmy approached the desk clerk and asked whether the telephones were still working. It appeared that, for the moment, they were—but only essential calls were allowed.

"I was thinking of my husband in the hospital," Emmy said.

"The hospital is still functioning, Mrs. Tibbett. We are in touch with it and also with the police. If there is no urgent message—"

"No," said Emmy. "No urgent message."

Half an hour later, while Emmy was lying fully dressed on her hotel bed, trying to snatch some sleep despite the screaming inferno outside, the main telephone cable of St. Mark's Island came down to earth with a crash. Nobody was in touch with anybody else any longer.

The night seemed to last forever. It was hard to believe that wind could make such a shattering amount of noise. It was impossible, of course, to look out of the taped and shuttered windows, but occasionally the cacophony outside was augmented by the wail of a siren, as an ambulance or police car battled through the chaos to the scene of an emergency. With the beginnings of daylight, around five in the morning, the wind began to abate. By eight o'clock, when Emmy got up and changed her clothes by the feeble light that was creeping through cracks in the shutters, the hurricane was packing winds of no more than fifty miles an hour over the Seawards. The lethal leading edge of the storm had screamed on out to sea and toward the apprehensive coast of the United States mainland.

There was no question of washing. The electrical pumps were dead and the taps dry. Feeling exhausted and filthy Emmy made her way downstairs, headed for the dining room, and hoped that the hotel cooked with gas and not electricity.

The dining room was well populated. Not only were all the hotel's residents and staff enjoying a hearty, gas-cooked breakfast, but many other St. Markians (notably those with electric stoves) had come in for a meal. The shutters had been removed from the big windows, and through the crisscross of protective tape it was possible to look out and get a first glimpse of the night's devastation.

The gardens of the hotel looked like a deserted battlefield. Trees, uprooted by the fury of the wind, lay around at drunken angles, stripped of their leaves. Streams of mud cascaded down the steep hillside toward the harbor, carrying with them the pathetic remains of what had yesterday been flowering shrubs. In the continuing gale the few surviving trees bent hopelessly toward the west, like creatures under the lash of a whip. What leaves still clung to them were blackened, as if burned.

Emmy, standing at the window, became aware of someone at her elbow, and turned to see Dr. Vanduren. "Look at the trees," she said. "Was there a fire?"

He shook his head. "No. That's salt burn."

"Salt?"

"Hurricane winds coming in from the sea carry enough salt to burn up vegetation," he explained. "We see it in Florida." A pause. "Well, we've been lucky."

"You call this lucky?"

"It could have been a lot worse. There are roofs off, of course, and telephone poles down and many roads impassable—but only five deaths that we know of."

Emmy said, "How do you know all this? Is the radio—?"

Vanduren shook his head. "No, the radio station is still out of action. Our only communication is by VHF and radio hams."

"Then how—?"

"Can't you guess? I've only just gotten back from the hospital." Vanduren smiled. "There are oaths and oaths, Mrs. Tibbett, but I guess the Hippocratic is about the most binding there is. In an emergency like this, a doctor can't simply crawl under the sheets and go to sleep, even if he is masquerading as an import-export broker. I came clean."

"You told them your name?"

"Not my real one. I just said I was a doctor—that was enough last night. I had the hotel inform the hospital just before the phones went, and they sent a jeep for me. It's quite a shambles down there—but mostly just fractures from falling trees and walls and cuts from broken glass."

"Did you see my husband?"

"I didn't see any of the regular patients—I was in the Emergency Room all night. However, I didn't forget you, Mrs. Tibbett. I insisted on coming back here for breakfast."

"What's that to do with me?"

"Just that there'll be a jeep along to pick me up and take me back in about half an hour. I thought you might like to ride along with me. There's no other way to get there unless you walk."

"Thank you. Oh, thank you so much, Doctor Van—"

"Venables, Mrs. Tibbett. Dr. Leonard Venables. Well, shall we have breakfast?"

17

It was a bumpy and somewhat scary ride. The young driver from the hospital handled the jeep with airy expertise, but most of the way the road conditions were nightmarish. Boulders, electricity poles, tangles of fallen telephone wire, sheets of tin roofing, all cluttered the streets of the battered island. Where roads had been paved, the weight of the rushing mud and water had cracked the surfaces into crazy ruts and potholes: the dirt roads resembled riverbeds, with cascading streams carving out rocky ravines over which the intrepid jeep leaped and bucked like a goat. The sides of the road were littered with overturned vehicles and such bizarre sights as a wheelbarrow resting upside-down on the roof of a truck or a wire fishtrap lodged in the window of a small wooden house. There was no sign of life. People and animals alike were taking shelter where they could find it, still not prepared to venture out into the desolation.

Dr. Vanduren had described the hospital as a shambles, but in fact Emmy was surprised to find how competently and methodically the staff members were coping against fearsome difficulties. The battlefield aspect of the grounds was already something that had become familiar, and so lost its power to shock. Inside, there were a lot of people, among them crying children and scared-looking mothers clutching tiny infants, waiting to see a doctor, but there was no panic, just a minimum of disorder. The hospital personnel looked gray with tiredness, but the nurses' caps and aprons were as white and starched as ever, and their smiles as frequent, if slower.

As Emmy and Dr. Vanduren came through the main entrance, the doctor was instantly accosted by a nurse, telling him that he was urgently needed in the Emergency Room. He gave Emmy a small, encouraging smile and disappeared down the corridor. As he did so, Dr. Harlow came hurrying out of one of the emergency wards, a sheaf of papers in his hand. He saw Emmy and said, "Ah, Mrs. Tibbett. Glad you're here. You should go and see your husband. Can't stop now . . ." He was gone.

Henry's small ward had been transformed. More beds had been brought in, so twelve patients were now crammed into the space which had been barely enough for eight. The newcomers—two of them children—were bandaged and had various limbs in plaster. The transistor radio still blared out music. The old gentleman still sat on the edge of his bed conducting his monologue, but—or so it seemed to Emmy—with rather more spirit and enjoyment than before. To the institutionalized, all and any excitement is a welcome source of exhilaration.

The screens around Henry's bed had been replaced, and Emmy slipped quietly between them, anxious not to disturb her husband. Despite what Dr. Harlow had said, she thought it likely that he might still be asleep. On the contrary, he was sitting up in bed, writing with feverish concentration on a large pad of lined yellow paper. He looked up as Emmy appeared.

"Oh, well done, darling. How on earth did you get here? They told me—"

"I have my methods." Emmy smiled. "You look a lot better. What's the great literary effort?"

Henry laid the pad down on the bed and said, "It's quite simple, darling. I've remembered."

"You have? Everything?"

Henry made a wry grimace. "How do I know? There may be a lot I still forget—but I've remembered the most important things."

"But how—?"

"It was the hurricane. Ask poor Dr. Harlow. He went through a hell of a night with me."

"I don't understand."

"Dr. Harlow explained to me that there are two sorts of amnesia: one caused by a concussion, the other by emotional trauma or drugs. You never get back memories lost by a concussion—which is why I can't remember anything about my last hours on *Windflower*, and I never will. But the other sort of amnesia can sometimes be overcome by triggering off the memory by applying the same sort of conditions that were in force when recollection was

182

destroyed. I've probably got that all wrong in medical terms—but what happened is quite easy to understand. I lost my memory in a hurricane, and it needed another one to jolt it back into some sort of working order. I don't suppose it's often that anyone goes through two hurricanes in a week—but we did."

"So what happened?"

"I don't remember a lot about last night," Henry admitted cheerfully. "Doc Harlow says that when the storm really started going great guns, I regressed—that is, I went absolutely crazy and began reliving the first hurricane over again. You can imagine that the last thing these unfortunate people wanted was a raving lunatic around the place—but there I was, and they had to put up with it. I'm trying to piece together from what the doctor and nurses heard exactly what I was reliving as far as the actual hurricane experience went—but that's not really important. What matters is that when it was all over, and I woke up and came to myself again, I found I could remember at least some things from the period before the first storm."

"That's wonderful, Henry."

"I'm not sure that it is. It's pretty grim, and action will have to be taken right away—and a fat lot of hope there is of that with every policeman and official on the island entirely concerned with the hurricane. However, we can but try."

"Well . . . tell me."

Henry wrote a final word, then drew a line at the bottom of the text with a flourish. He handed the pad to Emmy. "You'd better read it. Screens have ears. We're not private."

Emmy took the pad and started to read. When she had finished, she looked at Henry for a moment and then said, "I . . . it's fantastic. Are you absolutely sure, Henry?"

"Absolutely. I heard them discussing it all."

"But . . . have you any proof at all?"

"There's the *Katie-Lou*. That's why I knew I must remember the name."

"Yes, I know. But that's just a load of . . ." She caught Henry's warning eye and amended quickly, "That's just one cargo. It has nothing to do with—all this."

"It's a part of it. But not, as you can see, the serious part."

Emmy hesitated again. Then she said, "Henry, I hate to say this, but . . . well, you were very ill, you know. Could it possibly all be just a part of your hallucinations? I mean, it's such a farfetched—"

She stopped. Henry's face had taken on a look that she had never seen before. A hard, sneering expression, totally unlike him. In a strange voice he said, "Oh, yes. If you survive, you'll tell them the story. Do you think anybody will believe you? You poor idiot . . . nobody will believe you, ever . . ."

Emmy leaned forward and took his hand. "I'm sorry, darling. Of course I believe you."

Henry's face relaxed. He passed a hand over his brow. "I was off again, wasn't I? Well, if you don't believe me, I'm really sunk."

"I just said I did."

"That's good. The thing now is to arrange a meeting with the Governor. I don't see any point in talking to anybody lower, do you?"

"No," said Emmy. "Unless we can convince Sir Alfred—" Emmy looked at the thin cotton screens and remembered the apparently harmless patients occupying the rest of the ward. She decided to say very little. "We do have," she added, "a useful ally."

"An ally?"

"A doctor. Do you remember that I told you I had seen him at the marina?"

Henry looked at her blankly. "At the marina? When? I don't remember anything about a doctor."

Emmy said, "All right. It doesn't matter. But there is someone on this island who can help us. Now, you try to get some rest, and I'll try to get the Governor to listen to us. May I take this?" She indicated the yellow pad.

In the moment of Henry's hesitation, Emmy remembered vividly Dr. Vanduren's remark, "It's unfortunate that we have to trust each other." She felt a spurt of anger that a purely moneymaking concern should have the power to cause even a momentary doubt in a relationship of love and trust that had taken a quarter of a century to build up. Then she remembered what she had just read and was aware that it was not only money at stake. It was power, and power is the great corrupter.

Then Henry smiled, squeezed her hand, and said, "Yes, darling. Take it. After all, it's in my mind now—I can always write it down again. Just don't lose it."

Emmy said, "I'll be back when I have anything useful to report."

Transport on the island was minimal and strictly official. No chance of a taxi, Emmy was informed by the hospital receptionist. No buses running. Might get a ride, but probably have to walk.

It was not so dreadful. Fortunately, the hospital was on the same side of town as Government House, and it took Emmy little more than half an hour to walk up to the wrought-iron gates and small sentry box that guarded Her Majesty's representative.

A polite black manservant asked Emmy to wait—not, this time, in the shabbily elegant drawing room, but in a small and sparsely furnished waiting room. After about twenty minutes, the Governor's secretary appeared—a neat, attractive island girl, as beautifully coiffed and turned-out as if Hurricane Beatrice had never been. She informed Emmy that the Governor was sorry, but she must realize that he was far too busy today of all days to bother about anything but the hurricane damage.

Emmy said that she quite understood, but that this business was even more serious than the hurricane.

The secretary smiled, with a little less friendliness, and repeated that she had her instructions and there was nothing to be done.

Emmy fell back on her last line of attack and proffered Henry's yellow note pad. Would the secretary agree to take this to the Governor and ask him to read it?

Reluctantly, the girl took the pad and left the waiting room. Ten minutes later, she was back to say that the Governor would see Mrs. Tibbett briefly.

Sir Alfred Pendleton was in his office, sitting in shirt-sleeves at his desk. He was obviously exhausted, worried, and angry. Henry's notes lay on the desk in front of him, and as Emmy came in he slapped the pad crossly with the palm cf his hand.

"Mrs. Tibbett," he said without preamble, "last time we met I asked you and your husband to leave these islands alone. That was before we were hit by a severe hurricane. Do you think I have nothing better to do than waste my time on this sort of drivel?"

"Sir Alfred, it isn't drivel—it's true."

Controlling himself with an effort, the Governor said, "Just consider the facts, please. Your husband became involved officially in these islands while investigating the disappearance of a lady who had not disappeared at all." Emmy opened her mouth to protest, but he silenced her with a gesture. "He then proceeded to have a mental breakdown, in which he behaved irrationally and irresponsibly, incidentally breaking the law. Do you deny that?"

"No, but—"

"He had a miraculous escape during the first storm and entered the hospital, claiming amnesia. And now . . . *now* . . . he maintains that he has recovered his memory and comes up with the biggest taraddidle of nonsense that I've ever heard in my life. Frame-ups, police corruption, rebellion, independence from Britain, plantations of marijuana, drug capital of the world, Mafia money . . . my dear Mrs. Tibbett, you must think me very naïve. These are the ravings of a madman. Now please get out of my office, and as soon as the first plane can take off, take your husband back to England for a long convalescence, which is what he undoubtedly needs."

The Governor mopped his brow and glared at Emmy. She said, "Sir Alfred, I firmly believe that all this is true."

"Then you're as crazy as he is. There's not a shred of proof—"

"There's the *Katie-Lou,* sir. In Bob Harrison's yard. You'll see it says there that she's loaded with marijuana, and that she's to be the decoy which—"

"Mrs. Tibbett, I have tried to be both patient and fair, but—"

"The boat's there, Sir Alfred, I saw her myself. If you'd just have Inspector Ingham search her—"

"There's no question of any of my policemen being spared for such a—"

"Or Mr. Harrison. He could make a search. You can contact him on VHF radio. The dope won't be hard to find. It's supposed to be found."

The Governor gave an exasperated sigh. "Oh, very well, Mrs. Tibbett. I presume Harrison has the owner's permission to go on board."

"He must have. He's been doing repairs."

"And he isn't on your husband's list of suspects?" added Sir Alfred, with heavy irony.

"You know he's not."

"All right, I'll arrange it. Go back to the waiting room and I'll let you know what happens. I'm not denying we have a drug problem, and if we can make a good haul, I'll be happy. But you realize that even if we do, it won't prove any of Tibbett's other wild allegations."

"It'll be a beginning," said Emmy. "Thank you, Sir Alfred."

It was another hour before the secretary again entered the waiting room to tell Emmy that Sir Alfred would see her. The girl spoke in a curious way, as if with satisfaction. Emmy followed her into the Governor's office.

Pendleton was still at his desk, but he looked more relaxed. To

Emmy's surprise, Inspector Ingham was also there. Henry's notes were on the desk.

"Well, Mrs. Tibbett," the Governor said, "we went further than you asked. Inspector Ingham himself went to the yard and searched the *Katie-Lou*."

"He did?"

Slowly, Sir Alfred went on, "And he found nothing, Mrs. Tibbett. Nothing at all that would not be among the normal equipment of a cruising yacht. From Mr. Harrison he learned that Mr. and Mrs. Carstairs, the owners, had intended to return from St. Thomas today to pick up the boat—but naturally the storm has delayed them. However, the boat is repaired and ready for the water and will be launched just as soon as conditions allow."

Ingham put in, "As soon as the Carstairs let Harrison know when to expect them, he's arranging for the boat to be provisioned by Anderson, and they'll be able to take her right away. It's all perfectly straightforward."

"Of course it is," snapped Sir Alfred. "Goodness me, these poor Carstairs people have suffered enough through your husband and his crazy friends without being falsely accused of drug-running in the bargain. Mrs. Tibbett, I hope you are satisfied and that you will now go away and leave us to get on with our jobs."

There was nothing Emmy could say. She simply nodded and left the office.

The wind had dropped to little more than a strong breeze, although the sky was still overcast and rain fell steadily. It was a wet walk up the hill back to the hospital, and Emmy made it sadly, burdened by both failure and doubt. Henry's story *was* fantastic and difficult to believe. The *Katie-Lou* had seemed to be the only checkable thing about it—and that had proved to be wrong. Either that, or Henry was wrong to surmise that Inspector Ingham was on the side of the angels.

As soon as Henry saw her face, he said, "No good?"

"Worse than no good, Henry." Emmy told him the bad news.

"So what did you do?"

"What could I do? I just came away."

"What about my notes?"

"Oh . . . I never even thought. They're still on Sir Alfred's desk."

Henry thought for a moment, then said, "I don't know whether that's good or bad, but it may be important. If the wrong person sees them—"

"Who is the wrong person?"

"I wish I knew. Could be anybody. Could also trigger off some action."

"Action?"

"Against you and me and the Governor. Anybody who saw those notes. Meanwhile—" Henry suddenly broke off. "Go over again just what was said—when Ingham was there, I mean."

Emmy repeated the conversation as accurately as she could remember.

Henry threw off the sheet and climbed out of bed. "Get my clothes," he said.

Emmy said, "Don't be silly, Henry. You don't have any clothes here. You were flown over by helicopter in those awful pajamas from the Golf Club."

"This is ludicrous," said Henry. "Go and buy me some clothes, for heaven's sake."

"Henry—there aren't any shops open. You've no idea what it's like out there."

"Well, the hospital must have something. I've got to get out of here, and I can't roam the streets in green silk pajamas."

"O.K.," said Emmy. "I'll do what I can."

It proved quite difficult to get a message through to Dr. Venables in the Emergency Room, but fortunately the stream of casualties was beginning to thin out, and after half an hour or so of waiting in the corridor along with the walking-wounded, Emmy was rewarded by the appearance of Dr. Vanduren, wearing a white coat rather too small for him over his own clothes. Emmy explained her predicament, and the doctor's first reaction was, not unnaturally, a question.

"What is it that he's remembered?"

"Almost everything," Emmy said. "I can't possibly explain here and now. In essence, it's that your so-called masters have a horrifying and very ambitious plan for these islands. To engineer independence and then, in fact, to take over the islands."

Dr. Vanduren gave a small and unamused laugh. "They could do it, too," he said. "Your husband thinks he can stop them?"

"He hopes so, if he can act fast enough. In the meantime, he has to have some clothes."

"Clothes? How do you mean?"

Emmy said, "He wants to leave the hospital, and all he has is a pair of green silk pajamas. O.K., go ahead and laugh, but really it's not funny."

"Nice to have something to laugh at for a change," said the doctor. "Well, now, I don't know what I can . . . I suppose I could get him something from the hospital orderlies' cupboard in the way of white pants and a white jacket . . . no, that might be a bit conspicuous, all dressed up in hospital gear. No, say, I've had an idea. . . ."

So it was that Dr. Vanduren alias Venables finished his morning's work in the Emergency Room with nothing but his trousers under his white hospital coat, which he kept on for his jeep ride back to the hotel at lunchtime: and Henry Tibbett, strictly unofficially, discharged himself from his ward and went out into the streets of St. Mark's in white hospital trousers topped by a holiday-bright cotton shirt several sizes too large for him, bearing the label of a Miami Beach men's shop.

18

I**T WAS MIDDAY** before Henry and Emmy, on foot, made it to Bob Harrison's yard. The weather by then had definitely improved. The rain had stopped, and although the sun could not penetrate the dense cloud layer above, there was a feeling of warmth and recovery in the air. The gate of the yard was open, and the Tibbetts could see Bob making the rounds of his property and inspecting it for damage.

Considering all things, the yard had been lucky. Only one boat had been blown off its cradle, and the damage was minimal. A few mooring lines had parted, causing some boats to damage themselves by crashing against the pontoons, but Bob looked reasonably cheerful as he waved in greeting.

"Glad to see you up and around, Mr. Tibbett," he remarked. "Heard you had a bad time in *Windflower*. Haven't been able to get her off the beach as yet—what's left of her. Never fear, she's well insured."

Emmy noticed, with gratitude and relief, that Bob seemed to accept Henry's reappearance in the normal world without comment. She said, "Yes, we've all been lucky. How's the *Katie-Lou*?"

"The Carstairs' boat? Now, there's a funny thing. You'll not believe, but I had Herbert Ingham down here this morning, searching her for contraband. Beats me. Didn't find anything, of course."

Henry said, "When d'you expect the Carstairs to come and pick her up?"

Bob shrugged. "Depends on the weather. Be several days before anyone would want to put to sea, in my view. But, of course, if they're really anxious to get back to the States . . ."

"I gather," Henry said, "that Anderson is going to provision her for them."

"That's right. He does it for a lot of charter boats."

"Any news of the airport?" Henry asked.

"Pretty good, so I hear. Runways are being cleared now, and they hope to get flights operating again tomorrow."

Henry said, "My wife and I are staying at the Harbour Prospect. We're friends of the Carstairs. We'd be very grateful if you'd let us know when they are expected—that is, if you can get a message through."

"No trouble there. The telephone's working already. They tell me they hope to get the power on by this evening."

"Life goes on," said Henry, and Bob nodded in cheerful agreement.

The Tibbetts made their way back to the Harbour Prospect by the shortest route for those on foot—through the discotheque which had an entrance on Main Street. Normally it would have been closed at lunchtime, but on this unusual post-hurricane day the bar was open and doing a good trade. Henry and Emmy made their way up the now-familiar staircase at the back and through the devastated gardens to the hotel.

The dining room was open for lunch and was doing a brisk business. The level of chatter was high—everybody had a near-miss story to tell. The general verdict was that the Seawards had been extraordinarily lucky, and the atmosphere was full of the same cheerful camaraderie that prevailed during the Second World War among the survivors of an air raid. Well, we're still here. Did you hear about Mr. Harrigan's roof? I believe the Barkers lost their dinghy . . . roof's off the North End Yacht Club . . . can't drive to Turtle Bay, road's completely blocked . . . yes, old man, I tried this morning, and I can tell you . . . It was all comforting.

Henry and Emmy were just finishing lunch when Dr. Vanduren came in. He looked very tired, but his face lit up with a smile when he saw the Tibbetts. Emmy was glad to see that he had been able to change into another shirt.

He pulled a chair up to their table, sat down, and said, "Well?"

"Well what?" Emmy asked.

"Dr. Harlow is very put out," said Vanduren. "Says you had no business discharging yourself from the hospital just yet. However, he's too busy to make a big fuss. What have you found out?"

Henry was looking at Vanduren in amazement. He said, "What the hell are you doing here?"

"Didn't Emmy tell you?"

Quickly, Emmy said, "I told Henry there was a doctor here who

191

could help us. I didn't mention your name because we couldn't be sure of not being overheard."

"And the name, please, is Venables," said Vanduren. "All right, then. Let's have it. Emmy tells me—"

Henry turned to Emmy. "What have you been telling this man?"

Emmy said, "Darling, somebody has to trust somebody, or we can't get anywhere. It's taken the doctor and me a long time to come to trust each other. Right, Doctor?"

"Right, Emmy."

Henry still looked unconvinced. Emmy went on, "The doctor is here to try to find his daughter. He was mixed up in the sinister side of all this, but no longer. Henry, you have to trust him because he's the only person who can identify Janet—until that photograph arrives, which will be too late."

Henry said, "Have you had lunch, Doctor?"

"Sure. At the hospital."

"Then let's go up to our room—my wife's room, that is. We need to talk."

Henry made sure that Dr. Vanduren talked first. Allowing no interruptions or explanations from Emmy, he listened as the doctor told his story, from his daughter's presumed death to his blackmail by the Mafia to his final decision to come to the Caribbean and make an end to it all.

"And I have been trying to tell Emmy—Mrs. Tibbett—that she is too trusting, Chief Superintendent. This Governor—what do you know of him? What do you know of the Chief of Police? Maybe all these people were honest once, but with so much money at stake . . ."

Henry said, "All right. We'll trust each other. I don't like it, but there it is. How much has Emmy told you?"

"Nothing more than I've said."

"Here goes then," said Henry. He stood up and began pacing the room as he told his story. "This is what I have remembered. There may be more, but this is what we have to go on so far." He paused. "It's difficult to get this across, but you've had dealings with these people, so perhaps you won't find it so hard to believe. I overheard all this on *Windflower,* when they thought I was completely stupefied. Had I been normal, of course, I'd just have said nothing. But I was stoned and I had to make a big scene. They just laughed—they were high themselves, of course—and said that if I did tell anyone, I'd never be believed. After that, either they stepped up the dosage or I got a concussion because I simply don't remember any more."

"Well?" said Vanduren.

"The plan," Henry said, "is a takeover of these islands, no less. They've been used for some time as a staging-post for transporting drugs from Colombia to the United States, but that's small-time stuff. Your masters, as you call them, have been on the lookout for some time for a sovereign state of their own, and they plan to have it here."

"A sovereign state?"

"These islands," Henry said, "are ideal for the growing of cannabis. Why smuggle something which you can so easily raise on your own doorstep? Of course, the British Authorities wouldn't like it. So the British Authorities must go."

Vanduren said, "But that's—"

"Preposterous? Not at all. Look how many small islands have become independent recently."

"Yes, but the new government would also object to—"

"Not," said Henry, "if the new government was just a collection of puppets manipulated by organized crime."

"All right," said Vanduren. "I'll go so far as to agree that such a plan might be possible. But there are such things as elections, you know, and people are not—"

Henry said, "The people of these islands—especially the young people—are being carefully groomed, Doctor. The drug problem is very difficult to control here because the stuff is virtually being given away. It is being handed round and smoked so openly that the police are forced to make big raids—like the one at the fish fry the other night—and to arrest a lot of young people. Many of them are the children of prominent local families. The pattern is being set for a revolt against police brutality."

"Brutality? Are the police brutal?"

"No, of course not. But there will be plenty of youngsters ready to swear they are, when the big event happens."

"What big event?"

Henry said, "It would have happened already, except for several things. The first was Miss Elizabeth Sprague, God bless her. By her intelligent and courageous behavior, she set me in action. I was a bother. I was too prominent an official just to be disposed of in the usual manner. So—very cleverly—they decided to draw my fangs by destroying my credibility. I was fed PCP and kept in a state of light intoxication for a period of several days, during which I behaved with typical PCP reactions—that is, I became euphoric, irresponsible, aggressive, and apparently crazy. I was then given larger doses to produce amnesia, but by a chance that nobody could have foreseen, I was saved. Saved from death at sea in Hurricane Alfred, which I still don't understand, and saved from forgetfulness by Hurricane Beatrice. The hurricanes also played their part by knocking the Mafia's time schedule to hell. As I said, the big event would have taken place by now."

"The big event being—?"

"The brutal murder by the police of two nice young visitors, whose only crime was to smoke a little grass."

Vanduren said, "I don't understand. I thought you said the police weren't brutal."

"They're not. This was a very careful and cleverly planned operation, and we happened to walk into the middle of it. First, there was the fish fry. The police were virtually dragooned into taking action by an anonymous tipoff, and anything so openly lawless had to be investigated. As many young people as possible were set up to be arrested. They were busted for smoking pot and taking other drugs, questioned, and released on bail. Many, if not all of them, in the forthcoming atmosphere of hysteria, will swear that they were mistreated by the police."

"All right. What about step number two?"

"That didn't go according to plan," Henry said, "thanks to the intervention of Miss Betsy Sprague. To go back a little, the *Chermar*—crewed by your daughter and her friend posing as the late Mr. and Mrs. Ross—had brought a cargo of drugs to St. Mark's, much of it for distribution at the fish fry. They were preparing to depart and scuttle the ship as usual, when Betsy turned up and identified Janet. That meant that she had to be disposed of. The obvious thing was to kill her and let her go down with the boat—but her absence would soon have been noticed, and that might have triggered off police actions and suspicions just when they weren't wanted—at the start of step two, in fact. So, using PCP, they put her into a state of amnesia for a couple of days and then sent her home. If Betsy hadn't made that telephone call to me—and if Miss Pelling's niece hadn't been allergic to cats—that would have been that. But as it was, I came into the picture."

"And put a spanner in the works?"

"Not really," said Henry, with regret. "I wish I had. I turned up, nosing around after Betsy and getting myself officially appointed to investigate her disappearance. Too bad. That was really annoying for the masters. So they decided not only to put me out of action and beyond the bounds of credibility, but actually to use me in their scheme." Henry paused. "I must say, they are very ingenious."

"I can think of a harsher word," said Dr. Vanduren. "Go on."

"Well," said Henry, "to go back to step two. The idea was to alert the police that a private yacht was carrying a large cargo of marijuana from St. Mark's to the United States."

"To alert them? How?"

"By using a childishly simple radio code. By leaving obvious clues around."

"How could they be sure the police would pick up the clues?"

"Because at least one member of the force," Henry said, "is actively working for the Mafia. O.K. You have the picture so far. First, the bust at the fish fry. Then the chase at sea of the suspected yacht. What happens? Plenty happens. The police launch locates the boat and hails it. The boat does not respond. After repeated warnings, the launch draws up alongside the boat, and officers board her. They find an extraordinary situation—a sort of *Marie Celeste*. A certain amount of marijuana, but not very much." To Emmy, Henry said, "I got that all wrong at first, darling. There'll only be a little on the *Katie-Lou*." He went on. "More importantly, they find the bodies of two young people, a man and a girl, beaten to death. The police try to radio a report back to St. Mark's but find that their radio is out of action, as is the one on the boat they have boarded. All they can do is take the boat in tow and bring her back to St. Mark's with her gruesome cargo. And tell their story."

Vanduren snorted. "Which nobody will believe."

"Exactly. Certain facts will be beyond dispute: that the *Katie-Lou* was suspected of carrying marijuana; that she was hailed and ignored police warnings, and so was arrested by force; that only a small quantity of marijuana was found; and that no radio report was made at the time. Also that the bodies of two American citizens, Katherine and Lewis Carstairs, were on board when the yacht was towed into St. Mark's, and that they had been brutally assaulted and killed. The police launch carries three officers. The two who boarded the boat will have only each other's word for what happened. The third officer, who remained on the launch, will have a different story to tell. This officer will report that the radio was never out of operation, that strange noises and cries came from the boarded yacht, that the other two officers spent the journey back concocting their story—you can imagine. There will be uproar—just the sort of situation to set off a revolution. There will be plenty of money and also weapons for the insurgents. The responsible politicians of the island will find it impossible to get their voices heard. When the dust clears, the islands will be independent and in the hands of the right people—from the Mafia's point of view. After that, the rest will be easy and extremely difficult to undo."

There was a long pause. Then Vanduren said, "Who will the dead couple actually be, do you know?"

"Katherine and Lewis Carstairs, of course," said Henry. "Their families will naturally identify them."

"But—"

"At the moment," Henry said, "they are calling themselves Jill and Harvey Blackstone—fictitious names—having been induced by money or drugs or both to switch identities temporarily with a young couple who had been smuggled illegally onto the island. We have been given a picture of the Carstairs as thoroughly respectable. In fact, they are well-to-do, but disreputable and deeply into drugs. However, the point is that they are at this moment being held prisoner somewhere. They will not be killed, you see, until just the right moment—that is, when your daughter and her friend leave the boat, and before the police arrive."

Quietly, Dr. Vanduren said, "Then we have to find them."

"We have to find them, and we have to abort the whole scheme," said Henry. "God, to think that we have all this information and not a soul will listen to us. The Governor and the Chief of Police have already strongly requested that Emmy and I leave the islands and never come back."

Emmy said, "At least the Governor has read your notes."

"Yes, and dismissed them as the ravings of a lunatic. I'm very lucky not to be in jail or a mental hospital. If it wasn't for the hurricane, I daresay I would be."

"Yes," said Vanduren, "Beatrice was a blessing in disguise, wasn't she?"

"In a way," Henry said, "but she's also tied up every police officer and other official on the islands. Anything we do, Doctor, we have to do on our own."

Emmy said, "By the way, does anybody have any money?"

There was a blank silence. Then Henry said, "I certainly don't. I don't even own the clothes I'm wearing. I thought you—"

"I have nineteen dollars and twenty-five cents," said Emmy, "and my bill here at the hotel must be well over a hundred already—not to mention the hospital and doctors' fees and—"

Dr. Vanduren held up his hand. "Please, please. Don't worry. It will give me the greatest pleasure to use some of the Mafia's own money to help outwit them. Allow me to take over the treasury."

"You're very kind," Henry said. "We'll repay you, of course."

"You'll do no such thing. I'm not about to accept honest money to replace . . . well, never mind. Forget about money. The thing is—where do we start?"

Henry said, "We start at the airport. We have to watch every flight as it comes in to know when the so-called Carstairs return to the Seawards. That's a job I think I shall have to do because Emmy only saw the couple once, in a darkened nightclub. I saw enough of them, I can assure you, never to forget their faces. You, Doctor, and Emmy must try to locate the real Carstairs. Obviously, they are on this island. I don't know how they were taken off the *Windflower* or by whom. My recollections are extremely hazy—I was heavily drugged by then. I know there were the five of us to start with, and then—" Henry passed his hand over his forehead. "Damn it, I *must* remember. The Carstairs . . . wait a moment . . . the Carstairs went ashore at St. Thomas in the dinghy. We were to wait for them at anchor. Jill and Harvey had been dropping acid—LSD—and were very high. And then the Carstairs came back . . . no, they didn't . . . somebody came aboard."

"Who?" asked Emmy. "You must remember who."

"I don't. I never saw who it was. I was down below . . . I don't remember any more until I woke up in hospital. The hurricane . . . everything . . . it's gone. But somebody was on that boat, and somebody sailed her back to St. Matthew's, beached her, and disappeared, along with the so-called Blackstones." He paused. "Beached her *before* the hurricane. Of course. That's how it was done. Everybody was much too preoccupied making preparations to notice a boat going ashore in an isolated bay. Then the Blackstones must have been taken ashore on St. Matthew's and brought over here during the lull between the storms. I've an idea—it's no more, but we have to start somewhere—two ideas, in fact, about where they might be. We'll have to split up, so we must arrange a series of rendezvous. Who's got a map of the island?"

Nobody had, but the front desk was glad to supply the whimsily drawn pamphlet that they gave to visitors. Henry laid it on the table and took up a pencil. "Now," he said, "here's the airport, and here's . . ."

The three heads bent earnestly over the little colored map. Outside the rain still fell, ambulances still wailed along near-impassable roads, and the enormous task of cleaning up began. In the bar downstairs, more near-miss stories circulated, more drinks were drunk, and the hurricane already seemed history. Only to the bereaved, to the relatives waiting at the hospital for news, to the exhausted salvage workers, to the Governor, to Inspector Ingham, and to the three people in the hotel bedroom did things seem to be as anxious and as desperate as ever.

19

LIFE WAS RETURNING to normal. The telephones were working again and electric power was expected by the evening. The desk clerk informed Emmy that limited numbers of flights in and out of the island were due to start later in the afternoon. The road to the airport had been given priority as far as repairs were concerned and was now open for at least one-lane traffic. Emmy called the taxi stand and asked for Shark Tooth. He answered in great good humor and told her that both he and his taxi had escaped damage in the hurricane. Certainly he would drive her husband out to the airport and then return to take her . . . where?

"I don't really know, Shark Tooth," Emmy said. "I'll explain when I see you."

Shark Tooth laughed richly. "Never had a fare like you, my dear," he said. "Mystery lady, eh? O.K. then. Be seeing you."

When Henry had departed for the airport, Dr. Vanduren set off on foot for the marina. Emmy waited in the lobby until the ever-smiling Shark Tooth reappeared, reporting that the road was rough but passable, and that he had delivered Henry safely. The airport, Shark Tooth said, was crammed with people trying to leave the island. Nobody seemed to know when flights would start, but the runway was in fair condition, and rumor had it that a plane from St. Thomas would soon be landing.

"And now, mystery lady, where we going?"

Emmy climbed into the back of the taxi and said, "I'm looking for a house. Up in the hills above the harbor—quite a bit higher than the hotel. I've only been there once, at night."

"Know whose house it is?"

"A woman called Pearletta Terry lives there. A policewoman."

199

"Sure, I know Pearletta's house. Matter of fact, I been there many time." Shark Tooth sounded positively disappointed that the mystery had proved so easy to solve. "O.K., let's go."

"D'you think the road—?"

"We'll try," said Shark Tooth.

The first portion of the road above the hotel was concrete and in fairly good order. Higher up, however, the steep dirt road deteriorated sharply, and the taxi struggled through deep ruts carved by torrents of rainwater. Emmy began to protest, but Shark Tooth grinned and grunted and gunned the engine and kept going. At last, however, a big tree that had fallen squarely across the road brought him to a halt.

Shark Tooth got out of the car and pointed upward. "There's the house," he said. "You can make it on foot from here." He paused. "Nobody there, I reckon. Nobody come up or down this road since the hurricane."

Emmy said, "Can you turn the car around?"

"Sure."

"Well, I'll go up on foot. You turn around and wait for me."

"O.K., my dear."

It was hard-going, scrambling over the fallen tree and on up the ruined road, but within a few minutes Emmy was standing outside the little house on its outcrop of rock, looking down at the harbor which, from this height, looked astonishingly normal. Emmy knocked loudly on the door.

Everything was silent and deserted. Emmy tried the door. It was unlocked. She pushed it open and went into the cheerful room that she remembered from her last visit.

Now, it was far from cheerful. The big plate-glass window that overlooked the sea had been smashed by the force of the wind. The careful Pearletta had taped it so that broken glass would not fly about—but its shattered remnants hung dismally, suspended by webs of thick paper tape. With the window gone, Beatrice had had a high old time with the furniture and fittings. Everything was awry and overturned—lamps smashed, chairs rolled over, papers everywhere. Pearletta was not going to have a very pleasant homecoming.

Emmy stepped inside. She called as loudly as she could, "Is anybody here?"

Silence. She began opening doors—a tiny, neat kitchen, a small bedroom, and a bathroom. All empty. In the bedroom closet, a spare police uniform and a selection of bright, pretty dresses arranged on hangers under plastic covers.

Feeling like a Peeping Tom, Emmy went back to the living room and began picking up some of the papers that had blown around. Among them was a small diary for the current year. The entries were mostly in the type of shorthand that people use when recording information for themselves alone. There were initials with times, indicating meetings—the letter *D* with four-hour spans, which Emmy took to mean spells of duty. On certain recent dates, which Emmy could recall, came the entry *SF,* with a time. So these were Pearletta's own loggings of the *Starfish* messages. Emmy turned the page and saw another of them. *D 8–12. SF 10.* She looked at the date. Tomorrow. *Tomorrow* . . . Emmy hesitated, wondering whether to take the diary with her, then decided against it. Henry had emphasized that she should leave no trace of her visit.

Next she went over to the shattered window and looked out onto the balcony, which hung out over the crag like a platform in space. There had been a couple of wicker chairs out there and a small table—all now twisted and wrecked by the hurricane. But there was something else, too. Broken and useless now, it lay among the debris—a small telescope that had been mounted on a tripod. A telescope through which one could look from this eagle's nest down at both the harbor and the marina. Emmy took her handkerchief and carefully polished any surfaces or doorknobs that she had touched. Then she left the house and went to rejoin Shark Tooth and his gallant cab. He dropped her back at the hotel and went off to the airport again to rejoin Henry.

At half-past four, Emmy and Dr. Vanduren met by arrangement in the hotel lounge. The doctor seemed jubilant.

"She's there," he announced.

"The *Ocean Rover*?"

"The same. I managed to get into conversation with the woman. As far as I could tell, she was alone on board. Say what you like about hurricanes, they do break the ice. Everybody was talking to everybody else. She told me they'd been lucky—got into St. Matthew's just before Alfred struck and slipped across to St. Mark's between the storms."

"That would fit," Emmy said.

"I mentioned that I'd heard that at least one boat had been lost—the *Windflower*."

"Any reaction?"

"Complete vagueness. She'd heard something about it—must have been a charter boat, she supposed. Then she changed the subject."

"I wonder—" Emmy began, but was interrupted by the girl from the desk.

"There's a telephone call for you, Mrs. Tibbett."

Henry's voice came urgently down the line. "They're here. The plane from St. Thomas just got in, and they're on it. No, don't worry, they haven't seen me. They're not through Customs and Immigration yet. I'm leaving now—expect me in half an hour or so."

Emmy made her way back to Dr. Vanduren. She said, "They've arrived."

The doctor's euphoria evaporated abruptly. He said heavily, "Janet? Is it Janet? Ah, well, we'll soon know. Is Henry tailing them?"

"Nothing so obvious. He's left the airport ahead of them. But he's pointed them out to Shark Tooth, who's going to make sure he brings them into town. Then he'll report to us where they are."

"Can you trust this man—this driver?"

Emmy shrugged. "Here we go again. I think so. I can't say more. I found him quite by chance, and he's been helpful and discreet up to now and prepared to do what I ask without question. You spoke to Dr. Harlow, did you?"

Vanduren nodded. "He wasn't happy, as you can imagine, but he's agreed to leave the screens around Henry's bed and not notify the hospital office until tomorrow that he's discharged himself."

"So that anybody calling the hospital would be told that Henry was still a patient there?"

"That's right."

By five-fifteen Henry was back from the airport, and it was only ten minutes or so later that Shark Tooth called Emmy.

"Marina," he said succinctly. "Lady made a phone call from the airport, then I drove them to the marina. They gone into Reception, booking a room most like. O.K.?"

"O.K.," said Emmy. "Thank you very much. Any conversation in the cab?"

"A bit. Something about a boat being ready tomorrow."

"Thanks a lot, Shark Tooth."

"That's O.K., my dear. You want me again this evening?"

"Hold on a moment. I'll ask Henry."

Emmy made her report. There was a quick conference, and she

went back to the telephone. "Yes, Shark Tooth. Can you come up here in about half an hour? We're going to the marina."

Henry's next move was a telephone call to Bob Harrison, whom he caught just as the latter was leaving his yard for the day.

"Mr. Harrison? This is Chief Inspector Henry Tibbett. You may know I'm here officially on an investigation, and two of our suspects have a boat in your yard, which they plan to take away tomorrow. Now I know this is an unusual request, but . . ."

The harbor entrance lights were twinkling red and green in the dusk when the Tibbetts and Dr. Vanduren arrived at the marina. The restaurant and bar looked inviting, with ships' lanterns glowing on the tables, and there was a light in the Harbour Master's office. Henry and Emmy waited in the shadows on the quayside while Dr. Vanduren approached the Reception desk. He spoke to the clerk, then came back to the Tibbetts.

"Yes, they checked in, just for the night. Now they've gone out again, and the girl said she saw them walking down the pontoon, looking at the boats."

Emmy said, "*Ocean Rover.*"

"I guess so." Vanduren took a deep breath. "Well, I guess I'd better go and get it over. You'll be there?"

"Out of sight but within earshot," Henry said. And then, "Good luck, Doctor."

Vanduren walked away in the direction of *Ocean Rover,* like a man going to the gallows. Henry and Emmy followed at a discreet distance and stationed themselves so that they were hidden by a moored boat, as close to the Montgomerys' yacht as possible. Golden lamplight spilled out through the open hatchway and into the cockpit.

"*Ocean Rover,* ahoy!" Vanduren's voice did not falter. Without waiting for an answer, he went on, "Sorry to disturb you. Can I come aboard? There's something—"

He was in the cockpit already and disappearing down the companionway into the cabin. For a moment there was silence. Then Henry heard him say, "Janet!"

And a girl's voice, slow and slurred but apparently unsurprised, said, "Hi, Dad."

Montgomery's voice, loud and full of bluster, began to boom astonished platitudes, but he was cut short by his wife. In her deep and unmistakable tones she said, "Shut up, William. Let me handle this. So you are Dr. Vanduren, the Florida connection? Close the hatch, William. There's talking to be done, and you never know who may be listening."

The hatch door slammed and there was silence. Henry and Emmy were already halfway up the pontoon, heading back to Shark Tooth and his taxi. As they passed his office, Elwin Anderson came to the door and stood framed against the light.

"Mr. Tibbett!" he said. "They told me you were in the hospital."

"I was," said Henry shortly.

The Harbour Master seemed about to say something else, but changed his mind. "O.K. then." He went back to his desk.

Henry and Emmy got into the taxi. "Police station, please, Shark Tooth."

"Police, is it now?" The driver grinned. "Beats me which side of the law you people are on."

Pearletta Terry was on duty at the desk in the outer office of the police station. She greeted the Tibbetts with a charming smile, although she looked very tired. She was sorry, however, but there was no chance of them seeing Inspector Ingham. No, he was not off-duty—they had all been working round the clock since the hurricane—but he was out on an incident, and she had no idea when he would be back. Perhaps . . .

Henry was past her and at Ingham's door before she could get to her feet to stop him. Ignoring her squeaks of protest, he threw open the door to reveal Herbert Ingham, his feet up on his desk, with a cup of coffee in one hand and a telephone in the other.

"Tibbett! What on earth—?"

Pearletta was hovering in the background. "I'm sorry, sir. I did as you said, but—"

"All right, Pearletta. Get back to your desk and be a bit more efficient next time." Ingham sounded like a man at the end of his tether. Then, to the telephone, "Yes, it is true, Sir Alfred, and what's more he's just come bursting into my office . . . yes, both of them . . . all right, sir, I'll call you back."

He slammed down the receiver. "Now, what do you want . . . sir?" He made the last word sound like an insult.

Henry said, "You've got to listen to me, Ingham. I've got proof now."

Ingham sighed. He said, "And I've got a warrant for your arrest and deportation, signed by the Governor. Don't you think we've got enough troubles on this island, without—"

Emmy said quietly, "Please, Inspector Ingham. Henry is right—you must listen to him. Even if you don't believe everything

204

he says, there's a double or triple murder that we can prevent if you help us now. You're a policeman. You can't just sit back and let two youngsters be killed."

For a long moment, Ingham looked from Henry to Emmy and back. Then he said, "Proof? What proof?"

"I'm not asking you," Henry said, "to take my unsupported word for anything. I know my credibility is in shreds, and I don't blame you for thinking I'm still crazy. So what I'm going to do is this. I'm going to tell you what is going to happen tomorrow."

Ingham raised his eyebrows. Crazy, he seemed to imply, was the word.

Henry went on. "At ten o'clock or thereabouts tomorrow, another *Starfish* message will come in. Pearletta Terry will be on duty, and she will log it and report it to you. This time, it will be very much more explicit than the previous ones. It will mention a boat, the *Katie-Lou*. It will make it perfectly clear that she is carrying—"

Ingham broke in. "My dear Tibbett, we searched the *Katie-Lou* this morning! She's—"

"I know. I made a mistake because my memory was still playing tricks. In fact, there will be a small quantity of marijuana on board, but the *Starfish* message will imply that it is a big and important cargo. It will also mention a specific rendezvous, probably for the afternoon. Naturally, you'll send your police launch to intercept the yacht. That is, you would do so if you didn't know what I'm telling you now—that the whole thing is a frame-up. Now, wait a moment"— Ingham was showing signs of interrupting—"all I'm asking is this. If things happen as I've said, if that message comes through as I've told you it will, will you believe me and take action at once? Before the *Katie-Lou* sails, in fact?"

Ingham said, "If such a message comes through, the *Katie-Lou* will already be at sea."

Henry shook his head. "No. She won't be ready."

"How do you know?"

"I just have the feeling. She'll still be at Harrison's yard."

"But the message—"

Impatiently, Henry said, "The message isn't intended for the *Katie-Lou,* for heaven's sake, man. It's intended for you. And if you fall for it, it'll be the end of your personal career, let alone a lot of other things. I don't suppose that photograph of Janet Vanduren arrived from England, did it?"

"Of course not—there's been no mail for over a week. In any

case, it's of no further interest. Miss Sprague is alive and well, and Miss Vanduren is dead."

Henry sighed. "I won't say any more for the moment," he said. "Will you let me go back to my hotel now and call me in the morning when that message comes through?"

"*If* the message comes through."

"You will, then?"

"Oh, very well. Get out of my office, if you please. Sir." Suddenly Ingham grinned, a flashback to his old self. "Man, what am I going to tell the Governor?"

Henry grinned back. "Tell him that you're too busy to arrest me now, but that you'll do it in the morning. Tell him that I'm at the Harbour Prospect with my wife, behaving myself like a good boy, and that I'm planning to leave on the first possible flight, which is what he really wants. See you tomorrow."

Pearletta Terry gave the Tibbetts a distinctly unfriendly look as they walked out through her office to the street, where Shark Tooth was patiently waiting.

Henry said, "Just down to the marina again, Shark Tooth, to pick up our friend, and then back up to the hotel."

The marina bar was a blaze of light, but the Harbour Master's office was dark. The sky was still cloudy, and big seas rolled in from the channel. There was no sign of Dr. Vanduren. In the protective darkness, Henry and Emmy made their way down the pontoon, hoping to get close enough to *Ocean Rover* to hear what was going on on board, even with the cabin doors closed. However, they need not have bothered to take any precautions against being seen, for when they got to the end of the jetty, the mooring was empty. *Ocean Rover* had put to sea.

Emmy turned to Henry in dismay. "What's happened? They've all gone—the Montgomerys and Janet and her father—"

"And the unfortunate Carstairs with them, if I'm not mistaken," said Henry. "But not, I hope, very far."

"What do you mean?"

"Well, as you said, we have to trust somebody, and we decided it was to be Dr. Vanduren. Of course, if he's been secretly on their side all along, then they'll be heading away from Seawards waters and it'll be too late to save the Carstairs. But if Vanduren is playing his cards right, then I think this is all part of the prearranged plan. I think we shall find *Ocean Rover* at Bob Harrison's yard. Come on."

For the second time, much to Shark Tooth's amusement, his cab approached Harrison's yard in the darkness. Peering through the wire fence, Emmy could see that *Katie-Lou* was no longer ashore on a cradle; she had obviously been put back into the water, awaiting the arrival of her owners. However, her whereabouts was not important for the moment. What was important was that the now-familiar silhouette of the *Ocean Rover* was clearly visible. She had not taken a berth, but was riding at anchor in the small bay, her dinghy trailed astern of her and a light was on in her cabin.

Henry sighed with relief. "Thank God for that. Let's hope that Bob keeps his promise and delays *Katie-Lou* in the morning."

20

HALF-PAST FIVE in the morning. The very first strands of light were creeping across the sky, turning it from black to palest pearly gray, when Henry awoke. Emmy was sleeping serenely beside him in their room at the hotel. No hurry now, he had said the night before, after telephoning Bob Harrison. They won't be able to leave until after ten, after the *Starfish* message. By then, Ingham will be convinced. The Carstairs are safe for the moment. Nothing we can do.

But now, Henry woke with a sudden sense of urgency, an instinct that his colleagues had often described as his "nose." It even crossed his mind that some sort of heightened perception—a remnant of his drug experience—might still be affecting his mind. Perhaps he had miscalculated, had been wrong to trust Vanduren and Bob Harrison. Whatever it was, he found himself wide awake and absolutely certain that something was wrong. He hesitated a moment, then woke Emmy.

"What . . . ?" Emmy struggled back to consciousness and looked at her watch. "Half-past five? Henry, what on earth—?"

"I don't know, darling. I just know that we have to get down there."

"Down there?" A ripple of alarm ran through Emmy's heart. She remembered that PCP can cause aftereffects, which recur even days after the last dose. Certainly Henry did not sound rational at the moment.

He said, "To the yacht yard. There's something wrong."

"But Henry—"

"Come on. Get up and dressed. There's no time to lose."

Emmy did not argue. In ten minutes they were both dressed and in the deserted hotel lobby. No smiling Shark Tooth and his taxi at

208

this hour, and the big front doors to the hotel were locked. However, ringing a bell marked NIGHT PORTER eventually produced a yawning black man, who opened the doors for them.

Outside, it was getting light with the suddenness of a tropical sunrise, reminding Emmy of the morning when she had seen Dr. Vanduren in St. Matthew's. As in a nightmare, time had stretched so that the days before the first hurricane seemed eons ago.

Henry said, "Down through the gardens. Quickest way."

There was no question, of course, of going through the locked and shuttered discotheque; however, a garden fence—not too difficult to negotiate—led to a narrow alley and eventually onto Main Street. From there, ten minutes' hard walking brought them within sight of St. Mark's Yacht Charter Services.

Everything seemed quiet and still, but as the Tibbetts approached the gate, Henry suddenly grabbed Emmy's arm.

"Stop!" he whispered. "Somebody's moving about in there!"

They froze in their tracks. Then they heard Dr. Vanduren's voice. He was making no effort to keep it low, obviously believing the place to be deserted. "Hi, Ed! I can't find one here. I'll have to try in that other shed. Back in a minute."

A moment later, Vanduren appeared, hurrying and dodging among the shrouded shapes of grounded boats. He reached Bob Harrison's office, and Henry saw him wrestling unsuccessfully with the locked door. On impulse, Henry stepped up to the wire fence and said in an urgent whisper, "Vanduren!"

The doctor whirled around, terrified. Then he recognized Henry and hurried over to the fence. "Tibbett! Is this a miracle or an answer to a prayer?"

"Both, I suspect. What's up?"

"I've only got a minute or so. Make this quick. Jan and Ed are on board *Katie-Lou. Ocean Rover* came round here last night. Ed boarded *Katie-Lou* for a checkout and found something wrong with the engine. We've been up all night fixing it. It'll be done in a few minutes. I'm supposed to be finding a plug wrench."

"But—"

"Don't interrupt. I don't have time. They're not waiting for Harrison to arrive. They've smelled a rat and as soon as the engine's fixed we'll all be away. Jan and Ed on *Katie-Lou,* the Montgomerys, the Carstairs—poor devils—and myself on *Ocean Rover.* Message goes out at ten."

"Where's the rendezvous?"

"Don't know. They didn't say and I didn't dare ask."

"How about you?"

"I think they believe I'm with them, but I've got to get back and act natural. Get this. The real rendezvous will be at half-past two, somewhere not far from the bogus one, obviously. That's when the Carstairs will be killed and put aboard *Katie-Lou,* while *Ocean Rover* makes off with the rest of us."

A man's voice called, "Hey, Doc, how's it coming?"

Vanduren shouted. "I'm trying to get this goddamn door open!" Whispering, he added, "There's a telephone and radio in the office. I was trying to get a message to you. Got to go now." He disappeared.

Henry and Emmy moved quietly away until they were out of sight and earshot of the yard. Henry said, "You were right. He is to be trusted."

"What do we do now?"

"They'll be off in no time. Somebody's got to go after them, or those two young idiots will be as dead as mutton."

"Inspector Ingham—?"

"You think he'd believe a story like this at six in the morning from *me*? Anyhow, even if he did, there's no time." Henry thought quickly. Then he said, "Unsatisfactory, but it's the only way. As soon as the boats leave, we break into Harrison's office. I take the keys to his launch and go after *Ocean Rover*—at a safe distance. My guess is they'll be under sail—make everything appear natural—so they'll be in sight for some time. You get on the telephone to Ingham and convince him if you can—otherwise we have to wait until the *Starfish* message at ten, which will certainly get him. Meanwhile, I'll keep in radio touch with you from Harrison's launch. Just remember though that everyone listening out in the Seawards will be able to hear what we say."

"Henry—"

"There's nothing else we can do. Dammit, we ought to have the whole police force and the U.S. Coast Guard and everybody else down here arresting these people, but so long as the authorities think I'm crazy, well . . . there you are. Listen!"

In the quiet of the morning, they heard the unmistakable sound of an auxiliary engine turning over, spluttering, then starting. A man's voice called out something unintelligible. Henry and Emmy arrived back at the wire fence in time to see an apparently serene and beautiful early-morning scene. Two graceful sailing yachts, their motors running quietly, puttering away from the yacht moorings and out into the bay against the light breeze, with trim and energetic crew members hoisting the big mainsails as they went. Not a sight to cause anything but appreciation and possibly envy in these delectable islands. Not, by any normal standard, in the least sinister.

"O.K.," said Henry. "Here we go. Over the fence."

"You lift me up first, and I'll find a ladder," said Emmy briskly. "I've done this before. E. Tibbett, the well-known breaker and enterer." Five minutes later they were both inside the compound.

The office—a small wooden building—was padlocked, but it proved a reasonably simple job to lever off the hinges with a stout chisel, which a workman had thoughtfully left beside one of the boats. The launch's keys were hanging on a board, labeled with the boat's name—MARK ONE—as though for the convenience of burglars. Emmy would have liked to wish Henry luck, to caution him, to get final instructions, even to kiss him for what might be the last time; but he was in and out of the office in five seconds flat, leaving her facing a telephone and a VHF radio, which she had no idea how to operate. She sat down at the desk and went into action.

Her first call was to the police station. An unfamiliar male voice informed her that Inspector Ingham was at home, snatching the first bit of rest he had had since Beatrice struck.

Emmy said, "Are you listening out on VHF?"

There was a moment of silence and then the voice said, "Sure, lady."

"There will be some messages from *Mark One*. Would you please be sure to log them? I may call you back and ask about them if I miss them myself."

"Who is this speaking?"

"Bob Harrison's yard," said Emmy, and she hung up quickly.

She looked at the radio with some trepidation and was relieved to see a simple-looking switch marked OFF-ON, and another marked RECEIVE-TRANSMIT. She set this to RECEIVE and switched on. Sure enough, she was rewarded by a crackling sound from the loudspeaker. And then Henry's distorted voice.

"*Mark One* to *Blandish*. *Mark One* to *Blandish*. Are you receiving me? Over."

Blandish was Emmy's maiden name. She switched to TRANSMIT, picked up the microphone, and said, "*Blandish* to *Mark One*. Loud and clear. Over." Decades ago, Emmy had been a controller in the wartime W.A.A.F. It was extraordinary how the years slipped away, how easy it was to be talking into a microphone again.

"*Mark One* to *Blandish*. Everything set for a good day's sail. I'll be in touch later. Out."

Emmy put the set back on RECEIVE and picked up the telephone again. This time she called Inspector Ingham's home number, which she found in the directory on Bob's desk. A soft-voiced lady answered.

"Inspector Ingham? Oh, he's just got to sleep. Unless it's really urgent . . . my husband has been . . ."

"I know he has, Mrs. Ingham," Emmy said, "but this really *is* urgent. I'm so sorry. Please tell him it's Mrs. Tibbett and I must speak to him."

Ingham's voice was sleepy and unfriendly. "Really, Mrs. Tibbett . . . ten o'clock this message is supposed to come through . . ."

"I know, Inspector, but things have changed. The *Katie-Lou* has left, and Henry's gone after her."

"He's—*what*?"

"I'm speaking from Bob Harrison's yard. Henry has borrowed Bob's launch and—"

"Mrs. Tibbett, I'm sorry. I may as well tell you that I've just had a call from Dr. Harlow, telling me that your husband discharged himself from hospital against medical advice and that his mental condition is probably still far from stable. If I get that *Starfish* message, naturally I will investigate it. Otherwise . . ." The line went dead.

It was by then nearly seven o'clock and the sun was up in a clear sky. Emmy dialed the number of Bob Harrison's home.

"Bob?"

"You just missed 'im." The woman's voice was pure London, quite unaffected by her move to this exotic clime. "Just left for the yard, 'e 'as. You'll catch 'im there in a few minutes."

"On the contrary, he'll catch me," Emmy thought, but aloud she said, "Thanks so much. I'll find him at the yard."

Then to the radio again. "*Blandish* to *Mark One*. *Blandish* to *Mark One*. Are you receiving me? Over."

"*Mark One* to *Blandish*. Loud and clear. Over."

"*Blandish* to *Mark One*. I'm afraid Herbert can't join the picnic, at least not until later on. Over."

"*Mark One* to *Blandish*. Never mind. I hope he manages to come later. He'd hate to miss it. Out."

Henry sounded positively cheerful. Indeed, against all logic, he was enjoying himself. *Mark One* was a sweet-running, beautifully maintained boat, and there was enough sheer pleasure in being on the water on a gold-and-silver morning to create a sensation of well-being. Also, he felt that his makeshift plans were succeeding quite well. He had radio contact with Emmy, and she had access to a telephone. He also had the two sailing yachts, *Katie-Lou* and *Ocean Rover,* well in view, while keeping far enough away not to attract their attention. He idled the motor and gave as good an imitation of fishing as could be done with no fishing tackle. His quarry had set sail due west, toward St. Matthew's, with a light wind astern. For the moment, nobody else seemed to be on the water. Henry had only to wait.

Bob Harrison's jeep pulled up outside the boatyard at twenty past seven. He was still fiddling with the key in the padlock on the gate when Emmy came out of the office.

"Mrs. Tibbett! How did you get in there?" Bob was genuinely astonished. "What's happening, then? Pity about *Katie-Lou*'s motor going on the blink," he added, with a grin and a wink.

Emmy said, "I'm afraid things haven't gone according to plan, Mr. Harrison."

"Bob."

"Sorry. Bob. They came into the yard last night in another boat, went aboard to check up, and found the engine wouldn't work. They've been up all night repairing it, and they left at about half-past six."

"Did they indeed?" Bob had opened the gate and was now inside. "Left without paying and broken into the office, too, by the look of it."

"No," Emmy said. "I'm afraid that was—"

"Well, if they're dangerous as well as dishonest, as Mr. Tibbett says, the thing to do is to go after 'em," said Bob. "Even if they're motoring. They can't do more than five or six knots with that little auxiliary. I'll get *Mark One*—"

"Bob," said Emmy. "I'm trying to tell you. Henry's already done that."

"Done what?"

"He . . . we broke into your office, and Henry's taken *Mark One* and gone after *Katie-Lou*."

Bob looked at her for a long moment, and Emmy was afraid that there might be an explosion. Then he said, "Has he, then? Does he know how to manage her?"

"He's done a lot of boating," Emmy said. "More sail than power, but he knows what he's doing, and we're in radio touch."

"You are?"

"On your radio," Emmy explained.

"Thank you very much," said Bob. "Perhaps you'd like to help yourself to my jeep and the petty cash while you're about it?"

"Bob, I—"

This time there was an explosion, but it was in the form of a bellow of laughter. "It's all right, my dear. Only joking. I don't suppose you'd like to tell me the whole story behind this, would you?"

Emmy said, "I'd love to and I will. But you may not believe me."

"Try me," said Bob.

"O.K. Well, it's like this . . ."

At the end of Emmy's recital, Bob scratched his head and said, "I can believe it. Thousands wouldn't, but I know these parts. A lot of youngsters here are getting . . . well, restless, like. The islands are too small for them, and they want a bit of excitement. Then there's the drug bit—smoking and snorting and all. You can't really blame the kids. They read about it and hear about it and it seems glamorous and the thing to do. But it didn't happen here on its own. Someone's behind it—someone with a lot of money."

"Organized crime," said Emmy.

"Well that wouldn't make sense if it was just to get the youngsters here hooked on pot," said Bob. "It's been puzzling a lot of us, and your story makes sense of what's going on."

"Of course," Emmy said, "the big boys don't appear down here. Too conspicuous. Their local representatives are the Montgomerys—"

"What?" Bob was scandalized. "The Colonel? Everybody knows him—"

"Exactly," Emmy said. "I'm reasonably sure he was never a Colonel and I doubt if he's even British. His wife certainly isn't. They've built up a very pretty façade, and their boat can act as mother-ship on these smuggling operations without attracting attention. On the island, the chief contact is—"

The radio crackled, and Henry's voice said, *"Mark One to Blandish. Mark One to Blandish. Over."*

Bob looked at Emmy inquiringly and raised his eyebrows. She said, "Blandish is me," and switched to TRANSMIT. *"Blandish to Mark One. Receiving you. Bob has joined the party. Over."*

"Mark One to Blandish. Good. Hope he enjoys himself. By the way, Bernie and Abby aren't together any longer. I'm sticking with Bernie. Out."

Emmy and Bob looked at each other for a moment. Then Emmy

said, "I see. Bernie is Montgomery—Monty's first name was Bernard. And Abby must be Dear Abby, Abigail Vanburen—which is near enough to Vanduren to mean Janet. The boats have parted company, and Henry is sticking with *Ocean Rover* because that's where the prisoners are being held."

The next radio message, which came through just after eight o'clock, was something of a surprise. A female voice. "*Katie-Lou* to *Starfish*. Are you receiving me? Over."

Mrs. Montgomery's voice was perfectly identifiable. "*Starfish* to *Katie-Lou*. Receiving you. Over."

"*Katie-Lou* to *Starfish*. I suggest we either abort mission or bring timing forward. Over."

Emmy exclaimed, "That can't be Janet Vanduren! That's not an American voice!"

After a moment of crackling silence, the radio spoke again. "*Starfish* to *Katie-Lou*. Impossible to abort at this stage. You have your cargo? Over."

A different voice, also feminine but this time American, answered, "*Katie-Lou* to *Starfish*. Yes, we have our cargo. Please give time and place of rendezvous. Over."

"*Starfish* to *Katie-Lou*. Time of rendezvous now brought forward to noon. Repeat rendezvous twelve noon. Place of rendezvous, Mango Bay, St. Matthew's. Repeat Mango Bay, St. Matthew's. We need sheltered waters for the transfer. Over."

"*Katie-Lou* to *Starfish*. Confirm rendezvous twelve noon, Mango Bay, St. Matthew's. Out."

Emmy flew to the telephone and dialed the home number of Inspector Ingham.

"Mrs. Ingham? I'm sorry, but it's Mrs. Tibbett again. May I speak to your husband?"

"I'm really sorry, Mrs. Tibbett. He's not taking any calls except from the police station."

"Oh, very well," said Emmy irritably, and she hung up. She called the police station.

"Duty Officer. Bob Harrison's yard here. Did you get that *Starfish* message?"

"Well—"

"Have you told Inspector Ingham?"

"I don't—" There was a metallic sound and voices in the background. Emmy judged that the telephone had been snatched from the young man's hand. Then a female voice said, "I am sorry, madam. We cannot divulge confidential information to members of the public." There was a click, and the line went dead.

Emmy looked at Bob Harrison. "They must have passed it on," she said. "I mean, that was the whole idea. What do we do now?"

The question was answered by the radio. Henry's voice was tense. "*Mark One* to *Blandish.* Position four miles southwest of Mango Bay, small cove, don't know it's name, behind Mizzen Point. Sea conditions reasonable to poor. Bernie awaiting first rendezvous. Get help if you can. I'm going in. Out."

Bob Harrison said, "I've only got an outboard dinghy, but I'm prepared to try. You coming?"

"Of course. But I have to contact Ingham first." Emmy was already dialing. "Mrs. Ingham? Look, this really is life and death. I have to . . . oh, he has? To the police station? . . . Thank you." She hung up and turned to Bob. "Can you take me to the police station at once in your jeep?"

"Can't you telephone?"

"Not safe," said Emmy briefly.

In the street outside the police station, cleanup work was already in progress. Gangs of men in trucks were carting away refuse, while others swept debris off the road. Emmy felt highly conspicuous as the only woman in sight, hanging around on a street corner. However, within a few minutes Inspector Ingham's familiar little black car drove up. As he got out of it, Emmy rushed to intercept him before he could go into the station.

"Mrs. Tibbett—I told you—"

Breathlessly, Emmy said, "About four miles southwest of Mango Bay, a small cove protected by Mizzen Point. We don't know its name. You must get there as fast as you can, Inspector. Henry's there in *Mark One,* on his own. Bob Harrison and I are going over in an outboard dinghy—"

"Are you crazy, Mrs. Tibbett?"

"No, no, no, for God's sake. There's been a lot of craziness, but this isn't it. This is real. *Please*, Inspector. So far there's only one boat, the *Ocean Rover,* but the *Katie-Lou* will arrive any moment. Just get out your launch and get there. You'll probably overtake us."

"I'll probably have to rescue you." Ingham was very angry. "The wind's dropped, but the swells are still high. Those are no seas for an outboard dinghy to be out in. I don't want any damned fool tourists drowning on me—"

"Then come after us," said Emmy, who then fled around the corner to Bob's waiting jeep.

21

IN THE SMALL BAY under Mizzen Point, which was locally known as Dutchman's Cove, *Ocean Rover* was at anchor, bucking and swaying in the waters, which, although sheltered, were still feeling the swell caused by the hurricanes.

Henry knew that he had no hope of making a surprise attack—the crew of *Ocean Rover* would certainly have heard his VHF message and be expecting him. However, this state of affairs had another side to it. The Montgomerys must also realize that the police, too, had picked up the signal, and—while Ingham might well disregard it as coming from a lunatic—if Henry should disappear or be found murdered, then there would be no doubt as to whom to blame. Also, they believed that Dr. Vanduren was their ally. Grasping at these two small straws, Henry maneuvered *Mark One* up alongside *Ocean Rover*.

At the sound of the motor, Colonel Montgomery came up on deck.

"Ah, Mr. Tibbett. We were expecting you, old man. Throw me a line and we'll tie your boat astern." His voice sounded perfectly friendly and normal. A minute later, Henry was on board *Ocean Rover* while *Mark One* streamed astern on a long painter.

"Come below." Montgomery's voice was harder and less friendly. "I think there are a few things we have to discuss."

In the cabin, everything appeared normal. Mrs. Montgomery was at the stove, preparing coffee. Dr. Vanduren sat at the table, studying a chart. As Henry went down the companion ladder, Montgomery's voice behind him said, "Just as a precaution, I have you covered and I won't hesitate to shoot if you try anything funny. Sit down, please."

Henry sat down next to Vanduren. Montgomery stood with his

217

back to the companion ladder. He held a revolver in his hand. He said, "You are a nuisance, Mr. Tibbett, but not a serious one. I understand from my young friends on *Katie-Lou* that you became rather too curious about certain matters on St. Mark's, and so we were forced to give you a little tranquilizer on your last visit to *Ocean Rover*. It was in the rum punch, of course. My friends followed you ashore and kept you fed with small regular doses, and I understand that the effect was most gratifying. As a matter of fact, you did us a service by getting Ingham and Pendleton worked up about the drug scene—precisely the tactics we were using ourselves. I admit we rather hoped you wouldn't survive the hurricane—but as Ed remarked, if you did it was highly unlikely that you would remember anything about your recent experiences—and even if your memory returned, nobody would believe you. I don't know what you think you have achieved by chasing us out here, but I'm afraid you've signed your own death warrant. Oh, I'm not going to shoot you if I can help it." He turned to his wife. "How's the coffee coming along, Martha?"

"A couple of minutes."

"Good. Dr. Vanduren, please be a good fellow and get the PCP from the fo'c'sle. You will be taking another drink with us, Mr. Tibbett. If you refuse your coffee, we will be compelled to knock you out and inject the drug—but one way or the other, you will get it. We will then put you into your launch, set the motor full ahead, and point her out to sea. I don't think that you will be heard of again."

Dr. Vanduren had disappeared through the door leading to the fore part of the ship. He seemed to be taking rather a long time, and Montgomery was showing signs of impatience when he finally reappeared carrying an envelope, which he handed to Mrs. Montgomery.

"Half a gram," he said. "That should do it."

"Thank you, Lionel," said Martha Montgomery. There was an eerie normality about the whole scene. She poured out a mug of coffee and stirred the white powder from the envelope into it, as if it had been sugar. Then she held the mug out to Henry. "Drink it."

Henry said, "You must really think I'm crazy. You dare not shoot me, and you surely don't think—"

Martha Montgomery said, "Come on, Lionel. The two of us can manage him while Bill gets it down him. In case he is found, the autopsy shouldn't show syringe marks."

Henry leaped to his feet, but the small cabin gave him no room to maneuver. Mrs. Montgomery, like an Amazon, got hold of one of his arms, and Dr. Vanduren the other. Bill Montgomery, still holding the gun, looked on almost benignly. As he struggled, Henry became aware of a whisper in his ear. "Drink it! It's harmless."

It flashed across Henry's mind that he had been dubious about trusting Vanduren from the start. A self-confessed dope-pusher, a doctor with a murky secret in his past. Now he had to decide whether or not to trust this man with his life. Decide? There was really no decision. He allowed himself to be overpowered and put up only token resistance as the contents of the mug were poured down his throat. It occurred to him that Mrs. Montgomery made very bad coffee.

When the mug was empty, the atmosphere in the cabin relaxed. Montgomery put down his gun and said, "I'll have a cup myself now, dear. How about you, Doctor?"

"Thanks."

Henry sat quite still, feeling nothing unusual, but not knowing when to expect the onset of symptoms, had the drug been genuine, nor at what point to start simulating them if Vanduren had really substituted a harmless powder. In the latter case, he had no idea of what form the symptoms should take. He let his head droop forward, feeling that this could hardly be wrong.

Vanduren said, "Interesting to see the reaction to such a massive dose. We don't seem to be getting the usual nystagmus and repetitive movements. I should say he'll go straight into a coma within a few minutes, maybe with spasmodic convulsions."

Henry's spirits rose. For a start, he still felt perfectly well. To go on with, Vanduren was quite clearly telling him how to behave. Coma within a few minutes? Spasmodic convulsions? So be it. He drooped his head still further. Then he executed what he felt was a rather artistic spasmodic convulsion, rolled his eyes, and collapsed with his head on the cabin table.

Vanduren said, "As I thought. I'll just take a look at him to make sure . . ." He bent over Henry, and as he did so whispered, "You take him, I'll deal with her. Now!"

The advantage of surprise in attack is well known. As a straight matter of physical strength, it is doubtful whether Henry and the doctor could have overcome the Montgomerys; but the impact of an apparently comatose individual and a trusted ally suddenly turning on their coffee-drinking hosts was shattering. This effect was aided by the fact that Vanduren threw his boiling coffee in Mrs. Montgomery's face, and that Henry was able to grab the gun, which Montgomery had laid down on the table while drinking his coffee. Henry was slightly built, but he had taken a course in unarmed combat, and Montgomery went down like a felled ox. As for the doctor, even the Junoesque Martha was no match for his huge physique.

Panting slightly, he said to Henry, "Cover her with the gun while I get rope. How long will he be out?"

"Only a minute or so."

"That's all we need."

Vanduren leaped up into the cockpit and returned seconds later with a couple of stout ropes. Martha Montgomery spat in his face as he tied her arms, but the doctor was unmoved.

"Now for you, my friend." The unconscious Montgomery was neatly trussed.

Henry said, "You're a marvel. What was it?"

"Bicarbonate of soda. All I could find. Now, come and help me free those wretched youngsters in the fo'c'sle."

Henry laid down the gun and was following the doctor through to the forward compartment when there was a shattering explosion and a bullet thudded into the ship's woodwork a few inches from Henry's head. A voice, which he recognized as that of the man who had called himself Carstairs, said, "Stay where you are and put your hands up, both of you. That was just to show you we mean business."

Turning slowly, with raised hands, Henry saw the man he knew as Carstairs coming down into the cabin, followed by his wife. Ed Marsham and Janet Vanduren. Ed nodded briefly toward the gun on the table.

"Take that, Jan. Don't hesitate to use it. I'll keep them covered while you untie Martha and Bill. Looks like we got here just in time. Then we'll deal with Kate and Lou. We'll make that noon rendezvous with time to spare."

BOB HARRISON'S OUTBOARD DINGHY was never intended to make the trip from St. Mark's to St. Matthew's through the choppy seas left in the wake of the hurricanes. Fortunately, the wind was astern, but the tiny craft rolled dangerously and the waves threatened to swamp her. Bob's main concern was that the outboard might get drenched, thus putting it out of action and leaving no means of propulsion except for a pair of oars; so Emmy spent the hair-raising trip hanging on to the boat with one hand and with the other trying to protect the motor from spray with an old oilskin.

Fortunately, as Bob pointed out, the rendezvous spot had been chosen at the point where the two islands were closest together, and so, although it felt like a century, it was only about half an hour before Emmy shouted, against the noise of the motor, "Look! There they are!"

"Aye," said Bob. "Both boats, with a couple of dinghies and the old *Mark One* all tied up astern the *Ocean Rover*. Well, my dear, here we go."

The dinghy was about a hundred yards from the anchored *Ocean Rover* when it happened. A big breaking stern wave accompanied with a sudden gust of wind whipped the oilskin out of Emmy's hand, and water cascaded over the outboard. The motor spluttered and fell silent, leaving the little boat rocking like a cockleshell, turning beam-on to the seas and threatening every moment to overturn.

"Oh, Bob, I'm sorry," Emmy wailed.

To her surprise, he grinned. "Not your fault," he said generously. "Best get those paddles out, and quick, get her nose up. Lucky we're nearly there."

As a matter of fact, the failure of the outboard was a blessing in disguise, since it ensured that Emmy and Bob would approach the *Ocean Rover* under the silent power of a pair of oars, with no telltale puttering of a noisy outboard. In consequence, the people on board, who had other things on their minds, were not aware that two additional passengers had added yet another dinghy to the duckling flock which now streamed astern and had climbed silently into the cockpit.

Ed Marsham was still talking. "Sure, we'll make the rendezvous, but there's plenty to do. Hurry up with those ropes, Jan. O.K. You all right, Bill?"

With much grumbling and picturesque language, Montgomery heaved himself into a standing position. Marsham said, "How come you let this happen?"

It was Martha who answered. "Your friend Dr. Vanduren," she said, "is apparently an undercover police agent. He was supposed to give Tibbett a half-gram of PCP, instead of which he gave him bicarbonate of soda and instructions how to act like he was going into a coma." Her voice was low and venemous. "Tibbett we can now drug properly and dispose of that way. It would be unfortunate if he were found with gunshot wounds. I don't think we have to worry in the same way about Dr. Vanduren."

There was a moment of silence. Then Marsham turned to Janet Vanduren. He said just two words. "Kill him."

Slowly, her voice slurred, Janet Vanduren said, "He's my father."

"You've killed before. You can kill again. What the hell does it matter who he is? He's in our way and he has to go. Kill him, or I shall kill you."

Like a small child, Janet Vanduren whimpered, "I can't. He's my father. Why don't you kill him?"

"Because it would amuse me to see you do it."

Softly, Dr. Vanduren said, "Come along, Jan. Be brave. Get it over with. You can do it."

"Dad, I—"

"He means it, Jan. I have to die anyway. Come on. Be a brave girl."

A dinghy oar is a useful weapon in that it can be used at quite a distance from its target, being over six feet long. It is not as a rule lethal, but as a breaker-up of tense situations it has few rivals.

Marsham had taken up the position formerly occupied by Montgomery, at the foot of the companion ladder, with his back to the cockpit. This was obviously the best point from which to dominate the cabin with his gun. It also meant that the dinghy oar wielded by Bob Harrison descended on his head with shattering violence.

Marsham staggered, then fell. Before the other occupants of the cabin had time to react, Janet Vanduren took aim and shot him as he struggled to get to his feet. For an endless moment, the dying man on the floor and the girl with the gun looked at each other, then, with the last of his strength, Marsham raised his gun and shot at her. She collapsed into her father's arms as Harrison and Emmy came tumbling down the ladder into the cabin.

Montgomery snatched the gun from Marsham's dead hand and said calmly, "Martha dear, I think it's time we left."

The gun was leveled at Bob Harrison, who faced it with a dinghy oar, like a caricature of a Home Guardsman facing the might of Nazi Germany. Henry did a quick mental calculation and said, "Let them go, Bob."

"But—"

"Let them go. Enough people have been hurt already."

Reluctantly, Bob lowered his primitive weapon, and a moment later both Montgomerys were in the cockpit. Twenty seconds later, Bob let out a roar of sheer fury. "They've taken *Mark One*!"

Sure enough, the sound of the launch's engine was unmistakable. Henry said, "I'm sorry, Bob, but it was the best thing. We'll get them in the end, don't worry."

"And what about my boat?"

Henry made a tiny gesture toward Dr. Vanduren and Janet. He said quietly, "What about his daughter?"

Bob looked, dropped his eyes, and said, "My God. I'm sorry."

Like a Pietà in reverse, Lionel Vanduren was holding Janet on his knees, cradling her in his arms. He said, "It's all right, Jan. You did right. Everything is all right."

Barely audibly, she said, "I really have killed somebody now, haven't I, Dad?"

"You mean—you didn't, before?"

"The old lady." Janet's voice was very weak. "I was supposed to kill her. I didn't. I couldn't. I took her ashore and to the airport and changed her reservation and put her in the hotel. I told Ed I'd killed her, but I didn't."

Very gently, her father said, "That was a very good, brave thing to do, Jan. What about Cheryl Ross?"

Janet shook her head feebly. "I . . . I had nothing to do with . . . I knew her, you see . . . it was the Montgomerys . . ."

"And Ed?"

Suddenly Janet began struggling, terrified. "Is he dead? Is he dead?"

"Yes, my darling. He's dead."

"It was Ed . . . he's one of them . . . he fooled us all . . . only got engaged to me . . . you a doctor . . . Florida connection . . . got me hooked on . . ." She clutched at her father's protective arms. "Don't leave me, Dad. He'll find me . . . he'll kill me . . . don't leave me . . ."

Vanduren bent his head. "Never," he said firmly. "Never again, Jan." Then he looked up and said to the others, "But she's left me. Poor Jan. She's dead." He buried his head in his daughter's long hair and wept.

IT WAS Henry and Bob Harrison who went into the fo'c'sle to release Katherine and Lewis Carstairs, who lay there trussed like chickens and waiting for butchery. It was Bob who navigated *Ocean Rover* and Henry and Emmy who brought *Katie-Lou* around to Mango Bay shortly before noon, to be met by the police launch from St. Mark's, with Inspector Ingham and Customs Officer Cranstone aboard. Henry was not at all surprised to see that Pearletta Terry was piloting the launch. She did not pilot it back to St. Mark's. Inspector Ingham had her under arrest, and Cranstone was at the controls.

Meanwhile, a radio report had ensured the arrest of Anderson, the Harbour Master—in whose delivery of stores was found the small amount of marijuana which had been put aboard the *Katie-Lou*. In an effort at plea bargaining, Anderson led the police to a large cache of drugs and a sizable arms dump in the hills of St. Mark's.

Mark One was found abandoned but in good condition about twenty miles north of the Seawards. A description of the Montgomerys and a warrant for their arrest were circulated throughout the area, but at the time of writing they have not been located. However, it is unlikely that they will operate actively again.

The Seawards incident was over.

Epilogue

THE TIBBETTS WERE DUE to leave the next morning. At the Anchorage Inn, a happy evening was in progress—a private dinner cooked by John Colville and his wife, served to a group of guests made up of Sir Alfred and Lady Pendleton, Inspector and Mrs. Ingham, Mr. and Mrs. Bob Harrison, Mr. and Mrs. Henry Tibbett, and Ebenezer Prout, otherwise known as Shark Tooth.

Dinner was over, and John had just proposed a toast to Miss Betsy Sprague, when the telephone rang. Margaret went to answer it.

"Yes . . . wait a minute while I get a pencil . . . yes . . . yes . . . I have that . . ."

The party at the table waited expectantly. At last, Margaret came back with a notepad in her hand. She said, "That was a telegram from London for Henry Tibbett. It reads: 'YOUR RESIGNATION ACCEPTED WITH GREAT REGRET STOP WILL NOT GAZETTE UNTIL CONFIRMED IN WRITING STOP HOPE YOU MAY RECONSIDER SIGNED ASSISTANT COMMISSIONER.' "

There was a moment of absolute silence. Then Henry said, "What in God's name—?"

Emmy was giggling hopelessly. "I forgot to tell you, darling. You don't remember now, but you sent a telegram resigning from Scotland Yard. You set up a company called the Henry Tibbett Investigation Bureau in St. Mark's, and you were going to live here and be a private eye . . ."

Henry said, "I see. So the recent case was not in the hands of Scotland Yard, but of the Tibbett Investigation Bureau, was it? Well, I think the sooner the bureau goes out of business, the better. After all, consider. It investigated the murder of a woman who was alive and well in her own home. It tracked down four criminals, two of whom escaped and two of whom killed each other. It—"

Sir Alfred Pendleton said, "It also just happened to save the Seaward Islands."

"For the moment," said Henry. "I wonder for how long."